VALLEY 12/29/2009 C:1
50690010723598
Goudge, Eileen.
Once in a blue moon

ONCE *in a* BLUE MOON

**Center Point
Large Print**

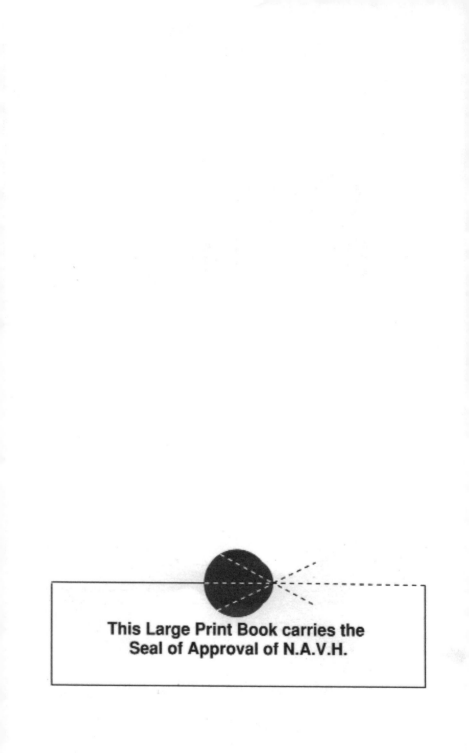

This Large Print Book carries the
Seal of Approval of N.A.V.H.

ONCE *in a*
BLUE MOON

Eileen Goudge

CENTER POINT PUBLISHING
THORNDIKE, MAINE

This Center Point Large Print edition
is published in the year 2009 by arrangement with
Writers House LLC.

The text of this Large Print edition is unabridged.
In other aspects, this book may vary
from the original edition.
Printed in the United States of America.
Set in 16-point Times New Roman type.

ISBN: 978-1-60285-627-1

Library of Congress Cataloging-in-Publication Data

Goudge, Eileen.
  Once in a blue moon / Eileen Goudge.
     p. cm.
  ISBN 978-1-60285-627-1 (lib. bdg. : alk. paper)
  1. Sisters--Fiction. 2. Ex-foster children--Fiction. 3. Domestic fiction.
    4. Psychological fiction. 5. Large type books. I. Title.

  PS3557.O838O53 2009b
  813'.54--dc22

2009027803

To my sister, Patty, who lives by the sea.

Those who inspire in us
the greatest affection are not always
those for whom we have the highest regard.

—From *Horace*, by George Sand

ACKNOWLEDGMENTS

FIRST AND FOREMOST, I would like to thank my dear husband, Sandy Kenyon, without whom this or any book would not be possible—at least not in any kind of reasonable time frame. Each fall when I kiss him good-bye and head off to my Pacific Northwest hideaway to beaver away for an extended period of time on the second draft of my manuscript, I am reminded all over again of why I fell in love with him. How many other husbands would be such a good sport and never once complain about having to eat takeout every night for more than a month?

Along those same lines, I owe a giant debt of gratitude to Bill and Valerie Anders, who have been so generous in allowing me the use of their guest house on Orcas Island.

I would also like to thank my publisher, Roger Cooper, and his caring staff; my editor, Francine La Sala, for her thoughtful and respectful comments and corrections, the delivery of which, amazingly enough, coincided with that of her second child; and, as always, my tireless and devoted agent, Susan Ginsburg of Writers House.

One small disclaimer: If I've taken liberties with what is a familiar part of the world to many of you, please chalk it up to literary license. I grew up in Northern California and still think of it as my home in many ways, but I've been away enough years to feel entitled to a certain amount of romanticizing. The same holds true for any small liberties I've taken in describing the workings of the state and local government as well as the various legal procedures depicted in these pages. When faced with the choice between strict authenticity and maximum dramatic impact, I always choose the latter.

PROLOGUE

Reno, Nevada, 1981

THE FIRST TIME Kerrie Ann disappeared was only the warning shot, as it turned out. Lindsay was fixing them something to eat and looked up from scraping scrambled eggs onto their plates to ask Kerrie Ann if she wanted ketchup with hers, only to find the folding chair in which her three-year-old sister had been sitting just moments before, swinging her small feet in their dirty pink Keds back and forth, back and forth, in that annoying way of hers that caused the chair's hollow aluminum frame to squeak like a rusty hinge, empty. The only indication that she'd been there were her stubby crayons, strewn over the tabletop next to the open Washoe County yellow pages, where she'd been coloring an ad for pet supplies—a cartoon dog begging for treats. It was as if she'd vanished into thin air: Tabitha playing games on *Bewitched*.

"Kerrie Ann?" Lindsay kept her voice low so as not to wake their mom. Crystal's shift ended when most people were getting up to go to work. Often she didn't get home until the sky was light, and then she would sleep straight through until the following evening. Crystal's one ironclad rule was that she not be disturbed during those hours. *Damn it, Linds. I bust my ass for a few lousy dollar bills off the craps tables, and I'm supposed to wipe your snotty little noses on top of it?*

Kerrie Ann wasn't in the living room when Lindsay checked. There was no muffled giggle from behind the sofa—an old nubby beige one that smelled of mildew and was marred by a coffee-colored stain in the shape of the African continent—where at night they slept toe to toe, Lindsay with her knees tucked up to give her sister more room. No singsong voice calling, "See if you can find me!" The only sounds were those of a car engine firing noisily in the parking lot below and the asthmatic gurgling of the window unit as it sluggishly stirred the hot, close air of room 22 in the Lucky Seven Motel without doing much to cool it.

Lindsay crept to the bedroom door and cracked it open as quietly as possible. Pale fingers of light poking through the drawn blinds traced the outline of the figure sprawled faceup atop the unmade bed. Crystal was still dressed in the clothes she'd worn to work the night before—tight white jeans and a stretchy purple top with spangles sewn across the front—her makeup smeared and her platinum hair mussed. Something winked at Lindsay in the darkness: the toe of a patent-leather high heel peeking like a shiny black nose from the hamster's nest of discarded clothing on the floor beside the bed.

There was no sign of Kerrie Ann. If she'd gone

in to use the bathroom, Crystal would have been up by now, cursing a blue streak and blaming Lindsay. Another of Crystal's rules was that they use Miss Honi's bathroom downstairs if they had to go rather than disturb her.

Lindsay checked theirs anyway, just to be sure. But Kerrie Ann wasn't on the toilet or playing hide-and-seek behind the shower curtain. Lindsay was tiptoeing back across the room when her mother stirred, eyelids flickering. She froze. But Crystal only muttered something in her sleep, then flopped over onto her belly. Lindsay reached the door safely, easing it shut. Leaning against the wall, she let out a slow breath. That had been a close call. What if her mother had woken up to find Kerrie Ann missing? You didn't want to get Crystal riled up before she'd had her coffee and first cigarette of the day. She'd never actually hit either of them, but when she was in one of her moods, things could get ugly very quickly. Lindsay was only in sixth grade, but she knew every curse word there was.

She was getting that tight feeling in her stomach again, a feeling that almost always had to do with Kerrie Ann. Before her sister had been born, when it had been just her and Crystal, she'd managed okay. By the time she was in kindergarten, in addition to being able to feed and dress herself, she could read street signs, count change, and order Chinese takeout over the phone. By third grade

11

she was doing most of the shopping and cooking. She was also well-versed in the facts of life, thanks to her mother's habit of bringing home strange men: Often Lindsay would wake to muffled thumping and moans in the bedroom or stumble into the bathroom in the middle of the night to find a naked man taking a whiz. She'd grown to accept it the way other children her age took it for granted that everyone had a mommy and a daddy. Some of the men had been nice. One, a bearded, heavyset man named Stan who was a fry cook at the all-night diner where Crystal sometimes caught a bite to eat after work, had shown her how to make a Western omelet. And she'd picked up a few phrases of Spanish from a blackjack dealer named Luis.

The summer Lindsay turned nine Crystal announced that she was taking some time off work. She grew fat, slept even more than usual, and was in a bad mood most of the time. The following winter she went off to the hospital. A day later she returned carrying a small, fleece-wrapped bundle. "Meet your new sister," she said, depositing the bundle in Lindsay's arms. Lindsay unfolded a corner of the blanket to reveal a small, scrunched-up face with a pair of bright blue eyes peering from its reddish folds. Eyes that fixed on her like a homing device. She and her baby sister stared at each other for a minute, taking each other's measure. Then the infant stiffened and began to howl loudly enough to bring old Mr. Huff stumping up from downstairs to see what all the commotion was about.

Life hadn't been the same since.

Now Lindsay had this whole other person to look after besides herself. And Kerrie Ann was a handful, no doubt about it. Her baby-fine, straw-berry-blond hair was perpetually snarled, and she'd whine and cry whenever Lindsay tried to unravel the knots using her fingers or the hair-brush. When Kerrie Ann was a toddler, everything she could put into her mouth—dirt, caterpillars, old chewed gum off park benches, once even a poker chip—had gone in one end and out the other. And she'd had every childhood ailment known to humankind, from earaches to allergic rashes to head lice.

Plus she was as slippery as a goldfish. In stores she was forever wandering off, and by the time Lindsay would track her down, her pockets would be stuffed with pilfered loot that Lindsay would then have to return to the proper shelves. At the park, where Lindsay took her on nice days when it wasn't too hot, her little sister was a blur, streaking down slides and scampering like a monkey over the jungle gym, from which she always had to be pried, wailing in protest, when it was time to go home. Once she'd chased a Mr. Softee truck, crossing a busy street to get to it. She might have been hit by a car or, if the nice lady who'd brought her back hadn't found her, still been out there roaming the streets, a red-haired menace to society.

Only at Miss Honi's was her sister content to stay put. Miss Honi Love, who lived in the unit directly below theirs, looked after Kerrie Ann during the hours when Lindsay was in school. But since she got paid only sporadically, Crystal being forever short on cash, and since she was a good-hearted woman who genuinely cared for the girls, it had developed over time into something far more than a job. The way Miss Honi fussed over Kerrie Ann, anyone would have thought she was her own little girl. And Kerrie Ann was just as devoted to Miss Honi. Lindsay would arrive home from school to find her little sister either playing quietly with Miss Honi's angel collection or curled up on Miss Honi's lap in the burgundy plush recliner in front of the TV. The two of them could sit like that for hours, Miss Honi smoking her Pall Malls and Kerrie Ann sucking her thumb, watching the dramas unfolding on *Days of Our Lives* and *All My Children*.

Sometimes Miss Honi told stories about what it had been like back in the day, when she'd been a top draw at gentlemen's clubs like Diamond Jim's and the Silver Dollar Lounge. She'd even shown them a photo of herself back then, all creamy limbs and Cleopatra eyes, her sculpted red-blond curls piled high atop her head, wearing spike heels and a spangled bikini bottom, a pair of tassels the only thing covering her breasts. She'd looked like a life-size party favor.

Now she was plump and middle-aged. She often joked that she'd be lucky to squeeze one of her big toes into that old costume of hers. She still liked to dress up, only now it was capri slacks and frilly, low-cut blouses that showed off her sizable bosom or sundresses with cinched waists in a variety of exotic prints. Miss Honi was inordinately proud of her dainty feet and owned several dozen pairs of shoes. Even relaxing at home, she wore marabou-trimmed satin mules, which Kerrie Ann loved tottering around in when playing dress-up.

It occurred to Lindsay that her sister might have gone to Miss Honi's. Where else?

She let herself out the front door, easing it shut behind her. It was late, the sun dissolving like a giant lemon drop into the far-off mountaintops, streaking the horizon with brilliant bands of cherry and tangerine. A handful of stars winked in the sky's deepening blue, and off in the distance, the casinos and clubs along the strip formed their own constellation, which cast a candy-colored glow over the streets around it. The club where Crystal worked was but a remote star in that constellation.

From where Lindsay stood, looking out over the railing of the balcony that wrapped around the top floor of the two-story motel, she could see the swimming pool below. It was fenced in, but the lock on the gate had long ago been pried open, and the manager, Mr. Boyle, hadn't bothered to get it fixed. It wasn't unusual when she came home from school for Lindsay to find a group of neighborhood boys gathered by the pool, drinking beer and generally being obnoxious. No one ever went for a dip, though. If there was one place in the U.S. of A. where you were likely to contract a tropical disease, Crystal was fond of griping, it was the pool at the Lucky Seven Motel.

It would also be easy for a three-year-old to fall in and drown.

Lindsay's stomach clenched as she set off in the direction of the stairway, her bare soles slapping against concrete still warm from the sun: a girl just shy of twelve, tall for her age with long, coltish legs brown from the sun and the nubs of breasts showing under the faded Garfield T-shirt she wore with her navy shorts. She walked fast, her dark brown ponytail bouncing at the nape of her neck, the curl at the tip going from a comma to an exclamation point with each forceful step.

She was so intent on finding her little sister that she was only dimly aware of noises drifting from behind the sun-bleached coral doors lining the walkway—the muttering of TV sets, a phone ringing, a mother yelling at her kids to shut up. Kerrie Ann was a pain in the butt, but she was *her* pain in the butt. She and Crystal were the only family Lindsay had. Lindsay didn't even know who her father was, much less where he lived. And her grandparents on her mother's side, who lived in Crystal's hometown in Ohio, apparently wanted nothing to do with either their wayward daughter or her illegitimate kids. Crystal hadn't seen or spoken to anyone in her family since she'd disgraced them by running off at the age of seventeen, when she'd been pregnant with Lindsay.

Lindsay could have found her way to Miss Honi's unit blindfolded. The scent alone, a potent mixture of perfume and cigarettes, would have been enough to guide her. She knocked on the door, and after a minute or so it swung open, her sister's babysitter materializing like an oversized nymph from the cloud of smoke that wafted forth. Miss Honi had been to the beauty parlor that day, and her hair, the yellow-red of marigolds, was piled atop her head in a mass of sculpted ringlets that added several inches to her already statuesque height. She was wearing a low-cut Hawaiian print sundress, which emphasized her ample curves, and a pair of color-coordinated lime-green sandals whose straps were decorated with rows of plastic daisies. The pendant on her necklace, sparkly pink stones in the shape of an angel, nestled in the cleft between her breasts, and a cigarette was propped decorously in the fork between two scarlet-nailed fingers. It was like encountering a neon sign in the middle of nowhere.

"Lord almighty, sugar, what's got into you? You look like you got chased here by a rabid skunk," she drawled, taking note of Lindsay's flushed face and the sweat beaded on her brow. She peered past Lindsay into the shadows beyond the porch light. "Where's my baby girl?"

Lindsay felt the bottom drop out of her stomach. "I . . . I thought she was with you."

Miss Honi grew very still. From the TV blaring in the background came the manic cackle of a laugh track. "Let me get this straight. You're saying you don't know where your sister is?"

Lindsay swallowed hard, blinking back tears. "I only turned my back for a minute, I swear. She was *right there*."

Miss Honi frowned. "Your mama know about this?"

Lindsay shook her head, saying miserably, "I was supposed to be watching her."

Miss Honi's frown deepened, her ruby-lipped mouth pursing the way it did when she had something to say but was too polite to say it. Something to do with Crystal, no doubt. Lindsay had overheard her talking on the phone once, muttering to whoever was at the other end, "Shoot me for saying so, but if motherhood was something they taught in school, she'da flunked that course."

Lindsay didn't have to ask whom she meant.

Miss Honi's upbeat tone didn't mask the worry on her face. "Don't you fret none, sugar. We'll find her. She can't have gotten very far, an itty-bitty thing like her."

Fleas were itty-bitty, too, Lindsay thought, but just try catching one.

Together they headed to the motel's office, where they found Mr. Boyle with his balding head bent over a racing form. "No, I ain't seen her," he informed them, muttering under his breath as he went back to circling his picks. "You folks oughta keep a closer watch on your kids."

"And *you*, mister, oughta watch your mouth." Miss Honi leaned down and thrust her face into his, eyes narrowed to emerald slits and her bonnet of marigold curls quivering as if from a strong gust. Before the stunned manager could react, she spun on her heel and sashayed out the door.

Lindsay didn't share her indignation. Mr. Boyle might be a mean old bastard, but he was right: She should've kept a closer watch on her sister. If anything were to happen to Kerrie Ann . . .

As if picking up on her thoughts, Miss Honi reached for her hand and gave it a squeeze. "She'll turn up. You'll see. She's got the Rocky Balboa of guardian angels looking out for her, that one." Miss Honi's angel collection wasn't just for show; she believed in angels the way Lindsay once had in Santa Claus, a million years ago.

And maybe there were such things, Lindsay thought. All those close calls from which her sister had escaped unscathed couldn't be chalked up to pure luck, could they? Like the time Kerrie Ann had tripped and fallen, charging down the stairs to the parking lot, and would have tumbled all the way to the bottom if one of her sneakers hadn't caught in the railing. And the time she'd swallowed a bunch of mothballs, thinking they were candy; if Miss Honi hadn't rushed her to the hospital, she might have died.

Lindsay struggled to keep up with Miss Honi as the tall woman clip-clopped across the parking lot in her high-heeled sandals at a rapid pace, making a beeline for the pool. It was deserted inside the chain-link enclosure when they reached it, with no sign of any recent activity, but they circled it nonetheless, with a grim sense of purpose.

On the far side of the fenced enclosure was the cinder-block shed housing the laundry facility, which consisted of a pair of coin-fed washing machines and dryers that were out of service as often as not. It was deserted as well. Not that Lindsay had expected to find her sister there, or anywhere on the premises for that matter. The Lucky Seven Motel wasn't a place where people got lucky; it was where they landed when their luck ran out. Except for the handful of year-round residents, like Crystal and Miss Honi, most guests stuck around only long enough to make the next score, turn around a losing streak, or get pawned valuables out of hock. Fights born of desperation were commonplace, and the police were frequently called in to settle disputes. It wasn't the kind of place where it was safe to wander around after dark. Especially for a three-year-old girl who didn't know enough to stay out of trouble.

Suppose Kerrie Ann had been kidnapped . . . or worse? What if at this very moment she was lying in a ditch somewhere with her throat cut? A fresh surge of panic caused Lindsay's chest to constrict, and she had to pause for a moment to catch her breath. *Please, God . . .*

They scoured the area. They knocked on doors. They walked up and down streets, calling out Kerrie Ann's name until they were hoarse. But as twilight gave way to nighttime with still no sign of her, Lindsay's panic crept over into despair. The night had become a vast ocean that seemed to have swallowed up her sister, and she felt as if she were drowning in it, too.

"You go wake your mama. I'll call the police." Miss Honi made no pretense of being upbeat this time. Lindsay could see that she was scared, too.

They were heading back across the parking lot when Lindsay caught sight of a black Labrador retriever in the back of a dusty blue pickup parked in front of one of the units. As they neared, the dog let out a yip and began to wag its tail. Some instinct drew Lindsay over to investigate. A wet tongue lashed at her outstretched hand, emboldening her to climb up onto the running board. She peered into the bed, and there, curled asleep on a dirty scrap of blanket, was Kerrie Ann.

Lindsay felt a rush of relief so intense that the world went a little gray for an instant.

Then Miss Honi spotted Kerrie Ann, too, and let out a cry. A moment later she was holding her "baby girl" tightly, muddy tears running down her cheeks, ruining her makeup, while Kerrie Ann blinked up at her sleepily, no doubt wondering what all the commotion was about. "I was playing with the doggie. It's a *nice* doggie," she said simply when asked what she'd been doing out here all alone. It was easy to figure out what had happened. She hadn't had her nap that day, because Miss Honi had taken her to the doctor for her checkup, so she'd grown sleepy and decided to curl up.

"Didn't you hear us calling you?" Lindsay cried in exasperation.

Kerrie Ann shook her head, and Lindsay knew she was telling the truth. Whether she'd been born that way or had merely learned to adapt to Crystal's comings and goings at odd hours, Kerrie Ann could sleep through anything. It wasn't uncommon for Lindsay to wake up in the middle of the night and find that her sister had rolled off the couch onto the floor without waking up.

She knew she should scold her sister for going off like that, but she was so relieved to see her that she didn't have the heart. Instead they all trooped back to Miss Honi's, where they polished off the leftover macaroni and cheese from the night before, along with a platter of sausages Miss Honi fried up. When Kerrie Ann had had her fill, she crawled into Miss Honi's lap in the maroon plush recliner. "Bob Barker," she announced in her clear, bell-like voice. *The Price Is Right* was her favorite TV show, and it had just come on. She fell asleep again in the middle of it, oblivious to the scare she'd given them.

Upstairs, Crystal slept through it all, oblivious as well.

A few weeks later, when Lindsay arrived at Miss Honi's after school to retrieve Kerrie Ann, there was a strange woman seated on the sofa. "Sugar, this is Mrs. Harmon," Miss Honi introduced her. She sounded upset. "She'd like to have a word with you."

The woman, short and thin-lipped with bobbed gray hair, explained that she was with Children's Services. "I'm sorry to have to tell you this, but your mother's been placed in custody," she informed Lindsay gently. "I don't know for how long—the charges are pretty serious." Later Lindsay would learn that Crystal had been arrested for selling cocaine to an under-cover cop. "But I don't want you to worry. It's my job to make sure you and your sister are well looked after until . . . well, for the time being. We have good homes lined up for you both."

Lindsay struggled to absorb what the woman was telling her. Crystal in jail? Homes for her and

Kerrie Ann? Why would they need homes when they already had one? Her mind was reeling, but she squared her shoulders and, with all the courage she could muster, looked Mrs. Harmon straight in the eye and said politely but firmly, "We're fine, thank you. We don't need anyone's help." She glanced toward Miss Honi, who gave her an encouraging nod.

"I'm afraid it's not up to you. Or me. It's the law," Mrs. Harmon said regretfully. "Now, why don't we go on upstairs and get your things?" She stood up, no doubt expecting Lindsay and her sister to follow.

But Miss Honi had other ideas. "They ain't going nowhere. I can look after 'em myself," she declared. Her hand dropped protectively onto Lindsay's shoulder. "Why, they practically live here as it is."

Mrs. Harmon cast her a dubious look. "Are you a relative?"

Miss Honi shook her head but didn't back down. "It don't make no difference. I couldn't love these girls any more'n if they was my own flesh and blood. They'll be just fine here with me until their mama comes home. Ain't that right, sugar?" she said, smiling down at Lindsay.

"I'm sorry, but it's out of the question. We have rules. You have to be licensed." Mrs. Harmon's tone grew brisk. "Please, Miss, ah, Love, don't make this any more difficult than it already is."

"There ain't nobody more fit to care for these girls than me," Miss Honi insisted, digging in her heels. "So if it's a matter of filling out some form, just show me where to sign."

"It's not as simple as that. For one thing, where would they sleep?" Mrs. Harmon glanced pointedly around the shabby two-room kitchen unit, identical to the one Lindsay and Kerrie Ann lived in upstairs except for the homey touches Miss Honi had added, like the plush recliner and lace doilies on every surface and the glass case in which her angels were displayed, angels of all shapes and sizes that she'd collected through the years, one of which, a delicate ceramic figure with gold-tipped wings, was presently cupped in the palm of Kerrie Ann's small hand as she sat cross-legged on the carpet, whispering secrets in its ear, seemingly unaware of what was going on.

"I'll make room," said Miss Honi firmly.

Mrs. Harmon remained firm. "Even if you could, how would you feed and clothe them when—if I may be frank, Miss Love—it looks as if you're barely subsisting yourself?"

Miss Honi's cheeks grew red. "We'd manage somehow. It don't take money to love a child."

In the end there was nothing to be done about it. The law was the law.

"Nooooooo!" Kerrie Ann wailed when Mrs. Harmon took her by the hand and began tugging her toward the door. She tore loose and darted over to

Miss Honi, clinging to her. "I want to stay with *you*!"

Lindsay noticed that in all the upset, her little sister had accidentally trampled the angel she'd been playing with; it now lay in pieces on the carpet, its head crushed, its wings severed from its body. In the years to come Lindsay couldn't think about her sister without seeing in her mind that poor, ruined angel.

But what would haunt her most would be the memory of Kerrie Ann crying out to her when it was time for them to go their separate ways— Lindsay to a foster home in Sparks and Kerrie Ann to one in another part of the state. A three-year-old girl in dirty pink terry shorts and a My Little Pony T-shirt, her face a knot of fear and confusion, her small body straining furiously against the adult arms holding her in check. Lindsay would never forget, either, the panic in her sister's voice as she begged her big sister not to let them take her.

It was the last she would see of that little girl.

CHAPTER ONE

Los Angeles, California; present day

*Y*OU GET OFF on pawing through ladies' underwear?" Kerrie Ann sniped.

The airport security guard glanced sharply up at her before resuming his search of her carry-on bag. She immediately regretted shooting off her mouth.

Why go looking for trouble when it was already on your ass like an APB on a stolen car? Here at LAX, of all places. Since 9/11, you couldn't look cross-wise at an airport official without being hauled off and strip-searched. And she was just the kind of person they would do that to. The kind likely to have a warrant out for her arrest or rock stashed in the lining of her suitcase. The only thing she wasn't likely to be suspected of was being a ter-rorist, but only because she was white.

Not just white but white-white. The kind of white that looked as if it never saw the sun because it was too busy soaking up the fluorescent lighting in some factory. She could almost hear the guard thinking, *White trash*. And who was she to deny it? Didn't she deserve to be looked down upon, to be the only one in line to have her bag searched for no apparent reason? It wasn't just that she looked the part, with her tattoo that snaked up one arm, pink streaks in her reddish-blond hair, and multiple piercings that had been enough to set off the metal detector. She was a world-class fuckup. She'd fucked up so royally, she'd had her kid taken away.

An invisible fist clenched about her heart at the thought. Annabella, Bella for short. Her six-year-old daughter, who wasn't hers anymore, at least not according to the state of California. Not until she could demonstrate that she was a fit parent. Seven whole months, and her only contact in all that time the twice-monthly visits supervised by

Bella's case-worker. And with her daughter in a foster home near San Luis Obispo, a three-hour drive each way, the trip alone was an exercise in frustration. Twice, on her way to visit Bella, the engine of her geriatric Ford Falcon had overheated, and once she'd blown a tire, which had eaten away at even those few allotted hours.

It won't be this way forever. She clung to that belief as if to a life preserver.

"All right, you're good to go." The guard, a swarthy middle-aged man, his cheeks pitted with old acne scars, zipped up her canvas carryall. But before she could snatch it off the table, he leaned in so they were eye to eye and said in a low, warning voice, "One word of advice, miss. Don't get cute. You get cute with us, you could find yourself in a whole lot of trouble. Got it?"

Kerrie Ann bit back a sharp retort. The dude didn't have anything on her, but he could still fuck with her, and she didn't want to miss her flight. She shot him a dirty look instead, waiting until she was out of earshot to mutter a few choice words under her breath.

The delay had put her a few crucial minutes behind schedule, and when she heard the boarding call for Flight 302 to San Francisco, she broke into a run. Why was everything so frigging *hard* all the time? If she didn't live all the way out in Simi Valley, if her friend Cammie hadn't gotten a ticket driving her to the airport, if she hadn't been singled out at the security check, she might have been one of those people leisurely strolling to their gate, a Starbucks coffee in hand. Instead she was weaving her way down the concourse like OJ's white Bronco with the cops in pursuit.

The story of her life. Wasn't she was forever running behind? A busted fan belt or blown sparkplug away from the breakdown lane at all times? At least once a week, she was late getting to work, delayed by car trouble, an appointment with her Legal Aid attorney, or a stop at the clinic where she submitted her weekly urine sample. And while Danny, her boss, wasn't unsympathetic—one of the advantages of working for someone in the program—she knew he was getting fed up with her excuses. She could hardly blame him, but what more could she do when she was already busting her ass just to stay afloat?

Would it be any different with the sister she was on her way to meet for the first time? Kerrie Ann had no idea what to expect when she arrived in Blue Moon Bay, and the pit in her stomach yawned at the thought. She hadn't even known about Lindsay until her attorney, Abel Touissant, had remarked the other day as they were settling into the booth at Denny's that was his ad hoc office until he could afford a real one, "You didn't tell me you have a sister."

Kerrie Ann stared at him, dumbfounded. "I do?"

"According to the state of Nevada. One Lindsay

Margaret McAllister." He pulled his laptop from its carrying case, and moments later they were looking at a blurry copy of a scanned document on its screen. He'd gotten hold of her old case file from Washoe County, thinking it might prove useful in her bid to regain custody of Bella. "Says here she went into foster care the same time you did," he went on, "only the couple who took her in must've adopted her because her last name was changed to Bishop in '83."

Kerrie Ann peered at the computer screen, struggling to process this startling revelation. "You mean all this time I had a sister and didn't even know it? Wow," she muttered in an awed voice.

Abel smiled at her. "This could be good for you."

Kerrie Ann didn't know about that. Whether or not it was to her advantage remained to be seen. She slowly shook her head. "I wonder where she is now."

"I have an address for her, in California," he said. "A town called Blue Moon Bay."

"It's somewhere up the coast, isn't it?"

"Just south of San Francisco. I vacationed there once as a kid with my folks. Nice place. Not much going on, but the scenery's awesome, and the people are friendly." He copied the address and phone number off the computer screen onto a slip of paper and handed it to her.

Kerrie Ann, in her present state, had no idea what she was going to do with the information, but she was glad her lawyer was taking her case seriously enough to dig up shit like that. Abel Touissant, twenty-four and fresh out of law school, might have come to her through Legal Aid, but he was as smart as any of those fat-cat lawyers with their fancy briefcases and high-rise executive suites. Better yet, he knew what it was to struggle. The eldest son of Haitian immigrants, he'd put himself through school on scholarships and by working nights and weekends. Maybe because of that, he didn't act like he was better than she; he always treated her as he would any client instead of one merely paying what she could afford.

"Thanks," she said, tucking the slip of paper into her purse.

"You should look her up."

"Maybe I will." Sure, and what would she say? *Hi, remember me? Your long-lost sister?* If this Lindsay had wanted a relationship with her, wouldn't she have been the one to get in touch?

Abel's brown eyes regarded her thoughtfully. "Seriously," he said, a bit more forcefully this time.

Kerrie Ann balked. "How do I know she'd even want to hear from me?"

"You won't know unless you look her up."

"And what would I say? 'Hi there. Long time, no see. And by the way, where the fuck have you been all these years?' Now, there's an icebreaker for you." As far as she was concerned, this was just another blank page in a family album that wasn't exactly a series of Kodak moments. "I don't even remember my mom. All I know is she died in prison. Hepatitis, I think—something drug-related." She gave a short, dry laugh. "So I guess I come by it honestly."

"Your sister might be able to fill in some of the blanks."

Maybe, but the last thing Kerrie Ann needed in her life right now was another complication. Also, niggling at the back of her mind, was the thought *What if she doesn't want anything to do with me? Why should she? Look what a loser I turned out to be.*

Two days later a hard dose of reality from Bella's caseworker propelled her to take action.

"The court is acting in your daughter's best interests. And until such time as you can demonstrate that you're competent to care for her yourself, she stays put," Mrs. Silvestre stated in no uncertain terms after Kerrie Ann shot off her mouth in a fit of frustration. "Be patient, Kerrie Ann," she advised in a less officious tone, closing the file in front of her. "These things take time. A child isn't a lost pet to simply be handed over."

Anger pulsed in Kerrie Ann like the vein throbbing at the base of her throat, but she resisted the urge to let loose with another curse. What purpose would it serve except to prove Mrs. Silvestre's point? She took a deep breath and said in a controlled voice, "I don't get it. I'm doing everything I'm supposed to. I'm staying clean. I go to meetings three times a week. I have a job and a place to live. So I don't get why Bella can't be with me. She's only six. She needs her mom." I *need her*, Kerrie Ann added silently.

Mrs. Silvestre, a small, bosomy woman with short, layered brown hair who brought to mind a robin with ruffled feathers, smiled at her wearily but not unsympathetically. "You've made strides, yes," she agreed. "But it's going to take more than a part-time job at Toys 'R' Us. And what about your living situation? Has that changed?"

"No, but I'm working on it," she said defensively. True, her current living situation wasn't exactly ideal—her friend Shoshanna was letting Kerrie Ann crash at her apartment until she saved enough money for a place of her own—but it was in a decent enough neighborhood, and her housemate wasn't a druggie. Meanwhile, Kerrie Ann was setting aside as much of each week's paycheck as she could. She walked instead of driving whenever possible and subsisted mainly on inexpensive staples like rice and beans. But what did this woman know? Did she have any idea how hard it was to save enough for first and last month's rent and security? Or how many rentals you had to look at to find something even halfway decent and affordable?

Clearly not, because Mrs. Silvestre was shaking

her head. "I'm afraid we're going to have to see more than willingness on your part, Kerrie Ann. Which I don't think is unreasonable considering the state of neglect your daughter was in when . . ."

Kerrie Ann tuned out the rest, not wanting to be reminded of what was still fresh in her mind. Could this woman heap any more shame on her than she already had on herself? Some days she was so filled with self-loathing that she could barely look at herself in the mirror. On those days, the only thing that kept her sane and sober was her twelve-step meetings, where she could at least derive some comfort from the shared experiences of others. Yes, she had only herself to blame. No one had put a gun to her head. But according to the Big Book, she'd been powerless in the grip of her disease. Powerless, too, where Jeremiah was concerned. Would she have gone down that road if she hadn't wanted so desperately to be a part of his life? If she hadn't felt that by refusing to get high with him she'd be cutting herself off from him in some way?

Before Bella was born, Jeremiah had been her whole world. She thought back to the night they'd met, eight years ago, when he'd picked her up hitchhiking. She was on her way to LA to see about a bartending job, and he invited her to crash at his place in Topanga Canyon. She never made it to LA. From that day on, they were inseparable. She was twenty-two and had been on her own for the past seven years, having run away from the last in a long line of foster parents (who'd probably been glad to see her go). Jeremiah did more than give her a home; he grounded her. With him she knew for the first time what it was to belong somewhere . . . and to someone.

Jeremiah was the lead guitarist in a rock-and-roll band called Urban Decay. The first couple of years, she went to every one of his gigs, even sitting in on practice sessions, just for the sheer pleasure of watching him perform. She didn't mind when other women came on to him; it only made him more desirable in her eyes. *She* was the one who got to go home with him at the end of the evening, the one to whom he'd make sweet love. She'd had her share of lovers before him, a lot of them one-night stands. But with Jeremiah, it was the real deal. She was in love. She loved everything about him: his face, his hands, his voice and low, seductive laugh, the fluid way he moved around onstage—sexier than any rock god—even the way he smelled, like their bed after a night of lovemaking. When they lay naked together, she never tired of running her hands over his skin, the golden brown of buttered toast, or threading her fingers through his dark, coiled hair that was like the pelt of some woolly beast. He was perfect in her eyes. Who cared if they were living from hand to mouth, or if their funky old house, built by some hippie who must have been stoned at the time, was practically falling down, or if the bills didn't always get paid on time?

The drugs were just part of the scene; at any given moment at least one member of the band was high on something. At first Kerrie Ann steered clear of all that, scared of ending up like her mom. But Jeremiah began pressuring her more and more. *You trust me, don't you?* he'd urge, wearing that sweetly innocent smile. *Would I do anything to hurt you?* Finally she gave in. In the beginning it was just the occasional party drug—pot, Ecstasy, poppers, a line of blow here and there. She stopped as soon as she found out she was pregnant, but after Bella was born, when it became clear that the train, meaning Jeremiah, was leaving the station without her, she started again. With a baby to care for, she couldn't go to his gigs like she used to. Without her keeping an eye on him, he began coming home later and later, sometimes not showing up until morning, and then occasionally smelling of perfume rather than just cigarettes and booze. She began to worry that he'd leave her for someone who wasn't so tied down or tired all the time. She'd do almost anything to keep him, and the one thing they shared, besides Bella, was drugs.

At first it was the best of both worlds. Taking care of her baby by day—sweet, precious Bella, whose chubby arms around her neck were the best high in the world—and by night, while her baby slept, getting loaded with Jeremiah and his band-mates. Not the hard stuff. That came later. By the time she was forced to admit to herself that she was hooked, it was too late: Quitting was no longer an option. Her extended season in hell, which began with that first rock she and Jeremiah smoked, led to four years in which she was lost to everyone, including herself.

No, she had no illusions about why her daughter had been taken from her. She just wanted Bella back.

Wordlessly Kerrie Ann dug a coin from the hip pocket of her jeans and plunked it down on the caseworker's desk. "My six-month chip," she said. "Do you know how freaking hard I had to work to get that? You ever tried pushing a wheelbarrow full of rocks up a mountain? That's what it's like. And do you know what gets me through each day? The only thing that makes it possible to keep putting one foot in front of the other? My little girl. Not an hour goes by, not a single minute, when I'm not thinking of her. When I'm not counting the days until I can be with her again." A tear rolled down one cheek, and she angrily brushed at it with the heel of her hand. She'd sworn she wouldn't break down in front of Mrs. Silvestre, and she'd be damned if she would.

The caseworker's expression softened. "I don't mean to sound unsympathetic," she said. "I just thought you should know what you're up against.

It's a high bar, Kerrie Ann. Yes, I can see you've come a long way, but you still have a ways to go." She paused as if in thought before adding tentatively, "Is there a family member who'd be willing to help out? Someone who could provide backup? The court might be more lenient in that case."

Which was why Kerrie Ann was on her way to her sister's now.

Lindsay Margaret McAllister Bishop. Kerrie Ann rolled the name around in her head the way she might an unfamiliar taste on her tongue. She wondered what this Lindsay was like. Was she married? Did she have kids? Had she made a success of her life, or was she struggling in some way? *If she's anything like me, she won't be much help.* And if she turned out to be a nice soccer mom living in the 'burbs? She probably wouldn't want her nice, tidy life muddied up by the mess Kerrie Ann had made of hers.

Either way, her long-lost sister dropping in out of the blue was certain to come as a shock. Kerrie Ann, figuring that a phone call wouldn't have the same impact as showing up in person, had decided to surprise Lindsay with a visit. It would be harder for her to say no that way.

Kerrie Ann had done a Google search, so she knew a little bit about her sister. The name "Lindsay Bishop" netted at least a dozen entries, most of them articles having to do with a piece of property Lindsay owned. "Local bookshop owner at center of land controversy," one of the headlines read. It seemed a hotel group with plans to build a fancy golf resort was trying to buy out property owners in that area. Lindsay was the lone holdout. So now Kerrie Ann knew two more things about her sister: that she owned her own home and business and that she wasn't a pushover. Which might or might not work in her favor.

As she boarded the flight to San Francisco, Kerrie Ann found herself wondering if this was a fool's mission. Why should her sister want to help out? Lindsay didn't know her. Maybe she didn't even want to know her. The fact was that in all these years she hadn't bothered to make contact. At least Kerrie Ann had an excuse for not getting in touch. What was Lindsay's? According to the records, she'd been eight years older than Kerrie Ann when they'd been shipped off to separate foster homes—old enough not to have forgotten that she had a sister.

She took her seat next to a petite, white-haired, grandmotherly type. They were buckled in, the plane readying for takeoff, when the old lady pointed to the wallet photo Kerrie Ann held clutched in her hand like a lifeline. "Your little girl? She looks just like you."

Kerrie Ann smiled tentatively. "You think so?"

Her seatmate leaned over to peer at the photo. "The spitting image."

Kerrie Ann knew the old lady was just being

polite. Her daughter looked nothing like her, except maybe around the mouth. If she was the spitting image of anyone, it was Jeremiah, with his burnt-sienna skin, curly dark hair, and striking amber eyes. The irony was that Bella had never known her dad. He'd split for parts unknown when she was just two.

In his absence Kerrie Ann had tried to harden her heart, but it was easier to hate herself than to hate Jeremiah. He wouldn't have left them if he'd been in his right mind, she reasoned; he'd been in the grip of the disease himself. Even all these years later, she missed him still. She'd been so wrapped up in him, it was almost as if he'd been part of her—an arm or a leg that had been chopped off. Closing her eyes as the plane taxied down the runway, she allowed her mind to travel back once more to the night they'd met.

"You take the bed, I'll crash on the sofa," he offered after they'd arrived at his place, adding with a sloe-eyed grin, "Wouldn't want you thinking I had an ulterior motive for giving you a lift."

"Why would I think that?" she replied with mock innocence. He could have anyone he wanted without having to scheme, and she was no exception. The minute she'd laid eyes on him, with his eyes that glowed like a cat's and body that made her want to jump his bones on the spot, she'd known she was in for a fun evening.

What she hadn't counted on was that it would be so much more.

"My guess is you've had your share of guys hitting on you." He looked at her, not like she was a piece of meat but admiring her as he might a beautiful piece of scenery.

"You mean because I'm not afraid to bum rides from strange men?" she replied, shamelessly fishing.

"You know perfectly well what I mean." His grin widened, showing an adorably crooked eyetooth. His eyes, she noticed, were the exact color of the tiger's-eye stone on the necklace she wore.

"So you think I'm hot, do you?" she teased, sidling up to him.

He laughed. "I'm not going to answer that on the grounds that it might incriminate me."

"Should I take that as a yes?"

"Take it any way you like." He played along, his eyes dancing. He still hadn't laid a hand on her.

"In that case, I have a suggestion—why don't we share the bed? That way neither of us has to wake up tomorrow morning with a sore back."

"That's assuming you plan on getting any sleep." Jeremiah slid an arm around her waist, pulling her in close to nuzzle her neck as he lightly traced the outline of one breast with a loosely clenched fist. She felt a deep inner tug, like a guyline being cut, sending her spinning.

Then he was kissing her, his lips soft against

hers, his tongue gently probing. He held her head cupped in his hands, his fingers threaded through her hair, his thumbs pressed lightly into the tender flesh below her earlobes. As if laying claim to her somehow. Before she knew it, they were struggling out of their clothes, trying not to trip over themselves and each other as they paused, breathless, between kisses to quickly undo a button, wrestle down a zipper, release a hook. From the start she knew it was going to be different than with the men before him—too many to count, starting at the age of fourteen, when she'd been seduced by a twenty-year-old relative of her foster family at the time. This wasn't just about satisfying an urge; it was way more intense. So intense it scared her. But it was a fun kind of scared, like riding the world's steepest roller coaster.

They never made it to the bedroom. They did it right there on the floor, on a ratty old carpet that might have been the softest down mattress for all she noticed. Not so much as if they were making love as *inhaling* each other. Her first high with Jeremiah, and not a joint or crack pipe in sight.

She gave a bittersweet smile at the memory, bringing her gaze back to the photo in her hand: the child who'd been born out of that love. It had been taken shortly after Bella's fifth birthday, one of those quickie studio portraits from Wal-Mart. She was posed against a backdrop of fall foliage, wearing the dress Kerrie Ann had bought for her first day of kindergarten, a yellow flowered one with a smocked front and puffy sleeves, and white patent-leather Mary Janes. Her curly dark hair was braided, little wisps standing out all over her head like the fuzz on a baby duck, and her smile as wide as a truckload of promises.

That had been a good day. They'd gone out for ice cream afterward, and then to the kiddie park. Kerrie Ann had managed to keep it together for the most part, having vowed for the umpteenth time that she was going to clean up her act. Didn't Bella deserve a mother who would look after her properly, give her the kind of childhood she herself hadn't had?

Her resolve lasted all of twenty-four hours.

Kerrie Ann was firmly in the grip of her addiction, dealing a little on the side to stay solvent and keep the supply coming, when a concerned neighbor alerted authorities to what was going on at her house. They found her living in squalor, the kitchen awash in dirty dishes and the floors strewn with refuse, an unkempt and underfed Bella dressed only in a pair of dirty underpants. The police searched the premises, but by sheer luck Kerrie Ann was between runs, so they didn't find any drugs.

Before she could breathe a sigh of relief, one of the cops, a tall, skinny guy with bad teeth, approached her, saying in a stern voice, "Ma'am, I need you to answer a few questions."

Kerrie Ann nodded grudgingly.

He looked at Bella. "That your little girl?"

"Yeah. Why?"

The cop ignored her combative tone. "Shouldn't she be in school?"

Kerrie Ann couldn't remember if it was a weekday, so she said the first thing that popped into her head: "She's sick." In fact, it was she who was sick. The jitters were setting in, along with the chills—she'd been on her way to meet her supplier when the cops had shown up.

"Then why is she running around half naked?" demanded his partner, a fat-bottomed woman with frizzy brown hair. She glanced at Bella, who was staring up at them with huge dark eyes, the fingers of one hand stuffed into her mouth—a baby habit she reverted to when upset—then brought her gaze back to Kerrie Ann, her expression one of contempt.

In a moment of terrible clarity, Kerrie Ann took in the squalid scene through the cops' eyes. She saw her daughter—really *saw* her—for the first time in weeks: how dirty she was and how thin she'd gotten, her ribs sticking out of her narrow brown chest like rungs on a ladder. She saw the stain on the seat of her underpants that had come from not wiping herself properly and having no one to do it for her, the crust of dried food around her mouth. When had she last fed Bella? When was the last time she'd tucked her into bed at night or taken her to school? She couldn't recall. There was only a terrible rushing sound in her head, like wind howling through a tunnel where calm and order had once been.

She watched the lady cop crouch down and begin speaking softly to Bella. It wasn't until she took Bella by the hand and began leading her toward the door that understanding kicked in. Kerrie Ann moved to block them. "Hey—where do you think you're going? That's my kid!" she cried. "Bella, come to Mommy!" It came out more as a shrill command than a cry of distress. Both cops looked worried that she might hurt Bella.

Even Bella's big, frightened eyes seemed to accuse her in some way. Bella began to cry.

Kerrie Ann took a lunging step toward her, wanting to console her, but the male cop quickly moved in, seizing her by the upper arm and commanding, "Ma'am, please." In a calming voice, he added, "We'll take good care of her."

"You can't do this. You have no right!" shrieked Kerrie Ann as the lady cop led Bella out the door, her partner maintaining a firm grip on Kerrie Ann's arm all the while. When she ran out of curses, Kerrie Ann began to plead. "Where are you taking her? Please, at least give me that." Her eyes were streaming, and phlegmy sobs erupted from her throat. The chills racking her body turned to uncontrollable shivering. She felt as if she were coming unglued.

"Call this number." He let go of her arm and fished a business card from his pocket, handing it to her.

Kerrie Ann saw the Children's Services logo on the card and felt herself hurtling back in time. The old nightmare playing itself over, this time with her child.

As soon as she could pull herself together, she drove to the county offices, where her pleas and entreaties were met with more indifference. All anyone would tell her was that Bella was in a safe place. The woman at the front desk suggested that Kerrie Ann get a lawyer, which only left her feeling even more at a loss. Whom could she hire? And how would she pay them? She was on her way to her supplier's—to satisfy a more immediate need—when, stopped at a red light, she spotted a billboard advertising a free clinic for those looking to kick a drug habit. Kerrie Ann would never know what caused her to head in that direction instead. In her twelve-step program they attributed it to her Higher Power, but for her it was simply a case of do or die—the choice between either stepping off a high ledge or retreating from it. Because the one thing she was sure of was that there would be no meaningful life for her without Bella.

She had little memory of the first week in rehab; she was in the detox ward for most of it, on meds that kept her so out of it, she barely knew what planet she was on. Gradually she emerged from the fog, and the days and weeks that followed were filled with meetings—meetings with her counselor, meetings with her peer group, twice-a-day twelve-step meetings—interspersed with a daily routine of menial chores and communal meals. All the while the desire to use again a constant beat on the boom box inside her head.

It was the longest month of her life.

She doubted she'd have gotten through it if not for Bella. She'd naively believed that if she could just get clean, that was all it would take to get her daughter back.

Her counselor at the clinic, Mary Josephson, a recovering heroin addict with twenty years of sobriety, suggested she call Legal Aid, and Legal Aid put her in touch with Abel Touissant. Days later she had a court date. But at the hearing, it quickly became evident that things weren't going in her favor. The judge, a portly middle-aged man, probably with children of his own, addressed her with such contempt that she felt as if she were on trial—which in a way she was.

"The child will remain in foster care until such time as the mother—" he scowled down at Kerrie Ann from the bench, "can demonstrate to the court's satisfaction that she's a fit parent." In addition to continuing with her twelve-step program, submitting to weekly drug testing, and taking a parenting class, she would need to find steady employment and "appropriate accommodations," he elaborated.

"How long? Weeks, months?" she tearfully asked her lawyer outside the courtroom.

Abel spoke with a directness she would later see as a sign of respect but which at the time felt like salt on her wounds. "I can't answer that. It's up to you." One misstep—a failed drug test, a lost job, a poor report from the caseworker—and she'd be back at square one, he warned.

"What if something happens that I have no control over?" she fretted aloud.

He smiled at her encouragingly. "You'll be all right as long as you keep your eye on the ball."

But Kerrie Ann soon discovered that good intentions weren't enough. Her résumé, which listed only a string of short-term jobs, was hardly an incentive for anyone to hire her. The part-time job at Toys "R" Us was the best she could do until she got her GED or some kind of occupational training. And without full-time work, how could she afford "appropriate accommodations"? Life was a series of dominoes: Knock one down, and the rest followed suit. If she could just get her legs under her . . .

Which was where her sister came in. Lindsay was the only card left to play. *Lord, don't let me fuck this one up, too*, she prayed. So much was riding on it. Already Bella was adjusting to life with her foster parents. During their scheduled visits, she would chatter on about her friends in school, the projects she was doing in her first grade class, and various fun excursions with the Bartholds. What would it be like six months from now, a year? Would her little girl stop asking when she could come home? However well meaning, the Bartholds didn't know and love Bella the way Kerrie Ann did. Would they remember that she was allergic to bee stings? Did they cut the crusts off her sandwiches the way she liked? Tell her it was okay when she wet the bed, that it happened even to big girls? To anyone who knew Kerrie Ann's history, she'd have sounded ridiculous airing such concerns. Yes, she'd fucked up. But she was still Bella's mom. No one could take that away.

Her thoughts returned to Lindsay. She still couldn't get over the fact that she had a sister. Even weirder was that she had no memory of her. How was it possible for those years to be a blank slate?

There was one recurring dream, though. In it she was a little girl again, snuggled on a woman's lap, her head nestled against a bosom more supremely cushy than the softest of pillows. In the dream, she never saw the woman's face. Nonetheless, Kerrie Ann knew that lap to be the safest place in the world. Each time she awoke from the dream, she would try to hold on to those feelings of warmth and comfort. At times, lying in bed with her eyes shut as she struggled to keep from surfacing, she could almost swear the woman was real, her presence was so strong. She'd even catch a faint whiff of her scent, a mixture of cigarette smoke and some flowery perfume. Kerrie Ann didn't think the woman in her dream was her mother. Maybe her sister would know . . .

Before she knew it, the plane was touching down at San Francisco International. Making her way through the terminal, she stopped for a hamburger and fries to quiet the growling in her belly—she'd skipped breakfast that morning—before heading for the rental-car center. She hated having to spend money on a car but didn't have much choice. Her old Falcon wouldn't have survived the trip to Blue Moon Bay, and if she'd taken a bus, she'd have been stuck overnight. And who knew what kind of reception she'd get?

Half an hour later Kerrie Ann was crawling through traffic on the Bayshore freeway in her rented Hyundai, her window down, smoking a cigarette. When she reached the exit for 92, she took the ramp marked Blue Moon Bay/Santa Cruz and soon was cruising along a less traveled route that wound through grassy, oak-studded hills. There wasn't a cloud in the sky, but along the horizon a line of fog crouched like a gray cat waiting to spring.

She was approaching the outskirts of town when she found herself enveloped in a soft gray mist. Not the dense fog she'd known on previous trips up the coast but one that merely blurred the landscape, giving it the look of a storybook illustration. The tall eucalyptus trees lining the road rose like Jack's magic beanstalk to disappear into the thicker fog overhead. Beyond stretched fields of cultivated flowers—roses, snapdragons, chrysanthemums, and dahlias with blossoms the size of teacups—where she could make out the indistinct shapes of toiling figures and several greenhouses that, from this distance, might have been glass castles. Directly ahead, a short distance from where the road merged with Highway 1, lay the sea. She could see it glinting where the sun had burned through the fog, a silvery sweep of ocean furrowed by long swells that sheared off into whitecaps as they drove in toward the cliffs.

The damp sea air rushing in through the open window brought pleasant memories of days at the beach, warm sand scrunching beneath her bare soles. In the distance, she could hear the booming of surf. Seagulls circled lazily above the cliffs. Kerrie Ann felt her anxiety ease a bit. In a place as majestic as this, surely there was room for one small miracle?

When she pulled into town, she parked in the first available spot and walked the rest of the way. After strolling for several blocks along a main drag lined with shops and eateries, she located her sister's bookshop on one of the side streets. Unlike some of the storefronts she'd passed along the way, with their cutesy signs and windows full of kitschy seaside souvenirs, it didn't appear to cater primarily to the tourist trade. It looked like a place that sold books to people who loved to read, as warm and inviting and a bit worn as a comfortable old sofa. The weathered sign over the gabled entrance advertised it as the Blue Moon Bay Book Café. There was a wooden bench out front, flanked by flower boxes from which bright pansies peeked like smiley faces. Peering in, she saw some customers browsing the aisles while others sat at café tables in back, sipping coffee and nibbling on baked goods. Displayed in the front window was an assortment of titles recommended for Mother's Day. Her heart constricted. For her, the holiday would be just another day without her daughter.

Hovering outside the door, Kerrie Ann felt as if she were about to step onstage to perform a part she hadn't rehearsed. Her heart was in her throat, her palms sweaty. Would her sister welcome her or want nothing to do with her? Or something in between—Lindsay making polite noises while counting the minutes until she left?

Only one way to find out. She paused just long enough to take in her reflection in the door's glass pane—pink-haired and tattooed, wearing black low-rise jeans and a pair of high-heeled boots, a red leather jacket over a knockoff Juicy Couture midi-top—before she pushed her way inside.

CHAPTER TWO

The previous day

ᗡO YOU THINK I'll ever find her?" Lindsay mused aloud.

"Who?" Grant replied without looking up.

"My sister."

It was late afternoon, and they were seated on the balcony of his condo, overlooking the marina in Pacifica. While browsing through the Sunday paper, Lindsay had come across an article about a brother and a sister in Germany, separated as children during World War II, who'd been reunited after a span of sixty-eight years. It had given rise to the spark of hope in her own breast, never far below the surface.

But when she'd remarked on it, Grant had only lifted his head from the sports section to murmur, "Mmm. Isn't that something?" She might have been commenting on the weather. With a sigh of frustration, she bundled up the rest of the newspaper and tossed it aside. Why, whenever she mentioned her sister, usually in the context of some new lead—a former foster parent of Kerrie Ann's whom she'd tracked down, or a response to a want ad she'd placed—did she get the feeling, even when he feigned interest, that Grant found the whole subject tiresome? As if she were someone in mourning who, in his view, should have moved on by now.

She stewed a moment longer before her innate sense of fairness won out. *Can I blame him?* she thought. He was a lawyer; he dealt in facts. And what evidence was there to support the hope that she'd one day be reunited with Kerrie Ann? Only scraps of information that had proved useless.

She leaned into him as they sat side-by-side on the chaise lounge. Between Grant's busy schedule and hers, their days off didn't often coincide, so she'd learned to savor each one as she did the all-too-rare sunny days in this part of the world. Today was a double bonus: a whole Sunday to themselves, with clear skies and temperatures that felt more like mid-June than May. Earlier in the day, they'd gone sailing with friends and were now enjoying a quiet moment alone before supper. An open bottle of pinot grigio sat on the small glass table in front of them. The sun, low in the sky, skewered by the tall masts of the sailboats moored in the marina, spilled its pinkish-gold light over the water below, turning it iridescent. Lindsay reached for her wineglass, the light from the setting sun sparking off its rim as she lifted it to her lips.

It wasn't just the article. These past few days, thoughts of her sister had been cropping up more than usual, as if a radio frequency on which Lindsay normally received only static were suddenly transmitting a clear, if intermittent, signal.

Why now, after all these years? She had no answer.

Grant finally abandoned the sports section when the light became too dim for him to read. "One of these days, I'd like a boat of my own," he remarked, gazing out over the marina. "Nothing fancy, just a nice little sloop. Enough room below deck for the two of us." He looped an arm around her shoulders.

"You could afford one now," she told him.

"Oh, so you think I'm made of money, do you?" He turned to her, his mouth slanted in a smile that, with the freckles spattered over his nose, made him look like a mischievous schoolboy. "Saving the environment has its compensations, I'll admit, but I'm afraid a fat salary isn't one of them."

"I was talking about my sister, and you're talking boats. Do you think there's a connection there?" Her lighthearted tone contained a gentle reprimand. Grant was the ideal boyfriend in many ways. He made few demands and loved her just as she was, so much so that he preferred the present, unvarnished Lindsay—jeans and sweatshirt, no makeup, her straight brown hair pulled back in a ponytail—to the stylishly dressed and made-up one who would stroll into the restaurant on his arm an hour from now. So why did she sometimes get the feeling that her concerns were fourth or fifth on his priority list? Was it simply that they'd been together so long that he no longer hung on her every word?

"We could always name the boat after your sister," he offered.

She frowned. "Be serious."

"I am. What better tribute?"

"She's not dead." Lindsay added on a fretful note, "At least, I hope not."

Grant reached for the wine bottle and refilled their glasses. Her mind traveled back to when they'd first met, three years ago at an Earth First! fundraiser at which he'd been the keynote speaker. She recalled how captivated she'd been by the sight of him standing at the podium. He wasn't, in the strictest sense, what she'd call handsome—more Sam Shepard than George Clooney—but he was so tall and poised and confident that he'd gleamed up there like a brandished sword, with his shock of blond hair and impossibly white teeth. Displaying just enough boyish enthusiasm to soften his heroic contours, he spoke urgently of the need for each individual to take measures in combating pollution: a modern-day Jason out to slay the Gorgons of corporate greed.

"I hope I didn't bore you with my speech," he said to her later on, after they were introduced. "Nothing sets the cause back like a preacher on his soap box." She assured him that she'd found his speech interesting, if a bit too long, to which he replied with a laugh, "You're the first honest person I've spoken to tonight. Lindsay, is it? Lindsay, will you sit and have a drink with me? I promise, no more preaching. I want to hear all about *you*."

On that night she had the feeling that if another woman at the function stripped off all her clothes and went streaking through the crowd, Grant wouldn't even have noticed, he was so focused on her. In the days and weeks that followed, too, he listened with rapt attention to her stories, laughed at her jokes, made a point of reading books she recommended; he even pretended to enjoy himself when dragged along to the local farmers' market, which he only later confessed he found about as fun as flossing his teeth (having grown up on a farm, he didn't see the appeal).

Now she wondered how she'd managed to drift away from the center of that focus. Was it simply inevitable when a couple had been together as long as Grant and she?

He handed her glass back to her. "Who knows? You may get lucky yet. Just like the brother and sister in the article." So he had been listening. If not for his patronizing tone, she might even have thought he was sincere.

"You make it sound like I'd have as much chance of spotting the Loch Ness monster."

At her sharp remark, he eyed her in puzzlement. The breeze picked up just then, lifting a lock of blond hair off his forehead. His blue eyes shone in a last burst of sunlight. "Did I say something wrong?"

"No," she conceded. "It's just that I get the feeling you don't think I'll ever find her."

He hesitated before saying gently, "Did it ever occur to you that maybe she doesn't want to be found?"

She felt herself tense. "Why would I think that?"

"It just seems to me that otherwise she'd have surfaced by now. Maybe there's a reason she's remained underground," he went on in the same maddeningly reasonable tone.

"Such as?"

"She could be in trouble with the law."

Lindsay responded quickly, "I wouldn't care if she was in trouble."

"Yes, but *she* doesn't know that." At the dark look she shot him, Grant shook his head, wearing a bewildered look. "I don't understand. You've been looking for your sister for God knows how long. Certainly as long as I've known you. So why are you getting so worked up all of a sudden?"

Lindsay's shoulders slumped. "I don't know." She sat for a moment chewing on her lip, watching a sailboat far out at sea gracefully tacking its way toward the marina, its sails bellying out as it leaned away from the wind. "Her birthday's coming up. It got me thinking, is all."

"I'll tell you what. When the day comes, why don't I take you out to dinner, and we'll celebrate—raise a glass to your sister in absentia. How about that?"

She brought her gaze back to Grant to find him beaming at her as if to say, *Problem solved.*

You don't get it. You don't get it at all. She bit back the caustic words. She wasn't normally given to displays of temper and rarely lashed out in anger. Logic, reason, carefully constructed arguments—those were her weapons of choice. Only, who was being unreasonable here? Kerrie Ann had been missing for more than a quarter of a century. Was it Grant's fault that he saw her search as futile? That he was unable to comprehend the deep ache she still felt (though he rarely saw his own sister, who still lived in his hometown of Grantsburg, Wisconsin, she was still very much a part of his life) that defied the passage of time and seeming absence of any hope?

She sighed once more, raising her glass to her lips. "I guess it's easier to dwell on the past than face what's happening in the present." She was referring to the current thorn in her side: the Heywood Group. Men in suits whose skulduggery was cloaked in corporate jargon but who were no better than a band of pirates trying to rob her.

"What's the latest from Dwight?" Grant asked.

Dwight Tibbet was her lawyer. When she'd gone to Grant for help in fending off the Heywood Group, he'd referred her to an old friend from law school who specialized in land disputes and who, Grant assured her, was more qualified than he to handle the matter.

59

"There's talk of their invoking eminent domain." She spoke in a low, controlled tone, determined not to spoil the day's mood any more than she already had.

Grant frowned. "They don't have the authority."

"No, but the county does, and I have it from a reliable source that at least half the commissioners are in bed with those slimeballs."

"It's just a scare tactic."

"Guess what? It's working." She felt sick just thinking about what would happen should the Heywood Group and their cronies prevail. Her only recourse would be to battle it out in court. And what chance would she, a mere property owner, have against the united front of a government body and a hotel group with virtually bottomless pockets?

"So have you changed your mind about accepting their offer?"

She shot him an indignant glance. Didn't he know her better than that? "I'm not *that* scared." The latest offer from the Heywood Group was more money than she'd see in a lifetime. Certainly more than her property would fetch on the open market. But what price could be placed on the joy of waking up each morning to the view out her window, or being lulled to sleep at night by the sound of the surf? On a more practical level, where would she go if she were to sell out? The house she'd inherited from her adoptive parents, set on twenty acres of oceanfront property, was the only real home she had ever known.

No; if those pirates seized control, it would be over her dead body.

"Well, I'm sure Dwight knows what he's doing. He'll shut it down." Grant put an arm around her shoulders as she began to shiver. "Cold? Do you want me to get your sweater?"

She shook her head, resolutely swallowing against the bitter pill that refused to go down. No sense boring her boyfriend to tears with her problems. Today was supposed to be a respite from all that. "No, I'm fine. It's nice out here." With the setting of the sun had come the cool air of evening, but she didn't feel like budging. How often did she get to just sit and relax?

"Shall I call the restaurant and tell them we'll be late?" he asked.

"No." She forced a smile. "Let's go eat." She wasn't hungry, but she supposed she would have an appetite once they got to the restaurant—they were dining at the Landing, her favorite waterfront eatery. "By the way, do you mind if I bring Miss Honi to the party tomorrow?" Grant was having some people over for dinner, a few of his clients and their spouses, and she thought her resident fairy godmother, as she'd dubbed Miss Honi, would enjoy an evening out. At an age when many of her contemporaries were content to stay home, the old woman never missed an opportunity to step out in a fancy dress and high heels.

Grant's expression remained neutral, but he hesitated a beat too long before replying, "Of course. The more the merrier."

For some reason, he and Miss Honi had never clicked. They were always polite to each other, but it was obvious to Lindsay that neither saw the other's appeal. Grant, despite his urban polish and Ivy League education, retained at core many of the old-fashioned values instilled in him by his small-town upbringing—about as far from the free-wheeling nightlife of Reno, Nevada, as the Promised Land was from Sodom and Gomorrah. Although he'd never said so to her face, Lindsay knew he was mystified by her decision to have someone who wasn't, strictly speaking, a family member move in with her. He didn't understand that for Lindsay, those ties ran deeper than blood.

She ducked into the bathroom, where she showered while Grant made some calls. He was still on the phone when she emerged, wrapped in a towel. From the garment bag she'd brought from home, she pulled her trusty black dress. She kept a toothbrush, a pair of pajamas, and a change of clothing at her boyfriend's, but other than that, she had yet to establish her presence in any real sense. Not that Grant spent much time here, either, which was why his condo, a short drive up the coast from her place, still seemed a bit sterile, almost like a model home, even though he'd lived there nearly a year. Now, standing before the closet door, zipping up her dress, she could see his reflected image in the mirror as he sat on the bed, the phone to his ear. He was looking her way but not seeing her, he was so deep in conversation. She couldn't help feeling the tiniest bit ignored. There was a time when her boyfriend couldn't keep his hands off her, when the sight of her naked would have been an open invitation and the bed an excuse to postpone their dinner reservation. Not that she was in the mood for lovemaking right now. Still . . .

I'm thirty-eight years old, she thought. *Why do I feel as if life is passing me by?*

Grant caught her eye as he was hanging up. He let out a low whistle. "Better hurry up or I won't be responsible for my actions," he said, getting up and strolling over to her. He planted a kiss on the nape of her neck as she struggled to fasten the clasp of her necklace. She smiled into the curtain of hair over her face as she stood with her head bent forward, his breath warm against her neck. Okay, maybe she wasn't going to be hanging it up just yet.

She turned to give him a real kiss, but he'd already moved past her and was reaching into the closet for his jacket. "Shall we?" he said, holding out his arm.

She smiled, doing her best to quell the tiny bubble of unrest lodged at her center. Together they stepped out into the cool of the evening, where a handful of high-flung stars glimmered.

The following morning Lindsay was at work stacking books on the center island when she glanced up to find Miss Honi gazing thoughtfully at the display, her ruby lips pursed in disapproval. "Sugar, you got to save yourself before you can save the planet," she said at last.

"And what makes you think I need saving?" Lindsay tossed her a distracted smile, blowing at a wisp of hair tickling one of her eyelids that she couldn't reach with her arms laden.

"Here you are giving over valuable display space to books only a green Nazi would love, and you have to ask?" Miss Honi was taking a break after a spirited reading from *James and the Giant Peach* for a group of rapt preschoolers and their moms. She was seated in the chintz easy chair tucked into a corner by the front window, where she could keep an eye on things.

"How would you know if you haven't read them yourself? I'm sure some of these are very interesting," Lindsay defended her choice of titles. "And don't forget, Earth Day is a big deal around here." As if it would be possible to overlook with all the flyers circulating for the rally on Thursday, a small stack of which sat next to the cash register at the Blue Moon Bay Book Café.

"Sure, but folks want to be fired up, not put to

sleep." Miss Honi waved a hand dismissively toward the display. "We'll be lucky to sell half a dozen of those dust catchers. The rest'll end up in some landfill, polluting even more of the planet."

Miss Honi heaved herself from the chair and clip-clopped over to the island in her dainty, wedge-heeled espadrilles, from which her red-painted toenails peeked coquettishly. In her midnight-blue velour slacks and matching top, gold necklace the color of the hair piled in ringlets atop her head, and a whole percussion section of bangles jingling on her wrists, she was, as usual, impossible to ignore. As if to prove her point, she picked up a book bearing the less than scintillating title *Sustainable Agriculture for the Modern Age,* giving an exaggerated roll of her turquoise-shadowed eyes before replacing it on its stack.

What made it so aggravating was that, in her heart, Lindsay knew Miss Honi was right. If the book café was struggling financially, it was mostly her fault. Too often she was guided more by her social conscience or personal preferences than what she knew would sell. She forgot she was running a business, not teaching a course. If it weren't for Miss Honi, a self-proclaimed lover of "trashy" novels and tireless advocate for the kind of books that were a guilty pleasure for a number of their customers, they would surely have gone under by now.

But Lindsay didn't give in easily once her back

was up. Growing up, she'd had to be tenacious in order to survive, the proverbial weed pushing its way through the sidewalk. "Whatever we don't sell, we can always return," she reminded Miss Honi, adopting a breezy tone as she set out one of the more approachable titles, an environmentally friendly book aimed at kids titled *It's Easy Being Green!* "And if they end up in a landfill, I'm sure it'll be a sustainable one," she added with a wry smile. "Anyway, don't knock the green Nazis. We're going to need them if the Heywood Group has its way." A vocal show of support from one of those organizations would force the bastards into the public eye, where they'd have to explain why one of the community's last unspoiled stretches of coastline should make way for yet another bloated golf resort.

"It'd help, too, if your boyfriend got off his bee-hind," declared Miss Honi.

Here we go again. Miss Honi seldom missed an opportunity to take a jab at Grant. Lindsay lowered an armful of books onto the table and turned to face her. "What makes you think he isn't helping?"

Miss Honi snorted in derision. "Actions speak louder than words."

"Well, you'll be seeing him tonight, so you can tell him to his face."

"Oh, what's the occasion?" Miss Honi inquired idly.

Lindsay repositioned a book on its easel. "He's

throwing a party, and you're invited. Remember, I told you about it last night." Miss Honi must not have been fully awake at the time.

"A party?" Miss Honi perked up like an alley cat at the scent of chicken bones.

"It's for his clients," Lindsay went on. "They're part of a coalition that's trying to save some fish from extinction—the spiny-backed something or other. Grant's been working overtime on the case."

Miss Honi gave another snort. "Figures. The man don't have the time of day for his two-legged brethren, but give it fins or fur and he's all over it like a cheap suit."

If Grant was circumspect when it came to expressing his feelings about Miss Honi, she had no compunction when it came to voicing her opinion of him. While she'd allow that he was "easy on the eyes" and "smart enough to give lawyers a good name," she was convinced that Lindsay was wasting precious time waiting for him to marry her. "I know the type. You'll always come in second with a man like that," she'd say when pressed for an explanation. Lindsay always defended him, but the truth was, she had her own doubts. She and Grant had talked about moving in together, but Grant couldn't see himself living with Lindsay and her elderly and somewhat disreputable housemate, and under no circumstances would Lindsay ever abandon Miss Honi. If they couldn't agree on something as basic as that, she wasn't going to hold her breath as far as marriage was concerned.

"Well, if that's how you feel, I guess there's no point in your going," Lindsay said with feigned regret even as she smiled to herself, knowing what Miss Honi's reaction would be. She was as transparent as a Frederick's of Hollywood negligee. No one loved a party more than she. Once a performer, always a performer, even if no longer involved taking off her clothes.

The glint in Miss Honi's eyes gave her away even as her chin tipped up, setting her saucer-sized hoop earrings wagging. "Did I say that? Lord, can't a girl catch her breath without you putting words in her mouth? You tell him I'll think about it."

"Well, don't take too long."

After pretending to give it some thought, Miss Honi relented with a noisy exhalation. "What the hell. Count me in. It ain't like I got something better to do." Her expression turned briefly wistful, as if she were thinking about her most recent boyfriend. They'd been going hot and heavy for a while—even at the age of eighty, Miss Honi was nowhere near ready to "pack it in"—until, sadly, Charlie had dropped dead of a coronary one night while bowling with his friends. That had been six months ago, and Miss Honi hadn't yet taken up with anyone new. "You sure he won't mind my tagging along?" she asked.

"Of course not. He made a point of asking me to invite you," Lindsay fibbed. A little white lie wouldn't hurt, would it? "Everyone knows you're the life of the party." True enough, which was why Lindsay had her own, selfish reasons for wanting Miss Honi there. Gatherings of Grant's business associates tended to be dull affairs—green Nazis, for all their zeal, were a fairly humorless bunch, she'd found—and with Miss Honi to keep it lively, Lindsay could relax a bit.

Miss Honi was trying not to show it, but Lindsay could tell she was pleased to be asked. "That may be, but come party time these old bones are gonna need a kick start, 'cause it don't look like I'll be getting any rest before then," she bitched good-naturedly, watching a customer, a young woman in jeans and Polar fleece, approach the register with a stack of books in hand.

Miss Honi hurried off to ring up the purchase, and Lindsay went back to arranging her display. It had been a slow day so far, not that you'd know it from the number of people browsing the aisles or lingering at the café tables in back. The trouble was, she knew from long experience, a lot of those customers would leave without buying anything. The Blue Moon Bay Book Café was that sort of place: It encouraged reading for reading's sake, not just to sell books. If someone wanted to spend the whole day parked in an easy chair or at one of the tables in back with a book or their laptop, there was no one to discourage him or her from doing so. In the children's section, the more popular titles were as well thumbed as library books. But Lindsay wouldn't have it any other way.

Grant often chided her for not being more hard-headed when it came to business, but she couldn't part with the notion that books were for everyone, whether or not everyone could afford them. As a young girl, before she'd gone to live with Ted and Arlene, where would she have been without books? Her library card had been her lifeline and books her lone escape. Caught up in her imaginary worlds, she would see, looking out the window of the motel, not the flat gray parking lot below, its cars gleaming under the relentless Nevada sun, but the misty, windswept moors of *Wuthering Heights* or *Jane Eyre*. She would see caped figures on horseback riding to the rescue where disreputable-looking men in baseball caps and toe-sprung cowboy boots lurked. She could even convince herself that one day she and her sister would escape.

That dream had come true for one of them at least.

At the same time, Lindsay couldn't ignore the cold, hard facts. She had bills to pay and expenses to meet. Not only that, when her lease came up for renewal in December, it would probably mean an increase in rent. There was no question that if she were to accept the Heywood Group's latest offer, it would solve her financial worries. Not just in the short term: She'd be set for life. She could open another bookstore in addition to this one with that kind of money.

But at what price? The house and property she'd inherited from Ted and Arlene were all she had left of them. How could she give that up? Mornings, watching the sun come up over the mountains to the east, she was reminded of her dad and the leisurely hikes they had often taken, with Ted, an avid birdwatcher, pausing frequently to press the binoculars into her hands as he pointed up at some bird perched in a tree. In the evenings, watching the sun sink into the ocean, she would think of her mom, Arlene, and how she had loved to stroll on the beach, picking up seashells and bits of beach glass that were still displayed in decorative bowls and jars around the house.

"From the time I was little, I knew I would one day live by the ocean," Arlene had told her once, smiling at the irony of it—she, a girl from Minnesota for whom the ocean had been but a lesson in geography until a trip to the seashore with her parents when she was ten. They'd been standing on the beach in the little cove below their house, watching the waves pound into shore as a storm brewed. Arlene's long, graying brown hair, the color of salt-silvered planks, which she normally wore braided, was blowing in the wind, making her look, in her navy peacoat and billowy skirt, like a character out of an eighteenth-century novel—a sailor's wife keeping watch for her husband's ship. "I wanted to be where I'd always know it was there, even when I couldn't see it. Where I'd hear it whispering to me at night. Does that make sense?" She turned to Lindsay, her eyes bright and cheeks flushed. Lindsay, all of fourteen at the time but in many ways wiser than most adults, nodded in response. It made perfect sense. Didn't she feel the same way?

"I hope I never get married," she told her adoptive mom with all the passion of a young girl who hadn't even been kissed. "That way I'll get to stay here always."

All these years later the grown-up Lindsay smiled, thinking, *Be careful what you wish for.*

But would she have wanted anything different? This was where she belonged, where she'd always belonged, even before she'd known of this place. She was as sure of it as she was that her being placed with Ted and Arlene had been no accident of fate. To lose her home would be cruel enough, but to be an accomplice in her own eviction—no, it was unthinkable.

She'd be a traitor to the community as well. Not everyone in Blue Moon Bay was as gung-ho about the proposed resort as those with a vested interest in the jobs and tax revenue it would generate. There were the recent transplants, like her closest neighbors, Bill and Janice Harkins, who'd moved here to escape such rampant development, as well as those like Ollie's dad, a third-generation fisherman, for whom a sprawling resort and all it would spawn—a plethora of Jet Skis and pleasure boats, kayaks and whale-watching expeditions—wouldn't be just the end of a way of life but a threat to his livelihood.

She glanced over at Ollie, manning the café in back. His full name was Sebastian Oliveira, but everyone knew him as Ollie. He caught her eye and grinned as he sent a cloud of steam hissing from the fancy La Pavoni espresso machine he'd insisted would be the best investment she could make—which it had been, though she suspected the increase in business had more to do with Ollie himself. Since he'd taken over managing the café, its revenues had doubled.

Ollie was one of those people for whom every obstacle was a movable object and every problem a challenge to be met. Whenever a customer approached the counter with a long face, he'd joke until he had the person smiling and laughing. In cases of true suffering, Ollie would do his best to console the person with a kind word or gesture. It didn't hurt, either, that he was cute in a goofy-kid-brother kind of way: tall and loose-limbed, with thick hair that shot straight up, like the bristles on a brush, and that no amount of gel could tame. She knew his parents well—his mother and Arlene had been great friends—and Ollie was a perfect mixture of both. He had his Irish mother's dimples and wide, mobile mouth and his Portuguese father's olive skin, black hair, and brown eyes—eyes that perennially forecast clear weather, however cloudy the actual skies might be. The thing that was pure Ollie, though, was his smile. If scientists could find a way of tapping into it, she thought, it would solve the energy crisis. There would be no further need for books like the one she was presently holding—*The Great Thaw: Global Warming and What the Future Will Look Like*.

She wandered over to have a word with him about tomorrow's event, for which he'd need to have a good supply of coffee and baked goods. She was expecting a sizable turnout for Wall Street wunderkind-turned-author Randall Craig, whose first novel, *Blood Money*, was the buzz book of the moment. It had been quite a score landing an appearance from him. Luckily for her, he was a local author—he lived just up the coast, in San Francisco.

Before she could get a word in, Ollie observed, "You look beat, boss." He smiled knowingly. "Don't worry; I have just the cure." From the glass display case alongside the marble counter, he withdrew a decadent-looking chocolate cake and slid a slice onto a plate. "It's my newest creation—chocolate with coffee whipped cream. I named it Devil's Slide." As in the aptly named stretch of Highway 1 just north of Blue Moon Bay. His smile widened into a grin, showing the chip in one of his front teeth from when he'd run afoul of an iron gaff at age fourteen, the one disastrous summer he'd apprenticed on his dad's boat.

"Mmm . . . hmmmnnhh," she mumbled around the bite of cake he forked into her mouth. It was delicious. She didn't know which was the biggest draw here—the books or Ollie's baked goods. She only knew that when he moved on, once he'd saved enough money for his own business, he'd be impossible to replace. "Divine," she pronounced when she could speak without spraying crumbs. "I'd eat the whole thing if it wouldn't go straight to my hips."

He heaved a sigh. "That's what skinny women always say." Women who watched their weight were the bane of his existence.

She laughed. "How do you think I *stay* skinny?" Admittedly it wasn't just that she managed to refrain from sampling all but a sliver here and there of Ollie's treats; luckily for her, she was built this way. Her boyfriend had once likened her to a Modigliani, all vertical and no horizontal, with her long lines and narrow features, her gray-green eyes that looked, he said, as if she were thinking deep thoughts even when she was doing nothing more intellectually demanding than going over a grocery list. He appreciated, too, that she wasn't the least bit flashy, though his image of her could be a bit confining at times. The night before, when they'd been leaving for the restaurant, he'd paused as they'd passed under the porch light and used his thumb to rub away some of the blush she'd applied to her cheeks. "There. Better," he'd said, smiling at his handiwork. Lindsay knew she should have felt flattered that he preferred her *au naturel*, but instead she was left feeling the way she supposed teenaged girls must when their parents disapproved of the way they were dressed or thought they were wearing too much makeup.

"What's the latest from your lawyer?" Ollie inquired as he was returning the cake to the display case.

Lindsay dabbed at her mouth with a napkin. "Nothing, but if he phones, it'd better be good news. I'm afraid today's quota for bad news is already filled." She'd heard earlier in the day from one of her customers, a real estate agent named Helen Adair, that the county tax assessor had submitted a report favorable to the Heywood Group. Which didn't bode well for her. Any more news along those lines and she would have to officially write this off as a crappy day.

Ollie straightened. "Okaaay. So I guess you don't want to hear what happened with Randall Craig."

"What about him?" she asked with trepidation.

"The dude can't make it," he informed her. "He called a little while ago to let us know. You were busy, so I took the message. He said to tell you he feels terrible about it and that as soon as he has an opening in his schedule, he'll stop by and apologize in person."

"Great. Just what I need," she said with a groan.

"Yeah, I know. Sucks, doesn't it?" Ollie commiserated.

She frowned at him. "Why am I only just now hearing about this?"

"Well, as you can see, I've been kind of tied up," he replied good-naturedly, gesturing toward the customers packed in at the tables.

Even with his brow furrowed in sympathy, Ollie wore the look of someone completely in his element. However busy or backed up, he never became stressed and was rarely in a glum mood. Nothing warmed his heart more than the sight of people contentedly nibbling on his baked goods or sipping one of his cappuccinos or latte mocha supremes. It was hard to believe this was the same kid who, for a time back in high school, had fallen in with the wrong crowd. Nowadays the son who'd been such a worry to his parents was the only one of five siblings who'd remained home to look out for them in their advancing years.

She patted his arm. "I'm not blaming you. I'm just disappointed is all." She'd been counting on this event to bring in some much-needed revenue. She supposed the extra copies of *Blood Money* that she'd ordered—seventy-five in all, an astronomical number for a store this size—would sell eventually, but not in time to meet next week's payroll.

On a personal level, she'd been looking forward to meeting the author. *Blood Money* had hit the *New York Times* best-seller list hot off the press, and it had remained there, in the top five, for eight weeks and counting. It wasn't just a lot of hype, either. Months before publication she'd picked up the ARC—advance reader copy—intending only to skim the first chapter, and had found it impossible to put down. Normally she wasn't a fan of thrillers—she left those for Miss Honi—but this one, set on Wall Street, rang true as only someone who knew that milieu inside and out could have written it. It was smart and insightful, with prose that soared as often as it punched. Clearly she wasn't alone in her opinion. The movie rights had been optioned by Dreamworks, and there was talk of Matt Damon playing the lead. Which left Lindsay wondering now if all that success had gone to Randall Craig's head. Maybe the real reason he'd canceled was because he'd been offered a better gig.

"Anything I can do to help?" Ollie offered. "You know, like put up notices or something?"

"Thanks, but I've got it covered," she told him, already mentally composing the e-mail she would send to everyone on her mailing list. "There is one thing you could do, though . . ."

He straightened, wearing an eager look. "Name it, boss."

"Save me a piece of that cake. I have a feeling I'm going to need it."

Leaving Ollie, she headed to the stockroom to unpack a shipment of books that had arrived that morning. The rest of the afternoon she was kept busy tracking inventory and stocking shelves, waiting on customers, and taking phone calls with reps. Along the way, she stopped to chat with several of her customers: Marie Gilroy, who was looking for a book to bring to her mother in the hospital, and Ana Fuentes, one of the book-club ladies with whom Lindsay had become friendly. Ana loved swapping recipes with Ollie, and today she'd brought in her recipe for seedless-grape chiffon pie, neatly printed on a five-by-six index card. There was also diminutive, doe-eyed Fiona Kennedy from the shop next door, which sold a wide selection of New Age remedies. Fiona pressed a small, purplish crystal into Lindsay's palm, saying, "It's supposed to calm the nerves," no doubt in reference to Lindsay's David-and-Goliath battle against the Heywood Group. Lindsay thanked her and tucked the crystal into a front pocket of her jeans, thinking, *Who knows? I might need it, if not to settle my nerves then as ammo for my slingshot.*

She was distracted just then by the sight of a woman pushing her way in through the door. Thirtyish, wearing tight black jeans, high-heeled boots, and a red bolero jacket over a midriff-baring

T-shirt the same shade as the pink streaks in her hair. Her ears were pierced in so many places, it was a wonder there was any flesh left to hold the multitude of earrings. A rose tattoo snaked up one side of her neck, and she had on so much makeup, it almost obscured the fact that she was pretty enough not to need it. In spite of her tough-girl look, she seemed a bit lost.

She paused just inside the doorway, glancing about uncertainly, prompting Lindsay to approach her and inquire, "Is there something I can help you with?"

"I'm looking for the owner," she said in a voice at odds with her appearance—soft and somewhat tentative, with a girlish lilt to it. Lindsay noticed she had a slight overbite, which, along with her pouty lips and tousled hair, gave her a sex-kittenish look. Her skin was so pale that Lindsay could see the tracing of veins beneath. Her eyes were the color of a fresh bruise.

"That would be me." Lindsay smiled and put her hand out. "Lindsay Bishop. What can I do for you?"

The woman's fingers trembled slightly in her grip, and her palm felt damp. She was staring at Lindsay as if she knew her from somewhere. "I'm not sure, actually. I guess it all depends."

Lindsay wondered if it was a job she was after. That would explain the tentativeness. Didn't she know you weren't likely to get hired dressed like that, except maybe in a dive bar? "I'm afraid you're going to have to be a little more specific than that," she said, her smile stretching to cover her impatience.

The woman smiled in return—the hard, flat little smile of someone reluctant to commit to it wholeheartedly, perhaps for fear of appearing vulnerable. "You don't recognize me, do you? No, I guess not." A spark of disappointment flared in her eyes before settling into a more resigned expression.

Lindsay eyed her in confusion. "I'm sorry. Have we met?"

The damp hand slipped like cool water from her grip even as those bruise-colored eyes remained fixed on her. "You could say that. Actually, that's what I'm here to see you about. You see, the thing is—"

Before she could finish the sentence, she was interrupted by a cry of jubilation from the other end of the store. Both women, along with several customers, swung around at the sight of Miss Honi tottering toward them as fast as her high heels could carry her, her cheeks flushed and her bonnet of blond ringlets bouncing along with her breasts.

She threw her arms around the pink-haired woman, who was too startled to react. When at last Miss Honi drew back, it was to peer at her intently. "Lord have mercy, it *is* you," she declared. "I thought my eyes were playing tricks on me at first,

81

but here you are, real as can be." She turned to Lindsay with the flushed cheeks and shining eyes of one in the throes of an almost religious rapture. "It's like a miracle, ain't it? Our very own Kerrie Ann."

CHAPTER THREE

I KNOW YOU. YOU'RE . . ." Kerrie Ann stared at the old lady, frowning in concentration. Then it came to her in a lightning flash of recognition, and she realized she'd known it all along, the name tucked away like a stick of gum in her back pocket. This was the woman in her dream. ". . . Miss Honi?"

The old lady beamed at her as if she had just given the correct answer to the million-dollar question on *Who Wants to Be a Millionaire?* "I guess I ain't changed so much you wouldn't recognize your old pal."

Kerrie Ann took in the blond ringlets, the bright-red lipstick, the plump but still shapely figure decked in bling. "Yeah, but . . . but how did you know it was *me*?" she sputtered. According to her records, she'd been only three years old when last seen by Miss Honi—a lifetime.

Tears were running down Miss Honi's powdered cheeks, catching in their creases. One false eyelash had come partially unglued, and her mouth was stretched in a wide grin that wouldn't stay put. "As if I could ever forget that face! You're still my baby girl, ain't you?"

"It's been a long time." She spoke cautiously, not used to being welcomed with such enthusiasm. "People change."

Miss Honi brought a finger to the small scar on Kerrie Ann's chin, just below her lower lip. "You got that climbing out a window when you were two," she said. "Fell flat on your face and busted your chin wide open. Lord, you never seen so much blood. I just about fainted, but you barely let out a peep. I seen grown men make more of a fuss over a black eye. And you were just an itty-bitty thing." She pulled a crumpled tissue from a sleeve of her blue velour top and used it to dab at her eyes.

Kerrie Ann had always wondered about that scar. Now she knew. She just wished the rest of those years weren't a total blank. "I don't remember that," she said, frowning. "In fact, I don't remember much of anything. Until a few weeks ago, I didn't even know I had a sister." She turned to the woman to whom she'd been talking when Miss Honi had descended on her like a blond, perfumed tornado. "So you're Lindsay."

Kerrie Ann took note of how pretty Lindsay was, in a fresh-faced, not-trying-too-hard kind of way, with her smooth olive skin, blunt-cut brown hair that fell to her shoulders, and intelligent gray-green eyes, which at the moment were wide with wonder. Dressed in jeans and a button-down shirt, a cashmere pullover in a pale, buttery shade of yellow draped over her shoulders with its sleeves tied loosely around her neck, she appeared trim and capable . . . and like no one to whom Kerrie Ann could possibly be related.

Lindsay seemed equally at a loss. When she finally stepped forward to hug Kerrie Ann, it wasn't with the unbridled exuberance of Miss Honi's embrace. At the same time, her delight seemed genuine when she cried, "I can hardly believe it. Do you know how long we've been looking for you? Years! I'd just about given up hope."

"Seriously? You've been looking for me all this time?" In her experience, when someone tried to track you down, it wasn't a good thing; usually it had to do with a bounced check or unpaid bill. Like the time she'd skipped out without paying her rent, and her landlord had sicced the cops on her. She found it hard to believe anyone would go to such lengths just to be with her and could only hope Lindsay would conclude that she was worth the effort.

Lindsay nodded, her eyes bright with unshed tears. "You're not an easy person to find."

"I've moved around a lot," Kerrie Ann acknowledged with a shrug.

"You said you didn't know you had a sister. How did you find out about me?"

"Through my . . . a friend." Kerrie Ann caught herself before she could reveal that it had been her lawyer. Now wasn't the time to lay all that on her sister. She would have to play her cards right. "He helped me get a copy of my old records. You were listed as the next of kin. So I Googled you, and now here I am."

"Thank God for the Internet," said Lindsay with a teary laugh.

Kerrie Ann glanced about the shop, at the books lining the blond-wood bookshelves and attractively displayed on the islands. On the walls hung framed illustrations and posters. Mismatched easy chairs were tucked here and there, all of them occupied by customers. In the children's section, the shelves and benches were scaled to kid-size, and an Elmo-blue plush rug covered the floor, where several young children were busily paging through picture books or playing with toys from the basket in one corner. The aroma of coffee drifted from the back.

"Nice place you got here," she commented.

Lindsay smiled. "Thanks. It'll never make me rich, but I wouldn't trade it for anything."

Kerrie Ann slowly shook her head. "I can't believe I'm related to someone who owns a bookstore. I didn't even pass high school English. Shit, I couldn't tell you the last book I read cover to cover."

Lindsay looked slightly taken aback, and Kerrie Ann made a mental note to watch what she said from now on. Her sister was clearly more educated and . . . well, more of everything she wasn't. She felt a momentary urge to flee. Then Lindsay's hand closed gently about her wrist. "Let's head back to my office," she suggested. "We'll have more privacy there."

Kerrie Ann bit back her apprehension and forced a smile. Following Lindsay as she wound her way through the warren of bookshelves, she prayed her sister would be as welcoming once she learned the real purpose of this visit.

"How about some coffee?" offered Miss Honi, an arm tucked through hers. "You ain't lived till you've tried Ollie's. That's him over there." She pointed out a tall, lanky kid with a thatch of spiky black hair doing the barista thing in back. The café's marble counter and display case filled with baked goods stood next to a small seating area packed with tables and chairs. "Come on, I'll introduce you." She tugged on Kerrie Ann's arm, calling to Lindsay, "Hold up a sec. She ain't met the whole gang yet!"

The kid was finishing up with a customer when they descended on him. "Hey, Ollie. You'll never guess what the cat dragged in." Miss Honi nudged Kerrie Ann forward, beaming as proudly as a parent showing off her child.

He stared at her, transfixed, before breaking into a lopsided grin. "I don't know," he said, "but I think I'm in love."

He looked to be in his mid-twenties, only a few years younger than she, though from a distance she'd mistaken him for a college kid with his black-and-navy pinstriped suit vest over a vintage black Metallica T-shirt, jeans shredded at the knees, and a pair of bright orange Converse sneakers. Kerrie Ann decided he was cute if you went for the opposite of the darkly brooding, day-old-stubble type. Ollie was more boy band than heavy metal.

"Hey," she greeted him, smiling as she put out her hand.

His handshake was as enthusiastic as his manner. "Don't tell me. I've got it. Didn't you open for Maroon Five at the Cow Palace last summer? No, wait, you're that actress who's on the cover of this month's *Cosmo*." He was the perfect combination of sincere and full of shit. She was charmed in spite of herself.

Lindsay laughed and shook her head. "Ollie, meet my sister."

He dropped the act, his eyes growing wide. "Your sister? The famous Kerrie Ann? No way."

"So you know all about me, huh?" Kerrie Ann was secretly pleased to have been the subject of such rampant speculation.

"Are you kidding? It's been like the search for Bigfoot. Not that I'm implying . . ." Ollie reddened. "I mean, you're *gorgeous*. What I meant was, we were starting to think it was just a wild-goose chase. And here you are. In the flesh." The color in his cheeks deepened while he made a valiant attempt not to ogle the flesh in question. "Wow. This is *huge*."

"Nice to meet you, Ollie." Kerrie Ann finally managed to extract her hand from his grip. "I hear you make a mean cup of coffee."

He gathered his wits. "You heard right. So what'll it be?" He gestured toward the menu on the wall behind him.

"Just regular coffee. Black, no sugar."

He pointed at the display case. "How about something to go with it? Cake, cookies, muffins— what's your pleasure?"

She shook her head. "Nothing for me."

"Please, you're breaking my heart." He pulled a mock grimace, clapping a hand to his chest in dramatic fashion.

"I don't dare, with you comparing me to Bigfoot," she teased.

His blush spread to the roots of his spiky hair. "I didn't mean—"

Kerrie Ann laughed. "I know. And trust me, if I wasn't still full from lunch, I could eat everything in that case." Like most recovering addicts, she had an incurable sweet tooth. "Another time, okay?"

Ollie pumped coffee from a thermos on the counter into a tall cup and snapped on a lid. His gaze met Kerrie Ann's as he handed it to her. "I'm gonna hold you to that."

"You girls go on ahead," said Miss Honi, shooing Kerrie Ann and Lindsay along. "I'll catch up with you in a bit."

Kerrie Ann could see that Miss Honi was trying to give her and Lindsay some time alone, and she felt touched by the gesture. "Thanks for the coffee," she said to Ollie as she turned to go. She felt his eyes on her as she and Lindsay headed off.

The office was little more than a cubbyhole tucked in back behind the history section, with just enough room for a computer desk, a couple of chairs, and a bookcase crammed with what Lindsay informed her were advance reading copies of books yet to be released. Kerrie Ann lowered herself into the chair by the door, placing her cup on the floor. She blew out a breath. "Wow. Pretty weird, huh? This whole sister thing." She hadn't felt this nervous even during job interviews.

"It'll definitely take some getting used to," Lindsay agreed.

Kerrie Ann cocked her head, studying her sister. "You're not what I was expecting." For some reason she'd imagined Lindsay a soccer mom living with her family in the 'burbs and driving a minivan. But she wasn't wearing a wedding ring, which meant she was either divorced or single, and there were no photos of children on her desk.

Lindsay smiled, settling into her chair. "You're not how I pictured you, either. I didn't notice the resemblance at first, but now I don't see how I could've missed it. You look like our mother."

Kerrie Ann eyed her dubiously. "Is that a good thing?"

Lindsay was quick to reassure her: "She was pretty, like you."

"What was she like?"

Lindsay's brow furrowed, as if she were trying to think of something that was complimentary. "Well, she could be fun when she wanted to be. Though, to be honest, that wasn't too often. The fact is, she wasn't around much. Most of the time, I was on my own. That is, until you came along." She added in a matter-of-fact tone, "Did you know we have different dads? I never met mine, and I'm not sure Crystal even knew who yours is. She was sixteen when she got pregnant with me. Her boyfriend at the time, my father, dumped her when he found out. Her parents weren't too happy about it, either. So she ran away from home. That's how she ended up in Reno."

"You wouldn't happen to have a photo of her?" Kerrie Ann asked out of curiosity.

Lindsay shook her head. "Only the one on her driver's license. They sent it to me along with the rest of her things after she died." She reached for her purse on the desk, extracting a laminated card from an inner pocket, which she handed to Kerrie Ann without comment: a Nevada driver's license with an unflattering photo of a woman about her age, with bleached-blond hair worn in a '70s shag and hard eyes that didn't go with her soft, almost child-like mouth. Kerrie Ann stared at it for a long moment, then silently handed it back. She felt no emotion whatsoever—the woman was a stranger to her. "She was a stripper," Lindsay went on. "Miss Honi was, too, a million years ago. Though in her day, they were called exotic dancers."

Kerrie Ann wasn't surprised to learn that their mother had been a stripper. In her case, the apple hadn't fallen far from the tree. She'd never used her body to get money, but she'd done a lot of other things she wasn't proud of. "All I know is that she died in prison," she said.

Lindsay gave a slow nod. "I was fifteen at the time. My parents asked if I wanted some sort of memorial service, but I told them no. I didn't want to have to be sad. Besides, I couldn't think of anyone to invite."

"Your parents sound nice." Kerrie Ann retrieved her coffee cup and pried off the lid, inhaling the fragrant steam before taking a careful sip.

Lindsay nodded, her expression softening. "I wish you could have met them." Kerrie Ann gave her a questioning look, and she added softly, "They passed away—my mom eight years ago and my dad a few years before that."

"Oh." Kerrie Ann didn't know what to say. Should she offer her sympathies at this late a date?

"They were older," Lindsay explained. "They'd tried for years and years to have a child of their own, but Arlene kept miscarrying. By the time they decided to adopt, they were both in their fifties." She smiled at Kerrie Ann, adding, "I know what you're thinking. Most couples want a cute, cuddly baby, right? But they were looking for an older child, around the age their own children would have been. That's the kind of people they were."

"Lucky you." Kerrie Ann wondered what it would have been like to have had a real mom and dad. All she'd known was a succession of foster parents who'd ranged from well-meaning to plain mean.

But if Lindsay detected any bitterness in her voice, she didn't comment on it. "Yes, I was lucky," she said. "I had fifteen wonderful years with them."

"You must miss them."

"More than you know. I owe them so much. They saved me, in a way." Kerrie Ann gave a pained smile, all too aware that she stood as an example of how her sister's life might have turned out had the circumstances been different. "Ted was a biology professor. He used to take me on these long nature walks. It wasn't until I was older that I realized he wasn't just teaching me about nature; he was letting me know, simply by being there, that it was safe to trust other people. And my mom—well, there was no one quite like her. She was the gentlest person I ever met."

For Kerrie Ann it was like hearing about life on Mars. Growing up, the closest she'd come to a meaningful relationship with an adult was with David French, her foster father when she was twelve. He used to take her out for ice cream and talk to her about things—adult things. Then one day, as she sat beside him licking her cone, he asked if she'd ever been kissed by a boy. Shocked not so much by the question as by the fact of his asking her, she told the truth: "Bobby Winston kissed me once on the lips." David smiled as if they were sharing a secret and, when she was done with her cone, asked if he could braid her hair. She let him, but it creeped her out so much that she made excuses after that whenever he tried to get her to go off alone with him. A few months later she was sent to live with another family.

"What did she do for a living?" asked Kerrie Ann.

"She was a teacher—she taught music at our local high school and gave piano lessons on the side. She had also had this amazing gift of being able talk to anyone, any age, and have that person instantly feel like she was their friend. She always knew the right thing to say, and when it was best to say nothing at all." Lindsay's smile turned wistful. "They would have been so happy to know I'd found you. They always hoped I would." She picked up a framed photo off her desk, holding it out for Kerrie Ann to see. "I took this of them a few months after we moved here." The photo showed a pair of long-haired academic types posing hand in hand on the beach, he with wire-rimmed glasses and a graying ponytail, she a dead ringer for June Carter Cash. They were smiling the easy smiles of people with nothing to hide and few regrets. "They always said it was their favorite picture of themselves."

A seed of envy cracked open inside Kerrie Ann, quickly blooming into a noxious weed. Her sister hadn't just caught the brass ring; she'd gotten the whole frigging merry-go-round, while Kerrie Ann had been shuttled around like a hockey puck. "Technically, you didn't find me. I found you," she pointed out.

"A good thing, too. I'd just about given up hope. All those years, all those dead ends." *She must have loved me at one time*, thought Kerrie Ann with wonderment. She couldn't remember ever having been loved as a child. "I managed to get hold of your records from Children's Services, so I had addresses and phone numbers for your foster parents—the ones who hadn't moved, at least—but they weren't much help. I even tracked down your driver's license, only the address on it turned out to be an old one. When I phoned your landlord, he seemed eager to get hold of you, too. Something about back rent you owed?" Kerrie Ann felt her face grow hot under her sister's probing gaze. "Then, out of the blue, you turn up on my doorstep." Lindsay shook her head, as if in disbelief at the irony.

"Like a bad penny," Kerrie Ann said with a self-effacing laugh.

"Why do you say that?" Lindsay frowned.

"You might not be so happy to have me back in your life once you get to know me."

No sooner were the words out than Kerrie Ann wanted to snatch them back. What she'd meant to say was that she hoped they could become friends. Instead she was doing what she always did in a new situation: putting up walls and putting herself down. The years of being bounced from one home to the next, of always being the new kid in school, had taught her that it was better to reject before she could be rejected. And by putting herself down before someone else could, she could come across as dryly sardonic rather than the object of derision. It made for fewer friends, true, but it kept her from getting hurt.

"You're my sister," Lindsay said, as if that simple fact were all that mattered. But she sounded a bit apprehensive nonetheless.

Kerrie Ann put down her coffee cup and reached for her purse. "Mind if I smoke?"

Lindsay hesitated before replying, "We could go outside if you like. There's a service area out back."

"Never mind. It can wait." Kerrie Ann spoke more curtly than she'd intended. Her sister was trying, but it did nothing to ease her growing discomfort.

An awkward silence fell.

"I wonder what's keeping Miss Honi," Lindsay said, glancing at her watch.

Miss Honi. There was another mystery. "So what's the deal with her, anyway?" asked Kerrie Ann. "Is she related to us, or what?"

"Not by blood. But she was the closest thing. She used to babysit you when you were little."

Kerrie was reminded once more of her recurring dream. "So you stayed in touch with her all these years?"

"Not in the begining. I tried sending her a letter once, but it was returned. She'd moved away, too, and hadn't left a forwarding address. I didn't even know her real name—just the stage name she went by. I never forgot about her, though, and used to wonder what had become of her." Lindsay picked up a shiny brass paperweight off her desk, idly turning it over in her hand. "Then one day I came across this newspaper article about a retirement home for former show folk in Carson City. On a hunch, I phoned the director and asked if a Miss Honi Love was living there. By sheer luck, it turned out she was. So I flew out for a visit, and the next thing I knew I was inviting her to come stay with me. That was six years ago. She's been with me ever since. Frankly, I don't know how I'd manage without her."

"So it's just the two of you?"

"Plus a dog and two cats. We live just up the coast. My parents left me a house and twenty acres. You should see the view." Lindsay, as if not wanting to give the wrong impression, was quick to add, "They never could've afforded it at today's prices. They bought it when land around here was dirt cheap."

"Sounds awesome." Kerrie Ann recalled the articles that had popped up when she'd Googled her sister's name, about some hotel group wanting to buy her out so it could put up a resort. But since Lindsay hadn't mentioned it, she decided not to bring up what was undoubtedly a sore subject.

Lindsay must have been thinking about it anyway, because she lapsed into silence for a moment, wearing a preoccupied look. At last she brought her gaze back to Kerrie Ann. "But enough about me. Tell me about yourself. I want to know all about you."

"What do you want to know?" Kerrie Ann shifted in her seat, craving a cigarette more than ever.

"Everything! So far all I know is that you've traveled around a lot and that you take your coffee black."

Kerrie Ann gave a nervous laugh. "I don't know where to begin."

"Why don't we start with the basics? Are you married?"

"Nope." Kerrie Ann fiddled with the rhinestone-studded heart on a chain around her neck, a long-ago gift from Jeremiah. She wasn't sure why she still wore it. Habit, she supposed, or maybe sentiment. "What about you?" she inquired before Lindsay could ask if she had any kids. She wasn't ready to get into that just yet.

Lindsay shook her head. "I was engaged once, just out of college, but it didn't work out. Now I'm afraid my life's a little too complicated for most men, including my current boyfriend." She studied her hands a moment, as if contemplating the absence of a ring. But when she looked up, her expression was untroubled. Either she was happy being single . . . or hiding something. "Now that we've gotten that out of the way, what sort of work do you do?"

Kerrie Ann shifted her gaze to the cup of coffee growing cold at her feet. Talking about herself was like picking her way over a minefield, trying to decide which aspects of her past were safe to reveal and which were best skirted. "I'm in retail," she said, leaving it vague. "But I'm sort of between jobs at the moment." It wasn't an outright lie, although she hadn't officially given notice. She'd merely told her boss she needed time off to take care of personal business. Her future, at this point, was in Lindsay's hands.

Would her sister be willing to take her in? Vouch for her when it came time to go to court? It was a lot to ask.

"Oh, well. I'm sure something will turn up." Lindsay spoke with the nonchalance of someone who'd never had to worry about such things. "There's always a job for someone with a good head on her shoulders."

"Yeah, well, I didn't go to college like you, so I wouldn't know about that," Kerrie Ann retorted. She'd meant it to sound ironic, but it came out sounding bitter and resentful. The story of her life: Act first, pay later. Fearful of getting off on the wrong foot, she was quick to clarify: "Hey, no offense. I just meant that for some of us, it's not that easy."

Unexpectedly Lindsay's eyes filled with tears. "I'm sorry. I know you had it rough growing up. I wish I could've been there for you."

Kerrie Ann ducked her head, feeling embarrassed. Her life might suck, but she didn't want anyone's pity, least of all her more successful sister's. "I don't know what you could've done. I guess nobody asked us what we wanted, right?"

She glanced up to find her sister still eyeing her sadly. "No, they didn't." Then Lindsay brightened and said, "Well, now that you're here, let's make the most of it. You haven't booked a hotel yet, have you?" Kerrie Ann shook her head. "Good. In that case, why don't you stay with Miss Honi and me? I insist on it, in fact. We have so much to catch up on!"

Kerrie Ann leapt at the invitation. "I'd like that." Lindsay might not be so excited to have her stay once she learned the real reason for her visit, but what better way to get a foot in the door?

Miss Honi appeared just then, bearing a plate of chocolate-chip cookies. She held it out to Kerrie Ann, urging, "Go on, one won't kill you. Ollie said to tell you that if you're anything like your sister, he'll have to look for another job. Someplace where he's appreciated."

Lindsay laughed. "He has a thing against skinny women who are always on a diet."

"Amen to that," said Miss Honi, reaching for a cookie.

Kerrie Ann helped herself to one as well. "Tell him not to worry. I never count calories." She took a bite and at once forgot about the cigarette she'd been craving. It was the best chocolate-chip cookie she'd ever tasted, soft and chewy at the same time, bursting with a subtle mix of flavors. She looked up at Miss Honi. "Ollie made these? They're amazing."

Miss Honi beamed as though she'd baked the cookies herself. "I'll be sure to pass on the compliment. As if you didn't already make his day just walking in the door."

Kerrie Ann saw her sister's brows shoot up. Did Lindsay disapprove of the way she looked? She'd wanted to make a good impression, so she'd worn her best outfit, only now she wasn't so sure . . .

But there was only warmth in Lindsay's voice when she said to Miss Honi, "I was just telling Kerrie Ann that she's welcome to stay with us."

"Where else?" declared Miss Honi as if there had never been any question in her mind where Kerrie Ann would stay. "She can have my room."

"I wouldn't want to put you out," said Kerrie Ann. "Really, I don't mind sleeping on the sofa."

"No one's going to be sleeping on the sofa," interjected Lindsay. She turned to Kerrie Ann. "There's a daybed in my room." She'd had it installed while her mother was ill so she could stay with her at night, she explained. "As long as you don't mind bunking in with me."

Kerrie Ann assured Lindsay that any bed would suit her just fine. She was thinking of the years she'd spent on the road, when her bed had been wherever she could find a place to crash, often with some guy she'd met along the way.

"It's settled, then," pronounced Lindsay. "A nice quiet evening, just the three of us. It'll give us a chance to get reacquainted."

"Aren't you forgetting something?" said Miss Honi.

Lindsay eyed her in confusion, then groaned. "The party." She turned to Kerrie Ann, explaining, "My boyfriend is having some people over tonight. I told him we'd come—Miss Honi and I. But I can always call and cancel. I'm sure he'll understand once I tell him the reason."

"Or you could call and tell him you're bringing an extra guest," suggested Miss Honi. "It'd give us a chance to introduce your sister around, show her off a bit." She helped herself to another cookie, chomping down on it with relish, blissfully ignorant of the stricken look on Lindsay's face.

"I don't know . . ." Lindsay cast a worried glance at Kerrie Ann. "All those people. We wouldn't have much chance to talk."

Suddenly Kerrie Ann understood: Her sister was embarrassed by her. That was why she was making excuses not to take her to the party. The realization brought a hot surge of shame before defiance kicked in. "Actually, it sounds like fun," she said with feigned enthusiasm. "I'm always up for a party." The truth was, she seldom went to parties these days unless they were sober functions. But she'd be damned if she'd be hidden away like some ugly stepchild.

"That settles it, then." Miss Honi popped the last piece of cookie into her mouth.

Lindsay didn't say anything more, but her strained smile spoke for itself.

CHAPTER FOUR

DEAR GOD, A PARTY ON TOP OF EVERYTHING ELSE? Lindsay was still struggling to reconcile the two Kerrie Anns: the pierced, tattooed woman and the little girl she'd known. And now to be plunged into a social setting with clients and business associates of Grant's, having to make bright cocktail chatter while making sure her sister felt included? Her head spun just thinking about it.

There was another problem: The whole dramatic story of their reunion was sure to come out. Until now, only those closest to Lindsay, like Ollie and his mom and a handful of others, had known her history. No one else even knew she had a sister or that Miss Honi was anything but an old family friend. But tonight all that ugliness from her past would be on display, as if she were appearing on one of those ghastly let-it-all-hang-out talk shows she abhorred. People with whom she was barely acquainted would know about their mother's prison record and that she and her sister had been placed in foster care.

Besides, was it too much to ask that, after twenty-five years, she have her sister to herself for just one night?

Apparently so. Lindsay had been surprised and, yes, a bit hurt when Kerrie Ann had jumped at the chance to go to a party instead of spending some quiet time at home with her and Miss Honi. How was chitchatting with a bunch of strangers preferable to getting to know your long-lost sister? They had so much to catch up on—a lifetime's worth.

One thing was already abundantly clear: There was a world of difference between her and her sister. Lindsay had seen it the moment she'd laid eyes on Kerrie Ann, even before she'd known who the pink-haired woman was: She'd led a hard life. Lindsay only knew what she'd gleaned through the years—the succession of foster homes, a dozen in all, culminating in Kerrie Ann's running away at the age of sixteen—but it was obvious her sister had had a rough go of it. Lindsay had seen that same look of defeat mixed with stubborn pride in the faces of the people she'd met through the literacy program she was involved in, people who'd been deprived as children—and not just of an education.

At the same time, Lindsay could see glimpses of the Kerrie Ann she'd known. She just had to find a way to get to her. Even if it meant catering to her sister's wishes in this instance.

"Right," she said briskly. "I'll call Grant and let him know. Did you bring anything to wear? If not, we can probably find something in my closet that'll fit you." Though a few inches taller, Kerrie Ann looked to be about the same size as she.

Kerrie Ann regarded her dubiously, as if wondering what, in Lindsay's closet, could possibly be her style. "I'm sure I can throw something together," she said.

"Just between you and me, sugar, if it's drop-dead you're looking for, you'd best go hunting in my closet," said Miss Honi. At the warning glance Lindsay shot her, she tossed back, "Now, don't you go looking at me like that, missy. It don't hurt to strut your stuff when you got something to strut. If the good Lord wanted us gals looking like a pillow with the stuffing knocked out of it, He wouldn't have built us the way He did." She threw out her chest and ran her hands down her own not inconsiderable curves, eliciting a giggle from Kerrie Ann.

Lindsay kept her voice light as she replied, "Well, then, you two can be the peacocks, and I'll be the plain old sparrow. Lucky for me, my boyfriend likes me the way I am. Even without the stuffing." She cast a rueful downward glance at her own more understated bosom.

She was rising to her feet, reluctant to get back to work but knowing she'd go broke that much quicker if she didn't—there was probably a line at the register by now—when Miss Honi suggested, "Ladies, what do you say we head back to the house now? We can crack open a bottle of wine and kick back for some good old-fashioned girl talk before the party."

Lindsay arched a brow. "And just what do you

suggest we do, leave our customers to the honor system?"

"Ollie can mind the store—it's just for a few hours," said Miss Honi. "He's got enough energy for three people, that boy."

"He might have the energy of three people, but he can't be in three places at once." Lindsay shook her head. "No, I'll stay. Why don't you two go on ahead? I'll catch up with you later on." She tried to sound cheerful but couldn't help feeling left out when Kerrie Ann didn't offer to stick around and keep her company. Clearly she preferred Miss Honi's company.

"We can take my car," volunteered Kerrie Ann.

It was only then that Lindsay remembered her own car was in the shop. She'd dropped it off that morning on her way to work to have it serviced and was supposed to have picked it up on her lunch break. In all the excitement, it had slipped her mind. Now a glance at her watch told her it would have to wait until tomorrow; the mechanic, Mr. Mahmud, closed early on Mondays.

She almost said something but in the end decided not to. She could always catch a ride home with Ollie. No sense raining on their parade.

Kerrie Ann must have sensed something amiss because she paused to eye Lindsay thoughtfully on her way out, as if there were something more she wanted to say. Then the moment passed and she was gone, leaving Lindsay to wonder what role, if any, she would be playing in her sister's life. Would they grow closer over time as they grew more comfortable with each other, or would their relationship merely be one of getting together once or twice a year and exchanging cards at Christmas? For once she wished she could be more like Miss Honi. The old woman had taken Kerrie Ann into her arms and given her a good Texas-sized hug while Lindsay hadn't even recognized her own sister.

At the same time, a tiny splinter of worry pricked at her. She remembered Kerrie Ann's facetious remark about being a bad penny. Suppose it was no joke? Would the fulfillment of her wish become a case of being careful what you wish for?

"Thanks again for the ride, Ollie. I know it's out of your way," said Lindsay as they rattled over the private road to her house. It was late in the day, the sun a golden rind peeking over the fog bunched along the horizon. They'd been delayed by a last-minute influx of customers, those who hadn't heard about tomorrow's event being canceled and who'd wanted to snag a copy of *Blood Money* before they were all gone—the second time that day she'd been inconvenienced by the no-show Randall Craig. Now she'd have to hustle to make it to the party on time.

Ollie, his hands loosely curled around the steering wheel of his Willys, the World War II–era jeep he and his dad had restored, replied amiably, "No problemo. Hey, it's not like I have anything lined up for tonight. Not that I'd turn down an invitation to some cool party, even if it was, like, last-minute," he hinted broadly.

Lindsay cast him an indulgent smile. "Forget it. The last thing I need is to show up with an entourage." It was enough that she would have her sister and Miss Honi in tow.

"What, you'd deny me the chance to meet the love of my life? What if the perfect woman happens to be there, just waiting for a guy like me to show up?" He gave her a pleading look, which, with his big brown eyes and wide, mobile mouth, his hair even more wild than usual from the air blowing in through the window, only made him look like a shaggy dog begging for treats.

"I hate to break it to you, Ollie, but Julia Child's no longer with us," she informed him, doing her best to keep a straight face. "Besides, the only women who'll be at the party are clients' wives."

"Go on, mock me," he said in an injured tone as he slowed to ease the Willys over a pothole. "Why should you take me seriously? No one else does. Around here I'm just the muffin man."

"Who happens to make the meanest muffins in town."

"Thanks, but I'd rather be known as a stud muffin," he continued in the same vein. "My problem is, I'm too freaking *nice*." He spoke the

108

word as if it were an insult. "In school? I was always the one the girls confided to about other guys, the ones they liked. The way I see it, girls don't want nice, they want six-pack abs and day-old stubble. You know, the type of guy who'd rather have his girlfriend's name tattooed on his arm than have a meaningful conversation with her. Who keeps nothing but beer and maybe some thousand-year-old Chinese takeout in his fridge."

Lindsay refrained from reminding him of the time he'd come dangerously close to being that kind of guy.

"If you're trying to make me feel sorry for you, it's not working," she told him. "And for your information, there's nothing wrong with the way you are. I'll take nice any day over six-pack abs and stubble. Though I suppose my opinion doesn't count, since I'm so ancient."

He grinned, going along with the joke. "I happen to like older women. Take your sister, for instance—she's hot. Seriously, I can't believe you guys are related." He caught himself, his cheeks reddening. "Sorry, that came out wrong. What I meant to say was that you're nothing alike. It's like you grew up on separate planets or something."

"It certainly feels that way," Lindsay confessed.

"You must've about shit a brick when she dropped in like that, out of the blue."

"That's putting it mildly."

"Well, if *my* opinion counts, I think she's awesome." He paused before asking, with a casualness belied by the deepening color in his cheeks, "You wouldn't happen to know if she has a boyfriend?"

"Not that I'm aware of. Why?" Lindsay was growing uncomfortable with the direction this conversation was taking.

"Just curious." Ollie fell silent for a moment, his porcupine head bobbing as he mulled this over. "It's just . . . well, I was thinking I'd ask her out. How long is she in town for?"

"I'm not sure—she wasn't definite. But I'm afraid you're barking up the wrong tree." No sense in encouraging him. "She's not your type."

Ollie grew defensive. "Why do you say that?"

"Well, for one thing she's older—we've already established that."

"I'm twenty-four. How old is your sister?"

Lindsay did the mental arithmetic. "Twenty-nine."

"That's only five years."

"I'm not just talking about the difference in your ages. She's had a hard life, Ollie. She's not . . . well, she isn't the kind of girl you would have taken to the prom. Let's just leave it at that, okay?" She didn't want to be unfair to her sister, but Ollie should know the truth.

He wasn't so easily dissuaded, though. "So she had it rough growing up. That doesn't make her a bad person."

"I'm not saying she's a bad person. I'm just saying she may not be right for you."

"You mean because she's not like you?" An edge crept into his voice.

Ollie's right, she thought. *I'm measuring her by my own yardstick, which isn't fair.* Truth to tell, Lindsay was still recovering from the shock of encountering someone who bore no resemblance to the idealized picture in her mind—that of an adult sister with whom she could share confidences and discuss topics of mutual interest. In place of that was someone who, by Kerrie Ann's own admission, hadn't cracked a book in years and with whom Lindsay was as likely to share a confidence or an opinion as the same taste in clothing.

Once again she felt a twinge of guilt, wishing she were as accepting as Ollie. But wasn't she, too, a product of her upbringing? The first twelve years of her life had been about waking up each morning with a vague sense of dread, wondering what fresh ordeal was in store for that day. Was it any wonder she'd grown up needing to be in control? That she had trouble making friends—especially with people whose lives were in disarray? People like her former classmate Susie Larson, who'd recently gotten in touch. Lindsay had listened in sympathy while Susie had described the messy divorce she was going through, but she hadn't followed up when Susie had suggested they get together. Not because she didn't feel for Susie but because for her, it would have been like accepting delivery of a suspicious-looking package that might contain an explosive device.

At the moment she had enough turmoil of her own, with the battle over her land.

She gazed out at the darkening landscape, folding around her like the gentlest of arms, arms that for so long had cradled her against the brunt of life's storms and that, God willing, would continue to do so in the years to come. The fog of earlier in the day had retreated, revealing a semibarren vista matted with low-lying scrub and, off in the distance, windswept bluffs where the bent and twisted shapes of Monterey cypress stood silhouetted like so many hobgoblins. Beyond lay the ocean, gleaming like tarnished silver and rippling with long swells.

It was a view she never tired of. She recalled her sense of wonder, those first weeks after arriving here with her parents, in discovering that the picture-perfect ocean of *Baywatch* and *Beverly Hills 90210* was actually a living entity, its moods as mercurial as the weather. Playful one minute and treacherous the next. On any given day, calm waters and blue skies could give way to a storm that would whip those swells into green-mawed combers and send them racing in to smash against the cliffs, sending geyser-like spumes of spray high into the air. It had its own language, too, one that whispered its secrets in her ear. It told her to be patient, to have faith. That it had endured, and so would she.

She could see the house ahead, lit from within and shining like a beacon in the gathering darkness. It was modest compared to most cliffside homes in this area, small and low to the ground, built out of cedar, with a shingled roof and siding worn by decades of salt spray to the soft, silvery gray of the coastal grasses that blanketed the surrounding fields. It was also in need of repair: Its roof sagged, the front and back decks were riddled with dry rot, and more than a few of its shingles were missing. Even so, she wouldn't have traded it for a mansion.

"You're the best—I owe you," she thanked Ollie again when he pulled to a stop in the driveway. Her gray-muzzled Labrador retriever, Chester, short for Mr. Rochester, loped over on legs stiff with arthritis to greet her as she climbed out of the Willys, and she stooped to pet him.

Ollie stuck his head out the window as he drove off. "Have fun at the party!"

The party. Lindsay's heart sank once more at the reminder.

She walked in to find Kerrie Ann all dolled up for the occasion, her hair teased and moussed, glittery shadow applied to her eyelids, and her pouty lips glistening with a fresh coat of gloss. She'd changed into a pair of low-rise white jeans so tight they looked spray-painted on and an equally tight, scoop-necked pink T-shirt with shiny metal rivets spelling out the word "Bebe" across the front.

She'd traded the high-heeled boots she'd had on earlier for a pair of jazzy platform shoes.

She was a dead ringer for their mother.

"Is that what you're wearing to the party?" Lindsay asked in dismay.

Kerrie Ann, seated on the sofa with the ginger cat, Fagin, curled in her lap, looked up from the magazine she'd been leafing through to give her a wide-eyed look. "Something wrong with it?"

"No, it's fine," Lindsay lied.

Her sister's eyes narrowed. "I can change if you like," she offered with a notable lack of enthusiasm.

"No time now. We should get going." Lindsay glanced at her watch. "Where's Miss Honi?"

Ignoring the question, her sister asked, "Aren't *you* going to change?"

"I'll throw something on. It'll only take a sec."

Kerrie Ann regarded her with the same dubiousness Lindsay had shown a moment ago when eyeing her, as if wondering what sort of outfit she could pull together in so short a time. But, unlike Lindsay, she obviously didn't feel it was her place to comment. "Sure, whatever," she said with a shrug, going back to her magazine.

Lindsay's gaze came to rest on an old chipped saucer sitting on the coffee table. In it were several lipstick-stained cigarette butts. Kerrie Ann caught her eyeballing them and said somewhat defensively, "Don't worry. I smoked outside."

"I wasn't accusing you of anything," Lindsay replied, but her voice was tight.

Kerrie Ann set aside her magazine and languidly rose from the sofa, sending Fagin racing off to join his sister, Estella, who was batting around a stick of kindling by the fireplace. "Hey, you weren't kidding when you said this place was out of the way," she remarked, clunking her way across the room in her mile-high platform shoes to gaze out at the view from the picture window. She turned toward Lindsay. "It must get pretty lonesome, huh?"

"That's what I love about it," Lindsay said.

"Funny, I wouldn't have pegged you as the loner type."

"Because I work around people all day?" Lindsay smiled. "That's precisely why I need the peace and quiet when I get home."

Kerrie Ann contemplated this for a moment before giving a nod. "Yeah, I get it. Kind of like when I used to work at Hooter's. The last thing I wanted on my time off was to have some bozo hitting on me after all the frat-boy crap that got pulled on me during my shift."

Lindsay didn't quite get the analogy, but she replied nonetheless, "Exactly."

"Anyway, it's cozy."

Lindsay followed her sister's gaze, seeing the room anew through Kerrie Ann's eyes. Very little had changed since she'd lived here with her parents. The same tongue-and-groove paneling and scuffed plank flooring covered in a crazy-quilt assortment of hooked rugs, the same Arts and Crafts lighting fixtures and funky, mismatched furniture. Her gaze lingered on the built-in shelves on either side of the fireplace. One side was lined with books and old LPs of Arlene's—mainly opera recordings—the other with Ted's collection of geodes and fossils. Tucked into the corner next to the fireplace was the antique dentist's cabinet that held the smaller rocks and bits of fossilized bone. The only thing her parents had loved as much as music and nature was flea markets. The house was filled with treasures they'd hauled home through the years, while Lindsay's only contribution had been to install new wiring and upgrade the plumbing.

Kerrie Ann wandered over to the stereo cabinet and began flipping through Lindsay's CD collection. "So you're into classic rock, huh? Cool. Though I gotta admit, I can't quite picture you grooving to Steppenwolf. Goes to show, you can't judge a book by its cover." She studied Lindsay as she might a word or phrase in a book that she didn't understand.

Lindsay only smiled wanly and said, "Books and music are my two favorite things." She'd have been embarrassed for her sister, or anyone, to see her on those occasions when she cranked up the volume and cut loose, sometimes even dancing in her underwear. The only one who'd ever witnessed that was Miss Honi, who, even at her age, wasn't above dancing in her underwear right alongside Lindsay. "Anyway, help yourself. I don't know what kind of music you like listening to, but we have the full range—from Pavarotti to U2."

"Who's Pavarotti?"

Lindsay struggled to keep the surprise from showing on her face. Who hadn't heard of the late, great Luciano Pavarotti? But she only replied, "Oh, just an opera singer."

With that, she hurried off to change. When she returned a short while later, Miss Honi and Kerrie Ann were waiting by the door, Miss Honi decked in her evening finery: a long-sleeved ruffled silk blouse in the same shade of fuchsia as her lipstick and a full, peacock-feather-green taffeta skirt that rustled as she gave a slow twirl to show off her outfit. Her ersatz "diamond" necklace and matching earrings from QVC completed the look. The lone concession to age was sensible, low-heeled pumps. After being on her feet all day, she didn't intend to spend the evening hobbling around in spike heels, she informed them.

Lindsay felt almost dowdy in her black cocktail dress and pearls. "You certainly know how to make an entrance," she said, smiling at Miss Honi's inimitable flair.

"Nobody's going to be looking at us, that's for sure," Kerrie Ann complimented her. Lindsay sincerely hoped that would be the case. She didn't enjoy being the center of attention, and her sister . . . well, the less she stood out, the better.

Soon they were making their way up the coast along Highway 1 in Kerrie Ann's rented Hyundai. Pacifica was only a twenty-minute drive from Blue Moon Bay but a world away in some respects. Because it was close enough to the city to make it attractive to commuters, its population was for the most part upwardly mobile, whereas Blue Moon Bay's was primarily working class. Every square inch of the waterfront, it seemed, was chock-a-block with pricey developments like the recently built condo complex Grant lived in.

When they were in sight of it, Lindsay began the ritual of ticking off in her head all the reasons not to move in with her boyfriend: (1) *No privacy.* Each of the attached townhouses had its own deck, which meant Grant had a view not only of the marina but of his next-door neighbors, who liked to sunbathe in the nude. (2) *Too noisy.* Lying awake at night listening to the sounds of revelers partying on their boats was a far cry from being lulled to sleep by the sound of surf. (3) *No place to park,* she thought, finally, as her sister circled the adjacent parking lot for the third time in search of a space.

Before she could think of a fourth reason, they were at the door, being ushered in by a smiling Grant. He gave Lindsay a light kiss on the lips, murmuring in her ear, "Mmm. Don't you smell nice," before greeting Miss Honi with a peck on the cheek. "And you must be the famous Kerrie Ann," he said, turning to Lindsay's sister with a wide, welcoming grin. "Grant Holbeck. It's great to finally meet you. I can't tell you what a surprise it was when Lindsay told me the good news. We'd just about given up hope of ever finding you."

Speak for yourself, thought Lindsay. But her irritation was quickly swept away by her pleasure at seeing him. He looked handsome in his linen blazer and striped, open-collared shirt, his face tanned from yesterday's sailing expedition and his blue eyes sparkling.

"Nice to meet you, too," Kerrie Ann murmured as she shook his hand. Nervously she looked around at the sleek, contemporary surroundings, which were a far cry from Lindsay's digs.

"I'm honored that you decided to come," he said, taking her jacket. "I'm sure you and your sister have lots of catching up to do."

Which we'd be doing right now if it weren't for this party, thought Lindsay.

Kerrie Ann glanced at Lindsay, saying with an odd note of defiance, "I wouldn't have missed it for the world."

"Well, come on in. The gang's all here." He led the way into the cathedral-ceilinged living room, where the other guests, a dozen or so, were seated with their drinks on the chrome-and-leather sofa and chairs or standing by the fireplace, nibbling on the hors d'oeuvres being passed around. "What can I get you ladies to drink? White wine, champagne?"

"You can pour me some of that bubbly," said Miss Honi.

"Same here," said Lindsay.

"Do you have any Diet Pepsi?" asked Kerrie Ann.

No sooner had Grant moved off toward the makeshift bar than Lindsay noticed a slight, stoop-shouldered man with deep-set brown eyes and a receding hairline making his way toward them. Her lawyer, Dwight Tibbet. He greeted Lindsay and Miss Honi, and Lindsay introduced him to her sister, with whom he briefly exchanged pleas-antries before getting down to business. "Listen," he said, leaning in toward Lindsay, his intensity, as always, a bit unnerving, "I spoke with Professor Lever today about a geological survey he did on a similar site up near Yreka, and—"

He was interrupted by Grant reappearing with their drinks. "Talking shop again, Tibbet? Take the night off. It'll do you good," he urged, giving his old friend a comradely slap on the back. Dwight flashed him a smile that seemed a bit forced. One of the things that must madden Grant's colleagues, Lindsay thought, was the seeming ease with which he pulled off his wins. He put in as many hours as anyone but always breezed into the courtroom looking as relaxed if he'd just stepped off the tennis court. The tactic worked: The few times she'd seen him in action, he'd had the judge and jury eating out of his hand.

Grant steered Miss Honi and Kerrie Ann off to meet his other guests, leaving Lindsay and Dwight to finish their discussion. Her lawyer had been successful in his bid to halt further movement on the resort until a full environmental study had been done and was now busy putting together a crack team. They talked about the merits of one biologist and botanist over another while Lindsay fretted inwardly about what all this was going to cost her.

When she looked up again, Miss Honi was holding court with several men, the youngest of whom had to be at least forty years her junior. Across the room, Kerrie Ann sat on the sofa next to an elegantly attired woman Lindsay recognized as Amanda Newsome, the wife of Grant's partner, Paul. Amanda was attempting to chat her up, but from the looks of it, Kerrie Ann wasn't making it easy; her bored expression was that of a teenager forced to make conversation with one of her parents' friends. Lindsay was working her way across the room to rescue both when Grant summoned them to supper.

At the table, Lindsay was seated next to Amanda. Grant's partner's wife was a buyer for Saks Fifth Avenue, and over the first course—smoked trout on a bed of greens—they chatted about the latest fashion trends, Lindsay confessing, "I'm afraid I'm hopelessly out of step. I usually just wear what's in the closet. In fact, I can't remember the last time I went clothes shopping."

"Meaning you can still fit into your old clothes, which is more than most of us can say. A couple of babies and there goes the waistline." Amanda gave a rueful downward glance. "What about you? Do you see yourself having kids someday?"

"Sure, but first I'd need a husband." Like most single women her age, Lindsay couldn't ignore her biological clock, but unlike those for whom a husband or live-in boyfriend wasn't essential in making a baby, she believed a solid commitment to a partner had to come first. She knew from close observation what it was like being a single mom and what it could do to your children.

"Speaking of which, when are you and Grant going to make it official? Paul says there's an office pool betting on when you two decide to tie the knot." Amanda's brown eyes crinkled above the rim of her wineglass as she lifted it to her lips.

Lindsay felt her cheeks warm, though she was sure Amanda was being facetious about the office pool. She and Grant had discussed marriage, of course—maturely and intelligently, like two adults—but there were some major obstacles before they could take that leap. "Your guess is as good as mine," she replied lightly.

She glanced over at Miss Honi, who was

regaling the guests at her end of the table with the tale of how her car had been totaled after she'd unwittingly parked it in a construction zone. "It was the darnedest thing," she said. "Foreman called me up to say how sorry he was, though anyone with eyes in their head could see it was my fault. Well, next thing I knew, he was introducing me to his widowed dad. That's how I come to know Charlie, the dearest, sweetest man who ever lived—God rest his soul. He's gone now. Though it figures I'd find love at the end of a wrecking ball, given my history with men."

The comment was greeted by a round of chuckles, with Miss Honi basking in the limelight. She was never more comfortable than when performing to a rapt audience. *If only I could be more like her*, thought Lindsay. Fun-loving and not shy about saying whatever was on her mind, even if it was to a roomful of strangers.

Just then she caught sight of her sister at the other end of the table, scowling at Amanda's husband, who was seated to her right. In a voice loud enough for everyone to hear, she snapped, "No, I do *not* have a tattoo on my ass. And even if I did, you'd be the last person I'd show it to!"

An awkward silence fell over the table, and every head turned toward Kerrie Ann and the somewhat inebriated-looking Paul Newsome, whose face was the same shade as the plum-colored tablecloth. Lindsay heard a choked cry and turned to see Amanda's face drained of color. Her heart sank.

Paul attempted to make light of the situation, flashing a grin and giving the shrug of the misunderstood. Which only served to anger Kerrie Ann further. "You know what pisses me off the most?" she went on in the same loud voice, her eyes glittering and hectic stripes standing out on her cheeks. "Dudes like you, that's what. You think just 'cause you wear a fancy watch and went to college, someone like me is gonna fall all over you. Well, I have news for you, buddy—I ain't interested. In fact, you can kiss my sweet ass, 'cause that's the closest you'll ever get to it!"

The even deeper silence that ensued spoke louder than any words. Some of the guests became suddenly preoccupied with what was on their plates while others cleared their throats and reached for their wineglasses. Lindsay just sat there, feeling as if she were trapped in a nightmare.

It was Miss Honi who took matters in hand, defusing the situation with a dose of Texas-style irreverence. "Sugar," she drawled to Kerrie Ann, "if all men thought with the head on their shoulders, there wouldn't be no call for us gals to get our dander up over every dumb thing a fella says when he's had too much to drink." She waggled a scolding finger at the "fella" in question. "Somebody get that boy some good strong coffee. Either that or we'll have to hose him down."

The tension broke, and a ripple of laughter went around the table. Miss Honi had effectively reduced the offense to that of a naughty schoolboy, thus making it possible for them to move on. All except the unfortunate Amanda, who stabbed at her smoked trout with her fork as if were still alive and she needed to impale it before it could wriggle off her plate.

Somehow they made it through the rest of the meal, after which they retired to the living room for coffee and dessert. Miss Honi entertained some of the guests with more of her colorful tales. Lindsay managed to appear composed while fielding questions about various books currently on the best-seller list. Grant rallied as well, telling about a trip he'd taken to the Galapagos Islands the previous year at the special invitation of the Venezuelan government. No one appeared to notice Kerrie Ann, who'd retreated into a corner, where she sat sipping a diet soda and staring out the window.

Before long it was mercifully time to go. Wanting a moment alone with Grant before they took their leave, Lindsay followed him into the bedroom when he went to collect their coats. "I'm sorry," she said.

"You have absolutely nothing to be sorry for," he assured her.

"But my sister—"

He cut her off before she could finish. "There's

no need to apologize for your sister. I'm sure Paul had it coming. He has a bit of a reputation, if you want to know the truth." Grant drew her into his arms, dropping a kiss on the end of her nose. "Don't worry, this will all sort itself out."

She didn't know if he was referring to tonight's incident or the larger issue of her socially challenged sister. "How can you be so sure?" She stared down at the pile of coats on the bed, where the fuzzy white collar of Miss Honi's decidedly un-PC rabbit chubby was sticking out from under a chic sky-blue trench coat with a Saks Fifth Avenue label.

"Because I know you," he said.

It came rushing back to her once more, the years in which she'd had to shoulder the burden of caring for her little sister at an age when her only worry should have been getting good grades. She remembered how scared and overwhelmed she'd felt and was certain that if it hadn't been for Miss Honi, she'd have been crushed by the weight of all that responsibility.

What she wanted more than anything right now was for someone else—Grant—to take charge. But that wasn't going to happen. Besides, what could he do? Kerrie Ann was her sister, not his. Her responsibility. One way or another, she would just have to find a way to sort it out on her own.

CHAPTER FIVE

$\mathcal{K}$ERRIE ANN COULD TELL her sister was pissed off. Lindsay sat stick-straight in the passenger seat as Kerrie Ann drove, her silence speaking louder than any words. Even the normally talkative Miss Honi, in the backseat, was subdued.

Finally the tension became too much.

"Will somebody please just say it?" Kerrie Ann burst out. "You think it's my fault, don't you?"

"No one's blaming you, sugar," said Miss Honi. "That fella had it coming from what I could see."

Lindsay broke her tight-lipped silence to reply in a carefully measured tone, "Maybe so, but not everything has to be aired in public. Sometimes it's better just to . . . overlook certain things rather than make a scene."

Kerrie Ann couldn't deny that her sister had a point, but she bristled nonetheless. "Oh, so when some creep's got his hand on your thigh and is whispering in your ear that he'd like see what's tattooed on your ass, you should just compliment him on his tie?" she replied sarcastically.

"All I'm saying is that sometimes, in situations like these, you have to take other people into account."

Just then her sister could have been any of the countless schoolteachers who'd reprimanded Kerrie Ann over the years—for sounding off in class, wearing a skirt that was too short, smoking in the girls' bathroom, not handing in her homework assignment on time.

"I'm not saying the guy isn't a . . . that he didn't do those things," Lindsay went on. "But he also happens to be Grant's partner. And did you see the look on his wife's face? The poor woman!"

"I know somebody who'll be in the doghouse when he gets home," piped up Miss Honi, sounding almost gleeful at the prospect. "Kibbles and bits, that's what he'll be eating from now on."

"Why should I feel sorry for her?" Kerrie Ann's fingers tightened around the steering wheel. "She married him, didn't she? And I never met a guy like that whose wife didn't know the score."

"Even if that's true of Amanda, she wouldn't have wanted it broadcast to everyone at the table. She didn't deserve that. She's a nice woman."

"Really? I thought she was stuck-up." Kerrie Ann hadn't really thought that, but she'd felt so hopelessly out of her depth around the other guests—people far more cultured and educated than she, who measured their lives in accomplishments rather than failures—that it was easier to portray them in a bad light than to admit to herself that she was a loser.

It didn't help, either, that Lindsay was leaping to the woman's defense while ignoring the insult to her sister. "How would you know? You barely spoke to her. Anyway, that's not the point."

The feeble voice of reason in Kerrie Ann's head warned her to back off, but her temper got the better of her. "Yeah, but it kind of is," she said. "See, that's the thing. Here you are, all worried about *her* feelings, while I'm supposed to just suck it up?" She shook her head in disgust. "Story of my life. I was hoping it would be different with my own sister, but apparently not."

Lindsay didn't respond. But in the intermittent glare from oncoming headlights, Kerrie took note of the grave look on her face and experienced a mild rush of panic. It was the same look she'd seen, growing up, on the faces of the adults in her life whenever she'd pushed one of them too far. Then it was *So long, kid*, and on to the next stop. Would Lindsay send her on her way, too? Before she'd even a chance to tell her about Bella? Kerrie Ann felt panicky at the thought. But she probably deserved it. Already she was shaping up to be as lousy a sister as she was a mother.

But when Lindsay finally spoke, it was in a tone more hurt than accusatory. "I'm sorry you feel that way," she said. "But honestly, I can't imagine how I could've given you that impression."

Kerrie Ann glanced once more at her sister, at the clean, uncluttered lines of her profile, the under-stated gold hoop earring peeking from the sheaf of smooth brown hair that lay across her cheek. So pretty, so composed . . . and so utterly alien. She shook her head and said, "Look, I'm not the cute little kid you used to know. So let's do us both a favor and not drag this out. First thing tomorrow, I'll be on my way. No hard feelings, okay?" Better to make a preemptive strike than to be on pins and needles for the rest of the drive home.

Lindsay cast her a startled look. "Why on earth would I want you to leave? You just got here." She paused before continuing in a more conciliatory voice, "Let's not blow this out of proportion. I'm sure after a good night's rest, we'll be able to put it in perspective and move on."

"Amen to that." Miss Honi reached over the seat to give Kerrie Ann's shoulder a reassuring squeeze.

She felt guiltier than ever for having made such a royal mess of things—starting with having cornered Lindsay into taking her to the party in the first place. She should have known it would be a bust. She should have left well enough alone. "Sorry if I wrecked your boyfriend's party," she said. Apologies didn't come easily for her, but she managed to inject a note of sincerity.

It must have been enough to satisfy Lindsay because the tightness went out of her face. "You didn't wreck it." She gave a small, grudging smile. "At least no one can say it was boring. And I'm sure it's not the first time Paul's gotten chewed out for putting his hand where it didn't belong."

"Men!" pronounced Miss Honi. "Sugar, if you rounded up all the ones who pulled that on me, the line would stretch all the way from here to Tulsa." She chuckled to herself. "I remember this one time, back in the day, one of the customers followed me outside after my show. Tried to kiss me, and when I wouldn't let him, he wrestled me to the ground right there in the parking lot. Must've figured I owed him for the twenty he'd tipped me."

Lindsay said in a shocked voice, "You never told me about that!"

"What happened?" Kerrie Ann asked, wanting to know how the story ended. Through the years, she'd found herself in similarly compromising positions, so she knew it was sometimes best just to roll over and play dead. But somehow she couldn't see Miss Honi doing that.

She knew she'd guessed right when Miss Honi said, "When he dropped his trousers, I took one look and started to laugh—couldn't help myself. So I says to him, 'You're gonna rape me with *that*?'"

"You didn't!" Lindsay gasped.

"Believe it," she said, and Kerrie Ann didn't doubt it. The way Miss Honi had handled the creep at the party had shown her what the old lady was made of: There was a core of titanium beneath that candy-coated exterior. "It worked, too. His you-know-what shriveled up on the spot, and he slunk off like a whupped dog. I suppose I could've just as easily gotten myself killed—

though if he'd had a gun, it woulda been the only heat he was packing."

Kerrie Ann burst out laughing, and after a valiant effort to restrain herself, Lindsay joined in. It acted as a pressure valve, releasing some of the tension that had built up.

They arrived back in Blue Moon Bay shortly before midnight. As Kerrie Ann drove along the road to the house, the darkness was as vast and deep as the ocean she could hear murmuring in the distance, the only thing alleviating it the flash of feral eyes in the underbrush, reflecting the glare of her headlights. Even the stars were obscured; all she could make out were the dark shapes of trees and the house in the distance.

Kerrie Ann knew she couldn't put off much longer telling Lindsay the real reason she'd come. The longer she waited, the worse it would look; Lindsay would feel duped. But it was late, and they were tired, and after the incident at the party, it might be best to wait until morning. She was still debating the matter when she pulled up in front of the house.

Before long they were settled in her sister's room with the lights out, Lindsay in her antique pencil-post bed and Kerrie Ann in the daybed by the window. Lindsay had given her a flannel granny gown to wear—the shorty pajamas Kerrie Ann had brought were too flimsy for this climate—and though it was hardly her style, she was grateful for its warmth as she burrowed under the covers. But sleep wouldn't come; she was still too wired from the day's events and plagued by worries about the future. She knew what she had to do.

"Lindsay, are you awake?" she called softly.

"Mmm?" Lindsay murmured groggily.

"Um, there's something you should know."

"What?"

"When we were talking before, back at the shop, about families and stuff, I didn't tell you that I—" She broke off, reluctant to blow whatever goodwill she might still have left.

"I'm listening," Lindsay coaxed.

Kerrie Ann closed her eyes and blew out a breath. "I have a daughter. Her name's Bella. She's six."

There was a rustle of covers, and when she opened her eyes, she could see Lindsay sitting up in bed, a pale shape in her ruffled nightgown, framed by the dark wood of the headboard. "Why didn't you say something?" If she'd been sleepy a moment before, she was wide awake now.

"I was afraid you'd judge me."

"Why would I do that?"

"Because I wasn't a very good mom. Don't get me wrong—I love my daughter more than anything. But I . . . I messed up." Kerrie Ann held herself clenched against the tears that threatened. "I won't go into all the gruesome details. Let's just say I was into drugs. It got so bad toward the end, I pretty much checked out—even on my own kid."

"Where is she now?"

"Foster care. I lost custody of her six months ago after the cops raided my place."

"I'm sorry. That must have been hard," said Lindsay in a soft, faraway voice, as if remembering the day she and Kerrie Ann had been taken away under similar circumstances.

"You have no idea." Just talking about it made her feel sick to her stomach. "I was so scared. Mad as hell, too. But I don't blame them now—they were just doing their job. A good thing, too. It forced me to face what I'd become. That very day, I checked into rehab."

"I see." There was a beat of silence as Lindsay absorbed this new and disturbing piece of information. Finally she asked, "What about her father? Where is he?"

"Who knows? Jeremiah's been out of the picture for years. He left when she was a baby." Kerrie Ann fingered the heart pendant on her necklace, wondering for the umpteenth time where he was now. She didn't even know if he was dead or alive. "So you see, I have only myself to blame. Guess I'm like our mother in more ways than one."

"You can't compare yourself to her. She never gave a damn about us."

"What does it matter if the end result is the same?"

Lindsay leaned forward, asking, "The real question is, where do you go from here?"

"Believe me, I'm doing everything I can to get her back. I hired a lawyer, and I go to twelve-step meetings—just got my six-month chip. Plus I've been working hard to save up for my own place, something near a good school. But it hasn't been easy, you know?"

"Well, it sounds like you're doing all the right things."

"Yeah, but it's not enough. That's why I'm here. I need your help."

Her sister replied guardedly, "If it's money you need, I'll give you what I can, of course. But I'm afraid I don't have much."

Kerrie Ann bolted upright in bed. "You think I came to hit you up for a loan?" But why wouldn't Lindsay assume that? She didn't know her from Adam, and Kerrie Ann hadn't exactly demonstrated herself to be the kind of person who was above such things. She was quick to assure her sister, "I don't want your money!" Though what she was about to ask was an even bigger favor. Finally she bit the bullet and came out with it. "Listen, the thing is, I was told I'd stand a better chance in court if I had at least one family member as backup. I, um, was hoping that person could be you."

When Lindsay didn't answer right away, she hastened to add, "I know it's a lot to ask, and I won't blame you if you say no. I can't even promise I'll be on my best behavior all the time. I'll try, but sometimes my mouth has a mind of its own." As Lindsay had already witnessed tonight. "Just think about it. That's all I ask."

The ensuing silence rippled like water from a flung stone. Kerrie Ann remained bolt upright, wide-eyed even in her exhaustion, her heart thudding. Finally Lindsay's tired-sounding voice came floating toward her, "Let me sleep on it, okay?"

It wasn't the response Kerrie Ann had hoped for, but it wasn't what she'd dreaded, either. She lowered herself onto her back, staring up at the shadows scudding across the ceiling from the wind blowing through the branches of the tree outside. "Yeah, sure," she replied softly. "Well, good night."

No response. After a minute or so came the soft sound of snoring.

The following morning, when Kerrie Ann awoke, her head was throbbing as if she'd gotten hammered the night before. She saw that Lindsay's bed was made, Lindsay nowhere in sight, and wondered how long her sister had been up. She staggered into the bathroom to down some aspirin before she jumped in the shower. Twenty minutes later, dressed and made up, she wandered into the kitchen, where Miss Honi, in a flowered kimono, was cracking eggs into a bowl. Lindsay, in a track suit, her hair pulled back in a ponytail and her cheeks ruddy as if from the outdoors, was grinding beans for coffee, a sound that went through Kerrie Ann's head like a chainsaw.

"Morning," she croaked.

"Morning, sugar! Beautiful day, ain't it?" chirped Miss Honi, though a peek out the window showed only cloudy skies.

"Sleep well?" Lindsay turned to look over her shoulder.

"Like a log. I didn't hear you get up." Kerrie Ann yawned.

"I'm an early riser, so you'd better get used to it."

Kerrie Ann wondered what her sister meant by that. Was it an offhand comment, or had Lindsay decided to let her stay? "How early is early?" she asked, trying to play it cool.

"I'm usually up before dawn." Lindsay dumped the ground beans into the coffeemaker and filled the canister with water. "There's a path along the cliffs where I go running, and this time of day I usually have it all to myself." She paused, smiling to herself. "For me, it's like . . . I don't know . . . like being in church. Except for the ocean— it always lets you know it's there." Her smile gave way to a troubled expression as she gazed out the window at the rugged, windswept landscape. Kerrie Ann wondered if she was thinking about what she would lose if those fat cats she was up against got their way. Obviously this place was more to her than just a roof over her head.

"You're way more ambitious than me," she said. "I'd sleep till noon if I could get away with it. The only thing that gets me out of bed is the thought of that first cup of coffee."

"Coming right up." Lindsay switched on the coffeemaker. Moments later came its reassuring gurgle, and the fragrant smell of brewing coffee filled the air.

The kitchen, like the rest of the house, dated back to an earlier era. The cabinets were of some dark wood made even darker by years of use. The tile counters were chipped in spots, the avocado refrigerator and stove the kind that had gone out of fashion along with gas-guzzling cars and Farrah Fawcett hairstyles. In one corner, by the window that looked out over the yard, was a breakfast nook with built-in benches and a square wooden table. The table was set for three, with quilted place mats, stoneware plates and cutlery, a butter dish and pot of jam.

Lindsay showed her where the mugs were, and after Kerrie Ann had poured herself a cup of coffee, she hovered in the background, uncertain whether to pitch in. Watching Lindsay and Miss Honi move about the kitchen, weaving around each other in the confined space with the practiced ease of a choreographed dance number, she felt like the proverbial fifth wheel. Which made her even more aware of her uncertain status.

She'd finished her first cup and was refilling her mug when an acrid odor drew her attention to the stove—something was burning. Miss Honi grabbed a pot holder, snatching the smoking skillet off the burner. "That's the second time in less than a week," she pronounced with disgust as she scraped the burned eggs into the sink and switched on the garbage disposal. "Lord, you'd think a grown person could fix scrambled eggs without burning them." She turned to Kerrie Ann with an apologetic look. "Sorry, hon, but you should know up front I ain't much of a cook." She glanced beseechingly at Lindsay.

"Don't look at me," Lindsay said with a laugh. "I'm good at making coffee, and I can boil an egg. That's about it."

Kerrie Ann seized the opportunity to make herself useful. "There's a trick to it. I'll show you," she said, reaching for the egg carton and cracking half a dozen more eggs into the bowl. She whisked them together with practiced ease, asking, "Do you have any cream?"

"Cream?" echoed Lindsay, eyeing her dubiously while Miss Honi went to fetch some.

"Just a dollop. You'll see." Kerrie Ann dribbled some into the beaten eggs, whisking all the while, then threw in salt and pepper and a handful of dried herbs from the spice rack. When the skillet was scoured and sizzling with butter, she poured in the eggs, and turned down the flame on the burner.

"You cook them at a low temperature without stirring until they start to set. Then very gently, you fold them." When the eggs were the consistency of runny pudding, she used the spatula to nudge them into a heap. She did this several more times, then quickly removed the skillet from the heat and scraped the scrambled eggs, loose and creamy, onto the plates Miss Honi had set out, pronouncing, "Voilà."

Lindsay and Miss Honi stared at her as if she'd performed a magic trick. "Where did you learn to do that?" asked Lindsay.

"I worked in a French restaurant once," Kerrie Ann told them. "The owner, who was also the chef, had this rule that everyone on the line, from the prep station on up, had to know how to do the basics. He used to say that if you could cook eggs, you could cook anything."

"Well, you learned your lesson well," commented Lindsay when they were seated at the table, digging into their food. "These are the best scrambled eggs I've ever eaten."

Kerrie Ann felt herself blush. Usually when she was the center of attention, it was for all the wrong reasons. But she was glad she'd scored some points today. Maybe Lindsay would see that she could be of some use around here.

Kerrie Ann ate quickly, shoveling in her food. The night before she'd barely touched the meal— no wonder, with that creep feeling her up under the table—but this morning her appetite had come roaring back. In addition to the eggs, she put away four strips of bacon and two toasted English muffins before her stomach finally protested.

As soon as the table was cleared and the dishes stacked in the dishwasher, it was time for Lindsay and Miss Honi to leave for work. Kerrie Ann drove them into town, to the service station where Lindsay's Volvo was ready for pickup. She felt a fresh surge of anxiety watching Lindsay unbuckle her seatbelt and reach for the door handle. Lindsay hadn't yet said whether or not she could stay. Either she was still thinking it over or she was waiting for the right moment to break it to her that the answer was no. Probably the latter.

Kerrie Ann was wondering if she ought to head back to the house and pack her bag when Lindsay suggested casually, "Listen, why don't you come to work with us today? I'm sure we can find some-thing for you to do. Have you ever worked in a bookstore?"

"No, but I could learn." Kerrie Ann injected just enough enthusiasm into her voice, not wanting to appear too eager—or, worse, desperate.

" 'Course you can." Miss Honi beamed at her.

"Good. It's settled, then." Lindsay gave Kerrie Ann a small smile as she climbed out of the car. Kerrie Ann sensed that she wasn't entirely for-given for last night, but at least she was being given a chance to redeem herself. She was determined not to blow it.

At the book café, she was given the job of stocking shelves. Hardly a challenge, but at least she wouldn't have an opportunity to screw up. She'd just finished sorting the various books into alphabetical order when she was approached by a stout, gray-haired matron. "Excuse me," the woman said. "I was wondering if you could help me. I'm looking for a particular book, and I don't see it."

"Um, sure." Nervously Kerrie Ann glanced about in search of her sister, who was nowhere in sight. "What's the title?" Maybe she could handle this without having to call on Lindsay. If so, wouldn't that prove to her sister that she could be useful here as well?

"*Horace*, by George Sand," answered the woman.

"Horace who?"

"*Horace* is the title, dear. The *author* is George Sand."

"Never heard of him."

"Actually, it's a her."

"Oh, she must be one of the newer authors. Who can keep track of them all?"

Kerrie Ann spoke with the air of someone who read so many books, she couldn't possibly keep them all straight. She didn't realize her mistake until the woman replied, "Actually, if you have it, it would be in the Classics section. But please don't trouble yourself. I can find someone else to help me." She regarded Kerrie Ann with the kind but pitying expression one might bestow on a mentally handicapped person before drifting off.

Kerrie Ann felt as humiliated as she used to in school whenever she'd been called on in class and hadn't known the answer. *Stupid, stupid, stupid* . . . She ducked her head and crammed her hands into the pockets of her jeans so she wouldn't give in to the impulse to send something flying—a book, for instance. When she glanced up, she saw her sister at the other end of the aisle, conferring with the woman. The woman pointed her out and smiled, saying something to Lindsay that made her smile as well. Were they making fun of her?

"Hey, you okay?"

She looked up to find Ollie standing before her, and she just as quickly dropped her gaze so he wouldn't see the tears in her eyes. "I'm fine," she mumbled.

She felt the pressure of his hand on her shoulder, and when she looked up again, it was only to fall into the warm pool of Ollie's molten-chocolate eyes. "Don't worry—it won't last."

"What?"

"Whatever's bugging you. Whenever I'm bummed about something, I always tell myself, 'You won't feel this way forever.' Usually it works." He winked at her. "If it doesn't, don't worry; I have the cure."

She caught his meaning, and a tiny smile surfaced. "One with about a billion calories in it, I bet."

"You guessed right," he said with a laugh. "Listen, you wouldn't happen to know how to operate a commercial espresso maker, by any chance? Because I could use a hand in the café."

She felt her spirits lift incrementally. "I worked in a Starbucks once. I think I can handle it."

He flashed her a grin, and she decided that he was really quite cute in an offbeat sort of way. Today's outfit was black jeans, a vintage striped blazer over a purple Hard Rock Café T-shirt, and his signature orange sneakers. His black hair bristled like a thick, furry pelt. "In that case, you're hired. In a manner of speaking, that is—I'm afraid I can only pay you in tips."

"I've worked for less." She was thinking of the time, low on cash and desperate for work, any work, she'd spent a week picking oranges in the orchards of Escondido.

Though she was a little rusty, she got the hang of it right away. The espresso maker wasn't like the one at Starbucks, but learning how to operate it wasn't brain surgery, either, and before long she was handling it like a pro. She filled the coffee orders while Ollie doled out muffins and cinnamon buns.

It seemed no more than an hour had gone by when she glanced at her watch and saw that it was noon. "Is it time for our lunch break yet?" she asked when she'd finished with the last customer in line.

Ollie looked up at her as he returned a tray of muffins to the case. "You read my mind." He slid the glass panel shut. "There's a deli just down the street. What do you say we grab a bite to eat?"

"Can't. Gotta run." She pulled off her apron, tucking it out of sight under the counter.

"What's your hurry?"

"I have to get my rental car back no later than one o'clock or I'll be charged for an extra day," she explained.

"So does this mean you've decided to stay on a while?" Ollie darted her a hopeful look.

"I don't know. We'll see." That all depended on Lindsay. In the meantime, she had no choice but to return the car, with her finances stretched thin.

"Why don't I follow in my jeep and give you a lift back?" Ollie volunteered.

She paused as she was heading to the stockroom to fetch her jacket and purse. "Thanks, that's sweet of you, but I wouldn't want to put you out." The Dollar rental center was all the way over the hill in Burlingame, she informed him.

"The buses don't run very often along that route. You could get stuck over there for hours," he pointed out.

She wavered. "Don't you have to be back at work?"

"I can always close up for a couple of hours. It's slow this time of day, anyway."

"Lindsay won't mind?" Kerrie Ann cast an uncertain glance at her sister, who was ringing up a purchase at the register.

"Don't worry about her. I'll take care of it." Ollie sounded so relaxed and confident that she felt her anxiety ebb as she watched him head off, winding his way through the maze of shelves and displays toward the front of the store.

Minutes later he was back, saying, "We're good to go. Meet you out front in ten minutes, okay?"

She wondered why the delay when, as far as she knew, his vehicle was parked out back, but she only said, "Fine." She touched his sleeve as he turned to go. "Oh, and hey . . . thanks."

He grinned at her. *"De nada."*

Twelve minutes later he pulled up to the curb where her rental car was idling. She smiled when she saw what he was driving because it was so Ollie: an old-time jeep that looked as if it dated back to World War II, which apparently it did. "It's a Willys," he informed her on the ride back. He pronounced it "Willis." "My dad and I restored it. Took us a couple of years—the parts were a bitch to find—but it runs great now. Sorry about the noise, though," he said, raising his voice to be heard above the engine as the jeep groaned its way up the steep incline along Highway 92. "It can get a little loud at times."

Kerrie Ann didn't mind. Ollie was such good company, she soon forgot about everything else. It wasn't until talk turned to her sister that she remembered why she was here.

"I can't believe you and Lindsay are related. You're so different from her," he observed.

"Is that a bad thing?" She was instantly on the defense.

"No . . . of course not. I didn't mean—" He broke off, and twin spots of color appeared on his cheeks, which quickly spread to engulf his entire face. Gamely he attempted to explain, "Look, Linds and I go way back, and I love her to death—did she tell you she used to babysit me when I was a kid?—but I gotta admit I can't quite picture her with a tattoo, if you know what I mean."

"Or with pink hair?" Kerrie Ann fingered the ends of her own hair.

He expertly maneuvered the Willys around a sharp bend in the road. "What I'm saying is I think you're cool."

"I'm not sure Lindsay thinks so. Not after last night."

Ollie cast her a curious glance. "Why, what happened?"

She told him about the incident at the party, careful not to gloss over her part in it. "Lindsay was pretty pissed. In fact, I don't think she'd be too sorry if I were to cut my visit short."

"I'm sure that's not true. Why would she want you to leave after she spent all that time looking for you? Anyway, it sounds to me like the guy had it coming."

"That's just it. All that time she was looking for someone who doesn't exist. Let's be honest—I'm not what she was expecting. Not even close." When Lindsay had last seen her, she'd been just a cute little kid. Now she was a big fat loser.

Ollie frowned. "You act like there's something wrong with the way you are."

She was touched, but he didn't know her well enough to speak with any authority. "Let's just say I don't think I'm the kind of person my sister would choose to be friends with."

"Give her a chance," Ollie said. "It's true she expects a lot from people, herself more than anyone, but once she gets to know you, she's the best friend you could ever have."

Kerrie Ann wasn't sure that would hold true in her case. *Once she gets to know* me, *what if it only confirms her first impression?*

They were cresting the hill when, without warning, Ollie pulled into the scenic lookout at the summit. Her dire thoughts were at once eclipsed by the dazzling view. Below them, the land dipped in a grassy slope dotted with oak trees, at the bottom of which, nestled in the crook of a long, looping curve in the road, lay the reservoir, sparkling in the midday sunshine. It was sunny, but a breeze was blowing, carrying a hint of coolness from the ocean on the other side of the hill.

"I don't know about you, but I'm starved," he said. "How about some lunch?"

She smiled, thinking it must be his idea of a joke. "So, um, what—we're foraging for nuts and berries?"

"Nope. I have something a little more substantial in mind." He twisted around in his seat, producing a large paper sack from in back. "You have your choice between turkey and pastrami. Oh, and I hope you like coleslaw. It was either that or potato salad, and I pegged you as the coleslaw type."

She stared at him in surprise. "But how? . . ."

"I think I may have mentioned the deli down the street? Well, I got the manager to throw something together while you were waiting for me to bring the jeep around."

Kerrie Ann laughed. "Smooth move."

They climbed out, and Ollie rummaged in back, finding an old tarp to serve as a picnic blanket. Kerrie Ann fell in behind him as he set off down the slope. Watching him bounce along ahead of her, the tarp under one arm and the bag with their lunch swinging at his side, his orange sneakers beating a path in the grass, she felt absurdly happy for some reason.

At last they came to a stop under an oak so old

and huge that its lower branches curled down almost to the ground in spots. They spread the tarp over the grass and sat down to enjoy lunch. After the big breakfast she'd had, Kerrie Ann was surprised by how hungry she was. She polished off the pastrami sandwich, a small bag of potato chips, and half the coleslaw, washing it all down with a bottle of root beer. She was easing open the button on her jean skirt when Ollie reached into the bag one last time, saying, "And now for dessert."

She groaned. "I don't think I could eat another bite."

Ignoring her, he produced a pair of chocolate cupcakes, which she recognized as signature Ollie creations. She took a bite of hers just to be polite, intending to save the rest for later, but as soon as she sank her teeth into its pillowy perfection, she knew she was a goner. "Amazing," she pronounced after she'd gobbled it down. "What's your secret?"

He grinned and settled back on his elbows, stretching his long legs out in front of him. "There's no secret. You just have to know when to stick to a recipe and when it's okay to experiment. Oh, and you can't think of butter and cream as the boogie man."

She licked the last bit of frosting from her fingertips. "I don't know any other guys who are into baking, except for pastry chefs. I'll bet you got teased a lot in school."

"Mainly it was my brothers. Good thing I'm into cars, too, or I never would've heard the end of it."

"How many brothers do you have?"

"Three, plus two sisters. I'm the youngest, so I was gonna get picked on no matter what, but my brothers never stopped giving me a hard time over the fact that I preferred baking to getting my knees shredded falling off a skateboard or wiping out on the waves at Año Nuevo. Of course that didn't stop them from wolfing down everything I made. Even now they still put in requests for birthdays and stuff, or when Sean or Donnie or Stew get a craving for my peanut-butter cookies or Heath Bar–crunch pie or . . . you name it."

"I wish I had that kind of talent," she said. Or any talent at all, other than a talent for messing up.

"Don't you have any hobbies?"

"Not really." She didn't think being addicted to crack fell into the category of a hobby. "I moved around a lot as a kid, so I was never in one place long enough to join a club or get involved in any activity. I had a hard enough time just keeping my grades up. By the time I got to high school, I'd pretty much given up even on that. My junior year, I got Ds and Fs in every course except phys ed. I spent more time in detention than I did in class."

"You and me both." At the look of surprise she shot him, he said with a rueful laugh, "You think I was always this nice, cupcake-baking kid?

151

There was a time when my parents and teachers thought I was on the road to ruin. Which I suppose I was."

"You? I find that hard to believe."

"Believe it."

"But how? . . ."

"The usual way. When I was sixteen I got into drugs—pot mainly. It wasn't long before my grades were in the toilet and my parents on my ass. They gave me an ultimatum: If I didn't clean up my act, I'd be spending every weekend and school vacation working on my dad's boat, where he could keep an eye on me. Since I'm not exactly cut out for the family business—fishing isn't my thing—I chose door number one."

"Was it hard for you to quit?" She was thinking of the hell she'd gone through to get this far.

"No, not really. I wasn't as into it as some of my buddies. I mostly just did it because I wanted to be cool."

"You were lucky. It's not as easy for some of us." He turned to eye her curiously, and after a moment's hesitation, she confessed, "I'm in recovery, six months clean. But for me, it was like clawing my way up a cliff with my bare hands and no rope." She didn't tell him about Bella; there was no reason he had to know—she'd probably be gone soon. "So you see, with Lindsay it isn't as simple as you think. I'm not sure if she can deal with all my baggage. And I don't blame her. It's a lot to dump on someone all at once."

His brow wrinkled in sympathy. "She just needs some time."

"Maybe. We'll see." Kerrie Ann reached into her purse for a cigarette.

When she'd finished smoking it, they gathered up their trash and folded up the tarp. "What did you think of Lindsay's boyfriend?" Ollie asked as they headed back up the slope.

"He seems nice enough," she replied. The real question was, what did Grant think of *her*? Probably not much after last night.

"Yeah, Grant's a cool guy. I'm just not sure he's *the* guy."

"Why do you say that?" she asked.

Ollie thought for a moment. "You know how two people can be in love and it doesn't necessarily make sense? Well, it's the opposite with Lindsay and Grant. On paper it makes such perfect sense, you can't think of a single reason why they shouldn't be together. Except one, and it's the most important one—no fire."

"Yeah, well, I'm not one to talk—my own love life is nonexistent."

Ollie looked surprised. "You? I'd have thought you'd have guys lining up at your door."

Kerrie Ann hastened to set him straight. "The problem isn't with men; it's with me." She explained that in the twelve-step program, they warned against getting romantically involved in the first year of sobriety. Given her history, she wasn't taking any chances.

Ollie looked a little disappointed, and she felt a little bad for bursting his bubble. Not that he would have stood a chance, even under any circumstances. He was cute and kind of sexy, in his own way. But despite his less than squeaky-clean past, he was far too nice for her. She would only end up dragging him down.

"There you are," Lindsay greeted them when they arrived back at work a short while later.

"Hey, boss!" Ollie called as they breezed in through the back door, giggling like a pair of slap-happy kids.

"What's so funny, you two?" Lindsay's gaze dropped to Kerrie Ann's hand, which rested lightly on Ollie's arm. Kerrie Ann knew that look: It was the same expression worn by Kerrie Ann's foster mom when she'd been in ninth grade, when Jean Fowler had walked in on Kerrie Ann in the bedroom with her teenaged son. The next thing Kerrie Ann knew, she was on a bus to Carson City, where a new foster home awaited her.

Kerrie Ann let her hand slip from Ollie's arm. "Ollie was just teaching me how to say 'Bug off' in Portuguese." They exchanged another look, which prompted a fresh bout of giggles.

Lindsay smiled at them, but her smile didn't reach her eyes. "Well, thank goodness you're back.

I was beginning to think you'd had car trouble."
She was eyeing Kerrie Ann as if she thought it had
been trouble of another kind. Something to do with
her and Ollie, no doubt.

She thinks I'm hitting on him. Poor Ollie, the
unwitting prey of a depraved older woman. And
who would want such a dear, sweet boy to get tangled up with the likes of *her*? A former junkie who
couldn't even hang on to her own kid. Kerrie Ann
experienced a surge of anger. Who the hell was
Lindsay to judge her? What business was it of
hers, anyway?

The same contrariness that had gotten her into hot
water so many times in the past asserted itself once
more. Any thoughts of wanting to make a good
impression on her sister flew out of her head, and
before she knew it, she was leaning in to plant a
light kiss on Ollie's unsuspecting lips. "Thanks,
Ollie . . . for the ride," she said in a throaty voice,
giving him a sultry look that wasn't lost on Lindsay
as she whirled away, hips twitching in her tight skirt.

CHAPTER SIX

$\mathcal{L}$INDSAY DIDN'T KNOW what to think. Was something going on between those two, or was Kerrie
Ann just being flirtatious? Probably the latter. Just
from the way she dressed—today's outfit was a
short denim skirt, black cowboy boots with fancy
red stitching, and a yellow scoop-necked jersey

155

that showed more than the outline of her bra—it was obvious that her sister liked drawing attention to herself. So whatever was going on with her and Ollie was probably harmless. But Lindsay felt uneasy nonetheless. *What if it isn't so harmless?*

Lindsay knew it was none of her business, but she felt responsible for Ollie. He was the closest she had to a kid brother. She'd watched him grow from boyhood to awkward adolescent, shooting up faster than he could keep up with, so that he was perpetually lurching around in a body that was more like a bicycle he was learning to ride, on his way to becoming the bright, funny, outgoing young man he was today. She'd worried whenever he'd hit a rough patch or floundered in any way. And having observed over the years how he behaved around girls, she knew the difference between light flirtation and a major crush. She had no doubt that if his crush on Kerrie Ann were to cross the line into something more serious, it would spell trouble with a capital T.

Take last night, for instance. Even if her sister hadn't knowingly encouraged Grant's partner, she was clearly a lightning rod for that sort of thing. Poor Ollie would be in way over his head. In fact, it looked as if he was already in over his head. The expression on his face when Kerrie Ann had kissed him had told Lindsay all she needed to know: He had it bad.

What would it be like if Kerrie Ann were to

become a constant presence? Lindsay's first instinct, the night before when her sister had asked for help, had been to rush to the rescue. Having Kerrie Ann move in with her would also be a golden opportunity. A golden opportunity to forge a bond that might otherwise take years. At the same time, a voice of caution inside her head had warned her to look before she leaped. More and more she was beginning to see how she'd glossed over her childhood memories of Kerrie Ann, using them to create an imaginary grown-up sister who in reality had never existed. She was remembering how contrary Kerrie Ann had been as a child and how prone to outbursts of temper. How Lindsay had constantly chafed under the burden of caring for her. In the real-life Kerrie Ann of today, those traits had only been compounded by a drug habit and a six-year-old child in foster care.

On the other hand, how could she turn away her own flesh and blood? Deny her sister the chance to be reunited with her child?

She was distracted from her thoughts by Miss Honi, who sailed over to mutter ominously, "Looks like we got company." She pointed in the direction of a tall, white-haired gentleman, dressed casually but expensively in tan chinos and a cashmere V-necked sweater, who'd just walked in the door. Lindsay gave a start, recognizing him at once from his photo, though they'd never officially met: Lloyd Heywood, CEO of the Heywood Group and the man directly or indirectly responsible for making her life miserable.

He looked to be in his late sixties, with a refined, erudite presence that perfectly captured the white-shoe elegance sought by those who flocked to Heywood resorts around the world. An old-world elegance updated, of course, with such modern amenities as flat-screen TVs and wi-fi, marble baths equipped with Jacuzzis and Czech & Speake toiletries, and complimentary robes and slippers in each suite. The more scenic resorts had eighteen-hole golf courses exactly like the one the Heywood Group intended to build on what was now her land.

As Lindsay approached him, she felt as if she were encased in a blood-pressure cuff squeezing tighter and tighter with each step. It was all she could do not to shout, *Shame on you!* Instead she was careful to arrange her features in a pleasant, neutral mask. She pegged him as the kind of sharp operator who was good at reading opponents, and she didn't intend to give him anything he could use to his advantage. At the same time, she was keenly aware of how vulnerable she was. What chance did she stand against a barracuda like him?

Until now she'd dealt only with his representatives, Ben Hammond and Stacy Jarvis, but his presence had nonetheless been felt at each of those meetings. Every sentence that came out of their mouths, it seemed, began with "Mr. Heywood would like you to know . . ." or "Mr. Heywood is prepared to offer . . ." And, more recently, "Mr. Heywood deeply regrets any inconvenience . . ."

Inconvenience? That was when you had to park a mile away because the parking lot was full, or when you had to wait in line forever at the cash register, or have your phone call rerouted for the umpteenth time after spending too long on hold. It didn't begin to cover what these people had put her through. What they were *still* putting her through in their systematic and ruthless attempts to seize control of her property by any means.

It was like biting down on tinfoil when she introduced herself. "Mr. Heywood? I'm Lindsay Bishop. You're here to see me, I presume?" She spoke in the crisp, cool tone of a busy professional.

He gave her a smile so warm and avuncular that she was instantly thrown off guard. "Lindsay— may I call you Lindsay? So nice to finally meet you." His handshake was firm but not crushingly so. And his weapon of choice—a pair of laser-blue eyes—twinkled disarmingly. "I've heard so much about you, I feel as if I know you. And may I say you're every bit as lovely as advertised."

Gritting her teeth, she inquired, "Is there something I can do for you?"

"Actually, there is. I was hoping to persuade you to let me take you out for coffee, or perhaps an early drink. There's something I'd like to discuss with you." He spoke with the vaguely continental accent of someone born abroad. "Is this a good time?"

"I'm very busy at the moment, Mr. Heywood. You should have called ahead to make an appointment," she replied in a cool, dismissive tone. "Besides, I don't know what there is to discuss. As I'm sure Ms. Jarvis and Mr. Hammond have told you, my property is not for sale—at any price. So if you've come all this way to make me another offer, I'm afraid it was a wasted trip."

He regarded her kindly. "No trip is ever a wasted one, my dear. Even when one fails to accomplish his or her goal. Through the years, I've probably learned more from my failures than from my successes."

"Easy to say when your successes outweigh your failures."

He chuckled. "Well said. But I suppose it all depends on your definition of failure. In my book, he who consistently fails to take action stands to lose far more than he who takes risks. So what do you have to lose, Lindsay, by letting an old man buy you a cup of coffee?"

She hesitated and saw the flicker of triumph in his eyes: He knew he had her. But what was the point of stalling him merely for the small satisfaction she'd derive from it? Sooner or later she'd be forced to hear his latest proposal. Briskly she replied, "Twenty minutes, that's all I can spare.

Which I'm sure will be more than enough time." How many ways were there of saying no?

She noticed Miss Honi hovering nearby, giving him the evil eye, and before Lindsay could signal that she had the situation under control, her self-appointed avenger was barreling toward them like a lioness sensing a threat to her cub. She even looked the part in her wraparound jungle-print dress as she swooped down on the unsuspecting Lloyd Heywood.

"We haven't met. I'm Miss Honi Love." She extended her hand. "And you must be that Heywood fella we been hearing so much about. Nice of you to drop by. We was wondering when you was gonna pay us a call. Where I come from, it's only sporting when you're fixing to stab some-body in the back to be man enough to at least show your face." Her tone was sugarcoated but the look in her eyes pure steel.

"A pleasure, Miss Love." He grinned, seeming not the least bit put off. "I've heard a lot about you, too. Though I must say my colleagues' description doesn't do you justice."

"Something tells me that ain't a compliment," she said with a sniff.

"On the contrary. I assure you it's very much a compliment," he replied with apparent sincerity. "Would you care to join us? Your friend Lindsay and I were just about to step out for a cup of coffee."

"Don't know what for, when we got the world's finest right here," she said, gesturing in the direction of the café, where at the moment Ollie was serving up a slice of chocolate cake to a girl Lindsay recognized as Annie Saxon, a former high school classmate of his and one of his not-so-secret admirers, while Kerrie Ann operated the espresso maker, looking like a honky-tonk girl who'd stumbled into the wrong joint.

"I don't doubt that, but perhaps it would be more private elsewhere?" Lloyd suggested.

Miss Honi smiled flatly, her blue-lidded eyes glittering like an arctic sunrise. "Thanks for the offer, but I'll pass. Some of us got *real* work to do." With that she whirled and stalked off.

When Lindsay went to fetch her coat from the closet in back, Miss Honi rushed to intercept her. "You sure you know what you're doing? Because, sugar, I don't just smell a rat, I see him walking off with the cheese." Lindsay saw the worry in her eyes and knew Miss Honi had every reason to worry.

"In that case, let's hope he chokes on it," she replied with more bravado than she felt. "Can you manage on your own until I get back?"

"Sure thing," Miss Honi assured her. "Your sister can pitch in if I get backed up."

Lindsay hesitated, thinking of the incident earlier in the day with Leona Venable, a retired school-teacher who liked to boast that she only read the classics. Leona had found it amusing that Kerrie Ann hadn't seemed to know who George Sand was. And though Lindsay privately considered Leona to be the worst kind of literary snob and knew you didn't have to be a simpleton to make the mistake Kerrie Ann had made, could she risk a repetition of that kind with other customers? Or, worse, a flare-up like last night's? "I suppose it'd be all right, just this once," she said at last with some reluctance, once more reminded of the decision she would have to make regarding Kerrie Ann.

Miss Honi helped Lindsay on with her jacket. "Don't worry about us—we'll manage just fine. You just go on out there and tell Mr. Rat where he can stick his cheese."

The nearest coffeehouse, the Daily Grind, was mostly takeout and had only counter seating, so she suggested they go to the deli down the street, where Lloyd Heywood ordered coffee and a roast-beef sandwich and Lindsay a Diet Pepsi. When their order arrived at the table, she watched him sink his teeth into his sandwich with obvious relish, as if he hadn't a care in the world, as if they were just two friends catching a bite to eat, and felt a grudging admiration for him. What must it take to project that breezy confidence in the face of such high stakes? She took note of the stainless-steel Rolex on his wrist—pricey without being ostentatious, the accessory of someone who didn't believe in flaunting his wealth—and thought, *Nice touch*. He could rob you blind without looking like the greedy son of a bitch he was.

"Very tasty. The horseradish gives it a nice kick," he pronounced, dabbing at his mouth with his napkin. "I'll be sure to recommend this place to my associates." He smiled at her across the checked tablecloth as if it had been just an innocent remark instead of a reminder that he and his people were going to be around to torture her for the foreseeable future. "Do you eat here often?"

"Not as often as I'd like," she told him, taking a sip of her Pepsi that did nothing to quiet the roiling in her stomach. "Usually I bring a sandwich to work and eat it at my desk."

His eyes crinkled in understanding. "You know the old saying: 'When you work for yourself, you have a slave driver for a boss.' All too true, I'm afraid." He shook his head slowly, wearing a small, rueful smile, and reached for his coffee mug. "Take it from an old man, my dear—you should learn to enjoy life more. It goes by all too quickly."

"I'm afraid it's not an option for some of us," she replied stiffly.

"Nonsense," he countered in the same agreeable tone. He blew on his coffee before taking a careful sip. "Studies have shown higher productivity levels among workers who take longer vacations and more frequent breaks than employees who don't. So what you see as hard work and dedication is actually a case of diminishing returns. Which is why I make sure to build in plenty of recreation time. I'm an avid golfer. Do you play golf?"

"No, I don't. And I have no intention of taking it up." An edge crept into her voice. "What did you want to see me about, Mr. Heywood?"

He took another bite of his sandwich, regarding her bemusedly as he chewed. "All right, then, I'll cut to the chase," he said at last. "I have a proposition for you."

"I told you my property isn't for sale."

"Yes, you've made that abundantly clear, and I'm not here to beat a dead horse. What I have in mind is something far more interesting—and, I hope, attractive." His blue eyes twinkled like those of a merry Santa holding out the promise of untold delights on Christmas morning.

"And what would that be?" she asked warily.

"Come work for me."

She almost fell out of her chair. "You've got to be kidding."

"Please. Hear me out," he said, raising a hand to still any protests before they could form. "What I'm proposing is that we relocate your bookstore to the resort once it's built. You would continue to manage it as you see fit—no interference from us. The only difference would be that you wouldn't have to worry about overhead and you'd be paid a handsome salary to boot. I would also provide you with living accommodations on the premises. In exchange for which you sell me your land. For which," he was quick to add, "I'm prepared to make an extremely generous offer." He flashed an ingratiating smile. "What do you say, my dear? It would solve both our dilemmas, don't you think?"

Lindsay didn't know what to say. It sounded so reasonable, the way he put it: the perfect solution to her current financial woes. She would still have her business and a roof over her head, and in addition a secure income, which would take the stress out of doing what she loved. Plus she'd have the profits from the sale of her land to invest. The only catch—and it was a big one—was that it would mean giving up the solitude and serenity of her little piece of paradise: No more early-morning runs along the cliffs with only her dog as company; she'd have to contend with golf carts zipping by and tourists wandering about. There would be manicured greens where wildflowers and coastal grasses now grew. Instead of being serenaded by the sounds of the surf and the wind whipping in off the ocean, she'd have the sputtering of lawn-mowers, the crack of golf balls and thwock of tennis balls.

It would also place her squarely under this man's thumb.

It was all an illusion, she realized. A clever artifice designed to lure her into his trap. She would still wake up each morning to the same view, but it would be unrecognizable—the Ralph Lauren do-over of its natural state. And the book café? It would be patronized mainly by guests of the hotel, tourists who wouldn't be around long enough for her to develop any kind of relationship with them. The majority of the locals would no doubt stay away, deterred by the off-the-beaten-track location and fancy new digs. Not to mention she'd be at the mercy of corporate maneuverings, however many promises Mr. Heywood made to her now.

In that moment, she almost wished her sister were there to provide a few choice words on the subject. Instead she said in a polite but firm voice, "It's a nice offer, but I'm going to have to pass."

His laser-like gaze didn't waver. "Won't you at least consider it?"

"What would be the point? I'm not going to change my mind."

His smile faded. "In that case, you're making a grave mistake."

"Maybe so, but at least it'll be *my* mistake."

"One that will end up costing you dearly," he predicted. "Because this resort *will* get built, I assure you—it's just a matter of time. Of course there are always obstacles with any project this size, but I didn't get where I am today by caving in to every local official waving ordinances at me or every property owner digging in his or her heels."

He paused, pushing aside his plate and reaching for the check. "Let me leave you with one final thought: the Panama Canal."

She frowned. "What does this have to do with the Panama Canal?"

"Think of the achievement," he went on as if she hadn't spoken, "how staggering it is to this day. What it must have taken, and not just in terms of manpower. Think of the delicate negotiations, and the colossal feat of engineering. And that's not even taking into account the inhospitable terrain: the heat, the mosquitoes, the constant threat of disease. Then ask yourself this." He leaned in, his gaze locking with hers. "If such an enormous undertaking could be brought to fruition against such impossible odds, what's to stop me from building a mere resort?"

Lindsay all at once felt defeated. He was right, of course. What was *she* to a man like him but a temporary nuisance? A mosquito, to use his own analogy, that was almost certain to get squashed. Didn't men like Lloyd Heywood always get what they wanted in the end?

Lindsay was so unnerved when she returned to work that she could hardly concentrate on what she was doing. She dragged from one task to the next, putting on a smile with her customers that felt carved into her face, until finally, blessedly, it was closing time. As she locked up, she caught Kerrie

Ann eyeing her intently and was reminded that she had one more unpleasant duty: She was going to have to tell her sister that she couldn't move in with them. She'd made the decision on her way back from meeting with Heywood. It wasn't just that she and her sister were polar opposites who were bound to clash, as they had last night, or that Kerrie Ann had more baggage than the cargo hold of a jetliner. How could Lindsay help fix what was wrong with her sister's life when she couldn't even fix what was wrong with her own?

As soon as the three women returned home, Lindsay disappeared into the bathroom for long soak in a hot tub. When she finally emerged, wrapped in her terry robe, the air was filled with fragrant cooking smells. She hadn't given much thought to supper and was gratified when she poked her head into the kitchen to find Kerrie Ann, frying something in a skillet while Miss Honi chopped greens for a salad.

"I found some hamburger in the fridge." Kerrie Ann turned to look over her shoulder, saying in an ingratiating tone, as if aware that she was on thin ice, "I hope you're okay with sloppy joes."

"Sure, sounds good." In truth, Lindsay was too drained to care what she ate or whether she ate at all.

Leaving her sister and Miss Honi to finish making supper, she went to throw on some sweats. When she returned, the food was on the table along with a small bouquet of wildflowers stuck into a jelly jar. "Shall we say grace?" said Miss Honi when they were all seated.

Lindsay gave her a surprised look. They never said grace when it was just the two of them. But she supposed Miss Honi felt the need to honor the occasion of their first supper as a family. Lindsay felt a fresh stab of guilt, reminded of the uncomfortable task that lay ahead.

"Dear Lord, bless this food we're about to eat," Miss Honi began, her head bowed and her hands clasped in prayer. "And thank you for bringing my baby girl home to me. It's a blessing having her under our roof again after so long a spell." Lindsay caught the glimmer of tears beneath her lowered eyelids. "Thank you, too, for mending this poor ol' family by bringing these two sisters together just when I was beginning to think I'd never live to see the day. Amen."

Lindsay's fork, when she finally brought it to her mouth, felt as if it weighed a ton.

She was subdued while they ate. Kerrie Ann, as if picking up on her mood, kept darting anxious looks her way. If it hadn't been for Miss Honi drawing them into conversation with her blithe chatter, Lindsay and her sister might have been strangers seated next to each other on an airplane. When supper was over, Kerrie Ann leaped to her feet to clear the table before Lindsay could beat her to it. Lindsay knew she was doing her best to make herself useful, probably in the hope that Lindsay would keep her around, which only made her feel more guilty for what she was about to do.

She was stowing the leftovers in the fridge, steeling herself against the difficult conversation ahead, when a loud crashing noise caused her to whip around. Kerrie Ann stood by the sink looking down in dismay at a plate that lay in a dozen pieces on the floor. "I'm sorry," she said, dragging her gaze up to meet Lindsay's. She looked stricken. "It . . . it just slipped out of my hand."

"Don't worry about it, hon. It coulda happened to anyone." Miss Honi was already scurrying over, broom and dustpan in hand.

"But it didn't happen to just anyone." Kerrie Ann's voice rose, the strain of the past couple of days showing on her face. "It happened to *me*—the fuckup. Isn't that what you're thinking?" Her blue eyes homed in on Lindsay.

"No, of course not. It was an accident," said Lindsay, but her words sounded insincere even to her own ears. At the same time, in her mind, she was seeing a tiny spun-glass angel shattered at the feet of a small, frightened girl.

"Guess I must be prone to accidents, then," Kerrie Ann went on in the same self-deprecating tone as she stood facing Lindsay, her face flushed and soapy water dripping from her hands. "After all, it was an accident that I ended up here. One that's shaping up to be a regular three-car pile-up, wouldn't you say? Isn't that why you're not exactly welcoming me with open arms?"

"What's all this nonsense? We're family. Why wouldn't we welcome you?" Miss Honi straightened from sweeping up the shards. "Ain't that right, sugar?" Broom in hand, she swung around to face Lindsay.

Lindsay was suddenly at a loss for words. "Of course," she said lamely. "You're always welcome." *To visit*; the unspoken words lay heavy in the air.

"But not when I need help?" challenged Kerrie Ann. "Is that what you're saying?"

"Will somebody please tell me what all this is about?" Miss Honi demanded, hands on hips.

Lindsay could see there was no use beating around the bush. "Kerrie Ann needs a place to stay. She asked if she could move in with us," she explained to Miss Honi, not taking her eyes off her sister.

"Just until I get my little girl back," Kerrie Ann hastened to add.

"Your—you have a daughter?" Miss Honi turned to face Kerrie Ann, wearing a look of astonishment.

Kerrie Ann nodded. A deep pain flickered in her eyes as she gave the abbreviated version of the story she'd told Lindsay the night before. At the end, she turned her gaze to Lindsay, shoulders squared and chin tilted in a stance Lindsay recognized from the early years, whenever she'd tried to get Kerrie Ann to obey her and Kerrie Ann had stubbornly refused, a look that was part defiance and part appeal. *Either help me or put me out of my misery*, her eyes seemed to say.

Lindsay realized that she couldn't go through with it; her decision had been guided by her head, not her heart. And whatever Kerrie Ann's shortcomings were, she was still her sister. *My responsibility*, she thought, as she had so many times when Kerrie Ann was small. Even as misgivings rose inside her, flapping and squabbling like a flock of crows, she put a smile on her face and said, "You always have a home with us, for as long as you need it."

There were plenty of occasions to regret that decision in the days to come. It wasn't that her sister didn't make an effort, just that all too often her efforts fell short of the mark. "Not everyone can be as perfect as you," Kerrie Ann snapped one morning when Lindsay pointed out that she'd left her wet towel on the bathroom floor—again. Kerrie Ann accused her of failing to recognize all the times she *had* remembered to hang up her towel or the clothes that, more often than not, were left strewn over the carpet. Kerrie Ann didn't seem to understand that it wasn't about being courteous and respectful some of the time—you had to be that way *all* the time, unthinkingly.

Like with her smoking. Most of the time Kerrie Ann obeyed the house rule and smoked outdoors, but a few times Lindsay had returned home from her morning run to the telltale stink of cigarettes in the air. Each time she'd confronted Kerrie Ann, who'd confessed with a vaguely sheepish look to having been too lazy to get dressed and go outside. On one occasion, she blamed the weather, saying, "You expect me to stand outside in the pouring rain?"

"I don't care what you do," Lindsay retorted, not bothering to hide her annoyance, "as long as you don't stink up the house."

Whenever she found herself regretting her decision to take her sister in, she thought of Miss Honi. How would she have been able to look Miss Honi in the eye had she turned her sister away? Also, Kerrie Ann was making herself useful at the book café, where they'd agreed she would work until she found a paying job, though Lindsay suspected that had to do with the fact that she was partnered with Ollie, who brought out the best in people. She'd turned out to be a good cook as well. So at least Lindsay had the consolation of a decent meal when she arrived home tired from work, though it usually meant being stuck with a sink full of dirty pots and pans.

The week after Kerrie Ann officially moved in— with the arrival of several large cardboard boxes shipped from her former address—Grant phoned

Lindsay at work on Thursday to ask if she'd care to join him for dinner that evening. "I'm entertaining a couple of clients from out of town," he told her. "It'd be great if we could make it a foursome."

"Sounds tempting," she fibbed. She hadn't seen Grant since the night of the party, but dinner with clients wasn't exactly her idea of a romantic evening. "I'm going to have to pass, though. We're hosting one of the book clubs tonight, and I'm in charge." That part wasn't a lie, at least. "Miss Honi has a date"—with her new beau, a retired basketball coach she'd met at a recent literacy fundraiser—"and I can hardly leave my sister in charge."

"How's that going?" Grant asked somewhat cautiously.

Lindsay, seated at her desk in the office, glanced at the door to make sure it was shut before replying candidly, "Wonderful when she's behaving herself, not so wonderful the rest of the time." She sighed. "A lot of the time it's like living with a bratty teenager. It's not just that she doesn't always remember to pick up after herself. She doesn't *think*. This morning was the third time in a week I've had to take a cold shower because she used up all the hot water. It's even making me not like myself—I've become a hopeless nag."

"Is that supposed to be a warning?" he said with a chuckle. Grant hadn't given up trying to per-

175

suade her to move in with him and seldom missed an opportunity to inject a comment to that effect.

Ignoring this one, she went on, "The bottom line is that my sister and I are oil and water, and the two don't mix."

"No, but out of oil and vinegar comes salad dressing."

"What's your point?"

"That sometimes opposing elements can complement each other."

"That remains to be seen. At the moment, I'm just trying to cope." She sighed once more, burying her elbows in the pile of paperwork on her desk—much of it unpaid bills or invoices due—as she leaned forward with the phone to her ear, propping her head on the heel of her other hand. "It's not all her fault. It's this damn case, too. It's got me on a short fuse."

"What's happening with that?" he asked, the warm concern in his voice banishing any uncharitable thoughts she'd had about his seeming lack of interest in the case. It had been several days since they'd spoken, and she was eager to bring him up-to-date.

"The county board of commissioners voted two to one in favor of supporting the Heywood Group's proposition." Her lawyer had phoned that morning to deliver the bad news. "Assuming there isn't an endangered species on my property in need of protecting, the next step will be for them to establish eminent domain." She felt a fresh stab of panic at the thought.

"Don't let it scare you." His calm voice soothed her frayed nerves. "Remember, even if they come out ahead in court, it's only half the battle—they'd still have to get approval from the state, and that's a much higher bar." Making a case for eminent domain based on tax benefits to the community, he reminded her, was a far cry from what the concept had originally been intended for: to clear the way for the building of railroads and highways, dams and aqueducts.

"That may be, but even if they don't have a leg to stand on, they have the resources"—Heywood's deep pockets and influence—"to make up for it. What am I but a lone voice in the wilderness?"

"You're not alone," he reassured her. "You have Dwight—and me."

"For all the good it does," she grumbled. Catching herself, she apologized. "Sorry. I don't mean to sound so grouchy. I must have gotten out of the wrong side of the bed this morning."

"Or maybe a case of one too many in the same bed?"

"My sister and I are sharing a *room*, not a bed," she reminded him.

Though at times it did seem as if she were way too involved in every aspect of Kerrie Ann's life. There were her sister's frequent and often frantic phone calls to her lawyer. And her new twelve-step buddies—one a muscular biker type going to flab with a skull and crossbones tattooed on the back of his shaved head, the other a skinny ponytailed guy with bad skin and even worse teeth, a former "tweaker"—who'd begun showing up at the house to take Kerrie Ann to the local NA meetings she'd begun attending. If they were any indication of what was in store, Lindsay would soon have to put up with a parade of bikers and tweakers and God knew who else—just like the sketchy characters Crystal used to drag home. Lindsay shuddered at the idea. *It's only temporary*, she reminded herself for the umpteenth time. Just until her sister got back on her feet.

By the time she hung up, she was feeling a little better; sometimes it helped just to vent. She returned to work with renewed vigor. An hour later she'd just gotten off the phone with the St. Martin's rep, a jovial man by the name of Ed Cosgrove, when there was a knock at the office door.

"Come in!" she called distractedly.

The door cracked open, and a head of wavy brown hair streaked with gray at the temples poked its way in. It belonged to a strikingly handsome man—fortyish, keen gray-blue eyes under heavy brows, a generous mouth bracketed by lines—who looked vaguely familiar, though she couldn't place him. "I'm not disturbing you, am I? The lady at the register sent me back, but if you're busy . . ." He seemed in no hurry to leave as he stood there smiling at her like someone accustomed to being a welcome interruption.

"No, please. Come in." She stood to greet him. "What can I do for you?"

"Randall Craig." He put out his hand—sturdy, tanned, sporting a silver band with Celtic lettering on its middle finger. "You said if I was ever passing through, I should drop by."

Now she knew why he looked familiar: the author photo on the back of his book. What had thrown her was that he was much better looking in person. "Of course. It's just . . . I wasn't expecting . . . that is, I thought . . ." she stammered, flustered as much by his presence as by the impromptu visit. At last she managed to gather her wits and say, "Well, it's nice to finally meet you. Though, honestly, I didn't expect you to take me up on my invitation. I know how busy you must be." She'd thought it merely a courtesy call when he'd phoned last week to personally apologize for canceling his author event. She hadn't expected to hear from him again.

"Never too busy to make amends. I hope you weren't too inconvenienced."

"Not at all," she lied. "It's not the first time it's happened, and I'm sure it won't be the last." His eyes were the color of a foggy sky with the sun burning through, and his mouth, with its fuller bottom lip, made her think of biting into a plump

179

berry. "Anyway, it couldn't be helped." He hadn't elaborated over the phone except to say that it was an emergency having to do with a family member.

"It was my mother," he explained. "She had a stroke. Fortunately it was a minor one, but she was in the hospital for a few days while they ran tests. I felt I should be there."

"Of course." Lindsay felt guilty for having assumed he'd blown her off for a more important gig. "She's better now, I hope?"

"Her doctor expects a full recovery." He had only a few inches on her but seemed taller, and physically fit without the pumped-up look of a man who spent hours at the gym.

She caught herself staring and quickly snapped back into business mode. "Well, now that you're here, do you think I could get you to sign some books?"

"With pleasure—it's the least I can do. Just point me in the right direction." Randall reached into the inner pocket of his well-worn brown corduroy blazer and produced a fountain pen that looked equally worn: marbled blue, banded in silver, with the enamel rubbed off in spots.

She guided him through the warren of shelves to where the remaining copies of *Blood Money* were displayed on the New Releases table up front. "We've sold quite a few, as you can see," she said, indicating the sizable dent in one of the stacks. "In fact, it's our most popular title at the moment."

"I don't suppose you've read it?" He arched his brow at her as he uncapped his pen.

"Yes, though I admit it's not the type of book I normally read," she confessed. "But once I picked it up, I couldn't put it down—I was up half the night. It's interesting that the comments I've been hearing are mostly about the plot," *like a high-speed chase in a stolen car,* raved one of the blurbs on the back cover, "but what struck me most was the prose. It's almost . . . literary. Which isn't what you would expect in a thriller."

Randall looked as pleased as a schoolboy awarded a gold star by his teacher. "I appreciate the compliment. But I have a feeling you'd have given it to me straight even if you hadn't liked the book."

"Probably not. Honesty isn't always the best policy in my line of work," she replied with a laugh. "Though I try to be fair to my customers. If I don't think a certain title is right for someone, I'll say so."

"But you'll spare the ego of an author whose head is already swelled enough as it is?" he teased, his blue eyes sparkling.

"Now you're putting words in my mouth," she said. "I never suggested you had a swelled head."

"Even though I just now shamelessly cornered you into giving me a glowing review?"

He grinned and picked up a copy of his book, which he signed with a flourish and handed back to her, held open to the title page. Glancing down, she noted with surprise that it was autographed to her: "Lindsay, will you have dinner with me tonight? Humbly yours, Randall Craig."

"My treat," he said when she brought her startled gaze up to meet his. "The book, that is. I wanted you to have your own signed copy." He pulled out his wallet and extracted two crisp bills, handing them to her—a first from an author. "Now, about dinner . . ." He spoke casually, as if not wanting her to see it as anything more than a friendly invitation. "I'm on my way to Monterey for a convention, so I thought I'd stay in town tonight. And I was hoping you'd let me make it up to you for canceling on you the other night."

Lindsay knew from Randall's author biography that he lived just up the coast, in San Francisco. Not so far away that he couldn't easily have made the return trip and still gotten to Monterey in plenty of time tomorrow. She wondered if he'd arranged to stay just so he could have dinner with her. The prospect was appealing even if it was only a case of his wanting to make amends.

But there was still the problem of the book club she was hosting tonight.

Kerrie Ann could handle it, she decided. She and Ollie would be on hand anyway to supply the coffee and cake. Would it really be too much to ask that she keep an eye on things and maybe ring up a few purchases? Before she knew it, Lindsay was replying, "I'd love to have dinner with you, Mr. Craig." She suggested a little Italian place around the corner where she often took visiting authors. It was intimate without being overly romantic, so she wouldn't feel too guilty about accepting Randall's invitation after having turned down her boyfriend's. Not that Grant would have cause to object. *It's just business*, she told herself. And part of her business was getting to know authors. So what if the author in this instance happened to be charming and magnetic? That was entirely beside the point.

Lindsay arrived at Paolo's shortly before the appointed hour, and she was able to snag one of the coveted tables in back, by the wood-burning oven, before Randall showed up. An hour and a half later, aided by a bottle of red wine, a plate of antipasto, and some of Paolo's magical *fettucini al limone*, they were as content as two people could be.

"I didn't know they made pasta like this outside Italy," Randall said, tearing off a hunk of bread to mop up the last of the sauce on his plate. The look on his face was one of such genuine pleasure that she found herself warming to him in a way that was far from business-like.

"Whatever Paolo can't buy or grow here, he has shipped over from the old country—even the flour that goes into making the pasta."

"No wonder it tastes so good." Randall popped the morsel of sauce-soaked bread into his mouth and chewed, eyes closed as if in silent communion with the gods, before washing it down with a swallow of wine. "When I was a kid, we used to spend a month every summer in Italy with my dad's family," he told her. "They lived in the village of Montepulciano, just south of Siena. For my little brother and me, it was heaven on earth. We ate like kings, ran around barefoot all day long, and were spoiled rotten by our *nonnas* and *tias*."

She was reminded of the first time she'd felt the salty sea air against her cheeks and the sand beneath her toes, walking along the beach here in Blue Moon Bay. She had thought she must have died and gone to heaven. "So how does someone with an Italian father end up with a last name like Craig?" she asked.

He smiled. "Anthony's my stepdad."

"Ah, that explains it."

"I never thought of him as anything other than my dad, though," he went on. "One of the advantages of your mom getting remarried when you're young, I suppose. Though I'm sure it had more to do with Anthony being such a great guy. Also, I didn't see much of my real dad growing up." A note of bitterness crept into his voice, and he offered her a rueful smile. "Not that that doesn't have its silver lining. I think all writers—the good ones, anyway—are born out of some childhood angst, so I have him to thank for that, at least."

"If that's true, then I would've been a Pulitzer Prize winner if I'd ever decided to try my hand at writing," she replied with a short, mirthless laugh.

He cocked his head, his gaze locking on to hers. "So you had it tough growing up?"

Lindsay sensed he wasn't asking merely out of idle curiosity. Still, she was sorry she'd brought it up. Only the wine and Randall's easy company made her feel relaxed enough to venture into territory she normally avoided. "My childhood was kind of a mixed bag," she told him. "I think of it as being divided into two parts, like B.C. and A.D., only in this case, B.C. stands for Before California. I moved here with my parents when I was thirteen. Before that I lived in Reno with my mother and my sister—my real mother, that is." She paused to add, with a slow shake of her head, "It seems strange calling her that because I never thought of her as my mom. She was just Crystal."

"That bad, huh?"

Lindsay shrugged. "She wasn't entirely to blame, I suppose. She had me when she was young—just seventeen. Also, I don't think she was cut out to be a mom. She wasn't what you'd call hands-on. She worked nights and slept during the day, so I pretty much raised myself. Then when my sister was born, I was stuck raising her, too." She hastened to add, "Don't get me wrong, I love my

185

sister, but—" She broke off , thinking the past had come full circle in some ways.

"Sounds like you had a lot on your shoulders."

"It wasn't easy," she admitted.

"So what happened?"

"When I was twelve Crystal went to prison for dealing drugs. My sister and I went into foster care." Her tone was matter-of-fact, as if she were speaking about people and events unrelated to her. The years of loneliness and neglect had taught her to distance herself from those emotions.

Randall was just the opposite. His face was like a seismograph charting his every mood, and right now it showed deep empathy. "That must have been hard on you and your sister."

"More for Kerrie Ann than for me. I was placed with a couple who ended up adopting me. My sister wasn't so lucky. She was only three at the time, so the only life she's known was being bounced from one foster home to the next. I even lost touch with her for a while—years."

"But she's back in the picture now?"

Lindsay nodded, taking a sip of wine. "Here's the strange part—I'd spent half my life searching for her, and then a couple of weeks ago, she just showed up out of the blue. I hadn't seen her since she was this high." She held her hand out level with the table. "It was quite a shock."

Randall gave a low whistle. "I'll bet. Must've been some reunion."

"It was. Though not like in movies, where everybody hugs and then it fades to black." So many conflicting emotions had been stirred up by her sister's unexpected arrival. "I'm happy she's back in my life, of course, but it hasn't exactly been smooth sailing. It isn't just that we're at opposite ends of the spectrum in terms of how we were raised—we're very different."

"How so?"

She hesitated, not sure how to put it without portraying her sister unfavorably—she didn't want him to get the wrong impression. "Well, for one thing, Kerrie Ann's not much of a reader. I can't imagine my life without books, and my sister doesn't even know who Dostoyevsky is. Also, I have a long fuse, while she . . . well, rub her the wrong way and she goes off like a Roman candle." She paused to reflect, fingering the stem of her wineglass as she gazed off into space. "I know she hasn't had an easy time of it, so I try to be understanding even though I'm not always that patient with her. I keep reminding myself that she hasn't had all the advantages I've had."

"I'm sure it'll get easier with time," he said.

"If we don't kill each other first," Lindsay replied with a dry laugh, explaining, "Kerrie Ann's staying with me and Miss Honi for the time being, until she gets her own place."

His eyes crinkled in a wry smile. "And who, may I ask, is Miss Honi?"

"You met her—the older lady at the register? I guess you could call her my adopted godmother. She was our neighbor when I was growing up, and she used to keep an eye on us when Crystal wasn't around. Anyway, she's the only family I have left. Except Kerrie Ann, of course. I just wish it were as easy with my sister as it is with Miss Honi. So far we seem to spend more time bumping heads than bonding."

Randall nodded in sympathy. "My brother and I are like that, and we grew up under the same roof. He's a Republican, I'm a Democrat. He's a church-goer, and I'm a lapsed Catholic. But even though we don't always see eye to eye, it doesn't mean we don't care about each other."

Lindsay set her glass down, realizing she was ever so slightly tipsy. Tipsy enough, at least, to be able to look Randall in the eye without losing her train of thought. She regarded him for a long moment, liking what she saw. "Thank you," she said. "It's nice to talk to someone who under-stands. And who doesn't think I'm a terrible person for occasionally wanting to strangle my sister."

"That doesn't make you a terrible person. Just human."

He smiled and reached across the table to take her hand, giving it a squeeze. It might have been nothing more than a friendly gesture except that his fingers remained lightly curled about hers.

There was no denying it now. They'd crossed the line from business into a place she had no business being. She felt a slow heat building in her and could see from the way he was looking at her that business was the last thing on his mind as well.

What am I getting into here? I have a boyfriend. Reluctantly she withdrew her hand from Randall's and sat back. "It doesn't help, of course, that she showed up needing a place to stay when I'm about to be homeless myself—that is, if the powers that be have their way." Lindsay told him about her predicament, careful to keep it brief lest she spoil the pleasant mood.

Randall listened intently, his expression darkening as she spoke. Clearly he had a soft spot for the underdog. "How much do you know about this Lloyd Heywood?" he asked.

"Not much outside what you can find out by Googling his name," she said. "Except that he's a bastard—and a charming one at that."

"The worst kind," he muttered, his expression darkening further.

"You can say that again," she said, recalling Heywood's cunning attempt to lure her into his web. "But how do you defend yourself against a man like that? He's the one holding most of the cards. And he has deep pockets. He'll put me in the poorhouse if he doesn't first succeed in driving me out of my home."

Randall lapsed into a brooding silence, and she

wondered if he was thinking about a similar experience of his own. Something that might explain why he'd left Wall Street at the peak of his earning years for the uncertain fate of a first-time novelist—perhaps a venture with someone unscrupulous in which he'd gotten burned? But before she could ask, their waiter appeared to clear away their plates. By the time coffee and dessert—slices of Paolo's delectable *torta di nonna*—arrived, they'd moved on to other topics. He told her more about his mother, who, in addition to having suffered several strokes, was in the early stages of Alzheimer's. He confided how difficult it was watching the bright, articulate woman he'd known slip away by degrees. She spoke with emotion about what it had been like losing Ted and Arlene.

When the check came, Randall paid the bill, then came around to take her arm as she rose to her feet. Just then they could have been any couple heading home after an evening out. She felt herself warm at his closeness and took note of the envious looks from several female diners, who no doubt thought them romantically linked and perhaps wished they could be as lucky in love. At the door, Randall paused to shake the hand of the portly, middle-aged Paolo. "The last time I had Italian food that good was at my *nonna*'s table in Montepulciano," he complimented the chef-owner, whose passion for his cooking was evidenced in the liberally stained chef's whites that strained at his ample belly, adding in fluent Italian, *"Dal cuore mangiate l'alimento migliore."*

The older man beamed at him, exclaiming, *"Esattamente!"*

"What did you say to him?" Lindsay asked when they were outside.

"Roughly translated, it means 'From the heart comes the best food.'"

"I didn't know you spoke Italian." She was impressed. Languages weren't her strong suit.

"There are a lot of things you don't know about me," he said, offering her his arm as they set off along the sidewalk. He spoke in a companionable tone, but she couldn't help noticing the preoccupied look he wore.

Randall had offered to drive her home, and she was in no shape to refuse. Even if she hadn't given Kerrie Ann the keys to her car, she was too tipsy to be trusted behind the wheel. It wasn't just from the wine, she thought, holding on to his arm as they made their way to where his car was parked. It was also the nearness to Randall. She felt as she used to with the boys in school on whom she'd had crushes. A feeling she hadn't had in a very long time.

When they arrived at her house, Randall cut the engine instead of letting it idle. *Nothing is going to happen*, Lindsay told herself. Nothing *could* happen while they sat parked not more than a dozen feet from the house, light streaming from the windows and her dog barking excitedly. But she experienced a little thrill nonetheless. It felt like her high school years, coming home from a date with a boy she liked, knowing the evening wouldn't end without a kiss. "I had a nice time tonight," she told him. "Thank you again for dinner . . . and for the book." Tame words compared to what she was feeling.

"My pleasure. I hope we can do it again sometime."

"I'd like that."

"In the meantime, good luck with everything."

The relaxed mood at the restaurant had given way to self-consciousness on his part as well. She sensed him holding back. Maybe because of the earlier reference she'd made to her boyfriend. Was he merely being respectful of that? Or was he involved with someone as well? He hadn't mentioned a girlfriend, and there was nothing in his bio about a wife, which meant he was either unattached or purposely keeping her in the dark. If it was the latter, it would mean he had designs on her and was only biding his time before he made his move. She felt a trickle of furtive pleasure at the thought.

And what of her own motives? Wasn't she supposed to be in love with Grant? What would he think if he could see her now?

She lingered a moment longer until she was at risk of appearing obvious before saying, "Well . . .

good night." She leaned in to kiss Randall on the cheek and somehow connected with his mouth instead. The kiss was light, a fleeting sensation of lips brushing over hers, his warm breath tasting faintly of licorice from the anisette he'd had with dessert. But it might as well have been a passionate embrace. She felt a bolt shoot straight down through the pit of her stomach, and if she'd been standing, her knees would have buckled.

She was trembling when they drew apart.

Randall clearly wasn't unaffected, either. "Good night, then." His voice was low and husky, and his eyes searched her face.

Even after they'd parted, she lingered for a moment or two on her doorstep, shivering in her light jacket, listening to the sound of his engine receding into the distance.

Randall Craig had forgotten how dark it could get in these remote areas, where there were no streetlights or lighted storefronts to guide the way. There was only the glare of his headlights as he bumped over the dirt road in his Audi convertible, his hands clenched tightly about the wheel and his eyes staring straight ahead while he replayed the evening in his mind.

You should have told her, he berated himself.

He'd wanted to come clean, and a few times over the course of the evening he almost had. But they had been having such a nice time, it had seemed a shame to spoil it. Then at some point the realization had kicked in that it wasn't just the evening he didn't want to spoil.

Nothing about this day, in fact, was going according to plan. He hadn't intended to ask her out when he'd stopped to see her at her store. But chatting with her, he'd felt an instant connection that had taken him by surprise. She wasn't the type of woman he was normally attracted to, with her understated prettiness and what seemed an almost purposeful attempt to downplay her looks. Yet there was something about her that had made him want to get to know her better. A feeling that had only deepened over the course of the evening. He'd quickly discovered that Lindsay Bishop, aside from being smart and well read, possessed a unique talent: She listened. Not like the women he'd dated in the past—the polite show of someone busy formulating a response that would showcase her in some way, demonstrate how sensitive and caring she was. Lindsay listened in the deeply attentive way of someone taking in every word, those big, solemn eyes of hers fixed on him all the while as if he were the only person in the room.

Like when he'd been telling her about his mom. Any discussion of Alzheimer's, he'd found, generally had people squirming in discomfort and rushing to change the subject. But she'd seemed not the least bit uncomfortable with the topic, her quiet focus acting on him like a sedative, calming the anxiety he felt at knowing the worst was yet to come. Nor had she stepped in with platitudes or attempted to relate to what he was going through by dredging up some tale about a friend of a friend's cousin who was in similar straits. She'd waited until he was finished before saying gently, "It's hard to watch a parent go. Believe me, I know. At times it's all you can think about—the fact that they aren't going to be around much longer. But it helps to remember the good times, too. Once you get into the habit of it, you start seeing them for who they really are, not just as an old, sick person you're terrified of losing." It was the best piece of advice he'd gotten so far—the *only* advice that hadn't made him want to chuck some well-meaning but totally misguided person out a window.

With her he hadn't just been Randall Craig, Wall Street wunderkind turned best-selling author, but son of Barbara Craig and repository of worries as well as story ideas. Maybe because she'd known tragedy of her own. He thought of the old expression *Still waters run deep*. Lindsay Bishop was the stillest person he'd ever met.

Not that the evening had been a somber one, by any means. They'd laughed over some shared observation just as often as commiserated over some tale of woe. They'd discovered that they had a number of favorite authors in common, even obscure ones most people wouldn't have heard of. She'd told him about her adopted mother's love of music and treasured collection of LPs ranging from Mario Caruso to the Bee Gees, and he'd confessed to being a vinyl guy himself—a throwback in this digital age. And they'd both agreed that anyone who claimed to have heard the rumored Satanic message on the Beatles' white album played backward was either delusional or a liar.

Had he only known her less than twenty-four hours? It seemed longer than that.

So why didn't you tell her? The most important aspect of his life where Lindsay was concerned, and he hadn't had the guts to be up front about it. Suddenly the withholding of that information seemed more than just an attempt to portray himself in the most flattering light, like the careful editing of his bio: He was a cheat, a fraud. He'd encouraged her to open up to him, all the while knowing she'd want nothing more to do with him were she to learn the real truth about Randall Craig.

CHAPTER SEVEN

$\mathcal{A}$LL HER LIFE Kerrie Ann had relied on her wits to get by. Like the time a trucker with whom she'd hitched a ride had tried to fondle her and she'd escaped by flashing her breasts and kicking him in the groin while he was ogling them. And the time the cops had shown up at a friend's house where she was doing drugs, and she'd escaped through the back while they were busting open the front door. But there were some situations quick thinking couldn't get her out of. Like when her little girl had been taken from her. And the latest: Kerrie Ann had just learned that the Bartholds had put in a formal request to adopt Bella.

At first she was stunned, then outraged. *Who the fuck do they think they are?* But her outrage quickly gave way to panic. She knew *exactly* who the Bartholds were: an upstanding professional couple with a nice house in a leafy suburb who just happened to be black—as was her daughter. What if the judge decided that what was best for Bella was to be with her own people, not some flaky white chick?

The thought was like a knife twisting in her belly.

"Do I look okay?" she asked Ollie. It was Sunday, two and a half weeks after she'd moved in with her sister, and he was driving her to Oakview, a suburb of San Luis Obispo, to see her daughter—a four-and-a-half-hour trip. One she'd been making from LA every other week for the past six months but which today had her as nervous as if she were on her way to an audience with the pope. From now on, her every move would be even more carefully scrutinized, she knew. It was no longer just a matter of when she could get her daughter back but *if* she would be getting her back at all.

"You look fine," Ollie assured her.

"You're not just saying that?"

"You're kidding, right?" He took his eyes off the road long enough to shoot her a look of naked incredulity. "You? You're, like, an eleven out of ten. How could you possibly look bad?"

He'd missed the point entirely, but she smiled nonetheless. She couldn't keep from smiling when she was around Ollie. When she looked into those big brown teddy-bear eyes, it was hard to hang on to the belief that the world was a shitty place full of bad people out to get her.

"Thanks," she said. "And not just for the vote of confidence. I'm sure you must have better things to do on a Sunday than drive me to Oakview."

"Like what?" he replied without missing a beat.

"Like, I don't know, watch the Lakers beat the crap out of the Warriors?"

He snorted. "In your dreams, sister. The Warriors'll wipe the court with those bums."

"Oh, yeah? What makes you so sure?"

"I have one word for you—Baron Davis. That's all I'm gonna say. Game over."

"That's two words. And you still haven't answered my question," she said, staring at him with her arms crossed over her chest.

"You mean would I rather spend the day with you or hang around the house waiting for my mom to find some chore for me to do? Gee, that's a tough call." Ollie stroked his chin, adopting a look of deep contemplation as he steered the Willys one-handed around a slow-moving truck.

Kerrie Ann laughed in spite of herself. She was still nervous about what she'd find when they got to Oakview—would Bella be happy to see her, like always, or would the Bartholds have turned her head with a lot of talk about the wonderful life she'd have with her new mommy and daddy?—but she didn't feel as tense as when they'd started out.

"You like living with your folks?" she asked him.

"Sure," he said, then sighed. "I know—kiss of death, right? Guys my age who are still living at home have about as much chance of scoring with a chick as Quasimodo. Believe me, I'd love nothing more than to have my place, but they depend on me, you know? My dad's got arthritis, so he needs help with stuff he used to be able to do himself. Which means I have to be up, like, way early to help him offload the catch and put away the nets before I leave for work. I do my baking at night, so that doesn't leave much time for stuff like, say, a *life*."

"What about your brothers and sisters—can't they help?"

"They do what they can, but they all have lives of their own. I'm the youngest, which means I'm stuck. It was either take care of *numero uno*, knowing my parents would have to struggle on their own, or do the right thing. I knew I wouldn't be able to live with myself if I left them in the lurch. Which is why, at the advanced age of twenty-four, I still live with my folks." He looked over at her and added with a rueful laugh, "Pitiful, huh?"

"I think it's nice." Though admittedly there had been a time in her life when a grown man living with his folks would have had less chance of getting into her pants than a guy with a prison record. "Anyway, I'm hardly one to talk. Look at me—I'm living with my sister, and I don't even know how much help I am. Sometimes I get the feeling I'm doing more harm than good."

"I'm sure that's not true," Ollie said.

"Oh? What about the other night?" Kerrie Ann reminded him. "All I had to do was babysit a bunch of book-club ladies for a couple of hours, and I couldn't even manage that."

"Don't forget I was there, too. And how were we supposed to know one of them was a shoplifter?"

True, none of those women had looked remotely suspicious. They ranged in age from late twenties to early seventies, but they all appeared respectable and trustworthy, the kind of people you wouldn't think twice about turning your back on in a roomful of merchandise. And yet when she'd done just that, one of them had filched eighty bucks' worth of books. Worse, since no one was owning up to the crime, there was no recourse. After talking to some of the other ladies, she'd pegged the newest club member as the culprit—a young woman who'd arrived carrying an enormous handbag and who'd ducked out before the meeting was over, muttering an excuse about needing to relieve her child's babysitter—but without proof, there was nothing that could be done about it.

"Yeah, well, somebody's still gonna have to pay for it, and unless they catch the thief, that person will be my sister." Kerrie Ann sighed as she stared out the window at the landscape gliding past— they were passing through King City, along a stretch of highway lined with shopping malls, warehouses, and discount outlets—recalling the look of resignation on Lindsay's face, one that said, *I shouldn't have expected more from you*, which was worse than if she'd gotten pissed. "Let's face it, if I was getting paid for this job, I'd have been fired by now."

"Don't be so hard on yourself," Ollie said. "You're still learning the ropes, and that takes time. The important thing is you're trying."

"With my sister, I get the feeling that isn't good enough." Or, more to the point, that *she* wasn't good enough.

"She'll come around. I know her. It's just that change is hard for her, and this is a big one."

"Like it's so easy for me?" Kerrie Ann shot back with an obstinate tilt of her chin.

What she didn't say was that in many ways she loved her new life. Her sister's was the first real home she'd known. She'd even grown to appreciate the peace and quiet of country life, which had almost driven her up a wall her first week living there. And work, when she wasn't messing up, felt like a real job, not just punching a time clock. She only wished she didn't feel as if she were walking around on eggshells with her sister.

Yesterday, for instance, they had been getting dressed for work when she'd noticed Lindsay surreptitiously checking her out. Finally it grew unnerving, and she confronted her sister. "What? Do I have a stain on my skirt, a zit on my chin? Am I missing a button?"

Lindsay feigned innocence. "Did I say anything?"

"You didn't have to. It's the way you're always looking at me. Like you'd be embarrassed to be seen in public with me or something."

"That's silly. Why would I be embarrassed to be seen with you?" Lindsay ducked her head to button her blouse, but not before Kerrie Ann caught the telltale redness in her cheeks. *Busted*, she thought.

"Maybe because you think I dress like a tramp?"

Lindsay slowly brought her head up, and this time her eyes met Kerrie Ann's in a level gaze. "I don't think that. Though I *do* wonder why someone as pretty as you feels the need to show off. You don't have to, you know. Men would still look at you if you weren't wearing clothes that gave them X-ray vision." Pointedly she eyed the tight top and miniskirt Kerrie Ann was wearing.

It was Kerrie Ann's turn to blush. She refused to look away, though, because it would have been like admitting defeat. She went on staring at Lindsay in defiance until finally it was Lindsay who looked away. But her sister's words had hit a nerve. She found herself recalling when, at four-teen, she had blossomed overnight from a skinny, flat-chested kid into a fully loaded woman—how amazing it had felt to suddenly be noticed after years of being either ignored or treated like dirt. It had given her a sense of power she'd never before had, one that she could use to her advantage with the opposite sex. And, like a teenager learning to drive, she had sometimes driven too fast.

Getting dressed this morning, she'd been con-scious of the image she wanted to make. Bella's caseworker would be monitoring today's visit, as usual, and it was more important than ever that she not get any black marks on her report. So instead of reaching automatically for the clothes she felt most comfortable in, ones that made a bold statement in a world where she'd otherwise be fine print, she'd selected her outfit carefully, choosing a pair of midrise moleskin jeans and long-sleeved jersey top, suede ankle boots instead of her favorite kick-ass cowboy boots. The only jewelry she had on were the studs in her ears and the necklace Jeremiah had given her, which she never took off. Looking in the mirror, she'd hardly recognized herself. In her conservative (for her) attire, with the pink streaks in her hair fading and a touch of lipstick and mascara her only makeup, she'd felt as panicky as if she were standing on a high perch looking down. *Who are you?* she'd thought.

Now she looked over at Ollie and thought, *I'm still me.* With Ollie, at least. He was the one person besides Miss Honi who saw the real Kerrie Ann underneath it all. "I suppose I should be happy my sister didn't think *I* was the one who stole those books," she said.

Ollie flicked her a surprised look. "Why would she think that?"

"Oh, I don't know. Maybe because I've been accused of worse."

"What's the worst thing you've ever been accused of?" He looked intrigued.

"You know how most kids, if they get kicked out of school, it's for cheating on a test or copying somebody else's paper? Well, with me it was for screwing a boy in the janitor's closet during lunch break." She paused to gauge his reaction, but his expression didn't change—maybe he wasn't so innocent after all. "We would've gotten away with it except the janitor opened the closet just as the principal happened to be walking by. Talk about busted."

She'd expected Ollie to be scandalized, but he only laughed. "That's nothing," he said. "My junior year, me and my buddies got caught breaking into a house."

"Seriously?" Kerrie Ann couldn't imagine Ollie involved in anything criminal.

"It was actually a cabin out in the woods near Bonny Doon. It looked like nobody had used it in a while because it was all boarded up. Anyway, we thought it'd be the perfect place to party. Except the party turned out to be us and a couple of scary dudes with guns. Turned out the reason the cabin was boarded up was because they were using it as a meth lab. Which was lucky in a way because it wasn't like they were gonna call the cops on us."

"You didn't call the cops on them?"

"We didn't have to. Somebody else ratted them out before we could."

"Wow." She eyed him in amazement. "Who would have guessed you had such a dark past?"

"Why, because I don't seem the type?"

"Actually, no."

"Just how *do* you see me?" Ollie gave her a peculiar look as he braked to a stop at a red light. Just ahead was a white pickup pulling a horse trailer. She could see the horse's rear end through the slatted tailgate its tail switching back and forth in a lazy, contented rhythm.

"I think you're sweet," she said.

"'Sweet,'" he echoed in disgust, "is about the worst thing you can say to a guy. Right up there with 'I see you more as a friend' and 'It's not you, it's me.'"

She laughed. "Trust me, it's a compliment." She couldn't say any more than that without leading him on.

Would that be such a bad thing?

Kerrie Ann pushed the thought from her mind. She closed her eyes and thought of Bella instead. Would her daughter be excited to see her? She'd been shy the last time they'd spoken over the phone, but when Kerrie Ann remembered how happy her daughter was whenever she came to visit and how Bella clung to her when it was time to go, she felt a little less anxious. She couldn't wait to tell her daughter the good news about her new house and job and the fact that she now had an aunt and a—Kerrie Ann wasn't quite sure how to bill Miss Honi, but she'd think of something when the time came—which meant that when Bella finally came home, it would be to a *real* home.

Kerrie Ann kept her eyes closed, savoring the rare moment of calm. She let her mind drift, aware only of the warmth of the sunshine rippling over her, the now familiar rumbling of the Willys's engine, and the scent of new-mown grass drifting through the open window as they passed from King City's commercial district into the farmlands beyond. The rude, clamoring thoughts that normally kept her from enjoying such peaceful moments were far away.

She must have fallen asleep because when she opened her eyes again, Ollie was pulling into a parking space in front of the familiar stucco building, home of the group dental practice of George Barthold, DDS, where her visits with her daughter took place every other Sunday under the watchful eye of Mrs. Silvestre. "See you in a couple of hours," said Ollie as she climbed out.

She paused to look back at him, realizing that she hadn't taken into consideration until now that he'd be cooling his heels for the better part of the afternoon with nothing to keep him occupied. "Will you be okay on your own?" she asked. "There's a Cineplex in the mall over on Highland Avenue— maybe you can catch a movie. Or, I don't know, check out the shops."

"I'm cool," he said. "I'll just wait right here. That way, if you need me, you'll know where to find me."

Kerrie Ann was touched. When was the last time a guy had looked out for her? Not since the early days with Jeremiah. She quickly turned away so Ollie wouldn't see the gratitude on her face. "Nah, you go on," she said. "I'll be fine. You'd only get bored hanging around here."

"Got it covered." He brandished the iPod he'd fished from a pocket of his cargo pants. "I also brought plenty of reading material." With a flourish, he pulled a stash of magazines from under his seat—copies of *Food and Wine*, *Bon Appetit*, *Cook's Illustrated*.

She laughed and said, "In that case, knock yourself out."

Stepping through the front entrance after she was buzzed in, Kerrie Ann was met by a blast of frigid air—the air conditioner was always on at the group practice of George Barthold, DDS, as if he and the other dentists saw it as a way to numb patients before they got their anesthetic. Kerrie Ann thought she could use an anesthetic right now. She was sweating despite the cold, and her pulse beat in time to the clacking of her boot heels against the tiled floor as she made her way past the empty treatment rooms toward the day care center, thoughtfully provided for the patients and employees of the dental practice.

Through an open door at the end of the corridor drifted the sound of voices—a woman's and a child's. Mrs. Silvestre and Bella had gotten here ahead of her, as usual. She felt a swelling of excitement. She hadn't seen her little girl in several weeks—she'd had to reschedule the prior Sunday's visit due to a lack of transportation—and missed her so much that it was an actual physical ache. Smiling, she stepped through the door.

Bella sat at one of the low tables, drawing on a large sheet of paper with colored Magic Markers, while Mrs. Silvestre stood over her, admiring her artwork. They both looked up at Kerrie Ann, Mrs. Silvestre with a welcoming smile and Bella with a look of delight that quickly gave way to one of shyness.

Kerrie Ann fought the impulse to fly over and gather Bella into her arms. She knew that coming on too strong could cause Bella to retreat or even bring on tears. Their relationship had become so fragile that each word, each gesture had to be carefully measured. It wasn't just that Bella had a new life with the Bartholds; her trust in Kerrie Ann had been shaken. The mommy who was supposed to care for her had let her down. Kerrie Ann had explained, as best she could, that she'd been "sick" and that it wouldn't happen again, and while Bella seemed to accept that, she wanted to know why they couldn't be together now that her mommy was "all better." She was too young to understand why Mommy couldn't make that happen, so somehow that was Kerrie Ann's fault, too. The thought was like a splinter lodged in her heart as she made her way across the room.

She squatted down so she was at eye level with her daughter, struck anew by the miracle she and Jeremiah had created in this child. With each passing year, Bella grew to look more and more like her father. She had his toffee-colored skin and wavy black hair, his lean shape and long, graceful fingers that had turned liquid when he'd played his guitar. Her blue eyes and the shape of her mouth were the only features she'd inherited from Kerrie Ann.

"Hey, baby. What you got there?"

Shyly Bella held up the drawing for her to see. It was a picture of what looked to be a large fish tank, containing various aquatic creatures, including an octopus. "It's an aquarium," she said. "That's where all the fishes live. And whales and dolphins that do tricks."

"The Bartholds took her to Sea World," explained Mrs. Silvestre. She extended her small, plump hand to Kerrie Ann. Her brown eyes, beneath the wispy bangs that came down over her eyebrows, seemed to take in every detail of Kerrie Ann's appearance in the time it took for them to shake hands. Kerrie Ann must have passed muster because the caseworker's smile was a bit warmer than usual. "Apparently the whale act was a big hit."

Kerrie Ann felt another knife-twist in her gut. She should have been the one taking Bella to Sea World! But she bit back a caustic response and only said, "Sounds like fun."

"Well, I'll leave you to it. Just give a shout if you need me," said Mrs. Silvestre before heading over to the adult-sized table in the corner where her laptop sat like a square, glowing eye.

Kerrie Ann quickly became so wrapped up in her daughter that she forgot about anything and everyone else. They drew pictures together and, when Bella tired of that, constructed a castle out of Legos. A Barbie doll filled in as princess of the castle, Bella declaring, "She got locked up by a mean witch, and now the prince has to rescue her."

"Where's the prince? I don't see him," said Kerrie Ann, making a show of searching for him.

"You're not s'posed to, Mommy. He's *invisible*." Bella looked up at her with all the sage wisdom of a six-year-old. In her flowered turtleneck and denim jumper, with her curly hair in neat braids, she looked like the girls in school whom Kerrie Ann used to envy.

"Why is he invisible?"

" 'Cause. The witch put a spell on him."

"Why'd she do that?"

"So the princess wouldn't see him."

"If she doesn't know he's there, how is he supposed to rescue her?"

Bella giggled. "Mommy. Don't you know *anything*?"

Kerrie Ann smiled. "Guess I'm not as smart as you."

"He gots to *kiss* her first."

Bella went back to playing make-believe with the princess and invisible prince. Eventually she grew tired of that, too, and they sat and talked about other things: what she'd learned in school and the extracurricular activities she was enrolled in, like the dance class for which Carol Barthold had bought her a pink leotard and matching tights. As much as it pained Kerrie Ann to admit it, Bella was flourishing in the Bartholds' care. Would the judge see that, too, and decide in their favor? If it were only a matter of who was best equipped to raise Bella, it would be no contest: The Bartholds were the clear winners.

Kerrie Ann felt a pang, wondering if she would be there to buy Bella her first bra . . . or see her off to the prom . . . or dry her tears when she got her heart broken by some insensitive clod of a boy.

"Hey, I almost forgot, I brought you something," she said as they were settling into the beanbag chair with Bella's favorite book—*Eloise at the Plaza*. Kerrie Ann dug into her pocket and pulled out a small, brightly wrapped packet. "I picked it out just for you."

A look of shy pleasure spread over Bella's face. "What is it?"

"Open it and you'll see."

It was a small gilded sand dollar on a silver chain. Kerrie Ann had spied it in a souvenir shop down the street from the book café and thought it would be perfect. Her guess proved correct—Bella was delighted with it. "Is it a real shell?" she asked in an awed voice.

"Sure is. In fact, I'll bet it came right off the beach by my new house."

Bella eyed her in confusion. "What happened to the old house?"

"I moved, sweetie—to a whole new town. I was going to tell you over the phone, but I wanted to save the good news for when I could tell you in person. You should see this place! It's right by the ocean. You can see whales there, too, only not the kind that do tricks. And outside there's a ton of room to run around in. And here's the best part . . ." She broke into a grin. "Your aunt Lindsay says I'm welcome to stay as long as I like."

"Who's Aunt Lindsay?"

"You haven't met her yet." Kerrie Ann didn't add that neither had she until recently; it would only confuse Bella. "But she's nice—you'll like her." She would explain later about Miss Honi.

"Will I live there, too?" Bella wanted to know.

Kerrie Ann glanced over at Mrs. Silvestre. She was tapping away at her laptop, pretending not to listen, but from her alert pose it was obvious that she was tuned in to every word. "You bet," she said. "But not right away. First I have to get permission from the judge."

Bella looked up at her with big, solemn eyes. "When will that be?"

Kerrie Ann sighed. "Soon, I hope."

"But *when*?"

"I don't know, sweetie. It's not up to me. I wish it was."

"Can't you talk to the judge?"

"It's not as simple that. But I'm working on it. Mommy's trying as hard as she can."

Bella's lower lip began to quiver. "You say that every time."

"I know." Kerrie Ann felt on the verge of tears herself. "But I promise, as soon as the judge says it's okay, I'll come get you."

"How do I know you're not just saying that? Like the time you were supposed to pick me up from Katie's party and you never came?" Bella's eyes narrowed.

Kerrie Ann's memory of her own early years might be a blank, but her daughter had a mind like a mousetrap. Bella recalled everything, practically since birth. The incident she was referring to had happened when she was in kindergarten. While Bella was at her best friend's birthday party, Kerrie Ann took the opportunity to get high and was so out of it that she forgot to pick Bella up. Now she felt a resurgence of the old guilt. How could she have done that to her own child? She glanced again at Mrs. Silvestre, praying she hadn't overheard. All she needed was another black mark on her record.

"I was sick then, but I'm better now," she said, swallowing against the knot in her throat. "I promise it won't happen again. From now on, you can always count on me." She hugged Bella. "Okay? You're still my little girl, aren't you? And I'm still your mommy?"

Bella nodded, but her small shoulders sagged. "I want to come home with you *now*, Mommy. Please?" Her voice rose to a querulous pitch.

Kerrie Ann darted another glance at Mrs. Silvestre, who was looking straight at her now. Cautiously she ventured, "Don't you like it at George and Carol's?" She was careful to strike a neutral tone.

Bella shrugged. "They're nice." She never said more than that, as if not wanting to be disloyal, but the few times Kerrie Ann had seen her with her foster parents, she'd been affectionate with them.

"What about your friends in school? You like them, too, don't you?"

Another solemn nod.

"And I hear you have a new playhouse. How cool is that?" It killed Kerrie Ann to have to list the perks of life with the Bartholds, but she knew it was the best thing for Bella right now.

Her instincts proved correct because Bella brightened at once. "You should see it, Mommy. It has furniture and everything. And Carol made curtains. They said I could have a kitty, too."

Kerrie Ann smiled and nodded, and her heart broke a little more.

Before long their time was up. By then they'd polished off the bag lunch that Kerrie Ann had brought—tuna-salad sandwiches, apple slices, and Ollie's to-die-for chocolate-chip cookies—and had spent most of the remaining hour playing on the swings and jungle gym out back. Now she cuddled a sleepy Bella on her lap, reluctant to let go. Each time it became a little harder.

Finally she could delay it no longer, with Mrs. Silvestre making noises and glancing pointedly at her watch. "Time to go, kiddo. Mommy's got a long drive ahead of her." She kissed the top of Bella's head.

Bella clung to her, whining. "I want to go *with* you."

"Not this time, baby. But soon. I promise." Kerrie Ann choked back tears. It never got any easier.

Bella started to cry, and Kerrie Ann grew a little impatient. "Come on, baby. That's enough. You're a big girl. Much too big for this." She caught a sharp look from Mrs. Silvestre and quickly changed her tack. "Will you do something for Mommy?" she said more gently. "Will you draw me another picture? You can give it to me next time. I'd really like that."

Bella nodded in mute assent, turning her woeful, glistening eyes up at her mother.

Kerrie Ann thought her heart would break. With a last hug and a kiss, she fled the room before she could—what? Scream her frustration at Mrs. Silvestre? Grab Bella and make a run for it? All she knew was that if she didn't get out of there fast, she was sure to do something she'd regret.

Outside, Ollie's jeep swam into view through the tears clouding her vision. She was hurrying toward it, stumbling a little, when she noticed a dark blue Mercedes sedan pulling into a slot nearby. The car came to a stop, then the driver's-side door opened and a tall, dark-skinned man climbed out. George Barthold. A moment later his wife, Carol, emerged from the passenger side, a statuesque woman with her hair in tiny braids coiled atop her head like the elaborate headdress of some high priestess. Either they'd miscalculated the timing or they'd purposely arrived early to pick up Bella, with the intention of reminding Kerrie Ann who had the upper hand. No doubt the latter, she thought, starting to simmer.

They spotted her and exchanged a guarded look before approaching her. George Barthold smiled pleasantly as he shook her hand. "Hello, Kerrie Ann. Nice to see you. You're looking well." He was tall and distinguished-looking, just starting to go bald on top, with skin the same coffee-with-milk color as his wife's. The sort of dentist who would inspire confidence in a patient facing a root canal—which Kerrie Ann felt as if she were undergoing right now. "How did it go in there?" He gestured in the direction of the clinic.

"Fine," Kerrie Ann managed to reply through clenched teeth.

"We came a little earlier than usual," Carol Barthold explained, as if that weren't obvious. "One of the girls in Bella's class is having a party, and I know Bella wouldn't want to miss any of it." Her tone was friendly, if minimally so, but her haughty eyes told a different story. *Just because you gave birth to that child, it doesn't give you the right to ruin her life.*

Kerrie Ann felt her resentment bubble over. "No, we wouldn't want that. God forbid she should spend a few more minutes with her *mother* when she could be stuffing her face with cake and playing pin-the-tail-on-the-donkey with some stupid kid from her class."

George attempted to ward off a scene by saying with a wry chuckle, "Pin-the-tail-on-the-donkey? We used to play that back in my day. Now-a-days it's clowns and pony rides and video arcades." Behind his this-won't-hurt-a-bit smile, his expression was tense.

"You know what? This is bullshit. I'm not gonna stand here talking to you people like I don't know what you're up to," Kerrie Ann erupted. "You think you can take my daughter away from me? Bribe her with a playhouse and a kitten and a trip to Sea World so she'll want to stay with you? I'm her mother. She belongs with *me*, not with you two bozos. Got that?"

Carol's eyes flashed, and she drew in a sharp breath that caused her nostrils to flare. George, the more diplomatic one, turned to his wife and said, "Why don't you wait in the car, hon? I'll go get Bella." The proprietary tone with which he spoke of Bella hit Kerrie Ann like a slap in the face. If she'd been carrying something heavier than a purse, she'd have smashed that smile right off his face. And now he was looking at her, saying in his carefully modulated voice, "I understand that you're upset. But we all have to set our personal feelings aside and think about what's best for Bella. Carol and I believe that it would be best if she remained with us. I know you don't agree with that, which is why it's up to the judge to decide."

Kerrie Ann was so enraged, she was momentarily speechless. It wasn't until Dr. Barthold was halfway across the parking lot, headed for the clinic, that she found her tongue. In the heat of anger, she called after him at the top of her lungs, "Oh yeah? Well, you can kiss my ass!"

At that exact moment she happened to look over and see Mrs. Silvestre emerging from the building, holding Bella by the hand. She paused at the entrance, staring straight at Kerrie Ann, her round face registering shock that quickly hardened into a frown of disapproval.

Ollie did his best to console Kerrie Ann on the way home. "You couldn't help it. Who wouldn't be pissed off if someone was trying to take away their kid?" In a harsher tone, he added, "If it had been me, it probably would've ended with the cops being called."

At the image of genial Ollie being hauled off in handcuffs, Kerrie Ann let out a teary snort that fell short of a laugh. "No offense, but somehow I can't quite picture that," she told him.

"Oh, so you don't think I'm tough enough?" He looked a little put out.

"No, I don't, and you should be glad of it," she shot back irritably. "There are two kinds of people in this world, Ollie. The kind like you who spread sunshine everywhere they go. And the ones like me who turn everything they touch to shit."

Ollie guided the Willys into the left lane to avoid the traffic backed up at the exit they were approaching. "The only thing the matter with you is that you don't believe in yourself," he said.

She glared at him. "Give me one good reason why I should."

"Well, for one thing, because *I* believe in you. I see how hard you're trying. And not just with your kid. You should be proud of how far you've come and that you're still hanging in there. Not everybody in your shoes could say that, I bet."

Ollie was right about that, she grudgingly conceded. Though, like all addicts, she was never more than a slip away from falling off the wagon. "I wish I had your faith," she said.

"It's a little like baking a cake," he went on. "You don't always have to stick to the recipe. You just have to trust your instincts."

"Even if your instincts suck?"

"Deep down you always know the right thing to do, even if you don't always do it."

Kerrie Ann gave in to a small smile. "You're a smart guy, you know that?"

"I don't know about that," he demurred, reddening.

"You're pretty cute, too," she threw in.

Ollie's blush deepened. When he blushed, it wasn't just his cheeks; it was his whole face, from his Adam's apple to the roots of his electrocuted hair. "Glad you think so," he muttered, casting her a look of such pained longing that she wished she hadn't said anything.

She'd put her foot in it. Again. She had no business encouraging him. Unless . . .

Before she could take that thought to its inevitable conclusion, they were cut off by some asshole in a black Beamer going ninety miles an hour who nearly clipped them as he shot into the lane just ahead of them. Kerrie Ann uttered a curse, her thoughts returning to the Bartholds.

If only she'd kept her mouth shut! Mrs. Silvestre was probably filling out her report at this very minute, and Kerrie Ann knew just what it would say: *Difficulty with social interactions . . . lack of impulse control . . . needs to work on managing her anger.* She'd seen it all before on countless report cards and evaluation forms and performance reports through the years.

It was after dark by the time they rolled into Blue Moon Bay. Fifteen minutes later they were pulling up in front Lindsay's house. Ollie parked in the driveway and got out, walking her to the door. Kerrie Ann was opening her mouth to thank him and to apologize for being such poor company on the ride home when he did something completely unexpected and most un-Ollie-like.

He kissed her.

Kerrie Ann was so startled, she didn't resist. Even more surprising, she found herself responding. Ollie might not be a man of the world, but he certainly knew how to kiss. His mouth closed over hers with authority, his big, capable hands cupping her head, and she found herself melting into him. It had been so long since she'd been held like this by a man . . . since she'd been touched so tenderly . . . not since Jeremiah.

This time it was Kerrie Ann's cheeks that were on fire when they finally drew apart. "Jesus. Where the hell did *that* come from?" she murmured in a low, unsteady voice.

Smiling, Ollie replied, shaking his head, "Beats me."

She didn't doubt, from the look he wore, that he was as surprised as she was. "I'll let you off this time," she said with mock sternness. "But don't let it happen again." *At least not while we're within sight of my sister.* "Or next time somebody *will* call the cops."

"Yes, ma'am." He took a step back, but his smile remained intact.

Moments later he was strolling back down the path, whistling a tune, his hands stuffed in his pockets and a huge grin on his face.

CHAPTER EIGHT

OLLIE WAS MAKING A CAKE. Not just any cake; this would be his most magnificent creation yet. Kerrie Ann's birthday was tomorrow, her thirtieth, and this would be his chance to show her, with something she could see and taste and savor, exactly how he felt about her.

For the first time in his twenty-four years, Ollie was in love. There had been girlfriends in the past, but they'd been mere warm-up acts, he realized now. Kerrie Ann was different than any of them—the most beautiful, exciting woman he'd ever met. She'd been places, done things, he could only imagine. Yet there was a vulnerability to her, something almost . . . bruised. Despite his own relative lack of experience, Ollie felt oddly protective of her. With Kerrie Ann, he was a knight of yore looking out for his lady love.

Until last Sunday, he'd feared his passion was doomed to go the way of all hopeless fantasizing. But then something extraordinary had happened: a kiss that, for him, had been more like a cosmic event. And she hadn't pulled away or stiffened or made some lighthearted remark designed to fend him off. She'd kissed him back. For what had to be at least a full minute. *She'd kissed him back.* Like she was into it. Like she was into *him.*

Admittedly there had been nothing since to indicate that she saw him as more than a friend. At work she was her usual breezy, irreverent self, acting as if nothing was out of the ordinary. All she needed was more time, he told himself. Right now she was too preoccupied with her daughter to focus on anything else. He tried to see this as an opportunity rather than a setback. Simply by being there for her, helping her get through this rough patch, he would demonstrate that she could always count on him. And someday, years later, when they looked back on this, a gray-haired couple with children and grandchildren of their own, she would smile and say, *That was when I knew I loved you.*

So, he thought, *butter.* Eight tablespoons or ten? Should he go with the cake flour or the all-purpose? Or maybe do a torte—ground nuts and only a handful of flour? Yes, he decided, a torte. Layered with shaved chocolate and whipped cream. That would make a real statement.

As Ollie began assembling ingredients, the torte took shape in his mind. This was how he worked: a glimmer of an idea, a bagful of tricks, an array of ingredients that through some process he wasn't always aware of (to him, recipes were like riffs to a jazz musician) magically alchemized into what emerged from the kitchen later on. Then he would marvel at his creation, hesitant to take credit for something that seemed to have more or less taken shape on its own. Through the years he'd had his share of failures, but he didn't dwell on those.

Every haul has its share of garbage fish, his dad always said. You just had to be patient and wait for the big one, like he was doing with Kerrie Ann.

He'd finished toasting the hazelnuts and was using an old dish towel to rub off the skins when his mom walked in. Her gaze swept the countertop, scattered with bowls and utensils and ingredients, before dropping to the hazelnut skins scattered in a fine layer over the worn linoleum. Her mouth stretched in a wry smile even as she released a sigh of resignation. Frieda "Freddie" Oliveira had long since become accustomed to having her kitchen commandeered by her youngest son and finding it topsy-turvy, as much flour and sugar on the floor as in whatever he was making. Her only rule was that he clean up afterward. After thirty years of running a business that had her on her feet all day, the last thing she wanted when she got home was to chase after someone with a mop and a broom.

Which didn't change the fact that she had a soft spot for her youngest. "Need a hand with that?" she asked.

Ollie looked up at her with his smile that could melt a polar ice cap. "I'm good, Ma. Why don't you take a load off? I'll make you a cup of tea. Just let me finish this and I'll put the kettle on."

"Tea would be lovely." She reached for the kettle herself, but Ollie shooed her away.

"Sit," he ordered.

Smiling, she pushed back a wisp of curly red hair

dulled by age to the color of old copper as she settled into a chair at the kitchen table—one that had
come off an old steamer and had seen more turbu-
lence in the decades of feeding her noisy brood
than when sailing the seven seas. "You're getting
to be awfully bossy," she said, eyeing him with
affection.

Ollie grinned at her as he swept a handful of
crackling skins into the sink. "I had a good
teacher." It was a family joke that Freddie couldn't
walk past an empty chair without telling it what to
do.

She laughed. "I'll own that." She'd had to run a
tight ship with such a large brood, though her dis-
cipline had always been meted out with equal
measures of hugs and kisses. "Though Lord knows
where you get your knack for baking—it certainly
wasn't from me." Freddie was a "decent enough
cook," in her own words, but she had neither the
time nor the inclination for baking. "Or your dad."
She clucked and shook her head. "The one time I
let him loose in the kitchen, right after Tee was
born, he nearly set it on fire trying to fry chicken."

"Sounds like something Tee would do," he said
of his eldest sister, Theresa, who was famously
accident-prone.

"Well, you know what they say: The apple never
falls far from the tree."

If that was true, Ollie wondered which tree he'd
fallen from. Physically he was a mixture of traits

from both his parents, but in every other respect he might have been an alien dropped into this occasionally riotous but otherwise perfectly normal family. For one thing, he was the first in a long line of Oliveira men who preferred dry land to being out at sea. Even though his three elder brothers—a plumber, police officer, and sales rep, respectively—hadn't gone into the family business, they loved to fish in their time off. His sisters, too—Caty had once landed a thirty-pound snapper off their dad's boat, and Theresa, who lived in Idaho with her husband and kids, had taken up fly-fishing. Ollie was the only one in the family who disliked everything to do with fish except when it came to eating it.

Regardless, each weekday morning he was up before dawn to help unload the day's catch before making the rounds in the family van to the wholesale accounts. By the time he arrived at the book café, showered and dressed in clean clothes, he'd already put in half a day's work.

"She must be pretty special," observed his mom as she followed his movements about the kitchen. She had a knowing look on her face, even though he'd told her nothing about Kerrie Ann other than he enjoyed working with her. Either there was some truth in Freddie's claim, while he and his siblings were growing up, that she knew what they were up to even when she wasn't there to see it, or she had gotten an earful from Lindsay.

"Yeah, well, I told Linds I'd bring dessert. And since it's a birthday party and all . . ." He did his best to downplay it. All his mom knew was that Lindsay was having a little birthday gathering at her house on Sunday, to which he'd been invited. On the stove, the kettle began to hiss. He switched off the burner and poured boiling water into the teapot.

"I'm sure it'll make quite an impression." A simple remark, but worlds were contained therein.

"Hey, it's the big three-oh. Gotta go all out for that, right?" Ollie spoke blithely despite the ripple of unease in his belly as he fetched a mug from the cupboard over the sink.

His mom smiled and nodded. "Thirty? Is that all? I would've guessed older."

Uh-oh, here we go, he thought. "That's 'cause you don't know her."

"Well, she seems like a nice enough girl." It had been the universal statement through the years about any of his or his brother's girlfriends who, for whatever reason, hadn't met with her approval.

Ollie poured the tea, keeping a close watch on his mom as he set the steaming mug on the table in front of her. Her expression was neutral, but the grooves on either side of her wide mouth had deepened. She was probably wondering just how serious he was about this woman for whom he was baking a cake on a Saturday night when other men his age were out having fun.

"She *is* nice," he replied somewhat defensively. "Actually, we have a lot in common."

"Is that so?" A subtle lift of the brow, nothing more.

Recklessly he plowed on, "Yeah, she's cool. She gets me, you know?"

"Really? I wouldn't have thought so."

An edge crept into Ollie's voice. "How do you know? You only met her the one time." A few weeks ago when Freddie had stopped in at the store to pick up a book she'd ordered.

Freddie replied in the same mild tone, "I only meant that you come from such different backgrounds."

"Well, she can't help how she was brought up, can she?" He set the sugar bowl down on the table, hard enough to rattle the lid.

"No, I don't suppose she can." Freddie appeared to consider this as she helped herself to a spoonful of sugar, slowly stirring it into her tea. "But, son, if there's one thing I've learned in life, it's that most people can't escape their upbringing. I'm not saying she doesn't have her good qualities, but from what Lindsay tells me, she's seen more than her fair share of trouble."

Ollie felt the muscles in his shoulders tighten. Damn Lindsay. Why couldn't she have kept her mouth shut? "That's all behind her," he said in a gruff, clipped voice.

"Are you sure about that?" she asked, lifting the steaming mug to her lips.

He searched for the words to make her understand. It was important that he get this right. "Have you forgotten what I was like in high school? You and Dad didn't write me off. You gave me a chance to redeem myself. Shouldn't Kerrie Ann be given that same chance?"

"I haven't forgotten." Freddie's pale blue eyes locked with his over the rim of her mug. "But you were sixteen, and all you needed was a kick in the behind to set you straight. It's not as simple as that for some. There are people who struggle all their lives and never get it right."

His mother's words nagged at him long after she'd finished her tea and headed to bed.

"Oh, Ollie, it's magnificent!" declared Lindsay the following evening when she pried open the cake box to reveal what Ollie believed to be his finest creation yet: four layers filled with coffee-flavored whipped cream and glazed with bittersweet chocolate sprinkled with chopped nuts. "You really outdid yourself this time."

"You sure there ain't a naked lady in there waiting to pop out?" Miss Honi leaned in for a closer look.

"Do we have to wait until after supper to have a piece?" joked Grant, who earned a playful slap on the wrist from Lindsay when he extended a finger to sample the chocolate glaze.

The only one who was speechless was the

birthday girl herself. Kerrie Ann stared at the torte as if she'd never seen anything like it, while Ollie did his best not to stare at her. She'd never looked more beautiful. She was wearing black velveteen jeans and a bell-sleeved, midnight-blue top made of some semitransparent fabric shot through with gold threads that floated around her with each movement and through which he could see just the barest hint of a black brassiere. On each arm was a stack of colored bracelets set with tiny mirrored discs that jingled and flashed. He noticed her makeup was more toned-down than usual, allowing her prettiness to shine through, and that the pink streaks in her hair had faded to reveal more of its natural color—a pale strawberry blond. She smelled of some citrusy scent.

He adopted a nonchalant pose, but his mind and heart were racing. *Does she think it's too much? Am I coming on too strong? Should I have gotten her a nice card and a bottle of cologne instead?*

"I've never had anyone make me a birthday cake before," she said at last. Gone was the tough-girl expression she often wore. She looked soft and vulnerable, like that day he'd taken her to visit her little girl. In that moment he caught a glimpse of the little girl she herself had once been, a sad and lonely one for whom birthdays had probably been celebrated with a minimum of fuss. She turned to Ollie. "You didn't have to go to all that trouble."

He felt suddenly self-conscious. "Hey, it's not

every day a girl turns thirty. I think that calls for more than some lame card, don't you?" he said in an attempt to make light of it.

Kerrie Ann rolled her eyes, as if thirty was so old. "Don't remind me."

They exchanged a look, which wasn't lost on Lindsay from the sharp glance she shot them. He felt a flash of resentment. He'd always thought of Lindsay as a big sister, and maybe that wasn't far from reality since his own sisters, Theresa and Caty, had seldom missed an opportunity to put an oar in when it came to his love life.

They all retired to the living room, where they sipped drinks and nibbled on the crackers and cheese that had been set out. When dinner was ready, Lindsay summoned everyone to the table, apologizing in advance, "I can't promise it'll be the best meal you've ever eaten. I'm not as good a cook as my sister"—she gestured toward Kerrie Ann, who ducked her head to deflect the compliment—"but nothing got burned, and it appears edible, at least."

Grant remarked loyally, "I'm sure it's delicious."

"Who cares, as long as it's hot and there's plenty of it? I'm hungry enough to polish off that whole hog," said Miss Honi, gesturing toward the baked ham glistening at the center of the table. "It's this damned diet I'm on," she grumbled to no one in particular as she settled into her seat at the head of the table. "Ain't hardly enough to feed a Chihuahua."

Kerrie Ann whispered to Ollie, "She joined Weight Watchers." Which prompted him to remark chivalrously, "Aw, come on, Miss Honi. You don't need to lose weight. Guys like ladies with curves."

It was all the encouragement she needed. "In that case, I'll have two helpings of everything and a nice big piece of that cake to top it off. I can always go back to dieting tomorrow."

"Or not," Kerrie Ann chimed in. "I agree with Ollie. You look just fine, Miss Honi."

"Apparently you're the only one who thinks so." Miss Honi shot Lindsay a mutinous look.

"*I* think you look just fine, too," Lindsay defended herself. "I'm just concerned about your health is all. Remember what the doctor said. If you don't do something about that high blood pressure of yours, he'll have to put you on medication."

Miss Honi's scowl gave way to a contrite look. "I know, sugar. And I promise to be good. Starting tomorrow. Tonight, though, I'm gonna enjoy every bite of this feast you cooked."

While everyone else took their seats, Lindsay headed back into the kitchen to fetch the rolls warming in the oven. Grant followed her and carried out the remaining platters, which were passed around. It was obvious that Lindsay had gone to a lot of trouble. The food was as tasty as it was plentiful. In addition to the baked ham, there were mashed potatoes, candied baby carrots, and steamed brussels sprouts.

"I have to say, Linds, this meal rocks. You really outdid yourself," Ollie commented. He turned to Kerrie Ann to add, "You see? We had to wait until you were here for her to show her stuff."

Kerrie Ann smiled at her sister. "It was nice of you to go to all this trouble."

"It was no trouble at all," Lindsay demurred. "We haven't celebrated a birthday together since you were little. That alone makes it a special occasion." Her face glowed in the candlelight.

Miss Honi reminisced to Kerrie Ann, "Every year on your birthday we'd make a little party, your sister and me. We'd boil up a mess of hot dogs, and I'd make one of them Duncan Hines cakes." She darted Ollie an apologetic look. "Well, at least it was *something*."

"Where was our mom during all this?" Kerrie Ann asked.

"Who knows? Probably at work." Lindsay spoke lightly, as if to deflect what, for her, was clearly an uncomfortable subject. Ollie had noticed she didn't like talking about her childhood.

"Not out doing drugs when she should've been looking after her kids?"

Kerrie Ann's remark was greeted by silence. Ollie sensed the barb had been aimed more at herself than at their mother, but he saw the muscles in Lindsay's jaw clench.

"There was some of that, too, I'm sure," she said. "Would anyone like more potatoes?" She offered up the bowl of mashed potatoes with a bright smile pinned in place.

Grant came to the rescue. "I wouldn't say no to another helping," he said heartily as he reached for the bowl. "Don't know when I've had tastier mashed potatoes. What's the secret?"

"Buttermilk," answered Ollie and Lindsay in unison.

The tension broke, and everyone laughed.

When supper was over and the dishes cleared away, the torte was carried out, ablaze with candles. They all sang "Happy Birthday," Kerrie Ann pretending to be embarrassed while looking secretly pleased. Even the dog and cats gathered round, Fagin and Estella winding in and out between legs while Chester barked excitedly at all the commotion. Then the torte was served and everyone fell silent except for the moans of ecstasy that greeted each bite. Even Ollie was impressed. He just hoped he'd hit the intended mark with Kerrie Ann.

After the presents were opened—a jungle-print scarf from Miss Honi, perfume from Grant, and a pretty if somewhat plain sweater from Lindsay—Lindsay suggested a game of Monopoly. Ollie was on the verge of sinking into a chair at the card table in the living room when he surprised himself by announcing, "Actually, after all that food I could use some fresh air." He turned to Kerrie Ann. "What do you say? Are you up for a walk?"

"Sure, why not?" she said.

He took note of the anxious look Lindsay darted them but decided to ignore it. Who cared if she had a problem with it?

No sooner had they stepped outside than he turned to Kerrie Ann. "Is it just me, or did you notice a chill just now?" His tone made it clear he wasn't referring to the temperature outdoors.

Kerrie Ann shrugged, pausing to light a cigarette. She'd thrown on a blue Patagonia parka belonging to Lindsay, with the leopard-print scarf Miss Honi had given her wrapped jauntily around her neck. She took a deep drag and blew out a jet of smoke, saying, "What did you expect? I'm the woman with the checkered past and you're the wide-eyed innocent. That's how my sister sees it, anyway." She sounded more resigned than angry.

"I'm not as innocent as you think," replied Ollie defensively as they set off along the path to the cliffs.

"I didn't say it was what *I* thought. By the way, that was a delicious cake."

"It was a torte, actually."

"What's the difference?"

"Cakes are made with flour and a torte with ground nuts and only a little bit of flour." He stuffed his hands into the pockets of his windbreaker, wishing he'd thought to wear a warmer coat. It got cold out here at night, much colder than inland, with the wind blowing in off the ocean.

"It's a little more trouble, but I wanted to make you something special for your birthday."

"It *is* special." She added in a softer voice, "But let's leave it at that, okay?"

He caught her meaning and replied testily, "You mean because of Lindsay?"

"Yes and no. It's not that I feel like I have to answer to her. But she's right, Ollie. I'm no good for you. You've got your whole life ahead of you, and I'm still picking up what's left of mine." She shook her head. "It would never work. I'd only drag you down."

"Don't *I* get a say in this?" Ollie was tired of others deciding what was best for him—his mother, Lindsay, and now Kerrie Ann.

Kerrie Ann didn't comment. She merely sighed and took another drag off her cigarette, saying, "This is my last one, I swear. I always said if I was still smoking by the time I hit thirty, I'd quit. So no more excuses, right?" She stubbed out the cigarette on the ground, then retrieved the butt and tucked it into the pocket of Lindsay's parka.

They walked in silence for a little while longer, the only sounds the rattle of tall weeds at their feet and the subwoofer thumping of the surf. Out on the ocean, a glittering band of moonlight stretched to the horizon. For some reason, it made him think of the Led Zeppelin tune "Stairway to Heaven."

Which was precisely where he was *not* going with Kerrie Ann.

Ollie was normally a sunny person, slow to anger and quick to forgive. Even as a child, he'd rarely thrown temper tantrums and almost never sulked. But a coal of resentment glowed inside him now. He was sure she wouldn't be saying these things if it weren't for her sister. On top of that, he had his mother and her dire predictions. *To hell with them both*, he thought.

Before he knew what he was doing, he had Kerrie Ann by the shoulders and was pulling her around to face him. "Listen, I'm sick and tired of everyone telling me what to do. I'm a grown man, and I don't need permission from your sister, even if she is my boss. Also, for the record, I don't think you're a bad influence. As a matter of fact, I happen to think you're pretty damn awesome."

"You do, huh?" Kerrie Ann stared back at him with a flat, unreadable gaze.

"Yeah. Do you have a problem with that?" Ollie was almost shouting, he was so worked up.

The hint of a smile. "You're not just saying that because it's my birthday?"

In reply, he drew her into his arms and kissed her. And this time Kerrie Ann didn't just allow it; she responded in kind, winding her arms around his neck and pulling him even closer, opening her mouth to his. A mouth so soft and warm and willing it was all he could do to remain upright, his knees were wobbling so. She tasted faintly of cigarette smoke, which for some reason only excited him further. And she yielded in his arms just as she had in his fantasies.

If they'd been indoors, behind a locked door, there was no doubt in his mind what would have happened next. Instead he held on to her as if the next strong gust would otherwise have sent them sailing over the cliff. They stood that way for a long while, Ollie with a hand cupped protectively about her head, Kerrie Ann with her face buried against his shoulder and her hair, whipped by the wind, flying up around his face.

"Happy birthday," he whispered in her ear.

Kerrie Ann was confused as she let herself back into the house after seeing Ollie off. What was happening? she wondered. In the beginning, Ollie had merely been someone fun to hang out with; she'd known he had a crush on her but never imagined it would go beyond that. All that had changed with their first kiss. Since then she'd found herself thinking about him way more than she should have, and in ways that weren't exactly G-rated. She'd managed to disguise it with a friendly aloofness at work, but tonight, when he'd kissed her again, there had been no holding back. She'd found herself wanting more. Ollie might not be a man of the world, but he wasn't a little boy, either. There had been nothing tentative about the way he'd taken her in his arms or the kisses that had gone through her like hot water through brittle ice.

He might not be as experienced as she, but he instinctively knew what a woman wanted and just how to deliver it.

What it meant exactly she didn't know. But she suspected it was more than just that she was sexually deprived. And that troubled her. Because the last thing Kerrie Ann wanted was to break his heart.

She walked in to find Lindsay, Grant, and Miss Honi seated around the card table, engaged in a spirited game of Monopoly. Lindsay looked up to inquire, "Where's Ollie?"

"He had to get home. He said to thank you again for dinner." Kerrie Ann kept her face averted as she returned Lindsay's jacket to its peg by the door, fearing her expression would reveal that her evening stroll with Ollie had been more than that. It was the same reason Ollie had ducked out early.

Lindsay seemed a bit taken aback. "Really? I wonder why he was in such a rush."

Kerrie Ann shrugged. "Beats me."

But Lindsay wouldn't let it go at that. "He must have said something. It's not like Ollie to just take off without a word. I hope nothing's wrong."

"He's a big boy. He can take care of himself." Kerrie Ann spoke more abruptly than she'd intended, and when she looked around, she saw her sister wearing a perplexed frown.

But Lindsay didn't comment, for which she was grateful. All she said was, "Care to join us?"

Kerrie Ann wandered over. "Who's winning?"

"Your sister," Miss Honi grumbled good-naturedly. "She's already got a hotel on Park Place and I can't get off Baltic Avenue to save my life."

Grant smiled up at Kerrie Ann. "Monopoly brings out her competitive streak."

"I can see that," said Kerrie Ann, her gaze dropping to the tidy bundle of colored bills at Lindsay's place.

"Don't let her fool you," teased Grant. "Behind that mild-mannered exterior is a will of iron."

"Which means she usually wins and the rest of us have to eat dirt," laughed Miss Honi.

"If only it worked that way in real life," Lindsay said with a sigh. "I can get a hotel on Park Place, but I can't seem to keep a hotel *off* my own land. Maybe I should just challenge Mr. Heywood to a game of Monopoly, winner take all. I win, he has to back off."

"What happens if you lose?" posed Grant.

"I'd rather not think about that." The party mood at once gave way to a more somber one.

Kerrie Ann excused herself and was heading to bed when she heard Miss Honi say to the others, "Know what? I think I'll turn in, too. All that food I ate is putting me to sleep. Why don't you two go on without me? I already know how this is gonna end, and it ain't pretty."

Miss Honi caught up with her in the hallway. "You ain't seen my newest angel yet. It just come in yesterday's mail," she said, tucking her arm through Kerrie Ann's. For Miss Honi, eBay was an even bigger weakness than fattening food. "Come have a look. She's the prettiest one yet."

Entering Miss Honi's private domain, Kerrie Ann felt, as always, like Dorothy stepping out of her black-and-white world into Technicolor Oz. It was a room as colorful and eccentric as Miss Honi herself, hung with lace curtains and decked with more bright, shiny objects than a Christmas tree. A dozen or more prisms suspended from lengths of fishing twine hung in the window, where they'd catch the morning light. The walls were hung with bright paintings depicting scenes of cozy domesticity. A full-length, gilt-framed mirror that might have come out of an Old West bordello was propped in one corner, reflecting the spray of peacock feathers in a brass urn opposite it. The double bed was covered in a quilted baby-blue spread and piled with throw pillows of every shape and variety, at the center of which was a lace-trimmed red satin one in the shape of a heart.

But the thing that commanded the most attention was the glass display case that spanned one wall. It contained Miss Honi's angel collection, a hundred or more angels ranging from the size of a thimble to ones too large to fit in the case (those were displayed on the dresser top) and made of every material from papier-mâché to the finest porcelain. They came from all over the world. "A regular

United Nations," Miss Honi liked to boast. Punched-tin angels from Mexico, painted wooden ones from Russia, spun-glass ones from Austria, and from Italy brightly colored ceramic ones. There was even a brass candleholder from Ireland with a ring of tiny cherubim that twirled when the candles were lit.

"Don't she have the sweetest face," said Miss Honi, carefully removing the newest angel from the case and placing it in Kerrie Ann's hand—a small one made of porcelain with amazingly life-like features. "Kind of reminds me of you when you were little."

"I've been called many things in life, but never sweet," replied Kerrie Ann with a self-effacing laugh. She sank down on the bed, studying the angel cupped in her palm. It stirred a hazy memory from the past. She dimly recalled holding just such an angel in her then much smaller palm.

"Don't get me wrong; you were a regular little monkey. Weren't nothing could make you stay put. Nothing but these angels. You'd sit and play with them for hours on end. Once a wing broke off one of them wooden ones," she gestured toward a grouping of carved balsa angels, glued together in spots, "and you cried like there was no tomorrow. You told me you were sad 'cause she wouldn't be able to fly back to heaven with only one wing."

"I must have been pretty young if I still believed in heaven," Kerrie Ann said.

"You don't now?" Miss Honi looked sad for some reason.

Kerrie Ann shook her head, handing the angel back to Miss Honi. "I'm not even sure I believe in God. The way I see it, if there is a God, He must be pretty fed up with me by now."

"God ain't in the business of giving up on folks. Least of all the ones who need Him most." Miss Honi brushed a stray lock of hair from Kerrie Ann's cheek, tucking it behind her ear as she might have when Kerrie Ann was little. "We all done things we're sorry for. But you got to look ahead. If you don't believe in God, have faith in yourself."

Kerrie Ann smiled. "You sound just like Ollie."

"Well, that boy's got a good head on his shoulders, even if you got him so cross-eyed he can hardly see straight."

Kerrie Ann gave a guilty start. She'd been so busy worrying about what her sister would think, it hadn't occurred to her that Miss Honi had eyes in her head, too. And even though those outlandishly lashed, turquoise-shadowed eyes were filled with nothing but warm concern, Kerrie Ann felt the need to explain, "I'm not leading him on to feed my ego. I know that's what Lindsay thinks, but it's not like that. I . . . I really like him."

"Who wouldn't. There's a fella who knows how to treat a lady."

Kerrie Ann couldn't have agreed more. "With

most guys, I was lucky if they even remembered to wish me a happy birthday, much less thought to make me something."

Miss Honi smiled knowingly. "That's Ollie for you. Been like that ever since I've known him. Though Lindsay tells me he went through a bad spell in high school when he fell in with the wrong crowd and ran wild for a time. Between you and me, I was glad to hear it," she confided with a throaty chuckle. "A little streak of rebellion in a boy like that is like pepper on a steak—gives it a nice kick. Least we know there ain't nothing soft about him."

Kerrie Ann thought about the firm stand he'd taken with her tonight. No, there was nothing soft about Ollie. "When I was that age I didn't know what I wanted out of life. I just knew I wanted out," she said.

"And now here you are, right where you belong." Miss Honi's expression was so kindly that Kerrie Ann was tempted to crawl into that warm, ample lap the way she had as a child.

But she knew she wouldn't rest until Bella, too, was back where she belonged. "I just wish my little girl were here," she said, her eyes filling with tears.

Miss Honi patted her knee. "She will be."

"I don't know. I may not get a second chance."

"Don't you worry about that. Just be ready when the time comes."

"What makes you so sure they'll give me another chance?"

Miss Honi, her lips curled in a small smile, gazed down at the figurine in her hand and answered the question with one of her own: "Why do you think God made angels?"

CHAPTER NINE

*Y*OU'RE SURE YOU'RE ALL RIGHT?" Grant eyed Lindsay across the Monopoly board.

"Of course. I won, didn't I?" She held up a fistful of colored bills.

"I wasn't referring to that." He directed a meaningful glance at the darkened hallway down which Kerrie Ann had retreated a short while ago. The house was quiet; there was only the crackling of logs in the fireplace and gentle snoring of Chester at their feet.

"Oh." Her shoulders rolled in a small, resigned shrug. "You think I'm upset because my sister went for a walk with Ollie?"

"You said it, not me."

She sighed and began sorting the pink, blue, and yellow bills into their proper receptacles. "Okay, maybe I was a *little* upset. I know Ollie's a big boy and that he doesn't need anyone to look out for him, but I can't help feeling responsible to a certain extent. After all, I'm the one who threw them together. And the way my sister prances around half dressed . . ." Lindsay crammed the last of the bills into the box with more force than was necessary. "Of course he's going to be drooling over her—what man wouldn't be?"

"I can think of at least one."

She brought her gaze back to Grant. This was the first chance they'd had to talk, other than the banter exchanged at the dinner table and over the game. With a small stab of guilt, she realized she'd scarcely given him a thought all evening. Odd, she thought, when for the longest time it had seemed as if all she could do was complain about the fact that they didn't see other as often as she would like. She smiled at him and reached for his hand.

"I appreciate your loyalty," she said, "but I also happen to know that my sister's not your type."

Grant was too much a gentleman to say anything critical of Kerrie Ann, though his feelings were evident in the elaborate courtesy with which he treated her, the same that he showed Miss Honi and others whom he considered less cultured or intelligent than he. "How could she be when I have eyes for only one woman?" he said, his navy-blue eyes crinkling.

She played along: "I wonder who that could be."

"Oh, that's easy—she happens to be sitting in front of me." He laced his fingers through hers. "And while we're on the subject, may I remind you that it's been some time since we've shared more than a nightcap?" He glanced once more toward the darkened hallway.

"It might be awkward with my sister sleeping a few feet away."

"There's always my place," he reminded her.

Lindsay smiled seductively. "Just name the date."

"How about next weekend?"

"Sounds good."

He frowned. "Wait—no. Friday I'm flying to Seattle for a deposition, and I'll probably have to overnight."

"Are you free on Sunday?"

"Sadly, no. I have my cousin Daryl visiting from out of town."

"You don't want me to meet your cousin?"

Grant shook his head, wearing a long-suffering look. "Believe me, I'm sparing you. Daryl's a nice guy, but all he ever talks about is crop rotation and the price of grain and whether or not the Green Bay Packers are going to make it to the Super Bowl this year. You'd be bored stiff."

Lindsay thought, *Why not let me judge for myself?* But she didn't comment. "What about the weekend after that?" she asked.

Grant's brow, beneath the boyish lock of hair that had slipped down over it, rumpled in dismay. "No good, either, I'm afraid. We go to trial the following Monday. I'll be holed up the entire weekend."

They lapsed into silence, staring into the flames flickering in the fireplace. Finally Lindsay roused herself, folding up the Monopoly board and stowing it away in its box. "Let's put our calendars together. I'm sure we'll come up with something." She felt annoyed with him though she couldn't think why. She should be used to his busy schedule by now. For goodness sake, it wasn't as if he were chasing other women. He did important work, work that was noble, even. Why should he compromise that?

"I'll call you tomorrow as soon as I get to the office, and we'll set something up," he said when it was time to go. He gathered her into his arms, where she stood with her head nestled against his shoulder, breathing in the familiar scent of his aftershave. It felt good just to be held by a strong pair of arms, knowing that no harm could come to her—in the moment at least. Then he stirred, murmuring regretfully, "I should get going. It's a long drive."

At the door, they kissed good-bye. But as she watched his tall, lean figure disappear into the night, her thoughts strayed to another man, another night. She hadn't seen or spoken to Randall Craig since, but she'd replayed their near kiss so often in her mind that it had taken on a life of its own, become emblematic of some key element missing from her life. She realized then why she'd been so irritated with her sister tonight. It wasn't just because she felt protective of Ollie; it was the way Ollie looked at Kerrie Ann—the desire blazing in his eyes strong enough to incinerate anything in its path.

Lindsay wanted someone to look at her that way.

The following morning, as Lindsay was getting out of bed to go for her early run, she caught a flash of color out the window. A closer look showed it to be a man in a bright orange reflective vest peering into some sort of device set atop a tripod by the row of eucalyptus trees that marked the eastern end of her property. In her groggy state, she thought it must have something to do with the environmental study that had had a team of scientists tramping all over her land and the adjacent shoreline for the better part of the previous week. Then she realized what this one was up to and gasped. A surveyor—on her property!

"What is it?" Kerrie Ann muttered sleepily from her bed.

"Trouble, that's what," Lindsay replied grimly.

Minutes later she was racing out the back door, wearing a pair of sweatpants, flip-flops, and her blue Patagonia jacket, which she'd snagged from the coat rack on her way through the living room into the kitchen. Chester, snoozing in his bed by the stove, brought his graying muzzle up as she charged past and quickly fell in behind her, trotting at her heels as she made her way across the yard and into the grassy field beyond. She was moving so quickly, the old dog had trouble keeping pace.

When she finally reached the man in the orange vest, she was out of breath and had worked up a head of steam. "What do you think you're doing?" she demanded. Slowly he straightened to look at her. He was a middle-aged man with the beginning of a paunch, not at all threatening-looking.

"Just doing my job, ma'am." He bent down to give Chester a scratch behind the ears, "Hey, there, pooch. You're not gonna bite me, now, are you?" Chester responded by wagging his tail.

"Are you aware that you're trespassing on private property?" she huffed.

"That so?" He smiled as if he could argue the point but had decided not to. "Well, I'm sorry if I disturbed you, ma'am, but that's actually why I'm here—to find out exactly where the property line falls."

"You won't need *that*." Lindsay jabbed a finger at his device. "I can tell you right now that you're on my land. And as the owner, I'm asking that you leave this instant." When he made no move to decamp, she said more hotly, "Well? What are you waiting for?"

The man was wearing a navy bill cap emblazoned with his company's logo, and he lifted it to scratch his gray crew-cut head before withdrawing a cell phone from a flapped pocket on his vest.

"Let me call my supervisor, okay? This'll only take a sec."

Lindsay fumed while he made the call. She didn't buy for one minute that it was an honest mistake. Lloyd Heywood was trying to bully her, using any means at hand. Probably he thought that if he threw enough smoke bombs at her, eventually he'd wear her down. If that was the case, he didn't know her.

When the man was done with his call, he tucked his phone back into his pocket and said to Lindsay, "My apologies, ma'am. If you give me a moment to pack up my gear, I'll be on my way."

"Thank you," she replied in a frosty voice, then waited, hands on hips, while he folded his tripod and stowed the rest of the equipment in his carrying case. He lifted a hand in a halfhearted gesture of farewell as he ambled off, but she didn't wave back. Her sister would've flipped him the bird, she thought.

Kerrie Ann. As Lindsay started back toward the house, some of her irritation at having the morning's peace and quiet so rudely interrupted spilled over onto to her sister. She was still annoyed at Kerrie Ann for encouraging Ollie the night before when she knew perfectly well that it was wrong to do so. Was she on some kind of ego trip? Use him to boost her sagging self-esteem, then cast him aside when someone better came along?

Lindsay paused to take a deep breath, allowing her rising emotions to subside. It was hard to stay angry with the day stirring to life around her. The underbrush rustled with the movements of her dog and whatever small creatures he was chasing as he charged about like a young pup, snuffling the ground and peeing on every other bush. Overhead, seagulls circled lazily, their reedy cries counterpointing the rumbling bass of the surf. It was shaping up to be a nice day, the sun coming up in a sky the clear blue of the ocean swells gliding into shore. This time of year, the fog that rolled in most mornings seldom lingered, and with the early-summer months nearly upon them, they were enjoying mild temperatures as well.

Back at the house, she slipped on her Nikes and went for her morning jog, which helped let off more steam. But when she returned half an hour later, soaked with sweat and eagerly anticipating a hot shower, it was only to step inside to the sound of running water: Kerrie Ann had beaten her to it. She groaned and uttered a low curse.

She was searching the pockets of her jacket for a Kleenex with which to mop her brow when her fingers closed over something hard and stubby instead: a cigarette butt. Kerrie Ann's, no doubt. Her nose wrinkled in distaste. It seemed a symbol somehow of everything she'd been forced to put up with.

She spent the next fifteen minutes or so tidying

the kitchen, which was still in disarray from the night before. By the time Kerrie Ann finished her shower, Lindsay had washed and dried the last of the dishes, made coffee, and fed the animals. She managed to duck into the bathroom while her sister was getting dressed, and before long they were all climbing into her car and heading off to work without having exchanged more than a few pleasantries.

Lindsay was quiet during the drive as well, and Kerrie Ann, as if picking up on her mood, made no attempt to engage her in conversation. She chatted animatedly with Miss Honi while Lindsay pondered the wary dance of one step forward, two steps back she and her sister were engaged in. For brief periods, everything would be fine; then Lindsay would do or say something that would rub Kerrie Ann the wrong way, or vice versa, and they'd retreat to nurse that splinter of resentment until it either healed on its own or festered. Only with Miss Honi and Ollie was Kerrie Ann her relaxed, natural self. Which presented a whole different set of problems, at least where Ollie was concerned.

He was more vulnerable than ever, judging from last night's performance. And what if Kerrie Ann should do more than flirt with him? Look what had happened the last time he'd fallen in with the wrong element—it had nearly cost him his shot at college. He could slip back into that old self-destructive pattern and disrupt his entire life to chase after Kerrie Ann. His heart would be broken when she moved on—or, God forbid, what if Kerrie Ann became pregnant? It was too horrifying to contemplate.

The time had come to take matters in hand.

Lindsay waited for the right moment to pounce. Miss Honi was warning Kerrie Ann about the flood of job applicants that began each year around this time, with the approach of summer break, when Lindsay interjected, "That reminds me, I was wondering if you needed any help with your résumé." She cast a glance at Kerrie Ann, careful to keep her voice light. "You'll get a glowing recommendation from me, of course, but the rest may need doctoring. I'd be happy to give you a hand with that if you'd like."

"Are you saying you want me to look for another job?" Her sister spoke quietly, but Lindsay caught the edge in her voice.

"It's not a question of what *I* want. It's about what's best for you. And I'm sure you could use the money." Lindsay was paying Kerrie Ann a small stipend, but it was only enough to keep her in pocket money. She went on, "If you want me to make some calls for you, I can do that, too. I know most of the other shopkeepers, and there's always someone looking to hire extra help. Ginny Beal at Stitch and Sticks"—the yarn shop three doors down—"was telling me just the other day that she needs someone to fill in for her on her days off. It would only be part-time to start with, but she says it could work into something full-time. And I think you'd like Ginny." Lindsay prattled on, feeling guilty but also resenting the fact that she was being put in this position.

"What do I know about knitting?" Kerrie Ann sounded dubious.

About as much as you know about books, Lindsay thought. But all she said was, "You could always learn."

Kerrie Ann gave a dismissive laugh. "Somehow I don't see that happening. Anyway, I'm looking to make some real money. I was talking to one of the guys at my meeting, and he says they have adult ed at the high school three nights a week. I thought I'd check it out, maybe sign up for a class. Could be the start of a whole new career."

"That sounds like a fine idea. But," Lindsay forged on, "I'm sure some extra cash would come in handy in the meantime. And after all, this job was only supposed to be temporary."

Kerrie Ann's eyes narrowed. "Look, if you're firing me, just say so."

"I didn't say that," Lindsay hedged, reluctant to put it so bluntly.

"You don't want me embarrassing you in front of your customers? Fine," Kerrie Ann snapped. "Just don't give me a load of crap about it being for *my* benefit. Okay?"

Lindsay realized, too late, that now might not have been the best time to bring this up. Her sister had announced over breakfast that she'd quit smoking as of the night before, so she was bound to be more than a little on edge. But though a part of Lindsay wanted to drop the subject before things got ugly, she knew she had to see this through—for Ollie's sake as well as her own.

She drew in a breath and exhaled slowly before saying, "All right, then, I think it's time you looked for another job. Not," she was quick to add, "because you're not good at this one. Or because any of the customers have complained. As a matter of fact, several mentioned how helpful you were. But I can't keep on taking advantage of you like this."

"Now, sugar, don't you think you're jumping the gun a bit?" put in Miss Honi. "There's no rush, is there? And Lord knows we could use the extra help. If it's a matter of money, I'm more'n willing to have you take it out of my salary. You pay me too much as it is."

Lindsay knew she was only trying to help but felt annoyed with her nonetheless. "I'm not cutting anyone's salary," she said. "Besides, we *all* may be out of jobs before too long if Mr. Heywood has his way. It'd be nice if at least one of us had something to fall back on."

"I think I know what this is really about." Kerrie Ann didn't raise her voice, but its flat calm had an eye-of-the-hurricane quality. "It's about Ollie, isn't it? You think I'm a bad influence."

"No one thinks that," piped Miss Honi, but even she sounded weak and unconvincing.

The interior of the car grew close and hot, despite the cool ocean air blowing in through the vents. "This isn't about Ollie." *Not entirely, that is.* "But since you brought it up . . . no, I don't think you're a bad influence or that you'd ever intentionally hurt him." Lindsay chose her words carefully. "But you and he are in different leagues. And while I'm sure all this attention is very flattering for you, I'd hate to see him get his heart broken."

"Who says I'm gonna break his heart?" Kerrie Ann tossed back.

"Please." Lindsay rolled her eyes. Ollie was adorable, but he was hardly her sister's type. Lindsay would have thought Kerry Ann's new twelve-step buddies—Biker Dude and Tattoo Man, as she'd mentally dubbed them—would be more her speed.

Kerrie Ann glared at her. "We're not planning to elope, if that's what you mean. But I like Ollie. We have fun together. Is that a crime?"

"No, of course not." Lindsay struggled to maintain an even tone. "Everybody likes Ollie. But it's not all smiles and laughter with him. Underneath all that, he takes things pretty seriously. I always knew when he fell in love, he'd fall hard. But I hoped it would be someone who'd love him back."

"How do you know I'm not that person?"

Backed into a corner, Lindsay was forced to admit, "Somehow I just don't see it."

Kerrie Ann slowly shook her head, wearing a disgusted look. "And what makes you such an expert, huh? You hardly know me." The jab found its mark, and Lindsay winced. "But, hey, if you're gonna be dictating my social life, maybe I should just move out."

Lindsay, still irritable from her earlier encounter with the surveyor, snapped, "Why don't you?"

There was a sharp intake of breath in the backseat, followed by the click of a seatbelt being unbuckled. When Lindsay glanced in the rearview mirror, all she could see was a quivering mound of golden curls. "Girls, this ain't no way to act," scolded Miss Honi. She was leaning in so close, Lindsay could smell the toothpaste on her breath, mingling with the stronger scent of her perfume. "You're family, and family oughta stick together no matter what. Lord knows what I woulda done without my sister Annie." Annie, long gone now, was the only member of her family who'd stuck by her all those years ago when Miss Honi, then Sue-Ellen Dondlinger, was being ostracized by the townsfolk after having been caught naked with the preacher's son. To Kerrie Ann, she said in a gentle tone, "Your sister means well. It ain't just Ollie she's looking out for—she cares about you, too." She gave Lindsay's shoulder a not-so-gentle squeeze, saying to her, "And sugar, if you don't ease up on that gas pedal, you'll put us all in an early grave."

Lindsay glanced at the speedometer and saw to her chagrin that she was doing seventy in a fifty-five-miles-per-hour zone. Luckily there were no cops around. She eased her foot off the gas pedal and let out a pent-up breath. She felt spent, and the workday hadn't even begun. "I'm sorry," she apologized to her sister. "I didn't mean it. Of course I don't want you to move out."

But even as she said it, Lindsay wondered if she was being completely honest. Life with her sister, she was discovering, was more complicated than she'd ever imagined it would be. A line from an old children's poem came to mind: *When she was good, she was very, very good . . . and when she was bad she was horrid.*

"I'm sorry, too," Kerrie Ann offered grudgingly. "This quitting-smoking thing's a real bitch. I guess it's making me into one, too." She treated Lindsay to a half-assed smile. "By the way, thanks again for last night. It was a nice party. Notice I'm wearing the sweater you gave me?"

Lindsay had noticed. Kerrie Ann was wearing the rose-colored cotton cardigan unbuttoned far enough to show several inches of cleavage, with nothing but her bra underneath.

· · ·

Work proved a welcome distraction. With paper-work to weed through and inventory to sort out, appointments with reps, and a steady stream of customers, Lindsay didn't have a chance to dwell on the fight with her sister or the run-in with the surveyor. Still, she was grumpy all day, and her mood didn't improve even after she got home.

When the phone rang in the kitchen as she and Miss Honi were cleaning up after supper, Lindsay snatched it up with a growl of frustration, certain it was just another unwanted solicitor—they always seemed to call at the most inconvenient times or when she was bone-tired after a day at work—and answered with a brisk "Hello?"

"Lindsay?"

A ripple of excitement went through her even as she pretended not to recognize the familiar male voice. "Yes, this is she."

"It's Randall. Randall Craig. How have you been?"

She carried the phone into the next room, where she could converse in private. "I'm fine," she said, "and you?" Her heart was racing, and the room suddenly felt too warm.

Ever since they'd met, thoughts of Randall Craig had been darting in and out of her head like an errant child playing hide-and-go-seek. It was silly to fantasize about him, she knew. No different than when her female customers daydreamed about heroes of the romance novels. Besides, it wasn't as if she were desperate. She had a boyfriend, and though he might not always be as available as she'd like, he was kind and loving and, most of all, a known quantity. Nevertheless, she found herself pressing the phone closer to her ear while her other hand found its way to her heart as if to still its wild beating.

"Worn out," Randall replied with a laugh. "After fourteen cities in as many days, I can now reliably report that book tours are just a clever means of torture designed by sadistic publishers."

"Does that include booksellers, too?"

"No, of course not—they're the saving grace. Especially the ones who feed me." After a brief pause, he added in a more intimate tone, "I had a good time with you the other night. I've been meaning to call, but I haven't had a free moment until now. I only got back last night."

"Welcome home." She kept her voice light.

"Believe me, there's no better place after two weeks on the road."

"Has it been that long? I hadn't noticed," she lied. "I've been so busy."

"I'd like to see you again. You wouldn't happen to be free for dinner on Friday?"

"I don't know; I'll have to check my calendar," she said to buy herself some time. She felt giddy at the prospect of seeing Randall again but sobered instantly at the thought of Grant. She'd made no plans to be with him—he'd be tied up all weekend but she knew she'd felt guilty sneaking around behind his back.

"There's this little trattoria in my neighborhood," Randall went on. "Fantastic food. Maybe not as good as Paolo's but pretty darn close. The most sublime *spaghetti a la vongele* you'll ever taste."

She hesitated a moment longer before coming to a decision. One she knew deep down had been made for her the moment she'd heard Randall's voice at the other end of the line. Throwing caution aside, she replied, "It sounds tempting. And I believe I am free that night."

"Great! Why don't you meet me at my place around seven o'clock? We can walk from there." He gave her his address in Noe Valley, which she jotted down on a piece of scrap paper.

The following Friday, as she dressed for her date, Lindsay experienced few qualms. Those would come later, she knew. At the moment she was too busy fluttering about like a girl getting ready for her first prom. She'd tried on and discarded nearly every outfit in her closet and was on the verge of throwing up her hands in despair when Kerrie Ann stepped in and took charge like a commando on a mission.

"Here, try this on," she said, shoving a long skirt and paisley silk top at Lindsay.

Lindsay held the skirt up, observing dryly, "I didn't know you owned anything below the knee."

"Just try it on."

The length of the skirt turned out to be deceptive, as it had a slit up one side all the way to midthigh. The top was modest by comparison, but with its plunging neckline, it was still racier than anything in her own wardrobe. Nevertheless, she had to admit the outfit was flattering. As she swiveled from side to side in front of the full-length mirror, she marveled. Was that really *her*? Who would have guessed that under her Land's End exterior lurked a Victoria's Secret vixen? The only question in her mind was which of the two Lindsays would get the upper hand with Randall. In the end, she compromised by borrowing her sister's top and swapping the skirt for one of her own, a simple, straight black one that ended slightly above the knee.

The one area in which Kerrie Ann refused to compromise was the shoes to go with the outfit. They wore the same size, so Lindsay had no excuse not to try on the ones her sister thrust at her—a pair of black sling-backs with five-inch heels and red straps like racing stripes.

"Not on your life!" Lindsay declared after she'd taken a few unsteady steps in them. She collapsed onto the bed. "I'll look like a complete idiot wobbling around in these. That is, if I don't fall down and break my neck first."

"Not if you practice. Watch me." Kerrie Ann stepped into a pair of burgundy patent-leather stilettos and began strutting around the room with the ease of a beauty-pageant contestant.

Before Lindsay knew it, her sister had her by the elbow and was pulling her up off the bed and onto her feet. Amazingly, after a grueling ten minutes in which she continued to insist there was absolutely no way she was wearing those shoes, not tonight or any night, she found herself able to walk on her own without any help and with only a slight wobble to her step.

"I don't know if it's because I'm getting good at it or because my feet are so numb there's no feeling left in them," she said.

"Who cares? You look like ten million dollars. Isn't that all that matters?"

Lindsay thought she'd rather have the ten million dollars to pocket, but Kerrie Ann looked so pleased that she refrained from saying so. In the end, Lindsay didn't have the heart to deny her the pleasure of seeing her flat-footed big sister off in the shoes that she seemed to think would make a Cinderella out of her—if Lindsay didn't fall on her face and crack her skull.

"Thanks," she said as she dabbed on perfume. Her gaze met Kerrie Ann's in the mirror.

But her sister only replied with a laconic shrug, "For what?"

"For taking an interest, number one. And for not asking a lot of nosy questions."

Kerrie Ann arched a brow. "You mean about why

you're getting all dolled up for a guy who isn't your boyfriend?"

"Something like that."

"Don't worry. My lips are sealed."

"Not that I have anything to hide." Lindsay replaced the stopper in the perfume bottle and turned to face her sister. "I'm a bookseller. It's good business to get to know authors." She relied on the firmness of her tone to make up for her wavering sense of moral authority.

"I see." Kerrie Ann smirked. "So you get this dressed up for all your authors, do you?" She took a step back to survey Lindsay in her evening finery, her lips curling in a knowing smile.

Lindsay felt herself blush. "No, not all of them. But there's no law that says I can't mix business with pleasure."

"So you admit you're into this dude?"

"I like him, yes. He's good company."

"He's also pretty damn hot. I've seen his photo."

Lindsay risked a small smile, her blush deepening as she recalled the brush of Randall's lips over hers and how alive she'd felt in that moment. "He's easy on the eyes; I won't deny it."

"Well, have fun." Kerrie Ann, her arms folded over her chest, tipped Lindsay a conspiratorial wink as she headed out the door. "And for God's sake, try not to be too much of a Girl Scout."

Lindsay drove north along Highway 1 toward San Francisco, to the seductive beat of Bruce Springsteen's *Born to Run* album, which helped her unwind, as it always did, and made her feel like she belonged in the clothes she wore. Forty minutes later she was easing her Volvo into a parking spot that had magically opened up a block or so from Randall's place in the funky, outlying district of Noe Valley. Finding his address proved a bit trickier. She spent several minutes tottering up and down the sidewalk in her borrowed shoes before she finally located it, tucked behind one of the large, gracious Victorians that faced onto the street.

A converted artist's studio, painted white trimmed in robin's-egg blue, it stood at one end of a narrow brick courtyard bordered in oleander. She slowed as she approached. Through the floor-to-ceiling windows that faced onto the courtyard, she could see Randall moving about inside, dressed casually in khakis and a striped button-down shirt open at the collar. She watched him uncork a bottle of wine, then pause as his gaze turned inward. He stood that way for a moment, staring sightlessly ahead, wearing a small, preoccupied frown. What was he pondering that had him so deep in thought? she wondered.

Then he was greeting her at the door, all smiles. "So, you made it. My directions okay?"

"Your directions were fine. I even found a parking spot." She stepped into a room fragrant with cooking smells. Obviously they weren't going out tonight. She cast a wry glance at him as he was taking her jacket. "So this is the neighborhood restaurant you were telling me about?"

He flashed her a smile. "The place I had in mind was booked for a private party, so I decided to cook for you instead," he explained as he hung her jacket in the small coat closet. "No guarantees on the food, but you can't beat the location. Though it's a shame I won't be able to show you off. You look absolutely stunning." He stepped back to admire her, and Lindsay felt her cheeks warm. "I have to confess, I don't remember you being so tall."

She looked down at her feet. "It's these shoes. They're my sister's, and frankly they're killing me."

"In that case, why don't you take them off? There's no one around but me, and I promise I won't tell." He guided her to the sofa, where she sank down with a grateful sigh and eased off her shoes. Mellow jazz was playing on the stereo, and candles glowed. "There, that's better, isn't it? In fact, I think I'll join you." He slipped off his own shoes, a pair of brown suede driving mocs. "To be honest, I normally go barefoot around the house—one of the advantages of working out of your home." His smoky-blue eyes crinkled in a smile, and he reached for the open wine bottle on the coffee table. "Can I offer you a glass of wine? If you prefer white, I also have a bottle of pinot grigio chilling in the fridge."

"Red's fine," she told him.

He poured them each a glass. "I have friends who own a vineyard in Santa Ynez," he said. "They put out some very nice wines. This petite sirah is my favorite."

She took a sip, murmuring appreciatively, though she knew little about wine—one of the many things that set her apart from Randall. She glanced around the room. "I like your place. It has character."

"That it does." He followed her gaze, taking in the snug interior, with its tongue-and-groove wainscoting and old cypress flooring that resembled the deck of a boat listing slightly at sea. Piles of books were stacked beside built-in bookshelves crammed with more books. A large Chinese urn by the door held a potted ficus. The chairs and sofa appeared comfortably worn. "I lease it from the lady in the big house—Mrs. Adler. Her husband was an artist. This used to be his studio." He gestured toward a skillfully executed seascape on the wall. "That's one of his. He was quite good, as you can see."

She gazed at the painting admiringly. "What became of him?"

"He died some years ago. The poor old gal still hasn't gotten over it. They were married for over fifty years."

Lindsay sipped her wine. All this talk of long-term devotion was prompting uneasy thoughts of Grant. She said brightly, "So tell me about the tour. Did you do a lot of signings?"

"One in each city, and don't even ask which cities because it's all a blur at this point."

"Good turnouts?"

"For the most part. Except this one—Cleveland, I think it was—where only two people showed up." He gave a rueful laugh. "One guy must've felt sorry for me because he hung around the entire time. Turned out he was a tech geek, and when I said I was looking to upgrade my laptop, he told me which model to buy and where to get one at a discount. So even though I only sold a couple of books, all in all I'd say it was a good night."

"I wish every author were like you," she remarked. "Most are fairly nice about it when there's not much of a turnout, but a few get nasty. I'm not naming any names, but I once had an author storm off in a huff. He was mad because he didn't think I'd done enough to promote his event. As if it were my fault that it happened to be pouring rain that night!"

Randall shook his head. "Pretty shortsighted of him, I'd say. The first rule in touring is don't shoot at your own troops. We need you as much as you need us. Let me guess—I'll bet you didn't exactly go out of your way to feature his book after he went off on you like that."

"I wouldn't say I discouraged people from buying it, but they might have had a hard time finding it," she confessed.

Randall laughed and told her about the time early on, before the sales of his novel took off, when he'd sweet-talked a clerk at a Barnes & Noble into displaying *Blood Money* on the front table even though it wasn't part of any paid promotion. She didn't have to ask if the clerk had been female and found herself wondering if he'd gotten the woman to do more than prominently display his book. She felt a small stab of jealousy at the thought. Which was ludicrous, she told herself, since she hadn't even known him then and certainly had no claim on him now. Besides which, she had a boyfriend.

She once more resolutely pushed the thought of Grant from her mind, and soon she was coasting on the effects of the wine and Randall's easy company. Seeing him in his well-worn easy chair, his stockinged feet propped on the ottoman, it was hard to imagine him as a hard-driving Wall Street financier.

"Do you ever miss New York?" she asked.

He shrugged. "I miss certain things about it. Like, oh, I don't know, the smoked fish at Russ & Daughters and listening to live jazz at the Blue Note. Shakespeare in the Park on a clear summer night when the moon is out. But no, overall I don't miss New York."

"How long did you live there?"

"Almost fifteen years. I got a job on Wall Street right out of college."

"It says in your website bio that you were the youngest ever to make partner in your firm."

"Ah, yes, the fair-haired boy." He raised his glass as if to the ghost of that dear, departed young man. "What isn't in my bio is that I had to slave my ass off for ten years to get there. And for what? So I could make even more money that I was too busy to enjoy?"

"So you up and left? Just like that?"

"Just like that." His expression darkened, and once again she wondered, as she had the night at Paolo's, if there was something he wasn't telling her about that chapter of his life. Abruptly he changed the subject. "But you didn't come all this way to have me bore you with talk of finance. I want to know what you've been up to while I was away. How is it going with your sister?" He reached for the wine bottle and refilled their glasses.

She sighed. "Okay, I guess . . . except when we're at each other's throats." She told him about the fight they'd had earlier in the week and her concerns over the romance developing between Kerrie Ann and Ollie. "It's not all her fault, though. She tries, in her own way. Part of it's me—I tend to blow things out of proportion."

"Maybe because you're not starting with a clean slate."

"What do you mean?"

"You said you got stuck taking care of her when you were kids. I was just wondering if you might be harboring some old resentment."

Lindsay frowned. "Why would I hold that against my sister? She was just a baby at the time."

"It's easy to blame the nearest target when the person you're really mad at isn't around."

His words hit home, and she nodded slowly. "Crystal, you mean. You could be right. I was angry at her for a long time. I guess my sister could be stirring up some of those old feelings. I hate to say it, but she reminds me of our mother in a lot of ways." Lindsay tucked her feet under her, leaning into the sofa as she turned to face him. "What about you?" she asked. "Do you think you'll ever stop being angry at your father?"

Randall seemed to wrestle with his emotions before he replied, "It's different with me. My old man's still around to stoke the fire. Though I don't see much of him, I confess. Every once in a while he'll give me a call when he's in town, and we'll get together for a drink or a meal, but other than that he leaves me be."

"Still, he must be proud of what you've accomplished."

Randall shrugged and took a sip of his wine. "He doesn't consider it a real job. He thinks I just got lucky. Not like when I was raking in the dough on Wall Street—*that* he could respect."

Lindsay found herself disliking this man whom she hadn't even met. "It's not just luck. First you had to write the book when you didn't know if you would even get it published, much less hit it big. I had one author tell me it's like performing to an empty auditorium."

Randall gave a knowing laugh. "More like performing to an audience of one, which is tougher in a way since I'm my own worst critic. I suppose it goes with the territory," he added with a shrug.

"Except most authors aren't as talented as you."

He smiled. "Thanks. I just hope you think as highly of my cooking. Shall we?" He rose, extending a hand to help her up. "Supper's basically ready. I just have to throw a few things together."

Lindsay started to put her shoes back on, but he stopped her, saying, "No sense in being uncomfortable. Besides, I like you this way—it suits you." He regarded her for a long moment, his eyes communicating some unspoken emotion, then he turned and led the way into an alcove off the kitchen, where a small table was set for two.

Lindsay was grateful when he disappeared into the kitchen. It gave her a chance to collect herself.

Randall reappeared a few minutes later carrying a tray on which sat a conical clay *tagine*. He lifted the lid to reveal a mound of fragrant curried-chicken couscous and spooned some onto her plate. After she'd pronounced it delicious, he said,

"Good, because it's practically the only thing I know how to make." He explained that he'd once signed up for a cooking course but ended up attending only one session. He winked. "Don't tell anyone, though. My friends all think I'm a gourmet cook."

She smiled. "Don't worry; your secret is safe with me."

He passed her a basket of warm pita bread. "Ever been to Morocco? It's a fascinating place."

She shook her head. "I've never been anywhere, really. Mostly I just read about all the places I'd like go to someday." She glanced up at him shyly. "I must seem awfully provincial."

"Not in the least," he said. "You just haven't had the opportunity to travel. But all those places will still be there when you do get around to visiting them. So," he asked, leaning back in his chair, "where would you most like to go if you had to choose just one?"

She didn't hesitate. "I've always wanted to see Russia."

"Ah, the land of Tolstoy and Dostoyevsky."

She smiled. "What can I say? *Anna Karenina* was my introduction to literature when I was fifteen. I thought it was the most brilliant novel ever written. In some ways, I still do."

"Even though it ends tragically?"

"She chose love over what society expected of her. I see that as more brave than tragic."

"I didn't know you were such a romantic." His tone was teasing, but the gaze he directed at her across the table was as intimate as an embrace. She felt a light shiver go through her.

"Blame it on Tolstoy," she tossed back lightly. She didn't dare say more. In the mood she was in right now, flushed with the wine and Randall's company, it wouldn't take much for her to do as Anna Karenina had and throw caution to the winds.

After supper was over and the dishes cleared away, they retired to the living room for coffee and dessert—tiny cups of espresso and amaretti biscuits. She lingered over the first cup but said no to a second, murmuring, with some reluctance, that she ought to start thinking about heading back home. Before she could get up, he stilled her with a hand on her arm. "No, don't go—not yet." He paused, smiling at the concern that must have been evident on her face. "Don't worry. I wasn't planning to seduce you," he said, though his eyes told a different story. "I have a favor to ask. Feel free to say no if you think I'm imposing."

She was intrigued. "I doubt I'd think that. But I suppose you should tell me what it is before I promise you the moon."

"I wondered if you'd take a look at the novel I'm working on. I'm only a few chapters into it, and I haven't shown it to anyone, not even my editor. I trust you to give me an honest opinion."

"I'd be honored," she said.

Minutes later she was ensconced in the bedroom in back that doubled as his study, absorbed in the pages he'd given her to read. It wasn't at all what she'd expected. Unlike the pulse-pounding thrill ride that was *Blood Money*, this one had a slow, almost elegiac quality. She was immediately hooked nonetheless by the story of a teenaged boy, presumably a run-away, hitchhiking along a lonely stretch of highway in the pouring rain. The writing alone made her want to read on. It was so evocative that she felt the boy's exhaustion and fear of whatever he was running from. She felt the loneliness of the old man who stopped to give him a ride as palpably as if she'd been in that car, the rain sheeting down too fast for the windshield wipers to keep up with it. When she was done, she went in search of Randall, whom she found loading another stack of CDs into the player.

"It's good," she said. "I'm glad you didn't give me the whole thing to read or I'd have been up all night."

He straightened and walked over to her, taking her in his arms. "I don't suppose you'd be willing to stay the night anyway?" he asked softly. "I can't offer you the whole manuscript to read, but I know the author, and he might be persuaded to tell you how it ends."

He reached for her hand and brought it to his mouth, pressing his lips to her upturned palm. Lindsay began to tremble. She might have been standing there without a stitch on for how deliciously exposed she felt. She couldn't move; she could scarcely draw a breath. Any thoughts of an early departure, or of her boyfriend, faded from her mind. When he brought his lips to her mouth, it was no accident this time. The effect was electrifying. She had never before been kissed like this, as thoroughly and seductively as Anna by Vronsky. She sensed he was taking his time because he saw this not as the end of the evening but as the beginning in some way. Lindsay felt it, too, that quickening inside, like the point in a novel where she'd think, *This is where it gets good.*

She was so carried away, she was scarcely conscious of moving into the bedroom or of their clothes coming off. Both seemed to happen of their own accord. Then came a succession of exquisite sensations, each one melting into the next, as they lay tangled together on the bed. There was only Randall's touch and the brush of his lips as he caressed every newly awakened inch of her. She stroked him, too, trailing her fingers over his muscular chest, with its mat of curly hair, down to where his tan line ended and the pale flesh began . . . and below.

When he finally entered her, she tilted her hips to meet his thrust. Then they were two people moving as one. For Lindsay, it was a revelation. With other lovers—even Grant—it had been good but never *this* good. This was on a whole other plane. She felt a connection to Randall that was more than mere desire, that had its roots in something deeper.

Then she was coming in a blinding rush, and moments later he came, too, with a sharp cry of release. Afterward he didn't pull out right away. He held her tightly, as if fearful that she would slip away altogether once they drew apart. She could feel his breath coming in soft, noiseless bursts against her ear. Neither of them spoke. There was no need.

Even after they drew apart, they remained close, facing each other with their noses almost touching. Close enough for her to see, in the faint light spilling in from the hallway, the bristly patch on his jaw, the size of a small coin, where he'd missed a spot shaving.

"Did you feel that?" he murmured, his lips curling in a sleepy smile.

"What?"

"Oh, I'd give it about a nine point oh on the Richter scale."

She chuckled softly. "A best-selling novelist, and the best you can come up with is an earthquake metaphor?"

"Would a tsunami work better?"

"Trite."

"Okay, we'll just have to settle on mind-blowing, then. Not very original, I know, but it's the best I can do. My circuits are pretty fried."

She snuggled in close so that her head was nestled against his chest. For a long while, she was content to just lie there, basking in the afterglow and listening to Randall's heartbeat as it gradually slowed. "Tell me something about yourself that I don't already know," she murmured at last.

"What is it you want to know?"

"Something that will make you seem a little less perfect, so I'll know you're real."

She felt him tense, and she drew back to look at him. He appeared troubled, for some reason, but he was quick to shrug it off. "Oh, I'm real, all right. In fact, I'm about as real as it gets. So don't go putting me on any kind of pedestal." He spoke in a lightly ironic tone.

"Why, do you have something to hide?"

Lindsay smiled to let him know she was kidding. This time he didn't smile back. His eyes searched her face, still wearing that troubled look. Then he pulled her close and wrapped his arms around her. Even so, she shivered a little, as if a cool breeze had wafted into the room.

CHAPTER TEN

Do I LOOK OKAY TO YOU?" Kerrie Ann turned away from the full-length mirror. When Lindsay didn't answer right away, she bit her lip, frowning. "That bad, huh? Do you think I should change?"

"No, you're fine." Lindsay smiled. "It's just that

this is the first time you've asked for my opinion."

"So lay it on me, okay? 'Cause I don't want to go in there looking like someone who can't take care of her own kid."

Today's hearing was to decide whether Kerrie Ann should be allowed overnight visits with her daughter. The final decision on custody was still pending, but this was a crucial step. If the judge deemed her sufficiently reformed and she didn't blow it, she'd be halfway home. Still, in a life that was more about ifs than whens, Kerrie Ann knew better than to count on anything.

"Well, since you ask . . ." Lindsay stepped back to eye her more critically. "I'd lose the bracelets—all that jingling will be a distraction in the courtroom. The necklace, too. It's a little too . . ."

"Bling?" Kerrie Ann supplied.

Lindsay put it another way: "Do you have anything that isn't quite so . . . um, shiny?"

Kerrie fingered the heart-shaped pendant given to her by Jeremiah. She liked that it was shiny, with her initials spelled out in zircons. Besides, it had sentimental value. "I don't see what's wrong with it," she said, straightening her back and jutting out her chin.

Lindsay remained firm. "You can borrow my pearls," she said.

"And look like somebody's grandma? No, thanks." But Lindsay just stood there giving her the Look, as if to say, *This is no joking matter.*

Ordinarily it would have prompted another smart remark, but Kerrie Ann put a lid on it this time. Too much was at stake. "You got anything that's more my style?" she asked in a meeker tone.

Lindsay fished around her in her jewelry box before offering a teardrop pendant, gold set with an opal, on a delicate gold chain. "This will look good with what you have on," she said as she fastened it around Kerrie Ann's neck.

"Not half bad," Kerrie Ann grudgingly conceded as she checked her reflection in the mirror. "Thanks."

"No problem. It's only fair, since you helped me out the other night. Never mind that I nearly went lame in those shoes," Lindsay groused good-naturedly. "Honestly, I don't know how you get around in those things. I had to take them off as soon as I got there."

Kerrie Ann reached for her makeup kit. "Was that the only thing you took off?" She slanted her sister a coy look as she applied blush to her cheeks. All she'd gotten out of Lindsay so far was that she'd had a "nice time," which didn't explain the dreamy-eyed look she'd been wearing all week or the way she went all girlish and secretive whenever Randall phoned.

"None of your beeswax," Lindsay retorted, but her reddening cheeks only confirmed Kerrie Ann's suspicions.

She would have let it go, but she sensed something was troubling Lindsay. "If you're feeling guilty, don't," she advised. "You're not the type who cheats on your boyfriend because you want to try out a new flavor. I'm sure it happened for a reason."

"And what would that be?" Lindsay eyed her dubiously.

"Look, all I know is that you were out with a hot guy the other night and came home looking like you got royally—" She broke off at the warning look her sister shot her. "Anyway, I've never seen you look that way with Grant."

Lindsay threw up her hands. "You and Miss Honi. I swear, sometimes I think you two are in cahoots!"

Kerrie clicked the compact case shut and swiveled around to face her. "I can have my own opinion, can't I? Besides, I've got nothing against Grant."

"But?" Lindsay, hands on hips, waited to hear the rest.

"Clearly you're not getting enough."

The color in Lindsay's cheeks deepened. "Does everything have to be about sex?"

"I don't mean just sex. But that's a part of it, too. I mean, without it, what's the point? You might as well be hanging out with your girlfriends."

Lindsay surrendered with a sigh and sank down on the bed. "It's complicated."

Was it, or was she just making it that way? Kerrie Ann wondered. "So did you and Grant have a fight or something?"

"No, nothing like that." Lindsay sighed again. "You know how you can be going along and everything's just fine, then you meet someone and . . . and suddenly it's *not* fine? That's what happened with Randall. Grant doesn't know, of course, and that only makes it worse."

"So, you gonna break up with him?"

"Who, Grant?"

"No, Mahatma Gandhi."

Lindsay shrugged, turning her palms up in a helpless gesture. "It's too soon to say. There's a lot I still don't know about Randall—he's a bit of a mystery in some ways. And with Grant . . . well, at least I know what I'm getting. It may not be perfect, but it's enough. Or it was. Should I give all that up just because a meteor came crashing through my roof?"

"Depends on the size of the meteor," quipped Kerrie Ann. Lindsay cast her another sharp look, and Kerrie Ann added more seriously, "Isn't that kind of what happened with us? I sort of landed on you like a meteor."

"That's different—you're family."

"Yeah, but you didn't know me. And let's be honest, I wasn't exactly what you were expecting. But you took a chance on me, anyway. That says something, doesn't it?"

"Yes—that I wasn't going to turn my back on my own sister. This isn't the same."

Kerrie felt warmed by her sister's words. Did

that mean Lindsay was starting to accept her? "Maybe not exactly, but my point is that most of the time, you're better off just going with your gut. Yeah, I know, it can sometimes get you in trouble when you go off half cocked"—the way she had a habit of doing—"but you can also mess up by overthinking stuff."

"Well, there's no use dwelling on it. I don't have to decide today." Lindsay straightened her shoulders and stood up. "You *do* look nice," she said, giving Kerrie Ann a final once-over. "I'm glad you decided on that dress." It wasn't what Lindsay had picked out for her when they'd gone clothes shopping earlier in the week, a pantsuit that had made her look like a nun in secular clothing. Instead Kerrie Ann had struck a middle ground in choosing a polka-dot wraparound dress that complimented her figure without flaunting it.

"You mean that?" Kerrie Ann asked.

Lindsay smiled in a way that softened the angles of her face. "Yes, I do." She reached up to finger a lock of Kerrie Ann's hair. "I also think you look better as a blond than with pink hair."

Yesterday, with Miss Honi's help, Kerrie Ann had done a home color job on her hair, doing away with the last of the pink streaks. Not that she didn't still have a pink streak or two in her, but she'd seen the wisdom in not flaunting her inner wild child before the judge. It wasn't as big a deal as quitting smoking, which she still struggled with, though the nicotine patches helped, but it made her wonder if there wasn't a small part of her that was like her sister after all.

Kerrie Ann took one last look in the mirror, smoothing the front of her dress and applying a spritz of hairspray. *It'll have to do because this is as good as it's gonna get.* Aloud, she said, "I guess we should get going. It's a long drive, and I don't want to be late."

She wasn't due in court until three that afternoon, but San Luis Obispo was nearly four hours away by car, and she wanted to leave enough time in case of backed-up traffic or a flat tire. People like Lindsay could afford to show up late for a court date—it was no reflection on their character—but Kerrie Ann had lost that luxury when she'd lost her child.

Lindsay might have reasoned that it wasn't going to take six hours even if they had a flat tire along the way, but she only said, "Off we go, then. Why don't you round up Miss Honi while I go get the car? I'll meet you out front."

In the twelve-step program, Kerrie Ann had learned that you weren't supposed to pray for anything specific. Prayer, according to the Big Book, wasn't a Christmas-wish-list type of thing. You were supposed to just pray you'd make it through another day and leave the rest to your higher power. Not that she even knew who or what her higher power was. Growing up, shuttled from one foster home to the next, she'd been exposed to a grab bag of religions—Catholic, Presbyterian, Baptist, Pentecostal, Jewish—until about the age of thirteen, when it all became lumped together in her mind as one giant conspiracy with the single purpose of making her conform. It wasn't until she'd joined the program that she began to see faith in a different light. The words of one of the old-timers, a scruffy ex-con called Big Ed, often rang in her head: "It don't have to be Jesus. It can be anything you want—God, Mohammed, Buddha, or even freakin' L. Ron Hubbard. Hell, that doorknob over there." The bottom line, Big Ed had gone on to say, was that it was *yourself* you were praying to, the part of you that had gotten you this far and was keeping you on track. And who was to say that wasn't connected to God somehow?

So Kerrie Ann prayed. She tried to keep it general, but whenever she sat with her hands clasped in prayer, an image of her little girl rose in her mind. She knew she couldn't rely on her higher power alone. She had to somehow prove to the judge that she deserved a second chance. Because now, with the Bartholds complicating matters, the stakes were higher than ever. Even wearing the right clothes and saying all the right things, she couldn't begin to match what they had to offer with their fancy educations and highbrow careers, their nice home, their good standing in the community. And they were black. She knew that judges leaned in favor of placing children with adoptive parents from the same ethnic background. The same rule might apply here.

And what did she have to offer? Only her ninety-day and six-month chips from NA. She had no career, no savings to speak of, no home of her own, and at the moment no means of transportation. In short, she was in no position to provide for her child.

Except for one thing . . .

"Whatever anyone says, don't forget you're her mom," Ollie had reminded her the other day when they'd been walking on the beach. "And kids belong with their moms."

She warmed at the thought of Ollie. These past weeks he'd been doing his best to distract her from her looming court date: baking her special treats, even though she jokingly complained that he was making her fat, and thinking up fun activities. One day he'd taken her to the Boardwalk in Santa Cruz, where they'd ridden the roller coaster, screaming their heads off like a couple of maniacs. Another time he'd taken her to Big Basin State Park to see the giant redwoods. The night before last he'd treated her to dinner at a funky tavern owned by a self-professed film junkie, where they showed old black-and-white movies. That night it had been a '40s flick starring Bette Davis as a heartless vixen who got hers in the end by perishing in a fiery car wreck. The other patrons had cheered, but Kerrie Ann had taken no pleasure in seeing Bette's character go up in flames, however much she might have deserved it. She knew what a slippery slope life could be, how one wrong act could lead to another. She was in no position to judge.

Yesterday after work Ollie had driven her to Mori Point, just north of Blue Moon Bay, where they'd walked the unmarked trail that wound past a freshwater wetland and along craggy ocean bluffs. "You know the scene in *Harold and Maude* where Harold's Jag goes off a cliff? They filmed it right here," Ollie informed her as they stood on one of the bluffs, gazing down at the steep drop-off below, where surf foamed amid the jagged rocks.

"I don't think I've seen that one," said Kerrie Ann.

Ollie looked at her in disbelief. "Dude. That's tragic."

"What, the movie itself or the fact that I haven't seen it?"

"Both." He shook his head. "It should be required viewing."

"Well, since I missed it, why don't you tell me the plot?"

"It's about this guy, Harold, who everyone thinks is nuts. Like, he gets his kicks going to the funerals of people he didn't even know. Anyway, at one of those funerals he meets this kooky old lady named Maude. He's just a kid, but they fall in love, and then she dies." Kerrie Ann gave a snort of disgust and Ollie said, "No—it isn't creepy. They're kindred spirits, see? That's what's so cool about it. The point is, all that other stuff, like what society expects, is totally bogus when two people are meant for each other."

"Yeah, but think what would've happened if they'd gotten married instead," Kerrie Ann reasoned. "He would've had to go around introducing her as his wife, and then people would've thought he was even more nuts than they already did."

"So?"

"So you can only afford to do that when you have nothing to lose."

Ollie turned toward her, his eyes searching her face. "Are we still talking about Harold and Maude here?"

She realized the time had come to tell him. She said with regret, "I like you, Ollie. Not just as a friend. And, who knows, maybe in another time or another place . . ." She made a vague gesture. "But right now I'm not in a position where I can afford to piss people off. Such as my sister." She put up her hand, cutting off his protest. "I need her, more than I need you. That's the plain fact of it. So I think we should cool it for now."

Ollie eyed her mournfully. But, always sensitive to her needs, he merely said, "I guess I don't have a choice, do I?" He added that it was only until she got things sorted out, though, not for good.

For some reason, Kerrie felt comforted by that thought.

Her reverie was broken by Miss Honi piping up, "I don't know about you girls, but my stomach is telling me it's lunchtime. What do you say we pull over for a bite to eat?"

Kerrie Ann glanced at her watch and saw that it was almost one—they'd been on the road for over three hours. In a short while she'd be due in court. Any appetite she might have worked up fled at the thought. So much was riding on this. If the judge didn't see her as trustworthy even for something as relatively minor as overnight visits, what chance would she have when it came time to decide who was best equipped to care for Bella?

They stopped for lunch in Pismo Beach and arrived in San Luis Obispo with time to spare. Kerrie Ann's lawyer, looking more prosperous than usual in a new navy suit and tie, had arrived ahead of them, and she met with him briefly outside the courtroom while Lindsay and Miss Honi went inside to find seats. Minutes later she stepped through the double doors into her own private version of hell.

Court was in session, and the courtroom was packed with the usual motley assortment of people waiting for their cases to be called—lawyers and their clients accompanied by friends and family members, some of whom would be acting as witnesses. But in place of the familiar robed figure of

Judge Nickel sat a different judge: a slender, middle-aged black man with close-cropped salt-and-pepper hair. Her heart sank.

I'm screwed, she thought.

The only thing in her favor was that her lawyer was black as well. She shot Abel a panicked look as they slid in next to Lindsay and Miss Honi in the back row. He leaned in to murmur, "Judge Nickel had a stroke—it just happened, so it was too late to request a postponement. But don't worry. I'm told this guy's fair. He won't go hard on you just because . . ."

"I'm white?" she hissed back.

Abel gave a somber nod as if to say, *Among other things.*

The grave look he wore caused her to grow even more panicky. Was the incident with the Bartholds going to bite her in the ass? There hadn't been any repercussions—yet—but she didn't doubt that it had been significant enough for the caseworker to report it.

Before she could question him about it, the next case was called to the bench: a divorcing couple battling over custody of their two young kids. The wife, a mousy-looking brunette, wore a martyred air while her attorney did all the talking. "Your Honor, my client is a stay-at-home mom who's devoted her life to her children," began the gray-haired, grandmotherly lawyer. After extolling her client's virtues at length, she added, in reference to the kids, "It would be traumatic for them to be uprooted from the only home they've known and sent to live with a father who's so busy working, he scarcely has time for them."

Looking at the husband, Kerrie Ann didn't doubt every word said about him was true. He was a slick-haired, unpleasant-looking man with an even more unpleasant-looking lawyer. But appearances could be deceiving, she soon learned. "If my client, Mr. Henderson, is too busy working to spend as much time as he'd like with his kids, there's good reason for it," countered the husband's attorney in a voice thick with disdain. "He's been holding down two jobs, trying to pay off the gambling debts incurred by his wife." He jabbed a finger at the mousy wife, who shrank down in her seat. "*This* woman thought nothing of stealing food out of her children's mouths so she could troll the Internet placing bets while their hardworking father fought to keep the family afloat. She calls herself 'devoted'? I ask you, Your Honor, where does her devotion lie—with her children . . . or the online blackjack she was so enamored of?"

The judge's stern gaze fell on the red-faced wife. "I'd like to hear from Mrs. Henderson," he said, motioning for her to rise. When she was standing, he asked in the rumbling voice of Moses calling Pharaoh to account, "And just what do you have to say to these allegations?"

She stammered, "Your Honor, I . . . I admit I had

a problem at one time." A nervous glance over her shoulder at her husband. "But I've since joined Gamblers Anonymous, and I've been clean for over a year. Nothing is more important to me than my kids."

The judge appeared unmoved. "If that's the case, wouldn't the same have held true when you were gambling away their future?" he said, his eyes flashing with contempt.

After hearing from witnesses on both sides, including the wife's sister testifying on the husband's behalf, he ordered that the couple see a court-appointed mediator before setting a date for the final hearing. In the meantime, temporary custody was awarded to the father.

Watching the drama play out, Kerrie Ann felt her anxiety slip into full-blown panic. If the judge was that unsympathetic to someone who'd been hooked on blackjack, what would he say to a mother who'd regularly smoked crack in front of her five-year-old?

She glanced over at her sister, and Lindsay gave her a smile of encouragement. Miss Honi, on Lindsay's left, was in her mother-bear mode, sitting up straight as if poised to do battle, a fierce look in her eye.

When Kerrie Ann's case was called, Abel Touissant spoke briefly but compellingly. "Your Honor, my client has complied with every one of the court's stipulations. As you can see, her drug tests have all come out clean. She goes to twelve-step meetings three times a week. She also lives with her sister, who owns her own home and business, where my client is currently employed." He paused before going on, "I believe Ms. McAllister has proved herself worthy of unsupervised visits with her child. She's a good mother, Your Honor. All she's asking for is another chance, and I think she deserves that."

The judge peered down at Kerrie Ann from the oak-paneled bench, his face expressionless. She shifted in her seat, darting a nervous glance at the Bartholds, who were seated in the front row. George Barthold, in a conservative suit and tie, looked like someone you'd trust not just to fill your cavities but with your life . . . and Carol Barthold like someone who, if you were running for office, you would want as your campaign manager.

Kerrie Ann felt the knot in her belly tighten.

When Abel was done speaking, the judge called upon the court-appointed attorney representing Bella, a skinny woman with pop eyes and frizzy brown hair. "Ms. Travers?"

Skinny Minnie set aside the papers she'd been shuffling through and stood up. "Your Honor, in my opinion there needs to be further evaluation of the mother's, ah . . . suitability . . . before any changes are made to the current visitation," she said in her high, nasal voice.

"What's the basis for that recommendation, Ms. Travers?" he asked.

"The child's caseworker has expressed some concerns." She gestured toward Mrs. Silvestre, seated to her right. "Apparently there was an incident," she added darkly.

"Mrs. Silvestre?" The judge cocked a brow at the caseworker.

Kerrie Ann watched with mounting dread as Mrs. Silvestre rose to address the bench. "Your Honor, I'd first like to say that Ms. McAllister has made significant strides over the past seven months. And from what I've observed, there's a real bond between her and her daughter." She cast Kerrie Ann a look that was not without compassion. "What concerns me is her difficulty in managing her anger. The incident in question happened during a recent visit. I only came in at the end, but I noticed that Ms. McAllister was quite agitated and I was told she . . ." Color seeped into her cheeks. "She made a racial slur."

There was a collective gasp from the audience, and Kerrie Ann surged to her feet. "That's a lie!" she cried. The judge stared at her until she subsided into her seat. She realized too late that in shooting off her mouth, she'd only given credence to the accusation. Still, she quivered at the unfairness of it. Racial slur? She'd been accused of some terrible things but never that. Her own child was mixed-race. How the hell could she be racist?

"I'd like to hear more about this alleged incident, Mrs. Silvestre," said the judge. His expression was grim.

"It happened just after the child's foster parents arrived to pick her up." The caseworker turned to indicate the Bartholds, who looked to be very much the injured parties. "Ms. McAllister ran into them in the parking lot as she was leaving. Apparently words were exchanged. It became quite heated, from what I'm told. When I spoke with Dr. Barthold about it afterward, he said that she told him—" She broke off, looking embarrassed, before repeating with obvious reluctance, " 'You can kiss my white ass.' "

All eyes in the courtroom were on Kerrie Ann as she sat shaking her head in disbelief, struggling to keep from digging her grave any deeper with another outburst.

"Is this an accurate account, sir?" The judge addressed Dr. Barthold.

George Barthold stood up. "Yes, Your Honor, it is," he replied in a solemn tone.

The judge brought his attention back to Kerrie Ann. "What do you have to say for yourself, Ms. McAllister?" He eyed her as if she were something that had crawled out from the floorboards.

"I told him he could kiss my ass, yeah. But I never used the word 'white'!" she blurted.

Beside her, she heard Abel give a muffled groan and knew she'd once again said the wrong thing.

She turned her head to glare at George Barthold, hoping to shame him into coming clean. But she could tell from his stiff bearing and the deeply proud look he wore that he believed it to be the truth. It was the same look she'd seen on Jeremiah's face whenever some redneck asshole had called him the n-word. Deep down, she knew she had only herself to blame.

It was over within a matter of minutes. The judge declared, "Motion denied. Visitation remains as is until further ruling." Ignoring Kerrie Ann altogether, as if she were a subhuman species incapable of understanding, he advised her lawyer, "In the meantime, Mr. Touissant, I suggest your client take a course in anger management before we revisit this issue."

Kerrie Ann waited until they were outside the courtroom to ask point-blank, "How bad is it?"

Abel eyed her wearily. "Let's just say you didn't do yourself any favors today."

She was quick to set the record straight. "I'll own that, but I'm no racist. Yeah, I mouthed off when I shouldn't have, and I know that was dumb, but it had nothing to do with his being black."

"I know that. But the people in there don't know that." He jabbed a finger toward the courtroom. "And the judge certainly doesn't know that." He shook his head. "Like I said, you didn't do yourself any favors."

He was fed up, and she didn't blame him. "I

know," she replied, filled with remorse. "But does this mean I won't get custody? Because if that's the case, I might as well shoot myself now and get it over with." She felt miserable enough at the moment to do just that.

Abel's expression softened. "It's not as bad as all that. We lost the battle but not the war."

"But the Bartholds . . ."

"As far as they're concerned, it's far from a slam dunk. The court usually rules in favor of the biological parent, especially when the petitioners are non–blood relatives. That being said," he continued in a sterner tone, "I've seen cases where it's gone the other way."

His words struck dread in Kerrie Ann's heart. "Just tell me what to do. I'll do anything you say."

"Anything?" Abel arched a brow.

"You name it."

"Learn to rein in that mouth of yours."

Lindsay and Miss Honi did their best to console her.

"I could tell that man was lying through his teeth," Miss Honi staunchly proclaimed on the drive home. "The very idea! Why, there ain't a prejudiced bone in your body."

"It wasn't a complete lie," Kerrie Ann was forced to admit.

"Well, no sense crying over spilled milk. Best move on," Lindsay said briskly. She glanced at

Kerrie Ann in the rearview mirror. "What did your lawyer have to say?"

"That I should learn to keep my mouth shut."

"Good advice."

Ordinarily Kerrie Ann would have bristled, but she knew her lawyer was right. In fact, for the rest of the trip, she followed his advice, staring mutely out the window as she sat slumped in the backseat while Lindsay and Miss Honi conversed quietly up front.

"I wonder how Ollie's managing," Lindsay fretted aloud at one point.

"He can hold the fort down for one day. You know him—nothing fazes that boy," said Miss Honi in reply. "If it were a fire, he'd be the last one out after making sure everyone else had made it to safety."

Kerrie Ann suddenly wished Ollie were with her now. She longed for the comfort only he could provide.

They didn't get home until almost midnight, after stopping for a quick bite at a Friendly's along the way. Kerrie Ann was exhausted but doubted she'd get much sleep tonight. Her head was buzzing, and she felt twitchy all over, as if she were jonesing for a fix.

What I need is something to kill the pain.

The thought sneaked up on her as she brushed her teeth before bed. She froze, toothbrush poised over the sink, as she stared at her reflection in the

300

medicine-cabinet mirror. There were dark circles under her eyes, and her face was the chalky white of the toothpaste foam around her lips. She felt about as far from the tenets of the twelve-step program as Saul from Damascus.

She was shivering when she finally crawled into bed and pulled the covers over her head. Not just from cold. She never knew when the urge to use would strike—it came at odd times, mostly when her defenses were down—and now she did her best to shut out the insidious voice whispering in her head, *Just one beer. Where's the harm in that? No one ever has to know.*

She didn't get to sleep until almost four A.M. When the sun woke her, she was so wiped out, she wouldn't have been able to climb out of bed if the house were on fire. She felt hungover, too, like after a night of hard partying. With a groan, she burrowed deeper under the covers.

Lindsay, just back from her morning run, took one look at her and pronounced, "You're staying home today." Kerrie Ann was too weak to manage more than a feeble protest.

She promptly fell back to sleep. She woke hours later to pale sunlight streaming in through the window. Peering out, she saw patches of blue sky where the fog had burned off. She yawned and threw back the bedcovers, sending one of the cats, curled asleep in the folds of the quilt, leaping off the bed with a disgruntled meow. She was on her way to the kitchen to pour herself a cup of coffee when she was startled by a knock at the door.

They didn't get many uninvited callers this far off the main highway. She recalled Lindsay's troubles with those creeps who were trying to muscle in on her land and wondered nervously if it might have something to do with that. Only one way to find out . . .

She cracked open the door and peered out. But it was only Ollie, wearing faded jeans and an equally worn Harley-Davidson sweatshirt and holding a shopping bag with the book café's logo on it. He stood on the stoop regarding her sheepishly. "Did I wake you?" he asked.

"No, but you sure picked a fine time to drop by. I look like hell." She ran a hand through her tangled hair. The only thing she had on besides a pair of panties was an old T-shirt of Jeremiah's that barely covered her ass.

"Not to me you don't," he replied with apparent sincerity. She noticed he was having a hard time keeping his gaze from straying south. He thrust the bag at her. "I brought you some muffins. Blueberry—your favorite. You haven't eaten yet, I hope?"

"I haven't even had my morning coffee." She opened the door to let him in before making her way, yawning, into the kitchen. "Want some?" she asked as she reached for the pot. Even though she wasn't exactly in the mood for company, she was glad to see him.

"No, thanks," he said. "Actually, I'm on my lunch break. I just came over to see how you were doing."

"Is it that late?" She peered at the clock on the stove and groaned. Half past twelve. "I can't remember the last time I slept past noon." Memories of when she'd been using—back when time had no meaning and one day blended into the next—washed over her in a dirty gray tide.

"Sounds as if you needed it."

"Lindsay told you?" Her hand shook a little as she poured coffee into a mug.

He nodded, his easygoing smile giving way to a look of sympathy. "I'm sorry. I wish I could've been there. I would have come if Lindsay hadn't needed me at the store."

"It doesn't matter. There's nothing you could've done."

"What happened, exactly?"

"In a word, I blew it."

He came up behind her, wrapping his arms around her. She stiffened for an instant, thinking of her sister, but it felt so good to have his arms around her that she relaxed into him. They stood that way for a while, not speaking, spooned against each other, swaying slightly from side to side, Ollie's cheek pressed to her ear.

"It's gonna be okay," he murmured at last.

"How do you know?"

"I just do."

She swiveled to face him. "Just like you thought Madonna would never divorce Guy Ritchie?"

He grinned and gave a loose-limbed shrug. "Okay, so I was wrong about that. But I'm not wrong about this." His expression grew solemn, and he brushed his knuckles over her cheek. "You're Bella's mom. They can't take her away for good. Hey, I'm no lawyer and even I know that. Unless she's an ax murderer or something, the mom always gets the kid."

Kerrie Ann knew that wasn't always true, but his words had a soothing effect. She leaned in so her forehead rested against his, their arms loosely linked about each other's waists. She could feel Ollie's breath, warm and clove-scented. When at last he cupped her chin and tipped her head back to kiss her on the lips, it was with none of the windswept urgency of the night out on the cliffs. This time it was soft and sweet. She might still have been asleep, dreaming of better days to come, as she stood wrapped in his arms, her mouth opening to his like the petals of a flower to the sun.

Something stirred inside her. "Come to bed," she whispered.

Ollie did his best not to appear too eager. "Are you sure?"

"No one's home. No one will know." She took

him by the hand and gently tugged him in the direction of the bedroom.

Ollie needed no further encouragement.

If she'd expected him to attack her with most twentysomethings' lack of finesse, she was in for a pleasant surprise. Despite his lack of experience, he didn't make love like a novice. He took his time, the way she imagined he would baking a cake. *Sugar and spice and everything nice . . .* The words from the nursery rhyme came to mind, and she smiled to herself as she luxuriated in his arms, submitting to his feather-light kisses as they traveled over her body.

With the tip of his tongue, he traced the rose tattoo that snaked up her right shoulder and halfway up her neck before bending to kiss one breast, teasing the nipple with his tongue as he touched her below. A ripple of pleasure went through her, one she could feel all the way down to her toes. She moaned softly, reaching to pleasure him as well, but he gently pushed her hand away.

"No," he whispered, reminding her that he was still a kid in that respect—one with a hair trigger. Which only made her feel more tender toward him. He wasn't going to be greedy until he'd satisfied her first.

Snippets of memory, of the men before Ollie, riffled through her head like shuffled cards: the brief affairs, the one-night stands, the faceless men she'd gone home with after one too many drinks in a bar. Too many to count, but they all added up to one big fat zero. No, less than zero. Because with each mindless fuck she'd felt another piece of herself being subtracted until there was nothing left. Until she herself was as empty as all that meaningless sex.

Ollie made her feel newly minted. With him, she wasn't some marked-down piece of merchandise. Just the way he touched her, almost reverently, let her know she was worth something.

She returned the favor by kissing and stroking him all over. Behind his earlobes. Inside his elbows. The tender spots where his armpits met his rib cage, with their dark tufts that stuck out like the hair on his head. The soles of his narrow, long-toed feet. He was built like a long-distance runner, every well-defined muscle streamlined for maximum speed and efficiency. A runner who was taking it slowly this time, not rushing to get to the finish line.

The first time he brought her to climax was with his hand. She hadn't expected that, either—that he'd be so adept. She was still coasting on the thermals when he entered her. Minutes later she was coming again, this time along with Ollie.

Afterward he rolled off her, not with a murmur of contentment but with a cowboy whoop. "Man! Man, oh man. *Sweet.*" He grinned at Kerrie Ann. "You're really something, you know that?"

She was feeling vulnerable, so she hid behind a wisecrack. "Yeah, the question is *what*?"

"You don't know? You honestly don't know?" He propped himself up on one elbow, staring at her incredulously.

"No; why don't you tell me?"

She could see that he was struggling to come up with the words to express what was in his heart—a range of emotions scudded across his wide-open face like great, fluffy clouds across a prairie sky—before he finally gave up in and burst out with, "You're . . . you're *it*."

And somehow they were the perfect words.

The meetings took place every Monday, Wednesday, and Friday in the social hall of the Catholic church at the corner of Water and Harborview. Kerrie Ann usually caught a ride with one of her fellow twelve-steppers. Most often it was Big Ed roaring up on his Harley Fat Bob, helmetless and with the tails of his bandana flapping in the wind along with his ragged gray ponytail. Other times it was her sponsor, Lois, or the retired naval officer known as the Admiral, who always made her smile when he came tootling down the drive in his bright yellow Smart Car, looking like the world's oldest child riding a pedal car. Ray, the tweaker who'd given her rides in the past, had succumbed, like so many before him, to the pull of his addiction.

At the church Kerrie Ann would make her way down a short flight of steps to the basement, a low-ceilinged room floored in scuffed green-and-tan linoleum and lit by overhead fluorescent tracks, where for an hour or more she'd sit in a folding chair, with anywhere from a dozen to three dozen people, sipping bad coffee and listening to strangers tell their stories.

The stories varied only in the details. There was the young mother who backed out of her driveway while on meth and ran over her four-year-old boy, maiming him for life. The former airline pilot who lost everything to blow—wife, kids, job, savings—until one day he found himself living out of his Range Rover. The former beauty queen who, in eerie shades of Kerrie Ann's own mother, lost her kids to the system when she was sent to prison for peddling dope. People who, by all outward appearances, had little in common with each other but who shared a common bond: They had all been to the dark side and back.

In her first weeks of sobriety, Kerrie Ann had hung back, reluctant to share at meetings, but it had become easier over time. These people, wildly disparate though they might be, were the closest she had to a tribe. She could tell them things she wouldn't have felt comfortable confiding to anyone else, knowing she would get nods of understanding in return, not judgmental looks. In this room, there was neither shame nor pity. Here any sympathy was reserved for the former occupants of chairs that now sat empty.

On the evening of the day following her court date—the ragged edges of which had been eased only somewhat by Ollie—Kerrie Ann rose to her feet before a group of forty or so and took her turn at the podium. She stood tall and cleared her throat. She began to speak.

"Hi. I'm Kerrie Ann. I'm an addict . . ."

As she told her story for the umpteenth time, she felt another missing piece of her fall back into place. It didn't matter how many times she'd shared in meetings. Each time there were new people who hadn't heard her tale, and it was from their sad and knowing eyes, as much as from the wisdom of the old-timers, that she drew strength. *You're not alone*, those eyes said. *We're with you.* Parents, husbands, wives, brothers, sisters—all of whom had become alienated from loved ones due to their addiction. Sometimes they were reunited with those loved ones, sometimes not. But the message was always the same: *It's never too late. Keep the faith.*

Tonight she looked out over the motley assemblage and felt something akin to love wash over her. There was perky red-haired Sue, who had been sober twenty years and was their unofficial den mother. Big Ed, in his studded leather vest, with tats covering nearly every square inch of his two-hundred-eighty-pound frame. Devon, a former executive, who could make you laugh while cringing at the same time with her stories about trying to walk a straight line in the corporate world while stoned out of her mind. Little pug-faced Shorty, who'd lost a leg in 'Nam, but not his sense of humor. And Kerrie Ann's sponsor, Lois, a soccer mom with three young boys whose story of being busted in front of all the other moms when her stash fell out of her purse at a PTA meeting never failed to spark uneasy laughter and groans of sympathy.

Tonight there was someone new. She couldn't see his face—he was sitting in back, where a column partially blocked him from view—just long legs in blue jeans worn to snow at the knees and a pair of toe-sprung cowboy boots. It wasn't until the meeting came to a close, while others were gathering into small groups to chat or drifting toward the exit, that he got up and started toward her.

Recognizing him, Kerrie Ann froze.

It had been a long time, and the face that had been so gaunt when she'd last seen it was fleshed out now. But she'd have known it anywhere. That smile, too—the smile that had once lit up her entire world.

"Jeremiah," she breathed.

He didn't say anything. He just stood staring at her as if they were the only two people in the room. Then he lifted a hand in greeting. "Hey."

Kerrie Ann was speechless. "What are you doing here?" she asked when she found her tongue. Not very original. But it was all she could come up with in her present state.

His simple reply rocked her to the core: "I came to see you."

She could see him clearly now, as if she'd been looking at him through a blurred lens and he was coming into focus: his stripey-gold eyes, the color of tiger's-eye, which slanted up at the corners to give him a vaguely exotic, Keanu Reeves look; his smooth, cinnamon-butter skin and high cheekbones that could cut glass; the dark clock-spring curls erupting from his head. He was a bit older and heavier than she remembered, but he could still pull off the lean-and-mean rocker look that used to drive the girls wild.

"How did you find me?" Her voice was unsteady.

"I asked around. Your friend Shoshanna said to say hello, by the way."

"Bitch." But Kerrie Ann laughed when she said it. Now that he was here in the flesh—the fully restored Technicolor Jeremiah—she could forgive her former roomate for revealing her whereabouts. She only wished she could harden her heart so she could stay angry at him.

He glanced around the room, where people stood in postmeeting huddles. Big Ed had his arm around Weezie, who looked as if she were about to cry:

311

Weezie had just lost a son to the same disease that had nearly killed her. In another corner, Lois and Sue were sharing a laugh. And over by the refreshment table, the Admiral was deep in conversation with one of the newcomers, a pale, jittery young man whom she'd pegged as a tweaker. Jeremiah seemed at home in their midst—this clearly wasn't his first meeting.

He brought his gaze back to her. "You look good."

She bit her tongue before she could reply, *So do you*. Instead she shrugged and said, "Yeah, well, it's been a while."

"So do you want to go somewhere? For coffee?"

Not so fast, thought Kerrie Ann. Jeremiah had to do more than show up looking like a bounced check made good to earn her forgiveness. "There's coffee here. Help yourself." She pointed toward the battered urn on the refreshment table.

"Thanks, I already had some." He made a face, to which she responded with a knowing chuckle: The coffee certainly wasn't the draw at these meetings.

She came to a decision. "You got a car?" He nodded, and she said, "Good. You can give me a ride home."

They stepped outside into the cool of the evening, where a mist lay over downtown Blue Moon Bay. It looked like an old-time photo, the edges of the buildings blurred and their colors faded to a uniform gray. She felt as if she, too, had stepped from the present back into the past. She recalled other evenings like this one, accompanying Jeremiah to gigs. Even his movements, as he strolled along at her side, were as familiar as her own: his rolling gait with the little snap to it—a less exaggerated version of the cocky strut he used to do onstage.

"I know," he said with a chagrined laugh when they reached his car—an old boat of an '82 Cadillac, white with gold fenders, that made her think of Elvis in his pimped-out Vegas period. "It belongs to a friend of mine who's doing time. He's letting me use it until he gets out."

She wondered if his "friend" was an indication of the kind of people he hung out with. If so, it didn't bode well. But who was she to judge? She'd rubbed elbows with her share of lowlifes.

Soon they were roaring along Highway 1 in the Caddie. As they approached the turnoff for Lindsay's house, Jeremiah asked anxiously, "Do you have to get back right away? I was hoping we could go somewhere and talk. I know I have some explaining to do."

"What makes you think I want to hear it?" she snapped, but she didn't protest when he blew past the turnoff.

They drove all the way to Bean Hollow State Park, where they parked and got out. The beach was deserted at this hour. With good reason, she thought, shivering in her thin jacket as they set out along the sand, the cold wind off the ocean stinging her cheeks and sending her hair whipping about her head. They walked together in silence, the only sounds the booming of the surf and scrunching of sand beneath their bare feet.

When they finally took shelter behind a dune, Kerrie Ann was chilled to the bone and had to huddle next to Jeremiah to keep from freezing. She made sure only their arms were touching, though, and she sat with her knees to her chest. She didn't want him to get any ideas.

"You said you had some explaining to do? Well, go on, I'm listening." She wanted to lash out at him—five years without so much as a freaking phone call!—but all her anger seemed to have vanished. Weren't they two of a kind, she and Jeremiah? They'd both messed up. He was no more to blame for the way things had turned out than she.

He hunkered down into himself. She could feel him shivering. "It's the same old story. I went out and stayed out for a long, long time." His was the collective voice of countless meetings like tonight's. "For a while I was even homeless, living off the streets, scoring whenever I could. If it weren't for Father Tom, I doubt I would've made it." He explained that Father Tom was a former priest who worked with street people. "He got me into rehab."

"Where, in LA?" She felt a little sick at the thought that at some point she might have passed Jeremiah on the streets and seen just another homeless man, not knowing it was he.

"Nah, I was living in Phoenix at the time. Anyway, Father Tom pulled some strings and got me into Hillsdale, this state-run facility in Prescott. It's not fancy, but it's free, and the guy who runs it is good people. Twenty-eight days later, I walked out a new man." He gave an ironic laugh, and she understood because it had been the same for her, only in a different setting: That had been just the beginning of the climb up Mount Everest. "Just got my ninety-day chip." He dug the coin from his pocket and pressed it into her palm.

"Congratulations," she said without sarcasm.

"Thanks." His flat, cheerless tone told her he knew he still had a long way to go.

"So what are you up to these days?"

"Nothing much—just trying to make ends meet." He plucked at a tough blade of sea grass poking up from the sand. "I was on a construction crew, but I just got laid off. Right now I'm crashing at a friend's place in Echo Park while I look for work."

"What about your music?"

Jeremiah gave a derisive snort. "My music? The band, you mean. Let's see . . . Weiland's working at Office Max, and Mazierski's doing community service on a drug rap. Carlson's the only one who made it. He got a gig with a real band. They opened for Bon Jovi last summer at the Hollywood Bowl. But then, he was the only one of us who was any good."

"You were good!" Out of old habit, she rose to his defense.

He looked up at her, his lips curled in a small, sardonic smile. "Yeah? That must be why none of the scouts who came to hear us play ever signed me for a label. Hey, it's okay—I always knew deep down it wasn't in the cards. I stopped chasing that dream a long time ago."

"So is that what you came all this way to tell me?"

"No. I came to say I was sorry. And . . ." He took a deep breath and let it out slowly, "I know I don't deserve it, but I want to see Bella."

Kerrie Ann fingered the coin in her hand, seeing it now as more than an NA chip: It was admission for one. Jeremiah's ticket to gain entrance—into her life, and into Bella's life. And that scared her. How did she know if she could trust him? What if he wormed his way into Bella's heart only to leave her again? That was the last thing their little girl needed, especially now.

She spoke cautiously. "That might not be so easy to arrange."

He nodded. "Yeah, I gather." She winced, wishing Jeremiah hadn't been present tonight when she'd told all at the meeting. On the other hand, since he was in no position to judge, she was spared the scornful looks and recriminations she'd come to expect from others. "But it's only temporary, right? She'll be coming home soon?" Jeremiah's naive assumption cut her to the quick. How could she tell him it might be months, years? Maybe never?

"It could be a while," she hedged. "At this point, it's up to the judge."

"So we'll go to court. Show them she has a mom *and* a dad to take care of her." Clearly he didn't get it. To him, it was no more complicated than retrieving a lost puppy from the ASPCA.

"It's not as simple as that."

She told him the rest of the story: about her battle to win their daughter back . . . finding out she had a sister and Lindsay's taking her in . . . and Bella's foster parents' wanting to adopt Bella. She watched his expression darken as she described the Bartholds.

"Those assholes! They think they can just waltz in and take away our kid? We're her *parents*, for fuck's sake."

And what model parents we've been, she thought. A couple of recovering crackheads, one a neglectful mom and the other a deadbeat dad. "We screwed up, Jeremiah. Big-time," she reminded him. "When there's a kid involved, you don't always get a second chance."

"So we'll do whatever we have to. We'll fight this—together." Jeremiah cast her a hopeful look.

"In fact, I was talking to one of the guys at the meeting, and he says there's plenty of work around here if you're not too choosy. So I thought, why not? This is as good a place as any, right? And that way I'd be around, you know, in case you need me."

Kerrie Ann sat stone-faced while her mind whirled. Was this some kind of ploy to get back with her, or was it just about Bella? Either way, she felt uneasy at the thought of what she might be letting in if she were to reopen that door. So she struck a middle ground, saying with a shrug, "Sure. Whatever."

It wasn't a rousing show of support, but it was all the encouragement he needed. He broke into a grin. "Cool."

They were getting up to head back when she realized she was still holding his chip. She held it out to him. "Don't forget this."

"Hang on to it for me, will you?" He folded her fingers around it, holding her fist cupped in his hands while he stood gazing deeply into her eyes. "That way you'll know I'll be back."

Kerrie Ann debated a moment before shoving it into her pocket.

CHAPTER ELEVEN

I WONDER WHAT'S KEEPING your sister," Miss Honi fretted aloud. She was watching her favorite TV show, *Meerkat Manor*, but paying more attention to the clock on the wall.

Kerrie Ann should have been back from her meeting by now; it was well past the hour when she normally rolled in. She hadn't phoned, either. Amazing how one person could stir up more mischief than a whole pack of furry critters, thought Lindsay. "I wouldn't worry. She probably went out with friends after the meeting." Even as she spoke, she realized that she had no way of contacting those friends. She didn't even know any of their last names.

"This time of night?" Miss Honi didn't have to add that the only places open in Blue Moon Bay at this hour were bars.

"She could have gone to someone's house."

"Wouldn't she have called in that case? Last time I checked, her dialing finger weren't broke."

Miss Honi reached into the box of See's chocolates on the end table by the sofa. She'd been fairly good about sticking to her diet but still allowed herself a treat in the evenings. She selected one, popping it into her mouth. She frowned in thought as she chewed. In her pink satin dressing gown, with her golden bouffant swaddled in a sparkly hairnet, she looked like one of her angels—Kerrie Ann's own personal guardian angel. Though Lindsay had hoped the days of her sister needing to be looked after were long past.

She eyed the open book lying facedown on her lap. All day she'd been looking forward to curling up with the new T. C. Boyle novel, but it looked as if that would have to wait. "She's a grown woman," she reminded Miss Honi. "She doesn't have to check in with us every minute of the day. Do I phone you every time I'm going to be late getting home?"

"That's different. When it's you and that boyfriend of yours, I know there ain't nothing much going on."

Lindsay surrendered with a sigh, closing her book. "Grant and I have been together a long time. At this point, no, it's not a thrill a minute. But it's comfortable."

"So's an old pair of slippers."

"Well, I'll take sheepskin over satin any day," Lindsay said, wriggling her toes in her Uggs slippers while glancing pointedly at the old woman's marabou-trimmed mules.

"Hmmpf," grunted Miss Honi, reaching for another chocolate. She went back to watching the antics of the meerkats, which were apparently of far greater interest to her than Lindsay's love life.

If only she knew . . .

These days Lindsay felt as if she were leading a

double life. On the surface all was calm and orderly, but underneath she was a bubbling stew of emotions, all due to Randall Craig. She day-dreamed about him constantly, so vividly at times that she could almost feel his hands traveling over her . . . his lips against her skin . . . his arms and legs tangled with hers. At work, mindless tasks like stocking shelves and setting up displays had become delicious oases in which her thoughts and memories could roam free. Once, while meeting with one of the reps, a perfectly ordinary middle-aged man, she'd found herself captivated by the curly golden hair on his wrists, so like Randall's, to the point that she'd completely lost track of what he was saying. With a red face, she'd had to ask him to go over the list of titles one more time.

So far Grant was clueless, but she didn't know for how much longer. All she knew was that she wasn't ready to let go of him just yet. Grant was a sure thing, whereas Randall was still a mystery in some ways. Whenever she probed too deeply into his past, he grew evasive. Did he have another lover, or a wife hidden away somewhere like Mr. Rochester in *Jane Eyre*? Was he harboring the secret of a dark misdeed from his days on Wall Street?

Due to all of the above, she'd been keeping Randall at bay to some extent, using work as an excuse. They spoke regularly over the phone, and once, when he'd insisted he couldn't spend another moment apart from her, he'd driven down to see her and they'd met for lunch.

But that was about to change. Recently he'd approached an editor he knew at the *San Francisco Chronicle*, who'd given him the green light to do a piece on Lindsay's plight. It was publicity she sorely needed in the face of the disappointing results of the environmental study. But it would also make her relationship with Randall more or less official. Lindsay had invited him for lunch this coming Sunday so he could scout around and take some photos. And as soon as Miss Honi laid eyes on him, Lindsay knew there would be no living with her until she dumped Grant in favor of Randall—which wasn't going to happen, at least not anytime soon. She didn't relish the thought.

She set her book aside and rose from her chair by the fireplace. Chester, curled asleep at her feet, stirred and grunted before tucking himself back into a ball. "I'm off to bed," she announced. "If you want to wait up, fine, but if I don't get some sleep, I'll be no good tomorrow."

Miss Honi got up off the sofa and clip-clopped over in her mules to give Lindsay a hug and a kiss good night. She smelled of chocolate and Pond's face cream. Lindsay felt her worries recede. Miss Honi wasn't always a ray of sunshine, but her arms never failed to warm.

" 'Night, sugar. Sleep tight." she said.

Some time later Lindsay was dragged from a

deep sleep by the snick of the bedroom door opening. In the dim light, she could make out a shadowy figure—her sister—making its way across the room on tiptoe. Kerrie Ann looked disheveled and was weaving slightly, as if . . .

Lindsay bolted upright, suddenly wide awake. "Are you *drunk*?"

Kerrie Ann came to an abrupt halt. "Jesus, you scared me."

"Well, are you?"

"Have I been out getting trashed?" Kerrie Ann snorted. "I wish."

"It's not something to joke about." Lindsay fumbled for the switch on her night-table lamp.

Kerrie Ann threw up a hand to shield her eyes against the sudden glare. Exposed, she looked even more of a wreck, her hair tangled and her makeup smudged, a streak of what looked to be charcoal running down one leg of her off-white jeans. "Did I say it was? Jeez, Lindsay, lighten up. Why do you always have to assume the worst? For your information, I ran into an old . . . friend at the meeting. We went for a drive. I guess I lost track of time."

"It wouldn't happen to be an old boyfriend, would it?" Lindsay knew it was none of her business, but any new wrinkle in her sister's already complicated life had a way of involving her, she'd noticed. And she didn't want this to become yet another complication.

"You could say that." Kerrie Ann lowered herself onto her bed. Lindsay could see now that she was sober. But something was clearly amiss. "It was Bella's dad. I haven't seen him since she was a baby, and there he was, big as life. It was a shock, let me tell you."

"I can imagine. I hope you told him to take a hike."

"Not exactly." Kerrie Ann sat hunched over, shivering. As usual, she wasn't dressed for the weather. She wore a lightweight peach-colored jacket over a tank top and low-rise jeans that showed a slice of tanned belly. Scarlet-painted toes peeked from a pair of cork-heeled wedgies.

"So does this mean you've forgiven him?" Lindsay asked incredulously.

"I didn't say that, did I?" Kerrie Ann glared at her. "Anyway, it's not as cut-and-dried as you think."

"Why don't you explain it to me, then?"

"Okay, but first you have to get off your high horse. Seriously. I can't talk to you when you're looking at me like that."

Lindsay let out a breath, settling against her pillows. "All right. I'm listening."

Kerrie Ann reached for the crocheted afghan folded at the foot of her bed and wrapped it around her shoulders. "Look, I don't blame you for thinking Jeremiah's a scumbag. I'd pretty much written him off, too. But he's changed. He's clean now—ninety days. I know that doesn't sound like a lot to you, but believe me, it's something."

"That doesn't change the fact that he walked out on you and Bella."

"No, and it doesn't excuse it, either. But it wasn't like he meant to. He was whacked-out at the time. And when you're high, you do all kinds of things you wouldn't otherwise do." Kerrie Ann clearly spoke from experience.

"He could at least have stayed in touch."

Kerrie Ann regarded her as if from the opposite side of a gulf, as if the prospect of explaining it to someone who'd never been there was simply too enormous. "He was out there for a really long time. I mean *out there*. It got so bad he was even homeless for a while. That's when he went into rehab. When he finally sobered up enough to see what a mess he'd made of things, he went looking for me. He wants to get to know his daughter. To be part of her life."

"What about you? Does he want to be part of your life, too?"

"Maybe, but who says I want him back?"

Nonetheless, Lindsay felt compelled to ask, "Do you?"

Kerrie Ann was quiet for so long as she sat slumped on the end of her bed, her head lowered so her chin was almost resting on her chest, that Lindsay thought she might have drifted off to sleep. Then from the folds of the afghan came her muffled voice: "I don't know."

Lindsay bit her tongue before she could put in her two cents. What her sister needed more than advice was a little breathing room. "Well, I'm sure you'll figure it out," she said.

Kerrie Ann brought her head up, flashing Lindsay a grateful look, then rose to her feet. As she headed for the bathroom, Lindsay called after her, "I'll leave the light on!"

"What, you think I can't find my way around in the dark?" Kerrie Ann turned to look at her.

Lindsay smiled at her. "We all need a little help sometimes."

By the time Sunday rolled around, Lindsay's trepidation about having her family meet Randall had eased somewhat. Who knew? Maybe this would be the kick she needed to force her into making a decision. She remembered a piece of advice Kerrie Ann had given her: *Don't overthink everything.* Not that her sister was one to hand out advice, but she'd made a valid point. Lindsay knew she had a tendency to become mired. All that uncertainty, growing up, had left her fearful of change. But who was to say she couldn't overcome it?

The morning of the big day, he phoned to tell her he'd be late. "My father wants to see me," he explained. "He said it was important." Randall sounded less than thrilled.

"Of course you should see him," she said. "He's your father."

"By blood only."

"Still, family is family."

"Yeah, about that . . ." Randall cleared his throat. "Lindsay, there's something you should know. I would've told you sooner, but . . ." He let the sentence trail off. "We'll talk about it when I get there, okay? If I'm going to be any later, I'll let you know."

Lindsay hung up, wondering what he was being so mysterious about. Something to do with his family, he'd hinted. Some skeleton in the closet? Or was he indeed married, as she'd feared? Maybe he even had children. But she quickly chalked up her fears to an overactive imagination and decided she had enough real problems without inventing ones.

Lindsay didn't have a chance to dwell on it, in any event. Minutes later Kerrie Ann's former boyfriend showed up unexpectedly. Jeremiah had driven Kerrie Ann to Oakview the day before to visit their daughter, and he was returning a sweater she'd left in his car.

Lindsay had been fully prepared to dislike her sister's ex-boyfriend but instead was disarmed. Jeremiah wasn't the swaggering rocker she'd imagined. And he went out of his way to be ingratiating, showing them photos he'd taken of Bella with his camera phone. "She looks like me, don't you think?" he said proudly as he scrolled through the images. "Kerrie Ann, too—look at that smile.

She's gonna be a real beauty, just like her mom."

Lindsay and Miss Honi agreed: Bella was the most beautiful child either of them had ever seen. "I can't wait to meet her," Lindsay said. Ever since she'd found out about Bella, she'd been looking forward to the day when Bella could come for a visit.

"You'll love her. She's a sweetie. Smart, too. She walked right up to me and said, 'Are you my daddy?'" His smile widened into a grin. "Can you beat that?"

"I wouldn't call it smart. I'd call it ESP. Since she ain't seen hide nor hair'a you since she was a baby," Miss Honi remarked with typical acerbic flair.

Jeremiah looked appropriately chastened. "I know. I haven't been much of a dad. But I'm gonna make it up to her. She's my girl, you know? My other girl, I should say." He turned to Kerrie Ann, who blushed.

Lindsay and Miss Honi exchanged a worried look.

"Coffee?" Lindsay offered in an effort to change the subject. She didn't want to think about what else might have transpired on that trip to Oakview yesterday.

"No thanks. I should get going—I'm seeing a guy about a job," he told them. "Wish me luck, okay?" He flashed Kerrie Ann a meaningful glance before returning his gaze to Lindsay and Miss

Honi. "But hey, it was great meeting you both. I'm sure I'll be seeing you again soon." He shook Lindsay's hand, then Miss Honi's when she grudgingly offered it.

Kerrie Ann jumped up to see him out, and Lindsay didn't miss the proprietary hand that rested lightly against the small of her sister's back as they fell into step.

All right, so Jeremiah wasn't the devil incarnate, she thought. But he might still be a bad influence. Even if he meant well, he could end up triggering those old self-destructive patterns of Kerrie Ann's. Or he could fall off the wagon and drag her down with him.

There was Ollie, too. He'd be crushed.

Be careful what you wish for . . . Lindsay had wished for something or someone to distract her sister from Ollie, but she'd never imagined it would come at such a price.

At quarter to one, Randall phoned to let her know he was on his way. Twenty minutes later he pulled into the driveway just as she was attempting to coax Chester out of her flower bed, where he was frantically sniffing at a gopher hole. Randall came over and squatted down next to her. He whistled, and Chester crept out, tail wagging, to lick his hand. It seemed that Randall's seductive charm extended to the animal kingdom as well.

"How did you do that?" she asked, rocking back on her heels to eye him in amazement.

He stroked the old Lab's gray-flecked muzzle. "Dunno. Dogs just like me, I guess."

Randall turned to look at her. With the sunlight on his face, his blue eyes seemed even bluer. She could see the fretwork of fine lines at their corners, lines that curved down to meet his temples as his mouth stretched in a smile. It was all she could do to keep from kissing him.

"How did it go with your dad?" she asked as they made their way to the house.

Randall's expression clouded over. "All right, I guess."

"What was it he wanted to talk to you about?"

"Nothing much. Just family stuff." He appeared preoccupied, frowning down at the redwood-bark path as they strolled along, his hands jammed into the pockets of his olive-drab chinos. She sensed him holding back. When at last he raised his head to meet her gaze, his eyes were troubled and his brow furrowed. "Actually, that's what I wanted to talk to you about—"

Before he could finish, Miss Honi stuck her head out the back door to holler, "Sugar, you been hogging that boy long enough. Bring him on in so he can meet the rest of the clan!"

Lindsay turned to Randall with a grin. "That," she said, "is Miss Honi Love."

Randall and Miss Honi got on like a house on fire. Within minutes it was as if they'd known each other all their lives. Over a lunch of lasagna, garlic bread, and a tossed salad, she regaled him with her colorful tales. "We weren't called strippers in my day. We were exotic dancers," she told him in answer to his question about her former profession. "And none of that cheap stuff they go in for today. Wriggling 'round on fellas' laps and Lord knows what else. We were *performers*." She tipped her chin up in proud defiance. "I know some folks don't see it that way, but it's no mean feat to make each and every fella feel like he's got you alone in his bedroom, whispering sweet nothings in his ear, before you've taken off so much as a stitch. And we didn't take it *all* off, neither," she added with a sniff. "Where's the fun in that? You gotta keep 'em guessing."

"I couldn't agree more," said Randall, clearly amused.

"She's right. I went to a nude beach once, and it was a total bust," said Kerrie Ann. She caught the double entendre and laughed. "I don't mean there weren't a lot of bare boobs and, you know, other body parts. Just that it wasn't sexy. None of the guys were checking out even the chicks with hot bodies. Not like if we'd been wearing bikinis."

"What's sex without a little mystery?" said Lindsay, surprising herself. Normally she felt uncomfortable discussing sex, not wanting to be reminded of the days when she'd known far more about the birds and the bees than any child should.

"Amen to that." Miss Honi stabbed with her fork

at a wedge of tomato on her plate. "How d'you think I keep 'em coming back at my age? It ain't by waltzing 'round buck naked in broad daylight, that's for damn sure. Any fella what got a good look at that would run for the hills if he had any sense. But hell, what he don't know won't hurt 'im, right?"

They all chuckled over that, and when Lindsay glanced at Randall, she could see that he was thoroughly charmed.

Even Kerrie Ann, who been a little distracted since Jeremiah's visit, seemed to be enjoying herself. By the time coffee and dessert were served, the four of them were chatting like old friends.

"Where you been keeping this boy?" Miss Honi demanded of Lindsay as she helped herself to another slice of cake. "He's just what we need around here, the kind of man to shake things up." She cast Lindsay a significant glance before returning her bright-eyed gaze to Randall. "I hope you'll come see us again. Feel free to drop by any ol' time."

Before he could answer, Lindsay jumped in. "Randall's working on his new book, so I'm sure he'll be tied up for a while."

"Nonsense," said Miss Honi with a wave of her beringed hand. "Ain't no one ever too busy to sit down with friends for a cup of coffee and a piece of cake." To emphasize her point, she took another bite of Ollie's banana-streusel Bundt cake.

Lindsay gave Randall a strained smile. "I'm sure you get this all the time. People who think the creative process is like waving a magic wand when it's really just plain, old-fashioned hard work."

He grinned as he leaned back in his chair. He was enjoying himself—as was Miss Honi. The old woman clearly saw Randall as a welcome catalyst who would stir things up, put a wedge between Lindsay and Grant. If this were a Jane Austen novel, Lindsay thought, Miss Honi would have her practically married off to him by now.

"True enough," he agreed, "but if you're cooped up for too long, the writing tends to get a little stale. Besides, you never know, one of these days I might decide to make one of my characters a retired exotic dancer—a lovely lady of a certain age who hasn't lost any of her powers." He tipped a wink at Miss Honi, who, Lindsay noted with amusement, was still capable of blushing.

"If you ever want to write about life in the breakdown lane, come talk to me. I could tell you stories," said Kerrie Ann with a frankness that surprised Lindsay—her sister didn't usually talk about her former life to those outside the program. "Like, did you ever wonder why there's twelve steps in the twelve-step program and only ten commandments in the Bible? That's 'cause, with us, it usually takes a couple of extra knocks on the head. And most of us never do get it right."

"I may just take you up on that," he said,

chuckling. "In the meantime, mind if I borrow that quote?"

"Sure, help yourself." Kerrie Ann looked pleased.

Am I the only one around here who's managed to keep her head on her shoulders? thought Lindsay. Not that she was immune. With Randall, she felt as if she were a passenger speeding in a car, part of her enjoying the ride and part of her wanting to slow down.

"Why don't I show you around?" she suggested as soon as she could tear him away. "If you're going to take pictures, you should do it while there's still plenty of light."

"Ladies, will you excuse me?" Randall stood, eyeing Miss Honi and Kerrie Ann with regret. "Hopefully we can continue this conversation another time."

"Don't be a stranger, now, you hear?" Miss Honi gave him a twin-barreled hug.

"I'll cook you dinner some night," volunteered Kerrie Ann.

Even Chester seemed sorry to see Randall go. He stood by the door wagging his tail and gave Lindsay an aggrieved look when she told him, "No, boy. You stay here. I'll take you for your run later on. This is business." She placed emphasis on the word "business."

Outside, Randall dashed off to fetch his camera bag from his car. When he returned, she remarked wryly, "You certainly made a hit. Are you this good with all the ladies?"

"Only the ones that strike my fancy," Randall drawled in a fair imitation of Miss Honi's Texas twang. He reached to take Lindsay's hand as soon as they were out of sight of the house.

It wasn't long before they'd ventured past her tidily landscaped yard into the open field beyond, where the wildflowers were in bloom, spattering the tall grass with bright dabs of color: purple thistle and lupine, golden poppies, and the bright yellow heads of dandelions. It was late in the day, and the sky was as clear as the ocean sparkling off in the distance—a clarion call of a sky in which seabirds looped and wheeled like stunt aerialists and any stray clouds were quickly chased away by the gentle breeze that was blowing. Lindsay breathed in the salty air, thinking that if she ever had to leave this place, she'd probably wither away and die, like the native cypress that couldn't survive outside this climate.

They walked the length of the field, Randall pausing frequently along the way to snap photos. Finally they came to a stop at the culvert that marked her property line. On the other side of the culvert lay fields, now fallow, that until recently had been a working farm.

"You're looking at nine holes of a planned eighteen-hole golf course," she said, pointing out the weed-choked furrows. "You can imagine how happy the Heywood Group was at my being the lone holdout. My land sits right smack in the middle of their little Xanadu."

"A fitting analogy." At the quizzical look she shot him, Randall explained, "You may recall that Xanadu comes from the Coleridge poem about Kublai Khan, the grandson of Genghis Khan and the founder of the Mongol dynasty. A man who stopped at nothing when conquering foreign lands."

"Trust a writer to pinpoint the reference," she smiled, though she felt he was missing the point. "I'm afraid I'm too close to it to have any kind of perspective. For me, it's very personal." She sought to explain it. "Before I came here, all I knew about the ocean came from watching movies and TV. When I saw the real thing, I couldn't get over it—how wild it was. How majestic. You're always reminded of the danger as well as the beauty, and that somehow makes you feel more alive. Does that make sense?"

"Perfectly." Randall gazed in appreciation over the field, where the furry tips of buckwheat, which grew waist-high in spots, curtseyed to the breeze, toward the ocean beyond. Then he drew her into his arms and kissed her lightly on the lips. "I'll do whatever I can to help. You know that, don't you?" She nodded, not trusting herself to speak. Where had this man come from? "You're not alone. I have resources. I know people."

"Thanks. I just hope it's enough." She was sure that Lloyd Heywood had more influence than all of Randall's connections combined. "Not that I don't appreciate what you're doing," she hastened to add. "And normally I believe in the power of the pen. But I don't know if it's mightier than the sword in this case."

Randall's brow creased as he stared past her. When he brought his gaze back to her, the frown lines were still there. "Lindsay, there's something you should know. But first I want to tell you—"

Before he could finish, they were interrupted by the drone of a car engine. Lindsay turned to see a black Mercedes SUV making its way down the drive, trailing a plume of dust. "I wonder who that could be," she muttered. "Unless it's one of Heywood's goons. And I can't believe even *they* would stoop this low—on a Sunday." She was getting a funny feeling, though. God might have rested on the seventh day, she thought, but the devil's work was never done. "I'd better go see who it is."

Randall gripped her arm. "Don't."

She eased her arm from his grasp. "I have to. I can't just leave my sister and Miss Honi to deal with this."

"Let me handle it, then."

"I appreciate your gallantry," she said. "But if it's who I think it is, they won't settle for my second."

Randall fell into step with her as she headed back toward the house. She could see that he wasn't happy about it as he walked stiffly at her side, his mouth drawn into a grim line.

When they got to the house, the Mercedes was parked out front. Lindsay reached it just as the driver's-side door swung open and Lloyd Heywood, dapper in a pair of cream trousers and a fashionably creased linen blazer, climbed out. His gaze fell on Randall, and his mouth spread in a grin that revealed a row of gleaming porcelain veneers.

"Hello, son," he greeted him.

CHAPTER TWELVE

*L*INDSAY STARED AT HIM IN SHOCK. "This man is your *father?*"

For a second she thought Randall was going to plow his fist into the older man's smug, smiling face. Then he turned to her with an anguished look. "It's not what you think. If you'll just let me explain—"

"No." She put a hand up to ward him off as she backed away. "My God. So you've been lying to me all this time? Trying to trick me into going along with his scheme?" She swung around to face Lloyd Heywood. Randall's father. She could see the resemblance now—the same build, the same nose and mouth. The same charm that masked a cold, calculating eye. And she'd believed Randall truly cared for her. What a fool she'd been!

"Lindsay, please . . ." He reached out to place a hand on her arm, but she shrank away. Randall looked stung, but he gamely plowed on, "That's what I was trying to tell you before . . . about my family. Yes, I know I should have told you sooner. The only reason I didn't was because I knew this was how you'd react. I didn't want you to think I was connected to him in any way." He shot another murderous look at the old man.

"Please, spare me. I may be naive, but I'm not an idiot." She took another step back. "I get it now. You thought if you could get me all buttered up . . ." *and into your bed . . .* "you'd have me right where *he* wanted me." She glared at Lloyd. "That I'd just sign on the dotted line."

Randall looked stricken. "No, it wasn't like that. You've got to believe me."

"Why should I?"

"Because I care about you, damn it!" Bands of color stood out on his cheeks, and his eyes were wild. This was not the Randall who'd had her family eating out of his hand a short while ago.

She gave a hollow laugh. "You expect me to believe that? Oh, I admit you had me fooled. I must have seemed an easy mark—poor, naive Lindsay, locked away in her ivory tower with all her books. All you had to do was come riding up on your white charger."

"It wasn't like that," he continued to deny. "I wasn't part of any scheme."

Lindsay was too angry to listen. "Well, now that you've had your fun, I'd like you to leave. If either of you ever sets foot on my property again, I'll get a restraining order." She turned to fix the elder Heywood with a frosty gaze. "Anything you have to say to me from now on, you can say to my lawyer. As for you . . ." She turned back to Randall. "We're done."

If Randall was shaken, the old man appeared unruffled. "In that case, I won't take up any more of your time, my dear," he said, as avuncular as ever. "But in all fairness to my son, you've mis-judged him. We're not, as you seem to think, in cahoots." He tipped Randall a wink, as if in blatant contradiction of his words. Randall stared back at him with a flat, cold gaze.

Lindsay's head was spinning, and she felt slightly sick to her stomach. *I'm no better than my sister*, she thought. At least Kerrie Ann had reason to believe that Jeremiah was the answer to her prayers: He was the father of her child. With Randall, all it had been was sweet talk and the hope he'd sparked in her of something that was never going to be.

Tears rose, choking off any angry words on the tip of her tongue. "Go." This time it was more a plea than a demand. She couldn't bear to look at him a minute longer. It hurt too much.

Randall made one last attempt. "Can I call you later? Five minutes of your time, that's all I'm asking. Will you give me that much? Please. You don't know the whole story."

Lindsay shook her head. "You'd only be wasting your time."

"You should listen to what he has to say," advised the elder Heywood in the same unruffled tone. "If you're looking to hang on to all this—" he gestured around him—"my son might just be your best bet. That way we could keep it all in the family." He glanced about with an appreciative look. "And I must say, I can't think of a nicer spot for a wedding."

"You bastard." Randall took a menacing step in his direction.

"Now, now, is that any way to talk to your father?" Lloyd feigned a hurt look. "And here I was only trying to help. Never let it be said that I stood in the way of true love. Now, where was I . . . oh, yes." He withdrew an envelope from the inside pocket of his blazer and handed it to Lindsay. "This is for you, my dear. Not another offer," he was quick to add at the contemptuous look she shot him. "It's a check. Quite a generous one, you'll see. All you have to do is sign the quitclaim my lawyer is drawing up." Lindsay moved to give it back to him, but he stepped back and put up his hands. "If you decide not to cash it, fine, we'll do it your way, but give it some thought at least. It would solve your money worries, and at the end of the day you'd still have your business."

She drew in a sharp breath. "What do you know about my business?"

"I know enough," he said. "I know, for instance, that you've had to borrow against your house in order to make the payments on your bank loan. I also know that your lease is up for renewal at the end of the year and that you're most likely looking at a substantial increase in rent. Don't look so shocked." He smiled. "You didn't honestly think I wouldn't find out everything I could about you? If I get what I want, it's because I do my homework."

This time Randall lunged at him, fists clenched, but the older man was as nimble on his feet as he was in his dealings. Before his son could lay a hand on him, he turned and climbed back into his shiny black SUV. Moments later he was backing out of the drive.

In a daze, Lindsay started back toward the house, trying not to stumble as she blinked back tears.

Normally she would have tried to put on a game face, but she could see as soon she walked in that it would be useless. Her sister and Miss Honi had witnessed the entire scene—the looks on their faces said it all. Miss Honi rushed over to her, throwing her arms around Lindsay. "You poor thing! Why, if I'da had a shotgun, I'da run the bastard off myself!"

Which bastard would that be? Lindsay wondered.

"She wanted to give him a piece of her mind, but I told her it would only make things worse," said Kerrie Ann.

"You're right, it would have." Lindsay was grateful that for once her sister had shown some restraint. Extricating herself from Miss Honi's embrace, she patted the older woman's arm, as if Miss Honi were the one in need of consoling. "Don't worry, I'll survive. It's probably for the best. I mean, just imagine if I hadn't found out. I might have gone on thinking that Randall and I . . . that we . . ." She let out an involuntary little sob and squeezed her eyes shut as she fought to regain her composure. Finally she squared her shoulders, assuring them in a less than steady voice, "I'm fine, really. It was a shock, but I'll get over it. It's not as if we were . . ." She paused, gulping back another sob.

"Lovers?" Kerrie Ann supplied.

Lindsay gave her a blank look.

"Oh, come on," her sister went on. "It's no use pretending. We know the score. We weren't born yesterday." She nodded in the direction of Miss Honi, who nodded back in assent.

Lindsay bristled. "What is this, some sort of conspiracy? I thought you guys were on my side."

343

"We are." Kerrie Ann advanced on her, wearing a stern look. "Look, sis, I know you're used to sucking it up, but we're not gonna let you this time. So deal with it."

"What your sister's trying to say," Miss Honi translated, "is that we love you, and we ain't gonna leave you to wallow in your own mud."

"Who says I'm wallowing?" But Lindsay's protest was without much conviction. The truth was, she felt as if she weren't so much wallowing as drowning. She staggered over to the easy chair by the fireplace, collapsing into it. For a long while, she just sat there shaking her head. Finally she said in a hollow voice, "Please tell me none of this is happening."

Miss Honi lowered herself onto the footstool beside Lindsay's chair. "Wishing it ain't so won't make it go away. You got to face facts."

"What facts are those? That Randall's a lying bastard? I think that's been pretty well established," Lindsay replied bitterly, an invisible knife twisting in her gut at the thought.

"I don't mean him. You got bigger problems than that."

"Such as?"

"Such as what you're gonna do if the *real* bastard has his way. He's right about one thing—you could lose it all, and not just the ranch. You need to look at what's best in the long run."

"What are you suggesting?" asked Lindsay.

"You could sell this place." Miss Honi cast a mournful look around her. "I know. I don't like the idea any more'n you do. But sometimes you gotta know when to fold 'em."

"This is my home!" Lindsay cried. "I can't just *leave*."

"Sure, you can," said the older woman with her usual pragmatism. "You can do just about anything you set your mind to. Always have, ever since you were this high." She put her hand out level with the back of Lindsay's chair. "The way you looked after your sister when she was little, why anyone woulda thought you were her momma. And you barely old enough to look after yourself. A little setback like this ain't gonna change nothing. Before you know it, you'll be back on your feet."

Lindsay was touched by the show of support, despite the fact that this was hardly a "little setback." More like a major catastrophe. "I'm sure I'll manage if it comes to that," she said. "But damn it," her hands balled into fists, "I'm *not* going down without a fight."

"I been thinking . . ." Miss Honi looked down at the cat that had crawled into her lap, absently scratching it behind the ears. "I got a little bit of money saved up, thanks to you. Enough to get by, with my Social Security. I could get a little place of my own, somewhere in town, close enough so I could walk to work. Maybe it'd be easier if you had one less person to worry about."

Lindsay spoke firmly. "You're not going any-where—either of you." She cast a resolute glance at Kerrie Ann, who looked a little worried. "I'm counting on you both to get me through this. And if we lose . . ." She let out a sigh. "I guess we'll just have to cross that bridge when we get to it."

Miss Honi nodded, her eyes bright with unshed tears. She replied in a throaty voice, "I was kinda hoping you'd say that."

They both looked to Kerrie Ann, who stood silent. There was a time when Lindsay might have mistaken her flat expression for a sign that she didn't care, but over the past weeks she'd come to see it for what it was: a mask that hid a world of emotions. At last Kerrie Ann shrugged and said, "Whatever you guys want, I'm in. Hey, it's not like I have a choice." A corner of her mouth turned up in a crooked smile. "There's just one thing . . ." She looked down at the envelope containing the check, which Lindsay hadn't realized she was still holding. "Don't you want see how much it's for?"

Lindsay had forgotten all about it. Now, she pried it open, saying, "This is stupid. It's not like it's going to make a difference."

"You should at least know what you're playing for," her sister reasoned.

Lindsay withdrew the check from the envelope as Miss Honi and Kerrie Ann gathered around to have a look. They were all speechless.

Finally Kerrie Ann said in an awed voice, "I've never seen so many zeros on a check."

Miss Honi looked up at Lindsay. "He must think it'd be pretty darn tempting to someone in your shoes."

"He'd be right." Kerrie Ann went on staring at the check, wide-eyed, before recovering her wits and casting Lindsay a contrite look. "I'm just saying. But hey, it's your money. Do what you want."

"It's not *my* money." Lindsay stuffed the check back into the envelope. "I have absolutely no intention of cashing this. If those two crooks imagine I can be bought off, then they don't know who they're dealing with!"

"Whoa." Miss Honi put out a hand. "Seems a little unfair, don't it, branding 'em both with the same iron. You can't be sure our boy was in on this." Lindsay wondered when Randall had become "our boy." Wasn't it obvious that he was as much the enemy as dear old dad? "Don't you think you oughta at least hear what he has to say? He don't strike me as the type to pull the wool over someone's eyes. 'Specially not someone he's sweet on."

Lindsay wavered for an instant but remained firm. "But that's exactly what he did—he lied to me."

"Lindsay has a point," Kerrie Ann put in.

"Thank you." Lindsay cast her a grateful look.

"All I'm saying is, don't rush to judgment," advised Miss Honi. "Remember, innocent until proven guilty."

"That's only in court," Lindsay said. "And even if he wasn't in on it, why didn't he tell me who he was?" She recalled that he'd been on the verge of telling her when his father arrived, but she dismissed it as a case of too little, too late. "All that time I was going on and on about the evil Lloyd Heywood, he never said a word. Not one word. If it wasn't an outright lie, it was still dishonest."

"You of all people should know what it's like to want nothing to do with your kin," Miss Honi said darkly.

Her words gave Lindsay pause. It was true that she'd wanted nothing to do with Crystal; she'd refused to even write to her in prison. But she'd never purposely misled anyone about her mother. And Randall hadn't just misled her; he'd led her to believe that he cared about her, which made it worse. She felt doubly betrayed. How could she ever forgive that?

"Does she know you're my son?" Randall's father had asked earlier when they'd met for a late breakfast at his hotel.

They'd been sitting out on the bay-view terrace. The morning sun was breaking through the fog, and though it was still quite chilly out—chilly enough for the other hotel guests to opt for the glassed-in breakfast area fronting the terrace—the older man seemed perfectly comfortable outdoors in his lightweight slacks and linen blazer as he sat sipping coffee and nibbling on a Danish. He might have been on his way to a summer polo match. Randall, in contrast, felt chilled in his much warmer fleece-lined jacket and chinos.

"No—I've been waiting for the right moment to break it to her." Randall frowned into his coffee cup, which he cradled in both hands, more for warmth than anything else.

"I wouldn't wait much longer if I were you," Lloyd advised. "You wouldn't want her to hear it from someone else."

Randall didn't respond. He'd learned early in life to hold his cards close to his vest when dealing with his father. Starting in high school, when he'd phoned his dad with the exciting news that he'd gotten into Princeton. Lloyd had used it as an exercise in "character-building," agreeing to foot the bill *only* if Randall would work for him during the summers. Since Randall's mom and stepdad hadn't had that kind of money, he'd had no choice but to go along.

Meanwhile, Lloyd's two children with his second wife had never wanted for a thing.

Not that Randall was bitter. If character-building had really been his father's intention, that much had been achieved. After graduating from college, Randall had headed for the one place where he was likely to make a killing and thus beat the old man at his own game. In the end, though, Wall Street had come close to killing him, soul-wise. However much money he made, it was never enough. He became like the people he worked with: an eye always on the main chance, devoid of a life outside the Street. Getting off the phone one day after having persuaded a client to buy shares of an iffy stock his company was aggressively pushing, he realized to his disgust that he hadn't just beaten his father at his own game; he'd *become* his dad. He'd walked away from it then: the seven-figure income, the chic duplex in TriBeCa, the three-thousand-dollar Alan Flusser suits, the never-ending supply of women lured by the scent of money. There were those who'd probably seen it as a good move in a youth-driven business where anyone over the age of forty was considered past his or her prime—Randall was pushing forty by then—but for him it had been the only move.

But the old man was right about one thing: He *should* have told Lindsay the truth long before now. He was castigating himself even as he replied, "Who would she hear it from? I haven't even told my publisher. The only people besides Mom and Anthony who know I'm related to you are the people I grew up with." He'd taken his mother's maiden name, Craig, when he'd come of age. "Oh, and your family, of course. But since I'm not even on their radar screen, I doubt they'd much care." Randall couldn't resist the dig at his father's much younger wife and their children—a half-brother and half-sister who were all but strangers. In newspaper and magazine articles about his father, Randall, if he was mentioned at all, was referred to in passing as "an older son from an earlier marriage."

"Nonsense. Vicky is always saying she wishes you'd visit more often," Lloyd corrected, popping the last bite of Danish into his mouth and brushing the crumbs from the front of his jacket. "You really should, you know. Now that Brett and Tamara are away at college, the house seems a bit empty with just the two of us. We'd love the company." His father and his second wife had a spread in Woodside, just south of San Francisco, but Randall could count on one hand the number of times he'd been invited there in recent years.

"Right. Well, I'll have to see what I can do. I'm pretty busy these days." Where there was now apparently a welcome mat, he'd met with only excuses growing up. Scheduled visits that were put off time and again, due to some urgent matter of business his father had to attend to, or a crisis with one of the "children." As if he'd been a distant relation toward whom they'd felt only a vague sense of duty. For Lloyd and his wife, he'd been a bothersome reminder of Lloyd's first marriage, and for Brett and Tamara, a brother so much older that he was more a curiosity than anything. Now, all these years later, he was expected to feel like a part of the family? It was all Randall could do not to laugh.

"Why don't you give Vicky a call and we'll see if we can't set something up?" His father wasn't going to take no for an answer. But wasn't that just like him? Railroading those around him by sheer force of personality. It must just kill him, Randall thought, that Lindsay had proved so resistant. He started a bit, as if his father had read his mind, when Lloyd went on, "Oh, and bring your girl-friend. It'll give us all a chance to get to know one another. Clear the air, so to speak. I'm afraid we got off to rather a bad start."

Randall was quick to scotch the idea. "Not going to happen—she'd never go for it." He replaced his cup in its saucer so abruptly that some of its contents spilled over and made a show of consulting his watch. "Look, I should get going. I'm running late as it is."

He started to get up, but his father's hand clamped over his wrist. "Sit down, son." Blue eyes that were mirror images of his own blazed from the old man's seamed but still handsome face. "If you weren't so goddamn stubborn, you'd see that what I'm proposing is in your best interests, too."

Randall eyed him coolly. "Frankly, Dad, I've never known you to care about anyone's interests but your own."

"Despise me all you like," said the old man, "but

don't cut off your nose to spite your face. Think, Randall. What's her reaction going to be when you tell her? She'll imagine you're part of some sort of conspiracy. And why wouldn't she think that?" He let go of Randall's wrist and sat back, his gaze remaining locked on his son's. "But what if I weren't the enemy? If you were to bring her home to meet the family, have her to get to know us and see that I'm not such an ogre after all, then I'm certain we could work something out." Lloyd's blue eyes bored into him. "I'm not the enemy, son. And even if that's how you see me, if we could work together on this, it would serve both our purposes."

"You know what, Dad, why don't I ask her?" Randall replied in a voice thick with sarcasm. "I'm on my way over there now. I'll just casually lay it on her that you're my dad and see how she'd feel about a fun weekend in Woodside, getting to know the folks."

Something sparked in his father's eyes: a gleam of triumph. Randall would have recognized it for what it was if his mind hadn't been so clouded by anger and forty years of bad blood.

Now, as he drove away from Lindsay's, Randall saw everything with a cold, clear eye. He replayed his father's words in his head: *If we could work together on this, it would serve both our purposes.* Lloyd wanted Lindsay's land. And Randall wanted Lindsay. Both would use any means necessary to achieve their goal. In that sense, they were indeed father and son.

At the first stoplight, Randall punched in a number on his cell phone. A girlish-sounding voice picked up on the third ring. "Victoria? Hi, it's Randall. Yeah, I know, it's been a while." He gazed up at the traffic light that had just gone from red to green. "Actually, that's why I'm calling. I was wondering when you and Dad might have a free weekend . . ."

CHAPTER THIRTEEN

$\mathcal{A}$LL DAY OLLIE HAD BEEN ANGLING, without success, for a moment alone with Kerrie Ann. Business at the book café had picked up over the past week with the arrival of the latest installment in the popular *Dragon Hunters* series—the author of which was being called the next J. K. Rowling—and everyone working in the store had been crazed, especially after Lindsay had advertised that a limited number of signed copies was available. Teens and tweeners accompanied by parents had been streaming in and out all day. As a result, the café was thronged, and Ollie's dragon-themed cookies and cupcakes were disappearing as fast as he could stock the case. It wasn't just the kids, either; he and Kerrie Ann had been working double-time to keep all those flagging parents supplied with caffeine.

No, but the timing couldn't be worse, he'd made up his mind: Today was the day he was going to find out what, if anything, was going on between Kerrie Ann and her ex-boyfriend. Ever since Jeremiah had arrived on the scene, she'd been making herself scarce; these days Ollie almost never saw her outside work. He'd taken her at her word when she'd told him Jeremiah was here only because of their daughter. Still, Ollie couldn't help noticing how, whenever Jeremiah called, Kerrie Ann went off into some corner where she could talk in private, and how lately, whenever she spoke of her custody battle, it was in terms of "we," not "I." Was Kerrie Ann being influenced by the fact that, overnight, Jeremiah had become a big hero to Bella? (Never mind the fact that he'd been a no-show for most of her life.) Was she buying into the notion that they could be a family again? Ollie hoped he was making too much of what might be an innocent situation, but at the same time he felt a sense of urgency: If he didn't stake his claim, sooner rather than later, he might never get the chance.

The day they'd made love was engraved in Ollie's memory—every tiny detail of that experience, down to the chipped polish on Kerrie Ann's toes and her belly-button ring with the turquoise stone that matched her eyes—but the following day at work, she'd acted as if nothing were out of the ordinary. Had she filed it away under "casual encounter," or was she merely waiting for the dust to settle, with her legal situation and with Lindsay, before declaring her true feelings for him? He prayed it was the latter.

"Need a hand with that?"

Ollie, roused from his thoughts, looked up at Kerrie Ann, who stood at his elbow eyeing him quizzically.

"No, I'm fine. Just lost track for a second there," he said as he slid four cupcakes onto a plate. "If it gets any more crowded in here, the fire department is gonna shut us down. Who knew dragons would be the next coolest thing to iPods?" He replaced a candy corn that had fallen off a cupcake—one of the dragon's fangs—before passing the order to the customer at the end of the line, a harassed-looking mother with four children in tow.

"Why don't you take a break? I can manage on my own for ten minutes," Kerrie Ann told him, raising her voice to be heard above the hissing of the espresso machine as she expertly manipulated its levers.

"No, I'm good." Ollie flashed her what he hoped was a nonchalant grin. "But I could go for some pizza later on, after we get off work. Feel like joining me? My treat." Kerrie Ann's gaze cut away, and he immediately kicked himself. Was it too obvious a ploy?

But she only said, "Sure. Whatever."

He wasn't sure if she'd remember, but when six

o'clock rolled around, it was she who said, as they were locking up, "What about the Flying Pie? Their pizza's good, and it's usually not a long wait."

"Fine by me." Ollie tried to act casual, even though his heart was racing.

"Good, because I'm starved."

They called out their good-byes to Lindsay and Miss Honi and within minutes were rattling along Shore Drive in Ollie's Willys. The Flying Pie pizzeria was in a strip mall, where the turnoff for downtown intersected with the feeder road for Highway 1. When they arrived, they settled into a booth in back. Looking across the table at Kerrie Ann, Ollie felt his spirits rise. *Alone at last*, he thought. He broke into an involuntary grin.

"What's so funny?" she asked.

"Nothing," he said, his grin widening.

"Then why do you look like you just won the Daily Scratch jackpot?"

"I'm in a good mood is all."

"After the day we just put in? If you weren't such a straight arrow, I'd say you were on something."

"Chocolate and caffeine. I must've inhaled enough fumes to have me flying high the rest of the week."

She laughed. "You're such a dork." She said it with affection, though.

"Wanna split a large?" he asked after they'd perused the menu.

"Yeah, sure," she replied distractedly.

"Pepperoni with mushroom, right?" Ollie had made a mental note of her preferred toppings when they'd had pizza delivered to the book café, the day the two of them and Lindsay had worked late setting up the *Dragon Hunters* display.

"You remembered." She looked pleased.

He shrugged as if it were no big deal. "Me? I'm an anchovy man. It's in my DNA. If you're an Oliveira and you don't like seafood, you might as well join the circus."

She wrinkled her nose. "Ugh. Don't you hate it when those little bones get stuck between your teeth?"

He mock-shuddered. "Worse than spilling Coke on the remote control."

She laughed again, and this time she looked at him—*really* looked at him—for the first time in days. "You're a funny guy, Ollie. I'm surprised some smart girl hasn't sewed you up by now."

His heart sank. What was *that* supposed to mean?

"He walks, he talks, he'll even bake you cake," Ollie quipped. His smile felt like something caught in freeze-frame. It wasn't that he hadn't had his share of girlfriends. He had women who came on to him at work, too. But he couldn't imagine being with any of them. For him, there was only Kerrie Ann. She was so beautiful—even more so lately, as if her beauty had been a neglected plant that, with a little care, had started to bloom. Taking in her glowing eyes and skin, her hair, restored to its natural color, falling in soft waves about her shoulders, he dared to wonder if he'd had a small role in bringing that about. And if not him, who? Jeremiah?

When their pizza arrived at the table, still bubbling, Kerrie Ann dove in as if she hadn't eaten in a week. Ollie's appetite, however, had waned.

"What's the matter?" she asked when she noticed he was only picking at his slice.

"Nothing." He shrugged, pushing aside his plate. "Long day. Guess I'm a little tired."

"Okaaaay." Obviously she wasn't buying it. He watched, mesmerized, as she caught a strand of cheese hanging off the slice in her hand and twirled it around her finger before popping it into her mouth. It was strangely sexy, and Ollie felt a stirring in his groin.

"Kerrie Ann . . ." He leaned—no, lurched—across the table to take hold of her free hand, nearly knocking over her Diet Pepsi in the process. "There's something I need to know. Are you . . . is there? . . ."

She caught his drift, and before he could choke out the rest of the sentence, her hand slid slowly from his, like water through clenched fingers. She shook her head. "I want you to know, Ollie, I think you're an amazing guy," she said gently. "And that day at the house? I'll always remember it as something really special." Perhaps moved by the look of desperation he wore, she spared him further agony by cutting to the chase. "Look, there's no easy way to say this, so I'll just say it: Jeremiah and me . . . we're back together." She eyed him with compassion. "I'm sorry, Ollie. I would have told you sooner, but until just recently I wasn't really sure how I felt about him."

Ollie had to swallow several times before he finally found his voice, a voice that turned out not to be his after all but that of someone making odd croaking sounds. "So what's the story? I kind of got the impression he wasn't too high on your mistletoe list. I mean, he cut out on you and Bella, didn't he? What kind of guy does that?" he asked bitterly.

She gave him a look that cut him worse than anything: It was the look you might give an old dog you were putting to sleep. "We were together a long time," she said by way of an explanation. "It got bad at the end, yeah, but that was just the drugs. Jeremiah's really a good guy. It just felt natural, you know."

Ollie swallowed again. "So you're . . . it's serious?"

She nodded, dropping her gaze as if she couldn't bear to see the anguish in his. "He found a place here in town. A job, too—on a construction crew. He wants me to move in with him."

So soon! It was a moment before he could choke out, "What about Bella?"

"My daughter comes first. I'm not making a move unless the judge okays it." He could see from the look on her face that this was one area in which she wouldn't compromise. "But the important thing is, she'll have a mom *and* a dad, which will look good in court. In fact, things are looking up already. My lawyer just called, and guess what? The judge is letting Bella come for an overnight visit. This weekend. It's all arranged."

"But I thought . . ."

"I know. Me, too. But apparently Abel convinced the judge to try it on a—" She frowned, as if struggling to recall the words.

"Provisional basis?" Ollie supplied.

"Yeah, that's it. Kind of like probation. I guess he could see that I'm trying. You know, like with my anger management course and everything."

"How's that going?" he asked in a dull voice.

"Not bad. The instructor's a cool guy. He has us do exercises and stuff, like acting out different scenarios, so we'll know how to handle it when it's for real. I only lost my temper once."

Ollie gave her a smile that felt as if it were held in place with toothpicks. "Well, that's progress, I guess. And hey, that's great news about your kid. You must be thrilled."

She nodded, her eyes shining, and he could see that she was struggling for his sake to contain her happiness. "It's just a small step, but at least we're moving in the right direction. And if it goes well, my lawyer thinks there's a good chance it could become a regular thing. We'll see." She gnawed on a thumbnail, the worry creeping back in. So much was still up in the air.

"I'm sure it'll all work out," he reassured her, as he had so often in the past.

She eyed him with gratitude. "I meant what I said, Ollie. You're an amazing guy."

You got that right—amazingly stupid, he thought. But all he said was, "Better watch out. If you keep telling me that, I might start to believe it."

"You should. Any girl would be lucky to have you."

Any girl except you. It was all he could do to sit there chatting with her like it was no big deal that she was breaking up with him. No, this didn't even qualify as a breakup, he thought, since they had never really been a couple to begin with. Just friends with benefits. "We should get going," he said as soon as she was done eating. "Unless dragons go out of style overnight, I have about a million more cupcakes to bake."

"As long as there are knights in shining armor, I don't see dragons going out of style," Kerrie Ann said lightly as she slid out of the booth.

"You sure you know what you're doing, sugar?"

Miss Honi and Kerrie Ann were in the kitchen cleaning up, Miss Honi washing while Kerrie Ann dried. "'Course not. When do I ever know what

I'm doing?" Kerrie Ann joked. At the older woman's look of concern, she added in a more serious tone, "Relax; I'm a big girl. And Jeremiah's behaving himself. There's nothing for you to worry about."

"Whenever I'm told not to worry, that's when I worry." Miss Honi reached up with a soapy hand to pat Kerrie Ann's arm. "I don't mean to ride you, hon. I got nothing against the boy—he's likable enough. And there oughta be a law against any fella that looks that good in a pair of jeans. But you know what they say: Two people in a shaky lifeboat is twice the chance of getting sunk. I'm just worried you're in for a dunking, that's all."

"Don't; I know how to swim," Kerrie Ann assured her. She finished drying the last of the pans and folded the dish towel over the drainer, giving in to a small, ironic smile as she recalled the days when she used to let dishes pile up in the sink and did the laundry only when she ran out of clean clothes. Now she was almost as tidy as Lindsay, and not just because of the dirty looks she'd get from her sister otherwise. Her life wasn't such a mess anymore, either. She was even daring to make plans for the future. She was taking an adult-ed class to earn her GED, and after that she was thinking about a career in nursing. Jeremiah was the last missing piece falling into place. Now, with Bella, they were finally the family she'd always wanted.

"Even when you know how to swim, it can sometimes be an awful long way to shore," cautioned Miss Honi, bringing her back to earth. "You got your little girl to think of, too."

Kerrie Ann grew impatient. "I *am* thinking of her. This is as much for Bella as it is for me. Don't forget, Jeremiah's her daddy."

"Ain't no denying that—she's the spitting image of him. But he walked out on you once, and who's to say he won't do it again? You willing to take that risk?" Miss Honi gave her a long, searching look.

"Yes," she said with a certainty she didn't feel. It was true that Jeremiah had walked out on her and might do so again. Also, there was a reason why romantic entanglements in the first year of sobriety were frowned on—especially between two recovering addicts. But if she wasn't a hundred percent sure she was making the right move, that was only because nothing in life came with a guarantee.

She felt bad about Ollie, though. Not just because she knew this was hurting him. She still had feelings for him. Feelings that had crept up on her so gradually, she hadn't noticed at first. Now she felt as if something irreplaceable had been lost.

"Okay, but don't rush into anything," advised Miss Honi. "You don't have to shack up with him just 'cause you're splitting the sheets." It was a moment before Kerrie Ann remembered that they were talking about Jeremiah. "If he means to stick around, he'll still be there when the time is right."

"How come you never got married, Miss Honi?" Kerrie Ann was eager to change the subject.

The older woman paused in sponging down the sink, her gaze turning inward. "Oh, I don't know. It wasn't in the cards, I guess. Not that I didn't have my chances. There was this one fella in particular . . ." She wore a small, remembering smile. "He said if I wouldn't marry him he'd keep right on asking till I said yes, even if it took years."

"Why didn't you?"

"I wasn't ready to settle down. Anyway, he moved on eventually. Found himself a nice girl, a secretary at his firm, who wouldn't raise eyebrows at the PTA, if you catch my drift. Turned out to be for the best. We both knew that I wasn't cut out to be a wife."

"I think you would've made a great wife," Kerrie Ann replied staunchly. She didn't know anyone more loving or loyal than Miss Honi.

Miss Honi flashed her a grateful look. "Thanks, sugar. But you didn't know me back then—I was quite the gadabout. Loved the nightlife. Loved being onstage. Figured I had myself a real career— not like the girls nowadays, with their store-bought bosoms and all that grinding in men's laps. By the time I'd been at it long enough to realize it wasn't all glitz and glamour, I was too old to get a husband—leastwise none I'da wanted."

"Didn't you want kids?"

"I had you and your sister, didn't I? I couldn'ta

loved either of you more'n if you was my own." Miss Honi grew misty-eyed. "Now, come give me a hug. No hard feelings? If this boy makes you happy, then I'll be the first in line to throw rice at your wedding." She opened her arms, and Kerrie Ann walked into them as naturally as if she'd been doing so all her life.

When Kerrie Ann drew back, her own eyes were moist. She quickly turned away so Miss Honi wouldn't see. "I should go change. He's picking me up in a few minutes." Jeremiah was taking her to tonight's meeting.

Fifteen minutes later she was roaring down the highway in Jeremiah's pimped-out Caddie. When they pulled up in front of the church, several people on the sidewalk turned to stare. Normally she'd have been embarrassed to be seen arriving at a meeting in a car that looked like it belonged to a drug dealer, but being around Jeremiah made her strangely reckless for some reason—she felt as if she were sixteen again, flouting all the rules.

Jeremiah let the Caddie idle at the curb. "What do you say we skip the meeting just this once?" He spoke casually. "We could grab a bite to eat and head over to my place instead, make an early night of it." At the look she gave him, he added, "Or not. Just a suggestion."

"I don't think that's such a good idea." It was a slippery slope, and she'd heard too many stories about what happened to people who skipped meetings. At the same time, she didn't think he'd meant anything by it; it wasn't as if he'd suggested they head for the nearest bar.

"You're probably right. I mean, there must be a reason we're here three nights a week. Like we're such hard cases we'd crash and burn otherwise." An impish smile tugged at the corners of his mouth.

"Speak for yourself," she said.

"Aha! So you admit you're not such a hard case." He was grinning now.

"I'm not admitting to anything."

"You just said . . ."

"I know what I said. You're twisting my words. And yes, we did—*do*—need to go to all those meetings. How do you think we got here in the first place? It sure isn't 'cause we like sitting on hard folding chairs, drinking shitty coffee and listening to a bunch of sad tales."

"You got that right." Jeremiah nodded vigorously, though she couldn't tell if he was simply agreeing that no one in their right mind would want to drink shitty coffee while sitting on a hard folding chair. "But there's such a thing as being too faithful, don't you think? What's the point of all those steps if, at the end, you're still stuck in the same place, listening to the same old shit? You gotta live a little. Come on, don't look at me like that." He leaned over to nuzzle her cheek. "Admit it, you'd rather have me make mad, passionate love to you."

Kerrie Ann opened her mouth to tell him thanks but no thanks, she'd go without him if he didn't care to join her, but an image of her sister rose in her mind just then—Lindsay, wearing her most disapproving face. She'd grown to love her sister, but there was no getting around the fact that Lindsay could be a stick-in-the-mud. The mere suggestion that Kerrie Ann might be in danger of becoming one, too, was enough to chase away the protest she'd been on the verge of uttering. Besides, Jeremiah was right about one thing: She could afford to skip a meeting now and then. It wasn't like the NA police were going to hunt her down and arrest her.

Also, she had to admit the prospect of making love was tempting. Jeremiah had never looked more fine, and she couldn't deny the desire he stirred in her. And since this weekend was going to be devoted to Bella, shouldn't they carve out some time for just the two of them?

"All right," she said. "Just this once."

On Saturday Kerrie Ann rose early, just as the sun was peeking over the horizon. Today was the day she was to pick up her daughter for her visit. She'd waited so long, and now it was finally here! As she tore around the bedroom like a madwoman, she was glad Jeremiah would be doing the driving. In her present state, she'd have been a menace on the road.

"Where's Snuffie? I have to find Snuffie!" she cried in a panic, kneeling to peer under the bed before darting over to the closet. Snuffie had been her daughter's favorite stuffed animal when she was a toddler, and Kerrie Ann wanted it to be waiting for Bella when she got to the house. It was the only toy of Bella's that she'd kept, and now it was missing.

"I'll look for Snuffie while you get dressed," said Lindsay, steering her back into the bathroom.

"Okay, yeah, good idea. Thanks." Kerrie Ann was reminded that she was still in her bathrobe, her hair wet. If she didn't hurry, she wouldn't be ready by the time Jeremiah arrived.

She was putting on her makeup when she remembered something else. Peanut butter! She'd forgotten to buy Skippy—the only brand Bella liked. All they had in the house was the chunky organic kind from the health food store. What kind of mother was she, forgetting something as basic as that? She groaned. Her hand was trembling so badly, she nearly jabbed herself in the eye with the wand as she brushed mascara onto her lashes.

When she'd finished applying her makeup and drying her hair, she found Lindsay on her hands and knees in the bedroom, pawing through the contents of the box that had been tucked into the back of the closet. "What is it now?" Lindsay asked in response to the dire look on her face.

"I forgot to get Skippy."

"I thought it was Snuffie we were looking for."

"Skippy, as in peanut butter," Kerrie Ann explained. "It's the only kind she'll eat."

"No big deal. I'll pick some up. I have to go to the store anyway."

But Kerrie Ann just stood there, shaking her head and chewing on her lip. "Thanks, but that's not the point. A good mom would've remembered." What if this was just the first of many such lapses, culminating in her daughter's slipping away from her altogether?

Lindsay stood up and walked over to her, placing her hands squarely on Kerrie Ann's shoulders as if to ground her. "You're a good mom. But even good moms aren't infallible. Besides, she'll be so happy to see you, she won't care about anything else."

"I just want everything to be perfect, you know?" Kerrie Ann had barely slept a wink the night before. It was so important that this visit go well. Their whole future depended on it.

"It will be," Lindsay assured her.

She looked tired as well. It had been two weeks, but she still wasn't over the shock of Randall's betrayal. (If you could call it that; Kerrie Ann wasn't convinced he'd set out to deceive her.) She wore the same haunted look that Kerrie Ann had when she'd come out of rehab. Kerrie Ann was reminded that she wasn't the only one with problems, and she touched her sister's arm lightly, saying, "Thanks. You're a pretty cool sister, you know that?"

A smile broke across Lindsay's face—the first real smile in days. "Go. I'll get breakfast ready while you finish getting dressed." Lindsay spun her around and gave her a gentle push.

By the time Kerrie Ann was ready, there was no time to eat, with Jeremiah due any minute. But her sister had anticipated that as well because she had the food packed up and ready to go. She thrust a bag into Kerrie Ann's hands. "It's just fruit and muffins, but it should tide you over until lunchtime. I packed enough for Jeremiah, too. Oh, and I found Snuffie—in Chester's dog bed. I'll have him all clean and spiffy by the time Bella gets here."

A wave of gratitude swept over Kerrie Ann, and she felt her throat tighten. "Thanks," she said gruffly, almost missing the old days when nothing short of serious pain could get her to cry. Life had been harder then, but at least she hadn't been forever in danger of puddling up. "Tell Miss Honi when she gets up to dust off that angel collection of hers. I told Bella all about it, and she can't wait to meet the gang."

Her sister smiled. "I have a feeling I won't have to."

The short beep of a car horn in the driveway sent Kerrie Ann racing out the door.

Jeremiah chattered nonstop on the drive, talking about all the fun things they'd do with Bella this weekend and in the months to come. "We could take her to the San Francisco zoo," he said. "Bet she's never seen a live giraffe."

"Of course she's seen a live giraffe," Kerrie Ann replied. "She's been to the zoo before." Did Jeremiah think Bella was still a baby or that she'd been on hold all this time?

"Okay, how about the water park?"

"Wrong time of year." There was still a nip in the air, and she didn't want Bella catching cold.

He shrugged. "I guess we'll have to settle for a movie and popcorn, then, at least for tonight. What's playing at the Rialto?" The Rialto was the lone movie theater in Blue Moon Bay.

"I think it's a Disney picture."

"What do you say?" Jeremiah looked pleased to have come up with a good suggestion.

"I'm sure she'd love it." Though, for all she knew, Bella might have already seen the movie. The thought brought a pang—she had once known everything that went on in Bella's life.

It was eleven fifteen by the time they arrived in Oakview. Kerrie Ann had phoned the caseworker as they were pulling into town, and now her heart leaped at the sight of Bella waiting with Mrs. Silvestre by the entrance to the dental clinic.

"Mommy! Daddy!" Bella came running toward

them, wearing a huge grin that showed the gap where she'd lost another tooth.

Jeremiah's reflexes were quicker than Kerrie Ann's, and he scooped Bella into his arms, swinging her up into the air as easily as if she were a toddler. Bella shrieked with delight while Kerrie Ann looked on with mixed emotions. It didn't seem fair somehow that Jeremiah, after having been a no-show most of Bella's life, should get a free pass. But mainly she was glad that he was back in the picture as well as grateful for the vast capacity for forgiveness that little children seemed to have. From the way Bella acted around him, anyone would think he'd been a constant in her life from day one. The moment she'd laid eyes on him, she'd been smitten. Already she was calling him "Daddy."

Jeremiah lowered Bella to the ground, and then she was dashing over to hug Kerrie Ann. "Mommy!" Her face glowed. "I thought you'd *never* get here. What took you so long?"

"It's a long drive, sweetie," Kerrie Ann reminded her. Holding tightly to Bella, she was gripped by an emotion more powerful than joy. A whole day and night with her little girl, and no one to peer over her shoulder! It was almost too good to be true. Something she'd once taken for granted but which she now saw as a gift.

She was careful to speak politely to Mrs. Silvestre. "I promise to take good care of her," said the newly humbled Kerrie Ann even as the old one ground her teeth at the injustice of having to make such a promise.

Mrs. Silvestre gave her a coolly appraising look. "I'm sure you will," she said. But this time it didn't grate on Kerrie Ann. She knew Mrs. Silvestre was only doing her job.

Then they were on the road again, Bella buckled into the backseat, all cares and woes set aside for the time being. They stopped for lunch at a McDonald's along the way, to the delight of Bella, who had Jeremiah rolling his eyes and making gagging noises at her description of the healthy meals Carol Barthold prepared every night. "I'm not even allowed to have French fries!" she reported. Then she caught herself, adding, "But I like most of the stuff she makes. She's a good cook." Clearly she felt some loyalty toward her foster parents. The realization took some of the buoyancy out of Kerrie Ann's mood, but as much as she wanted to despise the Bartholds, she couldn't work up more than heated indignation. They were taking good care of Bella, which was more than she'd managed to do. How would it look to them that Bella's first meal out with her mommy and daddy was junk food?

But soon she stopped fretting. They were having too much fun. She didn't even mind the umpteen choruses of "Row, row, row your boat" or Bella's endless knock-knock jokes. By the time they arrived back at the house, it felt as if they'd always been a threesome, and at the few stops they made along the way she imagined the people they encountered thinking what a nice family they were.

Lindsay and Miss Honi made a big fuss over Bella. Bella's eyes widened at the sight of the old woman with the bright red lipstick and blue eye shadow. But she took to her at once, content to have Miss Honi hold her hand as they headed inside. And Miss Honi was at her best. When Bella declared, with an air of superiority, after Miss Honi suggested a game of Old Maid before supper, "Old Maid is for babies. I'm *way* too old for that," the old woman merely laughed and said with a wink, "Well, sugar, in that case you'll just have to teach me another game because this old maid only knows a few tricks."

When it was Lindsay's turn, she squatted down so that she was at eye level with Bella, smiling at her warmly. "I want you to think of this as your house, too," she said. "You'll be sleeping in your mom's bed"—Lindsay had volunteered to sleep on the living room sofa tonight so that Kerrie Ann and Bella could be in the same room—"but you'll have your own set of sheets that no one else gets to use. They'll be yours whenever you come to visit. Your mom bought them especially for you. She's been so looking forward to this. We all have. We even made a special supper in your honor—fried chicken."

Bella's eyes lit up. "I *love* fried chicken."

Grant, who was in attendance as well, smiled at her and said, "Me, too. It's my favorite."

"Who are you?" Bella looked up at him curiously.

Grant glanced uncertainly at Lindsay, as if not quite sure what his role was, before answering, "You can call me Uncle Grant."

"I didn't know I had an uncle," Bella said.

"You didn't know you had an aunt, either," put in Lindsay. "But we've heard so much about you, and we're *so* happy to meet you!"

"Amen to that!" declared Miss Honi.

They all trooped into the house. Miss Honi unearthed a game of Boggle from one of the storage cupboards—a relic from Lindsay's girlhood—and enlisted Grant, Jeremiah, and Bella to play while Lindsay and Kerrie Ann got supper on the table. After much hooting and hollering and wild accusations of cheating, Bella emerged the winner.

"I'm afraid you had an unfair advantage, young lady," said Grant, pulling a serious face that didn't mask the twinkle in his eye. "Being as you're so much smarter than the rest of us."

"I am?" Bella regarded him just as seriously.

" 'Course you are, sugar," said Miss Honi. "Folks don't get smarter with age; they just get their heads crammed full of more stuff."

Kerrie Ann laughed. "What Miss Honi is trying

to say, sweetie, is that being a grown-up isn't all it's cracked up to be."

"Speak for yourself," sniffed Miss Honi. "I'm living proof that a few wrinkles don't mean you have to hang it up. Even us older gals know how to kick up our heels."

Bella, in a floral-patterned smock dress that tied in back, ruffled socks, and white patent-leather shoes, studied Miss Honi for a long moment, her lips pursed, before pronouncing, "*I* want to be like *you* when I grow up. I didn't know grandmas got to wear sparkles and stuff."

Everyone roared with laughter, Miss Honi loudest of all.

Bella was beaming when they all sat down to supper, and throughout the meal, the smile never left her face. She ate everything on her plate and seemed to revel in being part of such a large group, one that included Chester and the cats, to whom she kept sneaking scraps when she thought no one was looking. Kerrie Ann hadn't seen her look this happy since before . . .

She pushed away the thought. Things were going to be different from now on.

"So there I was, standing knee-deep in mud, looking at a dead alligator, of all things . . ."

Grant was telling a story about the time he'd traveled to a swamp in the Florida Keys to investigate an alleged case of toxic-waste dumping. Kerrie Ann tuned out the rest. Dinner hadn't set too well with her, and she was feeling queasy. All the excitement of the day, coupled with a lack of sleep, must be catching up with her. Or perhaps she was coming down with something. She couldn't even look at dessert, a vanilla cake with fudge icing. She excused herself from the table, barely making it to the bathroom before puking up the contents of her stomach. Afterward she staggered into her room and fell onto the bed with a moan.

Of all the times to get sick! If there were any way she could have dragged herself through the rest of the evening, she'd have done so, but she couldn't so much as sit up without her stomach threatening to capsize.

Miss Honi fussed over her, and Lindsay fetched her some Alka-Seltzer while the men kept Bella occupied in the next room. Kerrie Ann closed her eyes and drifted off to sleep. When she awoke, Jeremiah was standing over her. "You don't look too good," he said, peering at her with concern. "Why don't I take Bella to the movie while you get some rest?"

"But . . ." She started to sit up, and he gently pushed her back down.

"It's just for a couple of hours. We'll be back before you know it."

She felt a feather-brush of unease, but she didn't want to disappoint her daughter. It might be better if Bella weren't around her right now; whatever she had might be catching. Besides, what could go wrong? "You'll come straight home as soon as the movie's out?"

"You bet," he said.

She groaned, rolling away from him. She had so looked forward to this visit! *It doesn't matter what I do*, she thought, *the deck is always stacked against me.*

She drifted back to sleep, and this time it was the sleep of the dead. Hours later, when she was woken by a not-so-gentle shake, it was as if she were being dredged up from the bottom of a pond. She pried open her eyelids to find her sister standing over her, wearing a worried look. The room was dark except for the light spilling in from the hallway. Kerrie Ann's head felt as if it were stuffed with cotton balls, and her mouth tasted like something had crawled down her throat and died. "What time is it?" she muttered groggily.

"Almost eleven," Lindsay informed her.

"Where's Bella?"

"They're not back yet."

Kerrie Ann quickly calculated that it had been more than two hours since the movie had let out. She felt a pulse of alarm as she struggled into an upright position. "Did you try Jeremiah's cell?"

"At least a dozen times. I keep getting his voice mail."

"He must've forgotten to recharge it."

"Even so, you'd think he could've gotten to a phone by now."

"Maybe his car broke down." She didn't want to think about what else might be keeping him.

"I checked with the highway patrol. Nothing's been reported." Lindsay sank down on the mattress. "I didn't want to worry you. I know you're not feeling well. But frankly, *I'm* worried."

Kerrie Ann was worried as well, but some of the old obstinance kicked in nonetheless. "Why? Don't you trust Jeremiah?"

Lindsay gave her a searching look. "Do *you*?"

Kerrie Ann's first impulse was to defend him. Would she have sent her daughter off with a man she didn't trust, even if he was her father? Of course not. She *did* trust Jeremiah . . . or at least she had until now. At the moment, she didn't know what to think.

The alarm now clanging in her head sent her lurching off the bed. For a minute she thought she might throw up again, but she fought back the waves of nausea. She couldn't afford to be sick right now.

She reached for the phone, punching in Jeremiah's number, but, like Lindsay, all she got was his voice mail. "Damn!" She turned to Lindsay. "Can I borrow your car?" If nothing else, she could cruise the streets looking for them. Jeremiah's pimpmobile would be hard to miss.

"You're in no shape to be driving," Lindsay told her. "*I'll* go."

"No! She's my kid. *I'm* the one who let her go

off with that . . . that fuckup." She felt a sudden surge of anger toward Jeremiah. He might have a perfectly good excuse for the delay, but couldn't he at least have made sure his cell phone battery was charged?

"All right. We'll both go," Lindsay said, seeing that Kerrie Ann wasn't going to back down.

Kerrie Ann grabbed her jacket and cell phone and met Lindsay at the door. Grant had long since gone home. Only Miss Honi was there to see them off. The old woman stood in the entryway, in her pink dressing gown and hairnet, her lined face etched with concern. "Call if there's any news," she said as they raced out the door.

Soon the sisters were cruising the streets downtown in Lindsay's Volvo. At the Rialto, they asked the elderly ticket taker if he'd seen a man and a little girl who fitted Jeremiah's and Bella's descriptions. He hadn't.

Heading back to the highway, they drove south all the way to Davenport before turning back. The only abandoned vehicle they spotted along the way was a pickup truck with a blown tire down by Lighthouse Point. Nowhere did they spy Jeremiah's white Caddie.

Lindsay phoned the police as soon as they got back to the house, this time to report a missing child. By the time the cops arrived, Kerrie Ann was barely keeping it together.

"Ma'am, do you have reason believe your

daughter might've been kidnapped?" inquired the older of the two cops, a Hispanic man with a coal-black mustache and cropped gray hair.

Kerrie Ann shook her head, fighting back the waves of nausea rolling through her. She must have looked unsure because he exchanged a glance with his partner, a younger, skinnier guy with longish hair.

"So to the best of your knowledge, your husband—excuse me, ex-boyfriend—wasn't unhappy with whatever custody arrangements you two have?" asked the skinny cop.

"No." She wondered if she ought to inform them that she had no more legal rights than Jeremiah at this point but decided that would only complicate matters. "He . . . he had some personal problems, but he was getting his life together. Things were going good."

Lindsay put it more bluntly. "What she's trying to say is that he's a recovering addict."

Kerrie Ann gave her a sharp look, but Lindsay didn't flinch. *This is too important to mess around*, her eyes communicated. And she was right, of course.

The officers' expressions became even more grave, and they exchanged another look. The older cop scribbled something in his notepad. "That's helpful to know," he said.

"I don't think he—" Kerrie Ann started to say she didn't think Jeremiah was using again but quickly shut her mouth. She knew better than anyone how insidious the disease was, how it could fool you into thinking everything was fine when it wasn't. Could she truly vouch for him? The other night, when he'd talked her out of going to the meeting, she'd wondered if he was headed for a fall. They warned about it in the program: the tendency to think the worst was behind you once you were over the hump. Sometimes that was all it took.

"We'll let you know as soon as we hear anything," said the older cop as they were getting ready to leave. He gave Kerrie Ann a clumsy pat on the shoulder. "You'll get your little girl back, don't worry. Nine times out of ten, they turn up before we can even put out an Amber Alert."

Kerrie Ann wished she felt as confident. But she nodded, even mustering a tiny smile. She didn't want the cops to see her as some sort of hysteric. It might lead to more questions, ones for which there was no good answer. It wasn't until she'd closed the door behind them that she collapsed into her sister's arms, clutching her as she sobbed her heart out.

Ollie usually went to bed as soon he was finished with the night's baking. But tonight he was restless, so he switched on the TV in the living room instead. It was past midnight, and his parents had long since retired for the night; even so, he kept the volume down. His dad could snooze through a category 5 hurricane, but his mother was a light sleeper—the legacy of all those kids. Besides, there was nothing on that interested him; it was just something to keep him occupied. Otherwise he'd lie awake all night thinking about Kerrie Ann.

He flipped on the local all-night news channel with its reports of murder and mayhem, and storms brewing offshore—the perfect match for his present mood. His eyelids were growing heavy when he saw something that jolted him awake: an Amber Alert for a six-year-old girl with last name of McAllister. A photo of a dark-haired, dusky-skinned little girl flashed across the screen. He recognized her at once: Kerrie Ann's kid.

He stared in disbelief at the TV screen as the newscaster rattled on, "Last seen wearing . . . if you have any information . . ." He was aware of a tingling in his hands and feet, like some sort of itch. He felt an urge to do something—anything. But what? Nothing would be accomplished by going over to Lindsay's house. He'd only be in the way.

He switched off the TV and bolted upstairs to his room. He found what he was looking for on the Channel 4 web site: the same photo that had been shown on TV, along with all the pertinent information. Presumably Kerrie Ann's little girl was with her father, though it was unclear whether they were simply missing or if it was a kidnapping. There was a photo of Jeremiah as well, culled from some police file along with a record of his arrests through the years on various drug charges. Ollie felt a flash of anger. How could Kerrie Ann have chosen that loser over *him*? Not just a loser—a criminal. Possibly even a kidnapper.

He thought hard, his normally expressive face set in grim lines, his hands, knotted into fists, planted at either end of his keyboard like a pair of stone lions flanking the entrance to a castle keep. Gradually his face relaxed as an idea came to him.

He was getting up to throw on his jacket when he happened to glance at the digital time readout on his computer screen: five past one. He hesitated, then thought, *To hell with it*. As he made his way down the stairs, he heard a creaking noise on the landing above. He looked up as his mother stepped into the light, tying the sash on her robe and blinking at him sleepily.

"Ollie, is that you?"

"It's okay, Mom," he called up to her softly.

She moved closer to the banister, peering down at him, her sleep-blurred face growing alert when she noticed that he was wearing his jacket. "Where on earth are you going at this hour?"

He flashed her a mirthless grin. "Dragon hunting," he said.

Kerrie Ann paced by the phone, snatching up the handset every so often just to be reassured by the dial tone that it was still in working order. "Why is it taking so long?" she cried. "Shouldn't they have found her by now?"

"It's only been a couple of hours." Lindsay was curled on the sofa with her head resting on the throw pillows, but she looked tense, her face pale with dark circles under her eyes.

"Reminds me of the time you wandered off," piped up Miss Honi from the easy chair by the fireplace. "Your sister and me, we was tearing our hair out looking for you. Mercy, what a scare! And all that time there you was, sound asleep, curled up like a kitten in the back of a pickup truck."

Kerrie Ann knew she was only trying to put a hopeful spin on the situation, but it had the opposite effect. "Maybe I should've stayed lost," she muttered darkly. "None of this would be happening now."

Miss Honi, seeing that she was getting nowhere, rose to her feet with a sigh. "Why don't I make another pot of coffee?"

Kerrie Ann silently cursed Jeremiah. She'd run out of excuses for him, and a white-hot rage had settled in, fueled mainly by anger at herself for trusting him. What had she been thinking? Had she been thinking at all? Even if Bella was returned safe and sound, what were Kerrie Ann's chances of regaining custody after a fuckup of this dimension?

Her thoughts drifted to Ollie. Kind, decent Ollie,

who'd made her feel special and encouraged her to believe she could accomplish anything she set her mind to. She recalled how he'd calmed her fears the last time she'd felt in danger of losing her daughter and the infinite tenderness with which he'd held her. She clung to that memory as to a life preserver while she reached for the phone to make the call she'd been putting off. "Hello?" she said when a sleepy voice came on the line. "George, it's me, Kerrie Ann . . ."

The area known as the Flats had gotten its name from the long-abandoned railroad that ran through it like a stuck zipper; in the old days, before the highway had made the railroad obsolete, flats of transported goods had been regularly offloaded from the trains that had been the lifeblood of the community. Nowadays it was the closest Blue Moon Bay had to a slum, with its rundown houses and vacant lots, stray animals and motley assortment of stray humans.

Ollie couldn't recall the name of the street he was looking for, but after circling through the neighborhood, he came across a familiar-looking cul-de-sac that butted up against the old train yard. He cruised along slowly, his headlights washing over rows of small, flat-roofed houses in various stages of disrepair before he pulled up in front of the one at the end.

Moments later he was picking his way over the

uneven concrete path to the door, wondering if this might be the stupidest idea he'd ever had. Who knew if the guy even still lived here? It had been nine years since Ollie had last paid a visit to this address, and it hadn't been to form a lasting friendship. He knocked on the door with a sour feeling in his gut, reminded of a period in his life he'd just as soon forget. When after several minutes no one answered, he almost gave up and walked away. Only the thought of Kerrie Ann and her missing kid kept him hammering away until finally the porch light snapped on and a gruff male voice barked from inside, "What the *fuck*?"

There was the rattle of a door chain, followed by the door easing open a crack. A gimlet eye set in a grizzled face, which didn't look too happy at the moment, peered through the opening. "Do you know what time it is?" the guy growled. "It's two the fuck o'clock in the morning!"

"Sorry, man, but it couldn't wait. It's, um, kind of an emergency."

"What the—hey, don't I know you?" The eye peering out at him narrowed.

Ollie hadn't expected the dealer to recognize him after so long. He himself had only a dim recollection of that time—probably because he'd been stoned during most of it. "It's been a while," he answered cautiously, deciding the less said, the better.

The man's expression relaxed. "No shit. So what is it, kid? You running low on stash?"

"Nah. I'm looking for someone—guy by the name of Jeremiah. I wondered if you knew where I might find him. Light-skinned black, thirtyish, dark hair, brown eyes."

"The name don't ring a bell. But I see a lot of people. I can't keep track of them all."

"There's a missing kid involved."

That did the trick. The chain rattled, and the door swung open to reveal a middle-aged man with a pot belly and gray hair in a ponytail. Oddly, he appeared unchanged since Ollie's last visit, maybe because he'd seemed old to Ollie back then. "What d'you want from me? I told you, I don't know nothing." The dealer's voice took on a wheedling edge.

"Can I come in?" Ollie asked, and after a moment the man stepped aside to let him in. As soon as Ollie entered, the stinky-sweet smell of marijuana brought back a wave of unpleasant memories. Well, this wouldn't take long. "If you turn on the news, you'll see what I'm talking about," he said, gesturing toward the forty-inch flat-screen TV on the wall, an incongruous touch amid the ratty furnishings and scattered belongings.

The dealer didn't budge. "I'll take your word for it."

"The guy I'm looking for, the cops think he might've had something to do with it."

"Yeah? And what's that got to do with *me*?"

"Where would a guy like that go if he was looking to score crack?"

The dealer recoiled, throwing up his hands. "Hey, I don't deal in the hard stuff. That's ten to twenty, easy. Even if it's your first offense."

"But you know who does."

"Maybe." The man hesitated just long enough for Ollie to know he was on to something. "There's a guy, lives over in that new development—Heritage Acres? Heritage Oaks?—on Foothill Drive. Don't know him personally, but word gets around. He's new in town from what I'm told. Some of my customers, that's where they go when they're looking to expand their portfolio, if you know what I mean."

"You wouldn't happen to have an address?"

Ollie expected the dealer to scoff, but instead he disappeared into the next room, reappearing a minute or so later with a scrap of paper on which an address and phone number were scribbled. He thrust it at Ollie. "It's all I've got. Now, will you clear out so I can get some shuteye?"

It was supposed to be just a quick stop along the way, no different from ducking into a 7-Eleven for a six-pack, Jeremiah reasoned. He wouldn't leave her waiting in the car any longer than five minutes, tops. And it was a quiet residential street—the last place you'd expect to find your friendly neighborhood drug dealer—so she'd be safe. No harm done, and no one the wiser.

Only it didn't quite work out that way.

For starters, Bella put up some resistance.

"You're not supposed to leave little kids alone in cars. George and Carol said so," she scolded, sounding like a little adult—a pissed-off little adult—as she sat in the passenger seat scowling at him with her arms crossed over her chest.

"I won't be long," he told her.

"Why can't I come with you?"

"I told you, I'll only be a sec."

"It's dark. What if I get scared?" Her lower lip began to quiver.

Jeremiah felt himself growing annoyed. He wasn't used to being around little kids, and after the long car trip followed by dinner and a movie, the shiny-new-toy aspect of it was beginning to wear thin. Couldn't she cut him a break on this one small thing? "There's nothing to be scared of, baby," he told her, struggling to contain his impatience. "Anyway, like I said, I'll be back before you know it. So be good for Daddy, okay? Just this once? I promise I'll make it up to you."

Jeremiah knew what he was doing was wrong. Not just leaving his kid alone in the car but bringing her here in the first place. Kerrie Ann would skin him alive if she were to find out. He wouldn't have come if he weren't in serious need. Anyway, it was just this one time, he told himself. Okay, twice if you included last week's visit. And he could quit anytime. It wasn't like he was hooked or anything. Not like before. He'd never let it get that bad again.

Before his daughter could guilt-trip him any more, he jumped out of the car. "Stay put! I'll be right back!" he called to her as he jogged up the path.

The house was in a brand-new subdivision and resembled all the other cookie-cutter houses on the block—ranch-style with a stucco exterior and a newly seeded lawn into which half-a-dozen poplar saplings were stuck like birthday candles in a green-frosted cake. On the front door was a kitschy ceramic plaque with the name "Tucker" painted on it in flowery script. He smiled to himself, thinking that if any of the folks around here were told their neighbor was up to no good, they wouldn't imagine it to be anything worse than an illicitly hooked-up cable line.

He rang the bell, then waited on the stoop for what seemed an eternity, hands jammed into the pockets of his windbreaker as he jigged from side to side, whistling tunelessly under his breath. Finally the door opened, and he was greeted by a slender blond man in his late twenties who looked clean-cut enough to pass for the engineering consultant he billed himself as in order to allay suspicion about the high volume of traffic in and out of his house.

"Jeremy, right?" He stuck out his hand.

"It's Jeremiah."

"Either way, you're in the right place. Come on in. The party's just getting started." The man

Jeremiah knew only as Tucker broke into a grin. As Jeremiah was ushered inside, he could see that he wasn't the only visitor. Several other people were gathered in the tidy if somewhat spare living room. Tucker didn't bother with introductions, and no one seemed to notice or care. The rules of etiquette were different in places like this.

Jeremiah recognized one guy, though. Dan something. They knew each other from the meetings they both attended. It was only last week that Dan, a former corporate attorney whose career had gone up his nose, had shared at one of those meetings. But he showed no embarrassment at being seen sucking on a crack pipe—he was too far gone. He gave Jeremiah a friendly nod, as though they were just a couple of frat brothers running into each other at a campus function. When Jeremiah wandered over, Dan offered him the pipe.

"Go ahead. It's on me."

Jeremiah was sorely tempted but resisted. "Better not. My kid's waiting in the car."

No one raised an eyebrow. Dan merely shrugged and said, "Suit yourself."

Jeremiah looked at Tucker. "Seriously. I should get going." He dug into the pocket of his jeans and pulled out a wad of bills, the bulk of his last paycheck, holding it. "It's all here."

Tucker ignored the money. "What's your hurry? You just got here." He clapped a hand on Jeremiah's shoulder.

"Like I said, I got my—"

"Yeah, I heard you the first time. But see, here's the thing, I like to get to know my clients. Builds trust. And what's a business without loyalty, huh? For instance, how do I know you're not an undercover cop?" Tucker chuckled as if it were a joke, but his smile took on a less benevolent cast as he stood kneading Jeremiah's shoulder with enough pressure to make it just shy of painful.

Jeremiah gave a nervous laugh. "Come on. You know me."

Tucker appraised him coolly. "Do I?"

The last time Jeremiah had come with a buddy from work, one of Tucker's regulars, and there had been no screwing around. Now, desperate to be on his way, he thrust the money at Tucker one more time. "Look, I really have to get going. So can I have the stuff?" The clean-cut young man eyed the wad of bills with distaste, as if this were a tony club where it was considered bad form for cash to exchange hands. Jeremiah remembered too late that deals were done in the back room. Privately.

He felt an elbow nudging him in the ribs and turned to find Dan standing next to him, his doughy face flushed and his pupils so dilated that his pale blue eyes looked black. He thrust the pipe at Jeremiah once more. "Go on. What's it going hurt?" he urged in the voice of someone who'd come face-to-face with his own personal demons and decided they weren't such bad guys after all.

With Tucker's hard-eyed gaze on him and the stem of the pipe just inches away, Jeremiah closed his mind against the thought of his daughter sitting all alone out in his car and took a long, sweet hit.

Ollie cruised the streets of Heritage Oaks. It was one of the newer subdivisions, just east of Blue Moon Bay in the foothills of the Santa Cruz mountains, and all the houses looked exactly alike in the dark—the same facades, the same newly seeded lawns and spindly trees. He crawled along at a speed that would have made his ninety-year-old grandma seem reckless by comparison, peering out the window, trying to make out street signs. Even the streets were indistinguishable from one another, and for some reason, maybe because of the vaguely Italianate architecture, they were all named after various Italian cities and towns—Porto Fino, Ravello, Montenegro, Positano. Quaint, he thought. But where the hell was Florence Court?

It wasn't the sort of neighborhood where he would've expected to find a drug dealer. On the other hand, thought Ollie, if the dude was looking to hide in plain sight, what better place? Who would ever imagine a police raid on one of these quiet streets? Probably not even the cops themselves. In fact, Ollie was beginning to wonder if he was even in the right place.

He finally spotted the street sign for Florence

Court. His pulse quickened as he turned onto it. He found the address he was looking for, where several cars were parked out front, one of them an older-model white Caddie. Minutes later he was standing on the front stoop of a pinkish stucco house tricked out with decorative wrought iron, staring into a pair of cold blue eyes. The clean-cut man summoned by his knock was wide awake and fully dressed in cords and a light blue pullover. He might have been on his way to work.

"I'm looking for Jeremiah," Ollie told him.

"Sorry, you have the wrong address." The man started to close the door on him, but before Ollie knew it, his right foot, shod in a bright orange Converse sneaker, shot out to wedge itself in the door frame.

"I don't think so. In fact, that looks a lot like his car." Ollie pointed out the Caddie, which matched the description in the police bulletin. He knew that physically he was no match for the buff-looking man, so he used the only weapon at his disposal: his talent for running off at the mouth. "I mean like, dude, how many guys you know with a set of wheels like that? It kinda sets you apart from the pack, don't you think? Now, a guy like that, I'd say he's not your average dude. Like, he's probably into all kinds of shit that a guy who drives, say, a Volvo station wagon wouldn't be. Maybe even some illegal shit." He rolled his shoulders in an elaborate shrug. "Of course if you don't want to help a brother out, no problemo. You can always tell it to the cops. They should be here in, oh . . ." He pushed back the sleeve of his jacket to peer at his watch . . . "about three minutes."

He turned as if to go, and the man lunged forward to grab hold of his arm, jerking him back so hard Ollie nearly lost his balance. "You little shit. You're lying—you didn't call the cops."

Ollie pried his arm free, rubbing at the spot where it had begun to throb. "I guess that's for me to know and you to find out." He spoke calmly, but his heart was racing and he'd broken into a light sweat. *Get a grip, dude*, he commanded himself. *This is no time to be a wuss*.

"You don't know *shit*," snarled the man, who suddenly didn't look the part of Respectable Suburban Dude anymore. "In fact, if you don't get the hell off my property, I'll call the cops on *you*." It was a bluff. Ollie had seen the look of panic that had crossed his face.

Suburban Dude retreated into the house, slamming the door behind him. *Now what?* Ollie wondered as he stood shivering on the stoop, shifting his weight from one foot to the other in an effort to stay warm and wishing he'd thought to throw on something heavier than his Polarfleece jacket. *I believe this would be the time to stop screwing around and bring in the cops for real*, answered the cool voice of reason in his head. Ollie was pulling his cell phone from his pocket to do just that when the front door burst open and someone came hurtling out, helped along by a shove from the rear: a handsome, light-skinned black man with curly dark hair, wearing jeans and a faded navy T-shirt under an open, long-sleeved shirt: Kerrie Ann's ex. Ollie recognized him from his mug shot.

So violent was the shove that Jeremiah would have been sent sprawling if he hadn't fallen against Ollie, who grabbed hold of him to keep from losing his own balance. The door slammed shut again, and Ollie was left staring into the face of someone so whacked-out he probably didn't even know what universe he was in. Glassy, unseeing eyes stared back at him, so dilated it was like looking into the mouth of a tunnel. The arms he was gripping twitched spasmodically, as if he were holding a live wire.

Ollie gave him a little shake. "Dude. Where's your kid?"

Jeremiah blinked at him and drew back. "My kid?" He looked as if he'd forgotten he even had a kid, his face furrowed in the yellow glow of the porch light. Then faint comprehension dawned. "Bella, you mean. She's fine. I left her in the car."

"How long ago was that?"

"Dunno . . . few minutes maybe."

"Try a few hours," Ollie growled.

Jeremiah brought his hand up to peer at his watch, the old-fashioned wind-up kind with a braided leather strap so old it seemed fused with his wrist. He frowned. "Shit. That can't be right."

Ollie spun around, racing across the lawn to the Caddie. But when he wrenched open the door and peered in, there was no sign of Bella. She must have gotten tired of waiting and gone in search of her dad. She would have knocked on the door of the house first, to no avail. Ollie felt sick at the thought of the defenseless child standing on the stoop, begging to be let in, only to be shooed away. Where would she have headed next? Would she have tried walking back to Lindsay's? If so, she could be wandering the streets right now, lost. Ollie started to panic before remembering that it was a safe neighborhood with very little traffic at this hour. Also, how far could a six-year-old get on foot?

He straightened and swung around to find himself confronted by Jeremiah, who cried, "Hey, that's my car, man! What the fuck you think you're doing? Do I even *know* you?"

Ollie grabbed him by the front of his shirt, handfuls of checked blue fabric blooming from each fist like flowers pulled from a magician's hat. "Dude. Don't you get it? *Your kid is missing.*"

"Fuck." Full comprehension sank in, and Jeremiah stared back at him. He looked like a cornered rabbit, twitching all over, with his eyes bugging out of his head. But the seriousness of the situation must have overridden the high he was on because he said in a more lucid-sounding, if decidedly panicked voice, "So we'll find her, right? She's gotta be around here somewhere." He flicked Ollie a nervous look. "You're not gonna call the cops, are you?"

"We'll worry about that later. Come on." Ollie released him and started toward the Willys at a brisk jog. It would have made sense for Jeremiah to take his car as well, so as to cover more ground, but that didn't seem like the wisest move right now. And this way Ollie could keep Jeremiah from bolting until the police got here. He'd alert them as soon as he'd done a quick search of the vicinity. Bella couldn't have gone far, he told himself again.

Kerrie Ann wondered if she was dreaming. Incredibly, she'd managed to nod off while curled in the chair by the window, and when roused by the sound of a vehicle noisily rattling its way down the drive, it seemed at first to be happening in her dream. Then her eyes flew open, and she jerked upright. She felt momentarily disoriented, like in the old days, after a night of partying, waking in an unfamiliar place not knowing how she'd gotten there. But confusion quickly gave way to a thud of recollection: Her daughter was missing. That was why she was sitting here in the clothes she'd been wearing the night before, the phone clutched in her hand.

She struggled to her feet, wincing as her cramped muscles released their knots. Her sister had fallen asleep, too, and in the kitchen she could hear the tap running—Miss Honi making another pot of coffee, no doubt. Outside, the rattle of the approaching vehicle grew louder. Kerrie Ann ran to the door and jerked it open, darting out without bothering to slip on her shoes. In the darkness, the twin beams of headlights jounced their way down the rutted drive. Then the vehicle swung into view, and she saw that it was Ollie's Willys.

She felt a quick, hot burst of disappointment: not the police with her daughter. But her disappointment quickly gave way to a kind of relief. Ollie would make it better. He would help her through this. In that moment, as she stood there with her stomach seesawing and her arms wrapped around herself to keep from shivering, she couldn't think why she'd dumped him. He was the best guy she'd ever known. Maybe *too* good. Maybe the reason she'd chosen Jeremiah instead was because she'd felt she didn't deserve any better.

She ran to meet the Willys as it lurched to a stop. Watching Ollie clamber out from behind the wheel, she realized he wasn't alone. Someone was buckled into the passenger seat beside him—a small, droopy-headed figure. Kerrie Ann let out a choked cry. Could it be? . . . Then she saw that it was and let out a cry of joy, her heart taking flight.

"Bella!" She darted forward, mindless of the sharp bits of gravel digging into the soles of her feet. She was at her daughter's side within moments of Ollie's hoisting her from her seat, and then Bella was in her arms and the two were hugging each other while they both sobbed.

At last she turned to Ollie, managing to choke out, "Where on earth did you find her?"

"Asleep on somebody's front lawn. She'd gone looking for help and gotten lost." Ollie looked a little shaken himself, as if thinking of how close they'd come to a very different outcome.

"Oh, God." Kerrie Ann clutched her daughter more tightly to her.

"I saw on the news that she was missing. I thought I might as well join the search party."

"But how did you know where to look for her?"

"I didn't. Not at first. But I asked around, and that's what led me to your ex-boyfriend. He's fine, too, by the way, in case you're wondering. I dropped him off at the police station on my way."

"I don't give a shit about Jeremiah. He can rot in hell for all I care," replied Kerrie Ann through gritted teeth.

Ollie was glad to hear that she felt that way, though he was quick to inform her, "Not that it's any excuse, but I don't think he knew what he was doing. He was pretty high."

"Figures," she muttered.

The whole story came out once they were inside and Bella was tucked in bed. While the four adults sat drinking coffee in the living room, Ollie told how he'd tracked down Jeremiah's dealer. He played down his role, feeling a bit ashamed of his old connection, from the days when he'd been a druggie, too. The only thing that separated him from a guy like Jeremiah was that he wasn't a born addict. And it truly had been a lucky break, finding Bella on the lawn of a house not more than half a mile from the dealer's. Luckily, too, the sergeant on duty at the police station was an old friend of his family, so Ollie had been given the okay to bring Bella straight home.

All Kerrie Ann could think of was that, if it hadn't been for Ollie, her daughter might still be out wandering around, alone and scared. She recalled Miss Honi's words about there being an angel on her shoulder. Kerrie Ann now knew who her guardian angel was: She was looking right at him.

"I imagine that fella's neighbors got the surprise of their life when the cops showed up," said Miss Honi of Jeremiah's dealer. "And all that time, them thinking he was just the nice guy next door."

"Thanks to Ollie, it wasn't something worse than a drug bust," said Lindsay. "If he hadn't come along when he did . . ." She wasn't thinking only of what might have happened to Kerrie Ann's little girl; she was remembering the long-ago night when she and Miss Honi had searched frantically for the then three-year-old Kerrie Ann. So much had happened since then, yet they'd come full circle in a way. She could only hope the outcome in this case would be a happier one once all the dust settled.

Color rose in Ollie's cheeks. "It was just a good guess," he said modestly.

"No, it was more than that." Kerrie Ann looked at Ollie with tears in her eyes and said, "You were smart and brave and . . . and I don't know what I would do without you."

Ollie held her gaze as he sat there with his heart beating in slow motion. His present state of consciousness bordered on an out-of-body experience, but at the center of it all was a single clear thought: *She needs me.* He smiled at her. "Lucky for you, you don't have to."

CHAPTER FOURTEEN

𝒥HE FALLOUT WAS as Kerrie Ann had feared. The Bartholds, Mrs. Silvestre, and the state of California all held her personally responsible. Unsupervised visits with Bella were suspended for the foreseeable future, and the Bartholds were so cold to her over the phone whenever she called to speak with her daughter that she'd remarked bitterly to her sister that it was a wonder she didn't have frostbite. Her lawyer had informed her that her position was so shaky right now that the judge, if pressed to make a decision now, would most likely grant custody to the Bartholds. The only thing she had going for her, it seemed, were the once interminable and now welcome delays of due process. She was using the time to redeem herself as best as she could.

Jeremiah had gotten off lightly, all things considered; the Bartholds, bent on punishing Kerrie Ann, hadn't pressed charges against him. He wasn't so lucky where Kerrie Ann was concerned.

"It won't happen again, I swear," he'd pleaded, looking so repentant she'd felt a flicker of pity. Wasn't it the same face she'd so often seen in the mirror after having sworn not to use again, then breaking that vow? But she'd remained firm. "I hope not, for your sake," she'd told him. "But whatever you do, don't do it for me. We're done. And if I have any say in it, you'll never see Bella again."

Meanwhile, Lindsay was doing her best to forget Randall Craig. She hadn't returned any of his phone calls and had deleted all his e-mails, unread. He was history as far as she was concerned. A regrettable chapter in her life from which she'd learned a valuable lesson: Never trust a stranger offering candy. In this case, the candy had been Randall himself. He'd sweetened her up by charming, then seducing her. He'd made her feel desirable and filled her with romantic hopes and dreams best left to the pages of Danielle Steele novels. Even if he hadn't betrayed her, it would have run its course eventually, she told herself.

Maybe not this soon, but soon enough—like a sugar crash.

In contrast, what she had with Grant was solid and real, if not always exciting. He had his faults, sure, but he'd never been less than honest and aboveboard, which was more than she could say about herself. She counted herself fortunate that he'd never suspected anything—even if that was only because he hadn't been paying enough attention to notice. Better to be with someone like her boyfriend than with a charming trickster.

But no amount of rationalizing could change the fact that she missed Randall. She'd known him only a short while, but each moment had been like gold, to be hoarded and treasured in memory. She missed the sound of his voice over the phone. His infectious laugh and the stories he told that were like glittering threads shot through the otherwise muted tapestry of her life. Their spirited discussions about books they'd read, about which they didn't always agree. The way he frequently sought her opinion and always listened when she needed to vent frustration or voice a concern.

What pained her most was knowing that in all likelihood, she'd never again know the kind of passion she had experienced with Randall. Just the one time was all it had taken to awaken her senses and give her a delicious new awareness of her body. It was as though he'd drawn an erotic map to all its hidden recesses and nerve endings, setting a course that, once embarked on, couldn't be reversed. Making love with Grant, she'd often indulge in fantasies about Randall that left her burning with shame afterward. She told herself it was wrong, as well as unfair to Grant, but it was no good; she couldn't seem to keep her mind from straying.

The one bright spot was that business had picked up at the book café. The latest installment in the *Dragon Hunter* series had proved hugely successful and had spurred sales of other titles as well. And with the rise in profits had come a renewed sense of optimism. Cautiously she began to think that the future might not be so bleak after all. With a little bit of luck, she just might be able to hang on until her case was settled without losing either her home or business.

Nonetheless, she was haunted by the very real possibility that it could go up in smoke. Which was likely if Lloyd Heywood got his way. Each time her gaze fell on the check that she hadn't had the heart to either cash or tear up, she felt her stomach clench.

The day before they were due in court, Lindsay had lunch with her lawyer. They met at a small seafood place in Montera, where, over drinks and a shared appetizer of fried calamari, he explained tersely that there was a new wrinkle in the case. "I heard from Mike the other day." Mike Hubbard, a former colleague of Dwight's who now worked as a top-level aide to the governor, was his eyes and ears in Sacramento. "Apparently some new guy— fellow by the name of Curtis Brooks—just took over as head of the Lands Commission. Anyway, Mike has it from a reliable source that Brooks intends to rubberstamp this if the judge rules in the county's favor tomorrow."

Lindsay experienced a small jolt. "Can he do that?" She'd been told it was typically a long process—months, sometimes years if there was a back-lash in the community.

"It may be unorthodox, but it's not illegal. It does, however, suggest that this Brooks has some pretty influential friends."

Lindsay had thought herself immune to panic at this point, but a little alarm bell went off inside her head nonetheless. "Heywood," she said through gritted teeth.

"Most likely." Her lawyer frowned and sipped his drink.

"So what do we do?"

He frowned. "Legally our hands are tied. But it would help if we had some political juice of our own." Dwight nibbled on a piece of calamari, holding it delicately between his thumb and fore-finger. "All we'd need is the backing of one or two legislators."

"How would we go about getting that?"

"By lighting a fire under them." Becoming sud-denly animated, he leaned forward, propping his elbows on the table. "What's the one thing guaranteed to get an elected official motivated? Pressure from voters. We just have to make voters aware of what's going on."

"I thought that's what we were doing." There had been articles in the local press. There was also the piece Randall had planned to write, though that had most likely been scrapped by now. She felt a fresh stab at the memory of that ghastly day when he'd shown his true colors.

"Yes, but I'm talking mass scale. Major city newspapers, TV news, talk radio. Generate enough publicity and suddenly you're a *cause célèbre*. You're in *People* magazine. You're on *Oprah*. Everyone loves a story about the little guy going up against the corporate baddies who're out to screw him . . . or in this case, her. The public will eat it up. Then there won't be any sneaking this through; it'd be too much of a political hot potato." His brown eyes, which matched the conservative brown suit he wore, flickered with excitement.

Listening to him speak, she nodded slowly, taking it in. It seemed pretty far-fetched. What were the chances of her predicament becoming a *cause célèbre?* She'd promoted enough author events to know how hard it was just to get people to come to a book signing. This would be like that, only on a much larger scale. And in the unlikely event that she pulled it off—what then? The thought of being thrust into the public eye filled her with dread. Also, wouldn't it defeat the purpose? The whole point was to be able to enjoy the peace and serenity of her surroundings, which she could hardly do if she were running around the country appearing on TV and speaking to reporters.

"I don't know, Dwight," she said, shaking her head. "Somehow I can't see myself on *Oprah*."

Some of the fire went out of his eyes. "Let's just play it by ear, okay?" he said. "Who knows; maybe it'll go our way tomorrow." He didn't sound too hopeful.

Lindsay managed to hold it together for the rest of the meal. It wasn't until the drive home that she let loose some of her frustration. "Damn it!" she cried, bringing the heel of her hand down on the steering wheel hard enough to bruise it. Why *her*? Why not some other desirable piece of property where a resort could be built? And for that son of a bitch, Lloyd Heywood, to sink so low as to enlist his own son to seduce her into accepting his offer . . . Her eyes filled with helpless tears. It was one of those rare cloudless days, the sky the deep crystalline blue of late summer and the ocean glittering with a billion star points of reflected light, but she couldn't enjoy it. Over the course of lunch, the fledgling optimism of the past few weeks had given way to despair. All she could see was bleakness ahead.

At the first red light, she jammed a CD into the

player, and "Hotel California" came pouring from the speakers. She cranked up the volume, losing herself in its familiar rhythms. For her mother, it had been opera and classical music and for her father, jazz and rhythm and blues, but for her, rocking out to the Eagles . . . or the Grateful Dead . . . or Led Zeppelin was what helped clear her head. She sang along, closing her mind against the clouds gathering on her inner horizon.

Thank God she didn't have to face this alone. She didn't know what she would do without Miss Honi and Kerrie Ann. Lindsay's expectations had been so low during those first rocky weeks with her sister that it had been nothing short of a revelation to watch her blossom over time and become someone she could lean on, as opposed to someone who is always in need. Kerrie Ann worked hard and these days kept a low profile, though her "toned-down" look was still over the top at times. She pitched in around the house and even remembered to pick up after herself most of the time. In studying for her GED, she'd also developed an interest in reading—she'd recently discovered the Judy Blume books, which she couldn't believe she'd missed growing up. And despite her recent setback, she hadn't knuckled under. She'd faced the wrath of the Bartholds, the censure of Bella's caseworker, and the scolding from her own lawyer with an even-temperedness that had amazed Lindsay, given her sister's tendency to fly off the handle. She took full responsibility for allowing Bella to go off with Jeremiah, making no excuses. In short, she'd gone from acting like a bratty teenager to behaving like a grown-up.

There had been a change in her sister's attitude toward Ollie as well. She no longer batted her eyes at him only to leave him trailing in her wake like a lovesick puppy. Now they went on actual dates. Usually nothing more than grabbing a bite to eat after work or renting a DVD that they would watch over at her house. But, though Kerrie Ann continued to insist that they were just friends, Lindsay had seen the way they looked at each other. Regardless, she no longer worried that Kerrie Ann would either corrupt Ollie or crush him under her heel. It wasn't just that her sister had reformed; Ollie had proved himself to be more of a man than she'd given him credit for. If not for his quick thinking and brave actions, the scary episode with Bella might have ended tragically. If he could handle something like that, she didn't doubt he could take care of himself where Kerrie Ann was concerned.

Lindsay was calmer by the time she arrived back at work. She'd dried her tears and put her worries on the back burner. She had no time for dwelling on dire thoughts, with calls to make and customers to attend to, a meeting with her web designer, and flyers to send out for the book event they were hosting the following weekend.

She walked in the door and a voice fluted, "Lindsay!" She looked up to find Darla Humphrey bustling over. Darla, a retired schoolteacher with an inexplicable appetite for horror novels—the scarier the better—was one of her best customers and also among her most loyal supporters. She'd even started a petition to save Lindsay's land. Right now, though, it wasn't a petition she was holding but a magazine, folded open. "Oh, I'm glad I caught you. Do you know about this?" Darla thrust the magazine into Lindsay's hands.

It was the magazine section from the coming Sunday's *Chronicle*. Darla explained that her nephew, who worked at the paper, sent her an advance copy each week. In it was the article that had Darla so excited. The title and byline jumped out at Lindsay: "PARADISE INTERRUPTED, written and photographed by Randall Craig." The accompanying photo was the view of the ocean from her front yard.

Her heart bumped up into her throat as she scanned the opening lines.

This is Steinbeck country. Thirty miles or so south of San Francisco, along Highway 1, between the rocky fist of Devil's Slide and gentle reach of the Monterey Peninsula, lies a stretch of coastline so unspoiled, you have the sense, driving down it, that you're in the Northern California of *Tortilla Flat*.

Development has largely been a dream deferred or a threat unrealized, depending on one's point of view. Vast tracks of farmland still dominate, and the million-dollar ocean views are primarily left to passing motorists and the migrant workers tending those fields to enjoy. The California Coastal Commission makes sure most of it remains unspoiled. But there are unincorporated areas which fall outside the commission's purview. Such as the town of Blue Moon Bay, which has recently become the focal point in an ongoing war between the self-proclaimed prophets of progress and those who worship a more ancient god. At the center of it all stands the unlikely five-foot-six heroine who has become the David in this battle against Goliath. . . .

Lindsay slowly lowered the magazine and stared out the window, lost in thought. She remained that way for several long moments until Darla began to prattle. "Amazing, isn't it? Just the boost we needed. Keep reading; it gets better. I swear it almost seems like the man knows you. I don't mean just to interview you, but like you two were really close. But that's the mark of a good writer, I suppose, making it all seem so . . . well, *personal*."

Lindsay brought her gaze back to Darla. "May I borrow this? I'd like to take it home with me. I'm sure Miss Honi and my sister would love to read it, too."

"Keep it if you like. I can always get another copy," Darla replied, waving a plump arm expansively.

Lindsay took note of the faintly disappointed look she wore—clearly Darla had expected a more enthusiastic response—and gave Darla's hand a squeeze. "Thanks. What matters most, though, is that I have your support. I hope you know how much that means to me."

Darla flushed to the roots of her dyed blond hair. "Oh, well . . . I'm sure I only did what anyone would have," she replied, clearly flustered by the praise. "We're all rooting for you. Where would we be without you? Without this place?" She glanced around her, misty-eyed. "Stores like this are a dying breed." Oblivious to the look of discomfort elicited by her words, she gave Lindsay's arm a reassuring pat before heading back to the horror section.

Lindsay retreated to her office, where she could finish reading the article in private. Tears were rolling down her cheeks by the time she turned the last page. She didn't see how the man who'd written this piece could possibly be the same one who'd knifed her in the back. Struggling to make sense of it, she dropped her head into her hands. When she looked up, Kerrie Ann was standing at the desk.

"I brought you your mail." Her sister paused as she dropped the batch of letters on the desk, her eyes on Lindsay. "Hey, are you okay? You look like you've been crying."

"I'm fine." Lindsay spoke more brusquely than she'd intended.

"What? I'm the only one around here who gets to be a train wreck?"

"I didn't say that."

"You didn't have to." Kerrie Ann gave a sanguine shrug and scooted her backside onto the desk, where she sat perched as if at a tailgate party. "But hey, at least I know my life's a mess."

"I don't know if you've noticed, but you're not such a mess anymore," Lindsay observed with a wry glance at the relatively conservative outfit her sister had on—long skirt, knee-high black boots (a pair of Lindsay's), and a jeans jacket over a plain light blue camisole. "You don't even look like the same person. Four months ago, you wouldn't have been caught dead in that outfit."

"That's supposed to be a compliment?"

"Yes. Proof that you don't need tight clothes and gobs of makeup to show how pretty you are."

Kerrie Ann gave a snort, but she looked pleased. "Tell that to Miss Honi."

"That's different. Miss Honi's an entity unto herself."

"There you go again, throwing big words around. Oh, don't look at me like that; I know what it means. I read, too, you know." Kerrie Ann was only teasing, but Lindsay didn't miss the pride in her voice.

"All I meant was, you look great," she said.

Kerrie Ann flashed her a smile that quickly gave way to a more sober expression. "Yeah, well, looks aren't everything. I still have to prove to the judge that I'm not as hopeless as everyone thinks."

"I don't think you're hopeless."

"That's different. You're family."

Lindsay warmed at her use of the word "family." "Why not ask Ollie's opinion, then?" she suggested, hoping to feel her out a bit on the subject of Ollie, about which Kerrie Ann had been uncharacteristically closemouthed.

"I don't have to. You know Ollie; he never shuts up." Kerrie Ann's tone was light, but there was no mistaking the blush that crept into her cheeks. As if seeking a distraction, she seized upon the magazine folded open on the desk. "Hey, this must be the article Mrs. Humphrey was telling me about. Cool. I can't believe your boyfriend wrote it."

Lindsay was quick to correct her. "He's not my boyfriend."

"Whatever." Kerrie Ann eyed her thoughtfully before continuing, "Doesn't it make you wonder if maybe you were a little hard on him?" She brandished the article bearing Randall's byline. "I mean, he's obviously knocking himself out to get back into your good graces. How can you ignore that?"

"Easily." Lindsay moved to snatch the magazine from her sister's hand, but Kerrie Ann, grinning, held it out of reach. After several more attempts, Lindsay surrendered with good grace and plopped into the chair at her desk. "Look," she said, "I appreciate that he's trying to help, but it's too late—as far as he's concerned, anyway. I don't see how I could ever trust him again."

"It's not like he cheated on you," Kerrie Ann reasoned.

"In some ways, it's worse. He kept something from me that would've changed everything if I'd known."

"Maybe that's why he didn't tell you." Kerrie Ann slid off the desk, dropping the magazine into Lindsay's lap. "Honestly, Linds, for a smart person you can be really dense sometimes. The guy's obviously crazy about you, and people in love do all kinds of dumb things. It kinda goes with the territory, you know? Don't tell me you've never done anything stupid in the name of love."

"I haven't, actually," said Lindsay. The stupidest thing that came to mind was sending a Valentine's Day card to Billy Jarvis in the fourth grade, knowing he'd tease her mercilessly—which he had.

Kerrie stood, hands on hips, regarding her the way a teacher might a particularly slow-witted pupil. "Maybe that's 'cause you were never in love before this. Anyway, speaking of stupid, what do you call blowing off the perfect guy just 'cause he turned out to be not so perfect?"

"I don't know. What?" Lindsay replied glumly.

"Hello! I call it insanity after all the shit I've had pulled on me by guys not half as decent as Randall. Like, oh, I don't know, my ex-boyfriend, for instance." She refused to even speak Jeremiah's name. "But hey, suit yourself. It's your life . . . or should I say funeral."

Kerrie Ann left her with that thought as she sashayed out the door.

Lindsay somehow managed to make it through the rest of the day. By closing time, she was exhausted, not so much from work as from the effort to appear calm and collected on the surface with her mind in a muddle and her emotions all over the map. Ollie must have noticed she wasn't herself because he came over to her as she was closing out the register, handing her a cup of espresso. "Here," he said. "You look like you could use a shot."

"More like a shot of whiskey. But thanks," she said, downing it in a single gulp.

"De nada." He lingered as if something were on his mind. Finally he said, "Listen, we were wondering—Kerrie Ann and me, that is. Would it be okay if we took some time off tomorrow?"

She banged the register shut. "Tomorrow's not a

good day. I have to be in court, so we'll be short-handed as it is."

"Yeah, I know. That's why I'm asking. We thought you could use a little support from the home team."

Lindsay was quick to apologize. "I'm sorry, I didn't mean to snap at you. That's a really sweet thought, Ollie."

He leveled his gaze at Lindsay. "You don't always have to handle everything yourself, you know. In case you haven't noticed, we've got your back." As if to prove it, he took the empty espresso cup from her hand, saying, "One more for the road?"

Lindsay recognized the truth in his words. She *was* used to doing everything herself—a holdover from childhood—and thus she tended to forget at times that she wasn't alone. "I don't need any more coffee," she told him, "but I gratefully accept your offer to be my cheering section."

She was on her way back to fetch her jacket and purse when she heard a last-minute customer come in through the door, a man who greeted Miss Honi in a deep, familiar voice. Randall! Before he could spot her, Lindsay quickly ducked out of sight behind one of the tall bookshelves. Seconds later she was holed up in her office with the door shut, plotting an escape out the back, when Miss Honi rapped sharply on the door.

"Open up, sugar. You got company!"

Lindsay felt a flash of irritation. The woman would have rolled out the red carpet for Saddam Hussein! But it left Lindsay with no choice but to show her face. To hide from Randall would appear childish—or, worse, as if she were afraid she'd weaken at the sight of him. The fact that she was guilty on both counts only made her angrier. Why was he doing this to her? Why couldn't he just leave her alone and let the piece he'd written— admittedly a nice gesture—speak for itself: a last, eloquent *mea culpa?*

"I just wanted to drop this off," he said, handing her a bulky manila envelope. "It's the article I did for the *Chronicle.* I thought you'd want to see it before it comes out in Sunday's paper." She needn't have worried that he would throw himself at her and beg for forgiveness. His expression was pleasant, almost neutral, and far from the face of abject misery. Instead here was the Randall Craig with whom she'd fallen for: those blue eyes crinkling at her in faint amusement, the mouth hovering on the verge of a smile. As the envelope exchanged hands, his fingertips brushed hers in a way that electrified her.

She felt her resolve weaken, in spite of herself.

"Thanks, but I've already seen it," she told him. "One of my customers got a copy from someone who works at the paper."

He cocked a brow. "So what did you think?"

Lindsay, struggling to strike a balance between

cool remove and genuine appreciation, answered, "It's exactly what I would've written if I could write as well as you." To answer otherwise would have been dishonest, and she didn't intend to stoop to his level. Nor did she intend to pander to him in any way. Briskly she added, "But really, you shouldn't have gone to the trouble of dropping it off. I could've waited until the paper came out."

"Yes, but then you wouldn't have had it for your court date tomorrow."

"How did you know it was tomorrow?" Her eyes narrowed in suspicion. When he only shrugged in response, she knew: his father. Obviously he and Lloyd were in regular contact, if not cahoots. Not that it made a difference at this point. She'd had her fill of both men.

He glanced past her. "Mind if I come in?"

"Actually, I was just on my way out."

He grinned. "In that case, I'm glad I caught you."

She cursed inwardly as she stepped aside to let him in. "All right. But only for a minute." Why couldn't she tell him to take a hike? And why was her traitorous heart beating like that of a silly schoolgirl with a crush? If only turning her back on him were as easy as ignoring his calls and e-mails! She struggled to stay strong, maintaining a good distance and crossing her arms over her chest.

"I won't keep you," he said. "I just wanted to wish you luck."

Ignoring his attempt to butter her up, she replied

coolly, "Because I'm the one who needs it? Well, you're right about that. Your dad hasn't left anything to chance, has he?"

"No; that's not his style." She could see how unhappy he was beneath his facade as his eyes searched her face, as if for some small sign of forgiveness. "Look, I know what you think of me, but I need to set the record straight about one thing: I wasn't part of any conspiracy. The only thing my father and I share is the same DNA."

"Then why didn't you tell me you were his son?" She met his gaze squarely, her chin lifting.

"I tried . . . at least a dozen times."

"What stopped you?"

"I didn't want to screw it up with you. Ironic, isn't it?" Randall's mouth twisted in a pained smile.

Lindsay felt another chunk break away from the polar ice cap around her heart. Looking into his eyes, she saw nothing to suggest that he was a monster like his father. She saw only the face of a man who'd made a catastrophic mistake, one he deeply regretted. She wanted to forgive him— everything in her yearned to—but she couldn't forget that, whether or not he had purposely set out to deceive her, the end result had been the same. "The bottom line is," she said, "you *didn't* tell me. I had to find out from your father. Do you know how humiliating that was? Did you see the smug look on his face?"

Randall grimaced. "I know. I wish there was some way I could make it up to you."

"You already have. Consider us even." She dropped the manila envelope onto her desk.

He gestured toward it dismissively. "I would have written it no matter what." Despite herself, she couldn't help admiring the fact that he wasn't taking any more than his fair share of credit for what many would consider an act of contrition grand enough to wipe out any sins.

"Look, there's nothing you, or anyone, can do at this point," she said. "Thanks to your father, I'm looking at losing not just my home but my business. Whatever happens tomorrow, I know he won't quit until he's either run me off or bled me dry, whichever comes first."

"Even if he wins, it's just one step in a long process," Randall reminded her. "There's still hope."

"Is there? Really?" An appeal could take years to wind its way through the courts, and in the unlikely event that she prevailed, it would most likely be a Pyrrhic victory. The best she could hope for under those circumstances was that she'd have enough money left to make a down payment on another house. "Don't forget, your father has friends in high places. In fact, I'm told there's someone in Sacramento who's all set to rubber-stamp this if it goes through."

Randall all at once grew alert. "Where did you hear that?"

"I have my sources."

"What makes you think this person is connected to my father?"

"I don't know anything for certain, but I smell a rat. The timing is awfully suspicious, don't you think? This Curtis Brooks fellow gets appointed the new head of the Lands Commission right around the time we go to trial; then I hear he's poised to give your father's project the green light. Presumably he owes your dad a favor. Either that or he was bribed."

Randall fell silent, wearing a pensive look.

"Face it," she went on, "they have me boxed in. Even if I come out ahead tomorrow, it won't end there. They'll keep on pushing."

Randall's expression remained thoughtful, and he commented cryptically, "There may be another way around it. Don't forget, there's more than one way to skin a cat."

"True. But frankly, I'm out of ideas." She sighed and gathered up her jacket and purse.

"Maybe I can help. I don't suppose you'd consider having dinner with me," he said, eyeing her hopefully.

"Not a chance."

He looked disappointed, if not exactly surprised, but only said, "In that case, I'll have to settle for a good-night kiss." Before she could stop him, he had his arms around her and his mouth was closing over hers. She stiffened, but could no longer contain the feelings she'd been struggling to keep at bay, and for a beautiful, terrible moment she gave in to him. God, how she'd missed this! His mouth was warm and minty; he smelled of aftershave and of his own unique scent that seemed redolent of some old, happy memory. She kissed him back and went on kissing him until the feeble voice of reason in her head finally asserted itself. Even then it took all the strength she possessed to withdraw from his embrace.

"That," she said, pulling in a breath, "wasn't supposed to happen."

"Maybe not, but it did." He put a finger under her chin and tipped her head up to meet his gaze. "There's no use denying it. Admit it, you missed me. Maybe almost as much as I missed you." He gave a wistful smile. "Would it be so terrible if you were to give me another chance? I promise I won't let you down again."

She considered it briefly before slowly shaking her head. For some people, trust was something to be negotiated, but for her it was black and white: You either trusted someone or you didn't. Once a person had broken that trust, there was no going back. "I'm sorry," she said. "I just don't see how it could work."

"What would it take to change your mind?"

Seeing the pain in his eyes, she felt the crack in her own heart widen. "Even if I could learn to trust you again, I don't know that I could get past the fact that you're his son. Every time I looked at you, I'd see *him*. It's hard enough as it is. How will it be when he's robbed me of everything I own?"

Randall's jaw tightened. "He's my father; there's nothing I can do to change that fact. But he's not part of my life."

"Unfortunately, that doesn't change the fact that he's ruining mine."

"Lindsay . . ." Randall reached to put his arms around her.

This time she pushed him away before she could give in. "No. I can't. Please, just go."

The following morning at nine o'clock, Lindsay arrived at the courthouse, flanked by Ollie and Kerrie Ann. The courtroom was packed. The usual suspects, she thought, glancing around her. There were those who had been following the case since the outset and were fairly evenly divided into two camps: local business owners like Jerod Dorfman—a general contractor, who viewed the jobs and tourism the resort would generate as a way to boost their bottom line—and those who were firmly against any development that would spoil the rugged beauty of the coastline. In back stood a handful of reporters: John Larsen from the *Blue Moon Bay Bugle*, Melinda Knight from Channel 4 News, and several others Lindsay didn't recognize. At the respondent's table up front sat the attorneys for the county, a pasty-faced man named Newt Howland and a heavyset, middle-aged woman named Ann Wolf. They were accompanied by a pair of young associates and backed by representatives of the Heywood Group. At the plaintiff's table Dwight Tibbet sat alone, calm and in control as usual but looking seriously outgunned.

The judge had yet to show, but the bailiff, a balding, lantern-jawed man whom Lindsay recognized from previous court appearances, was on hand. The court stenographer, a pretty, curly-haired young woman was also a familiar face.

The only one missing was Grant, who'd phoned a little while ago to let Lindsay know he was running late.

She'd been a nervous wreck since she'd gotten up that morning, but now a strange calm descended over her. She had to face the fact that whatever the outcome, she wouldn't walk away a victor. Win or lose, the battle would go on. Were she to win, she would have the strength to forge on, knowing she'd have the advantage in the likely event of an appeal. But if she were to lose? She wasn't sure she would have either the strength or the resources to carry on.

She would just have to cross that bridge when she came to it.

She felt an elbow nudging her in the rib cage and turned toward Kerrie Ann, who muttered darkly, "If this doesn't work, we can always put out a contract on them." She cast a murderous glance at Heywood's posse. "I know people."

"Bite your tongue," Lindsay said. But it felt good knowing someone had her back.

Lindsay took her seat up front next to Dwight just as the bailiff called out in his booming voice, "Hear ye, hear ye! All rise for the Honorable Judge Davis! Court is now in session!"

The judge emerged from his chambers and took his seat: a not unattractive man in his mid- to late forties, with a full head of wavy brown hair going gray and intelligent brown eyes behind a pair of rimless glasses. She'd noticed on previous occasions that he had a habit of removing those glasses whenever he was making a point, usually in censuring one of the attorneys, as if he wanted nothing to stand between him and the full thrust of his gaze. It was one of the many little signals she'd learned to pick up on over the months he'd been presiding over her case. It was strange because she'd never sat down and had a conversation with the man, but she felt as if they were old acquaintances.

Once the formalities were dispensed with and the lawyers had made their opening remarks, witnesses for the county began taking the stand. The county assessor, a dour man in a dark gray suit, produced an impressive array of calculations regarding the projected tax benefits of the resort. A so-called scientist talked about the "minimal impact" on the environment. The COO of the

Heywood Group, a svelte blond woman around Lindsay's age, gave an account, aided by growth charts and glowing testimonials, of the positive impact on other communities where Heywood resorts had been built. Even the plainspoken Jerod Dorfman testified, speaking of the need for the jobs the planned project would generate.

"I got guys depending on me, all of 'em, like me, with mouths to feed. I don't see how a handful of tree huggers," he glowered at Lindsay, "should come ahead of working stiffs just trying to get by."

The burly contractor's words were met with a round of cheers from his sympathizers, which brought the judge's gavel cracking down in an effort to maintain order.

Then it was Dwight's turn to call witnesses. They seemed few and pitiful in comparison. A bearded environmental studies professor from UC Santa Cruz discounting the earlier testimony of his colleague by speaking of the potential harm to marine life by contaminants in the water supply. Local business owners who weren't eager to see the town overrun by tourists, one of whom was Ollie's dad. Alfonse Oliveira, looking as sturdy and weathered as a pier piling up on the stand, who talked about what it would mean to his livelihood to have the waters he fished clogged with kayaks, Jet Skis, and pleasure boats. "Got enough of that as it is," he groused. "Some days there's more folks out there than fish."

"So you're saying you'd be opposed to anything that made the problem, as you see it, worse?" Dwight clarified.

"Damn right." Alfonse's dark eyes, so like Ollie's, sparked in the rugged terrain of his face. "Fish are smart, see. Smarter than some people. They have the sense to stay away when something doesn't look right." He cast a pointed glance at the Heywood Group's blond COO, who clearly hadn't impressed him with her glorified charts and testimonials.

A ripple of appreciative laughter went through the courtroom, though there were those, including Jerod Dorfman, who were none too amused by the inference that they were mere lemmings lured by the promise of easy cash and a better life.

Lindsay was the final witness. After being sworn in, she climbed onto the witness stand and sat down, her hands folded in her lap, her gaze sweeping the packed gallery before settling on her sister and Ollie, who sat holding hands in the front row. Kerrie Ann looked almost as nervous as she. She flashed Lindsay a small smile, and Ollie gave Lindsay a thumbs-up. It was just the boost she needed. She squared her shoulders. This was her Waterloo . . . her last chance to make a stand. She had better make it count.

"I moved here with my parents in the early '80s, when I was just thirteen," she began in response to Dwight's questioning. "Before that I lived with my mother and sister in a motel just outside Reno. It wasn't anything like the life I have now, believe me. There was never any money, and whatever we did have went to feed my mother's drug habit. My sister and I were put into foster care when I was twelve and she was just three. I was lucky and got adopted by a wonderful couple—the Bishops. They're the ones who brought me to live here. Sadly, they're both gone now, but they left me the land they loved and that I came to love just as much." Lindsay, who in the past had been loath to tell her story, couldn't believe she was doing so now to a roomful of people, many of them strangers. "So you see, to me it's not just a deed to a piece of property. It's all those memories. Each time I look out my window or take a walk on the beach, I'm reminded of my parents." She choked up a little. "If I were to lose that, it would be like having to bury them a second time."

A few spectators were dabbing at their eyes by the time she climbed down from the stand. Even the judge seemed moved. Maybe, just maybe, this would go in her favor after all. . . .

"Court will reconvene at one o'clock," the judge announced when the morning's proceedings drew to a close. "I'll have a decision for you then."

Lindsay spent the next hour nibbling halfheartedly at the sandwich she'd ordered from the lunch cart, while Ollie and Kerrie Ann did their

432

best to keep her hopes up. She was too tense to respond with more than a nod or a murmur here and there. It didn't help that there was still no sign of Grant.

Before she knew it, they were all trooping back into the courtroom. The judge settled in at the bench and cleared his throat.

"Ms. Bishop, you argued very persuasively on your own behalf," he began, his benign gaze falling briefly on Lindsay before moving on to her attorney. "And Mr. Tibbet, I quite take your point that this isn't typical of most cases pertaining to eminent domain. However, it's not unprecedented, either. And Mr. Howland and Ms. Wolf made some excellent points as well. In a perfect world, we could preserve all the natural beauty we enjoy today without restricting any of the services we take for granted. And frankly, while I enjoy a good game of golf as much as the next man, I myself would choose such a world over the one we're in. But unfortunately, we don't live in a utopian society." He paused to remove his glasses, sending Lindsay's already racing heart into overdrive. "Like it or not, communities like this one depend on tax revenue. Schools, libraries, public works, social services all need it in order to survive . . . and thrive. Which means that inevitably we have to make some compromises. Which is why," he concluded, not without an air of regret, "I'm ruling in favor of the respondent."

Lindsay felt the room tilt a little to one side like a boat about to capsize.

Minutes later, the words of the judge still ringing in her ears, she made her way out of the courtroom in a daze.

"I'm sorry, Lindsay. I did everything I could." Her lawyer caught up with her in the corridor, placing a hand on her shoulder. With his grave expression, he looked more like a funeral director in his dark suit and polished black shoes.

"I know." Her voice seemed to come from very far away.

"I warned you it would be an uphill battle," he reminded her. "For once I wish I could say I was wrong."

"Me, too." She managed a small smile.

"It's not over, though. We'll file an appeal. I can start on it as soon as I get back to the office."

"Why don't you hold off on that for now?" she said. At the moment she didn't know what she wanted except for this to be over. Was anything worth all this grief?

"If you'd rather go with another lawyer, I understand. No hard feelings. I could even give you a few names—"

"No, it's not that. I don't think there's anyone who could've done a better job."

"Be sure and tell that to your boyfriend," he said in a weak stab at humor.

If I could find him, she thought. Whatever last-minute crisis had detained Grant, for which he would no doubt have a perfectly good explanation, the fact was that he was once again a no-show. Thank God for Ollie and Kerrie Ann. Lindsay looked around, and there they were, separating themselves from the stream of spectators emerging from the courtroom and heading straight toward her. Kerrie Ann's face was red, like it got when she was about to lose her temper. "Son of a bitch," she muttered under her breath. Lindsay didn't know if she meant the judge, the attorneys for the county, or the Heywood Group. Probably all of the above.

Dwight took advantage of the opportunity to excuse himself. "I'd better run. I have to get back to my office." She thanked him once more for his efforts on her behalf, which only caused him to grimace. "Save it for when we win on appeal," he said as he dashed off.

"I'm sorry, boss," said Ollie, eyeing Lindsay woefully. "Seriously, this sucks."

"That it does," agreed Lindsay.

"What your lawyer said just now? He's right, you know," said Kerrie Ann. "It's not over till it's over."

"Frankly, I'm not sure I have the stamina for another round." Lindsay drew in a deep breath and let it out in a long, ragged exhalation. "I think it's more likely we'll be looking for another place to live." It pained her, but she had to face facts. She couldn't go on like this much longer.

Kerrie Ann gave her a bolstering smile. "Don't worry. I'm an expert when it comes to that. I've changed addresses so many times, half the time I don't even know what zip code I'm in."

"As long as you're with me, you always know who to ask. Mine is engraved in stone along with my birth date and Social Security number," joked Ollie.

Kerrie Ann turned to smile at him, leaning into him when he slipped an arm around her waist. Lindsay was glad they were here, even if her cheering section was now a Greek chorus.

"It'll be all right," she said, putting on a brave face. "Anything is better than having this hanging over me."

"I know the feeling," said Kerrie Ann, and Lindsay knew she was thinking about her little girl.

"A miracle could still happen," said Ollie. "Like the Heywood Group could go out of business, or, like, they could discover your property is actually an old Indian burial ground."

Lindsay smiled. "I'm afraid neither of those things is likely to happen." A rabbit out of a hat was more likely.

Just then the lawyers for the county strolled into view. They'd briefly shaken hands with Dwight as he and Lindsay were leaving the courtroom but now were so busy congratulating each other that they breezed by without so much as a glance in Lindsay's direction.

"We should go," muttered Kerrie Ann, watching them retreat down the hallway, "before I start kicking some serious ass."

That was what finally broke Lindsay out of her torpor. "The last thing we need," she said, taking her sister's arm and steering her toward the exit, "is for you to get into trouble with the law."

Outside, the three of them descended the granite steps of the courthouse. Built in the late 1800s, it was one of the downtown's more venerable old buildings and boasted a dome, stained-glass windows, and interior oak wainscoting hewn from the canyon oaks native to the region. It was a bit run-down and showing its age, however, and there had been talk of converting it into a boutique shopping mall once more tourist traffic was flowing into the area and of building a new, more modern court-house adjacent to the county building on Ocean Street.

Nothing was sacred, Lindsay thought.

The house in Woodside had an interesting history. The onetime retreat of billionaire industrialist Bertram Goodwin, it was grand in the *fin de siècle* style, with turrets, fancifully carved pediments, and a stately entrance with a Doric-columned porte cochere. Goodwin had been eccentric in one respect, however: An avid naturalist, he'd collected exotic animals, which had been housed in a small zoo he'd erected on the property. So it was that as Randall Craig pulled up to the scrolled iron gates of what was now his father's estate, he could see, nestled among a copse of oaks in the distance, the stone lion's cage, nearly as large as the gatekeeper's cottage he'd just driven past. It seemed a fitting touch. Long abandoned, it nonetheless seemed to represent everything Lloyd Heywood stood for: Eat or be eaten. It was also a reminder to Randall of what he was up against.

It's going to be a long weekend, he thought.

He was greeted at the door by his father's second wife, a pretty, petite woman in her late forties with the unlined face and loosely tossed-and-buttered tresses of a woman half her age. She wore designer jeans and a cashmere sweater. A diamond tennis bracelet sparkled on one wrist. "Randall! How lovely to see you. It's been *ages*." She kissed him on both cheeks, continental style. Which was amusing, he thought, since Victoria Heywood had grown up Vicky Blunt, from Danbury, Connecticut, and had never even been to Europe until she'd married his dad.

"Thanks for having me," he said.

"Well, you picked the perfect weekend. The weather is supposed to be glorious. In fact, I thought we might all go riding on Sunday. If you didn't bring any boots, I'm sure we can find a pair that'll fit you. Don't you and your father wear the same size?" She ushered him inside, where the housekeeper, a trim, middle-aged Mexican woman he recognized from his last visit, took his bag. "Thanks, Maria. Why don't you put that in the guest room? Then we'll take our coffee out on the terrace."

His father's wife led the way through the oak-paneled foyer into a living room the size of a ballroom, done up in contemporary style that merely paid homage, with a scattering of antiques, to its beaux arts roots. Beyond was a sitting room cozily decorated in chintz and Ralph Lauren plaids, with a set of French doors opening onto a wide, semicircular terrace. It was adorned with statuary and stone urns spilling flowering plants, and stepped down in a series of smaller terraces—three in all— to the Olympic-sized pool below.

"How are the kids?" Randall asked dutifully as they settled into wrought-iron chairs at the patio table on the uppermost terrace. The last time he'd seen them had been five years before at his half-sister's sweet sixteen.

"Tammy's in France for the summer. She starts law school in the fall. Did Lloyd tell you she got into Columbia?" She flicked away an oak leaf that had drifted onto the table, leaning back in her chair. "And Brett's still at Swarthmore—just finished his sophomore year. Can you believe it? Seems like just yesterday they were in diapers, and now here they are, practically grown."

Randall might have been catching up on the lives of distant relations. It was hard to keep in mind that Tamara and Brett were his closest kin after his parents and little brother (also a half-sibling, but they'd grown up together, so Randall had never thought of Tim as anything less than a brother). "I guess you and Dad must be pretty proud of them," he said.

She beamed. "It's easy when you have such smart kids." Just then came the sound of a car pulling into the drive. "That must be your dad. I sent him to the store to pick up some things."

Minutes later Lloyd joined them on the terrace. "Hello, son." He shook Randall's hand before dropping a kiss on his wife's cheek. "Sorry for the delay, my dear. Next time you ask me to buy olive oil, you'll have to be more specific. There had to be at least twenty different brands."

"Well, I'm sure whatever you got is fine, even if it's not our usual brand. You like variety, don't you, darling?" There was a caustic note in her voice, though her expression remained sweetly smiling.

Trouble in paradise? wondered Randall.

"So how's our crusader? Still tilting at wind-mills?" Lloyd asked Randall in a faux-jovial tone. "Nice piece in the *Chronicle*, by the way. Could've used a bit more perspective, but overall very well written."

Randall bristled at his father's faint praise. "Thanks." It was an effort to maintain an even tone. "But I don't how much good it'll do." He'd read in the paper about his father's victory in court. "Congratulations, by the way. You always get what you want, don't you?"

"If I do, it's because a lot of other people want the same things." The maid arrived with the coffee tray just then, and Lloyd glanced at it dismissively before suggesting to Randall, "What do you say we head inside for something stronger? I don't know about you, but I could use a drink."

Randall gave a nod of assent. For once he and his dad could agree on something.

A short while later he and his father were ensconced in the den, Victoria having gone off to organize supper. Here the original baronial touches survived intact. It might have been the library of an exclusive turn-of-the-century men's club, with its oak paneling, original brass chandelier, and built-in glass-fronted bookcases displaying Goodwin's collection of rare volumes. The stuffed and mounted heads of trophy animals lined the walls. Goodwin, it seemed, had been an avid hunter as well as a naturalist; in those days people apparently hadn't seen the irony in being both.

"Have you spoken with your girlfriend recently?" Lloyd asked as he settled, whiskey and soda in hand, into the oxblood leather chair opposite Randall's.

"No," he replied tersely.

"Too bad about that." The old man shook his head with what seemed genuine regret. "But there are always bound to be casualties—one of the downsides of the profession. Nothing to be done about it, I'm afraid. And she has only herself to blame, really. I gave her every chance I could."

"Is that so?" Randall's voice was heavy with sarcasm. "You mean if someone were to make an offer on this place"—he gestured about him—"you'd be willing to give it up? Just like that?"

The old man chuckled. "I suppose it would depend on the offer."

"Are you really that mercenary?"

"Call it what you like. To my mind, it's just good business. I owe it to my shareholders, if nothing else."

"Where do you draw the line, Dad?"

"The same place we all do: when we've pushed the boundary as far as we can."

Gazking across the room at his dad, Randall recalled Lindsay's parting words: *Every time I looked at you, I'd see him.* Were he and his dad more alike than he cared to admit? He had his father's drive as well as a pit-bull tenacity when it came to achieving his goals. It was those qualities that had made him such an effective trader, and they were also what had brought him here today. He knew his father thought he'd come to repair relations and perhaps forge an alliance that would get Lindsay to accept the offer on the table and thus spare him any further legal woes, but the opposite was true: He intended to thwart his father any way he could. Since he knew persuasion wouldn't work, he was merely keeping his eyes and ears open for his main chance. If he could trick Lloyd into thinking he was willing to join forces with him, if only out of duress, the old man might reveal something he wouldn't otherwise. Something that would prove helpful to Lindsay.

Victoria called them to supper. Despite his black mood, Randall was touched that she'd gone to the trouble of making it herself, however simple the fare—filet and roast potatoes, a green salad on the side. Somehow he and his father managed to make it through the meal without any more tense exchanges. They spoke instead of the Napa winery Lloyd had invested in and the merits of various wines, one of which, a vintage merlot, had been opened in honor of the occasion.

Over dessert Victoria gushed to Randall about how much she'd enjoyed his book. "I got so caught up in the story, I didn't get a thing done that day. I even forgot I had a doctor's appointment."

"Believe me, that's the best compliment you can pay an author," Randall replied.

"I cried at the end. Not because it was sad but because I hated saying good-bye to the characters."

Lloyd looked up from spearing a forkful of the plum tart on his plate to remark, "Vicky tends to take everything to heart." He smiled indulgently at her. "You're too sentimental for your own good, my dear." It was becoming obvious that she'd also had a bit too much to drink.

She tossed back, "Well, at least I *have* a heart."

The jab was met by stony silence on Lloyd's part. Victoria flushed, falling silent as well, and for a while the only sound was the muted clinking of cutlery on china. Clearly they were having marital difficulties. Ordinarily it wouldn't have been of any concern to Randall, but it occurred to him that there might be a way to use it to his advantage. When his father suggested they head to the den to watch a golf tournament on TV, he seized the opportunity to help clear the table instead. He was carrying his second load of plates into the kitchen when he found Victoria at the sink, staring out the window with tears rolling down her cheeks.

She turned to him with a sheepish look. "I'm sorry. You must think I'm a terrible hostess."

"Not at all. Is there anything I can do?"

She shook her head. "No. But I'm glad you're here."

Sensing that she was holding back, he asked, "Would you like to talk about it?" It felt awkward reaching out to her; though she was closer to his age than her husband's, he'd never thought of her as anything other than his father's wife.

She gave a small, rueful smile. "You're probably the last person I should confide in. Your father would be angry if he knew. But right now I'm too angry at *him* to care."

"I kind of got that impression." Randall set down the plates he was holding and leaned against the counter, watching as Victoria dried her eyes. "So what did he do that got you so angry?"

"I'll give you a hint. She's got blond hair, and she's young enough to be his granddaughter." She spoke bitterly, her tongue loosened by the wine she'd had with dinner.

Randall was surprised. It hadn't occurred to him that the source of their difficulties might be another woman. Not that Lloyd was the faithful type—he had cheated on his first wife, Randall's mother, after all. But the old man was well past his prime, and if anyone was going to stray, Randall would have guessed it would be the much younger and still fetching Victoria. He saw that he'd once more underestimated his father.

He grimaced in sympathy. "I get the picture." He bit his tongue before he could add, *Now you know how my mom felt.*

She must have seen the accusation in his eyes, though. "You probably think I'm only getting my just deserts, and I suppose it's true," she said. "Back then I didn't think about who I might be hurting. I was too much in love. What goes around comes around, huh?"

Randall felt compassion well up in him. She wasn't a bad person, and she was hurting. "No one's blaming you. It was a long time ago." He paused before venturing, "So what are you going to do?"

"You mean am I going to divorce him?" She slowly shook her head, her eyes brimming with fresh tears. "I'm afraid he has me over a barrel. The prenup I signed would leave me practically penniless."

"Not necessarily." The wheels were turning in Randall's head.

"What are you suggesting?"

"There may be a way out," he ventured cautiously.

Before he could elaborate, Victoria shook her head in confusion, saying, "I don't get it. Why do you want to help me? Anyone would think you'd be glad to be rid of me. I'm the evil stepmother, aren't I? The home-wrecker responsible for your parents' divorce?"

"Let's just say it could be mutually beneficial."

She nodded slowly, folding her arms over her chest. "I'm listening."

The following day he had the distinct impression that Victoria was avoiding him. Another opportunity to be alone with her didn't present itself until Sunday. The day dawned bright and clear, as predicted. They were all supposed to go horseback riding, but at the last minute Lloyd got an important phone call he had to take, so he waved them on without him. Randall was relieved as he followed Victoria out of the house. Now was his chance to find out if she had given any thought to what they'd talked about.

The stable where Victoria boarded her Thoroughbred was a short distance away by car. They arrived just before noon. While she saddled up, Randall was given one of the trail horses to ride, a docile chestnut mare. He hadn't ridden in years, but it came back to him as soon as he eased into the saddle. Before long he and Victoria were cantering along the trail that wound its way through Huddart Park, sunlight filtering in a golden haze through the tall redwoods that crowded around them. They rode in companionable silence for a mile or more, Victoria leading the way. Randall waited for her to broach the subject of his father, but she didn't.

Did she regret having confided in him last night? He realized it had been naive of him to take her at her face value when she'd said she wanted a divorce. She'd had too much to drink and had merely been venting her frustration. How could he have thought a pampered woman like her, who'd been living in the lap of luxury for the past twenty years, would chuck it all? For what? Revenge? A chance at a better life?

Still, he had to know for sure. He waited until they were back at the stables and she was brushing down her horse. "Have you given any more thought to what we talked about the other night?" he asked.

"As a matter of fact, I have." She straightened and turned to face him.

"And?" Randall felt his nerves ratchet up.

"I still don't know if it'll work." She sighed, resting a hand against her horse's flank. "I'm not even sure if what you want exists."

"I'm not sure, either. We won't know unless you look for it."

"How would I even know where to look?"

"You were his secretary at one time. You must know where he keeps things."

"That was years ago! My job now is to play the company wife. That, and stay in shape so I'll look good on his arm when he's not off screwing one of his mistresses." The bitterness from the other night resurfaced. "Oh, yes, I'm sure there have been others. I just happened to find out about this one."

Some instinct prompted Randall to ask, "How *did* you find out?"

The question stopped her short, and a sly smile peeked from behind her scowling mask, that of someone who'd just spied a possible way out. "The usual way—by reading his e-mail."

Every Sunday afternoon Lindsay went walking on the beach. When the weather was sunny and warm, she was often joined by Miss Honi or Kerrie Ann. When it was gray, like today, she went with only her dog for company. The ocean in its many moods was the remedy for all that ailed. In the early years, when she was still getting over the trauma of having been torn from her sister, she had spent many restorative hours strolling along the shore, collecting shells and bits of sea glass with Arlene and stooping to examine tide pools with Ted.

"Every tide pool is its own little universe," her dad had explained, poking gently with his finger at a purple sea anemone, Lindsay watching in wonder as its delicate fronds contracted. "Each of these creatures has a purpose, and they all need each another in order to survive. Take this little guy, for instance." He picked up a small chambered shell scuttling across the rocks, seemingly of its own volition, and flipped it over so she could see the tiny claws wriggling underneath. "This hermit crab wouldn't have a home if not for the mollusk who kindly left him this one. When he's outgrown it, he'll move to the next. They're like people in that way—they learn to adapt."

She could see Ted in her mind's eye, his long, scholarly face with its neatly trimmed beard and warm brown eyes caught in nets of wrinkles. What would her life have been without him and Arlene? She recalled vividly the day they'd sat her down, after she'd been with them for about a year, and asked solemnly if she'd like to become their *real* daughter—in the eyes of the law, not just their own. She'd felt like the luckiest girl on earth.

Now she was like the hermit crab, faced with the choice of either clinging to the known and thus perishing . . . or moving on. In the days since the trial she'd thought of little else but was still no closer to a decision. If she continued her fight, she'd end up broke and would probably lose the house as well. Even if she could find another place nearby, it would be a loss. She would still have her Sunday ritual, but it wouldn't be the same. Gone, too, would be the thousand little things that connected her to Ted and Arlene. Gone her morning jogs along the cliffs, with the ocean sprawled at her feet like the kingdom of some mercurial potentate, one that with a wave of the scepter could give way to stormy seas just as easily as to the nearly impenetrable fog presently swaddling the shoreline.

The fog was a match for her mood right now. As she strolled barefoot along the cold, damp sand, she felt like the last person left on earth. Whenever she thought about what lay ahead, every muscle in her body contracted like the sea anemones her father used to poke. Her sister and Miss Honi had promised to help her look for another place, one big enough for all three of them. "Long as we still got each other, we'll manage just fine. Ain't nothing so bad that a pair of loving arms can't cure it," Miss Honi had consoled her. While Kerrie Ann's motto was "When life kicks you in the ass, kick it back." But Lindsay, though she appreciated their efforts, knew this decision, and its consequences, was hers alone. Could she face what the future held? Was she brave enough?

The answer, she realized, lay not in the future but

in the past. Her mind traveled back to the days when she'd been left to fend for herself and her little sister. She thought, too, of the business she had built from scratch and which she had somehow managed to keep afloat in these difficult times. And the David-and-Goliath battle she'd fought with all her might. The same person who had done all those things could do this, she told herself.

She was used to loss, after all. She'd lost all those years with her sister, and with the deaths of Ted and Arlene the only parents she'd known. Randall, too—she felt a fresh stab at the thought and quickly pushed it away before she grew even more depressed. And more recently, and somehow less painfully, her boyfriend of three years. The day of the trial, when Grant had shown up belatedly with, as usual, a perfectly valid explanation as to why he hadn't been able to make it in time, she'd realized, with a finality that took her by surprise, that it was over and had been for some time.

"I can't do this anymore," she told him. They were sitting on the wrought-iron bench in the pocket park adjacent to the courthouse. Grant had pulled into the parking lot just as she was getting ready to pull out and had come rushing over, tie flapping, apologizing profusely—something about an emergency injunction he'd had to deal with.

Misunderstanding, he nodded, speaking in sage, lawyerly tones: "Well, no one can say you didn't give it your best shot. It's perfectly understandable if you want to throw in the towel."

She was quick to set him straight. "I didn't mean the case. I meant *us*."

"What?" He blinked at her uncomprehendingly.

She placed a hand over his. "I'm sorry, Grant. It's not your fault. It's just . . . the way it is. We can't go on like this, with you always too busy to make time for me and me waiting for the day when it'll all magically work itself out. That's not going to happen—we might as well face facts."

"That's crazy. We can make it work. After all the time we've invested . . ."

"This isn't a business partnership. And even if it were, at some point, if a business is failing, you cut your losses and walk away."

"But I love you." He spoke urgently, and she saw pain in his eyes. It left her curiously unmoved.

"Yes—in your own way," she said. "But I'm afraid it's not enough for me."

"I thought we were going to be married someday."

"I thought so, too. But that 'someday' never seemed to come, did it?"

He continued to stare at her uncomprehendingly. That was when it dawned on her that, for Grant, theirs *had* been a working relationship. They just had different ideas of what they wanted out of life. She rose to her feet, not without some regret. She would miss his company and the comfortable rhythms they'd established. He was a good person. He just wasn't good for her.

"Good-bye, Grant." With that, she walked away.

Change, however painful in the moment, didn't necessarily have to be bad, she told herself now. Kerrie Ann had once accused her, in the heat of anger, of being a stick-in-the-mud. And Lindsay supposed it was true. But it wasn't fear of the unknown that had made her this way; it was intimate knowledge of what the unknown could bring. But there was a price to being inflexible. In an earthquake, it was the sturdy brick buildings that were first to tumble down.

Now that it was over with Grant, maybe it was time for her to move on in other ways as well . . .

Walking with her head down, lost in thought, Lindsay didn't notice that she wasn't alone on the beach. It wasn't until Chester began to bark excitedly that she looked up and saw the fuzzy outline of a figure making its way toward her through the dense fog. Just another lonely soul finding solace by the sea, she thought. Then, as it neared, the figure materialized into a man who looked startlingly familiar. She gave a gasp of recognition.

Randall.

What was he doing here?

Her heart took flight, and she wanted nothing more than to go racing toward him, as her shameless old Labrador was now doing. She came to a halt instead, watching Randall stoop to retrieve a piece of driftwood, which he pitched into a long throw, sending Chester chasing after it down the beach, before he continued on, his hands stuffed into the pockets of his chinos. He was barefoot, and his hair, the same silvery-buff color as the sand, stood up in windblown tufts.

"Let me guess. Miss Honi told you where to find me?" she said as he approached.

He shrugged, breaking into a grin. "She thought you could use the company."

"I see." Lindsay arched a brow, grateful for the effect of the chill air on her burning cheeks.

"I thought so, too. That's why I came."

"So you're not here to convince me to give you another chance?"

"I didn't say that."

She sighed. "Look, we've been over this already. What's the point of hashing it all out again?"

"Things have changed."

"What? I'm still at your father's mercy, and you're still his son. Nothing's ever going to change that." She spied a piece of sea glass gleaming amid a tangled skein of kelp and bent to pick it up, rubbing its grainy surface between her thumb and forefinger as she fought to rein in her emotions. Damn him. Why was he making this so much harder?

Even the sight of him was making it difficult as he stood smiling at her, his thick fair hair luffing in the breeze. "Maybe not," he said. "But I have something that might change how you feel."

He withdrew a folded piece of paper from his back pocket—a Xeroxed copy of a computer printout. She quickly scanned it. It was an exchange of e-mails between Lloyd Heywood and a man whose name she recalled from her lunch with Dwight—Curtis Brooks, the new head of the Lands Commission. It appeared innocent enough on the surface—Brooks merely thanking Lloyd for the all-expenses-paid vacation he and his wife had enjoyed at the Heywood resort on Maui and Lloyd promising in return to beat him the next time they played golf—but Lindsay was quick to grasp the significance of it. She jerked her head up to meet Randall's gaze.

"How on earth did you get this?"

"My father's wife. She did some snooping."

"Why would she want to help you?"

"At the moment she isn't too happy with him, either. It seems she caught him cheating on her."

Lindsay grimaced in sympathy. "Somehow that doesn't surprise me."

"Victoria's using it as leverage," he went on. "If it should get out that he bribed a public official, he'd lose everything, and he knows it. This way she'll get a decent settlement out of the divorce."

"And what's in it for you?"

"That remains to be seen." His eyes searched her face as if the answer lay there. "I had a little talk with my father, too. I told him I'd keep quiet if he ditched his plans for the resort." Lindsay's breath caught in her throat. "He let loose with some pretty choice words but in the end realized I had him over a barrel. He had no choice but to agree to it. Which means you get to keep your property, and I'm no longer welcome in his house."

Lindsay couldn't believe it. This was the miracle she'd prayed for. She tried to keep from grinning, but it proved impossible. The most she could manage was to keep from letting out a victorious whoop. "Will he ever forgive you, do you think?"

Randall appeared nonplussed. "No. And to quote Rhett Butler, 'Frankly, my dear, I don't give a damn.'"

"Still, he's your father . . ."

He shrugged. "Blood may be thicker than water, but it's not bullet-proof."

Lindsay shook her head slowly. "Does this really mean I get to stay? I won't have to find another place to live?"

Randall nodded. "With one catch."

"What's that?"

He grinned. "That you have an open-door policy when it comes to me."

Lindsay didn't trust herself to speak; she was too choked up. Instead she wordlessly stepped into the arms he held open to her. As she sank into Randall's embrace, a snippet from the Blake poem surfaced in her mind: *To see the world in a grain of sand . . .*

She was that grain of sand now, an entire universe unto herself on this vast beach, as she stood locked in the arms of the man she loved.

CHAPTER FIFTEEN

Seven months later

ONE OF THE BIGGEST SURPRISES of the past year had been Kerrie Ann's discovery that she liked to read. Since coming to work at the book café, she'd devoured all of the Judy Blume books (her favorite was *Are You There God? It's Me, Margaret*) and worked her way through the Anne of Green Gables and Boston Jane series, the Narnia chronicles, and the works of Elizabeth George Speare, Scott O'Dell, and Madeleine L'Engle before graduating to the likes of John Grisham, Stephen King, and her current favorite, Anne Rice. It was as though she were living her life in reverse through books, discovering worlds she'd bypassed growing up. In each book was a valuable lesson to be learned and usually a heroine with whom she could identify. Like Kit Tyler in *The Witch of Blackbird Pond* who is accused of being a witch in the days of the Salem trials. Kit stands to lose everything, including her life, but she's brave and eventually triumphs over adversity. Kerrie Ann had read the book three times, until the copy on sale at the Blue Moon Book Café finally grew so dog-eared that she felt compelled to purchase it.

As the date for her final custody hearing drew near, Kerrie Ann thought more and more about Kit Tyler. She, too, had been branded, though in her case not altogether unfairly. She'd also fallen prey to some unfortunate mishaps, like the one with Jeremiah. And she stood to lose what was most important to her: her child. But, like Kit, she knew she had to be brave and stay the course.

Over the past year, Kerrie Ann had gradually come to see that happiness was possible, if far from guaranteed. That good people *did* exist—like her sister and Randall, Miss Honi, Ollie, and her friends from the program. And that every once in a while, through a combination of hard work and luck, you got what you wanted.

She had never wanted anything more than this.

This was her last chance. If the judge failed to take into account the strides she'd made, she'd lose custody of Bella for good. And she didn't know how she would cope with that. It was one thing for them to be apart for a time, another for her to be forever robbed of the joy of waking up each morning to her daughter's sweet, smiling face.

Whenever she thought back to the Kerrie Ann who'd arrived in Blue Moon Bay nearly a year ago, packing not much more than a major attitude, that woman seemed like a whole other person, someone Kerrie Ann had no wish to become reacquainted with.

So much had changed since then. For one thing, she now had a real paying job at the Stitch and Sticks yarn shop down the street, one that had started out part-time but, as she proved increasingly indispensable, quickly became full-time. She'd even taken up knitting. It had been rough going at first, but she'd graduated from lumpy neck scarves to the afghan she was knitting as a wedding present for Lindsay and Randall, who were getting married in a few months. What she loved about knitting was that it soothed her mind while keeping her hands busy, and at the end she had something to show for it. She'd gotten others in her twelve-step program hooked, which had brought in a steady trickle of business from characters who must initially have seemed sketchy to the shop's owner, Ginny Beal: scary-looking bikers and ex-cons, recovering heroin addicts with old track marks on their arms. All of them people like her who were fighting to reclaim what they'd lost, day by day, stitch by stitch. Kerrie Ann jokingly referred to knitting as the thirteenth step.

In spite of her busy schedule, she still managed to put in some time each week at the book café, lending a hand at author events or during peak hours. It was small repayment for all her sister had done for her, she insisted whenever Lindsay protested that she felt like she was taking advantage of her. Kerrie Ann had noticed, though, that the protests were growing less frequent. The truth was, her sister needed all the help she could get. Business was better than ever now that she was able to devote all her energies to work. Also, word had spread among publishers, thanks in part to Randall, about her creative promotions and great turnouts, and more high-profile authors were going out of their way to make it a stop on their tours.

The publicity generated by the article in the *Chronicle* hadn't hurt, either. That had led to a segment on *60 Minutes*, which ironically had achieved what the planned and since scrapped Heywood resort had failed to: It had put their town on the map. Tourism was on the rise, and two new bed-and-breakfasts had opened in the past six months. It was small, steady growth as opposed to an overnight boom, but enough to allow for a general sprucing up of the shops and eateries downtown.

And in June Lindsay Margaret McAllister Bishop was going to become Mrs. Randall Craig. Lindsay had asked Miss Honi to give her away, which tickled the old woman to no end—she loved the idea of walking one of her girls down the aisle and was already planning her ensemble, which would no doubt include sequins and a pair of stiletto heels. Kerrie Ann was to be the maid of honor. "As long as I don't have to walk down the aisle in some butt-ugly old-lady dress. I've got a reputation to uphold, you know?" Kerrie Ann cracked, though secretly she too was delighted to be asked.

"Don't worry," Lindsay teased. "It won't be anything *I* wouldn't wear."

But if a large share of the credit for the new and improved Kerrie Ann went to her family and fellow twelve-steppers, a good part was owed to Ollie as well. First and foremost, if it hadn't been for him, that awful, endless night when her daughter had gone missing might have turned out very differently. And if she had the program and her own hard work to thank for her newfound sense of self-worth, she credited Ollie with opening her eyes to who she was as a woman. She now knew that she had something to offer besides her body. That she was someone a man wouldn't be embarrassed to introduce to his parents.

Which hadn't prevented her from balking the first time Ollie had brought her home to meet his. It was back in October, shortly after Lindsay had announced her engagement, and Ollie had insisted it was high time he properly introduce his parents to *his* girl. Kerrie Ann had done no more than shake hands with his dad the day he'd testified in court on Lindsay's behalf and knew his mom only to say hello to from the times she'd stopped in at the book café.

"What if they don't like me?" she fretted aloud on the way over.

"We'll just have to elope," Ollie teased.

"Be serious."

"I am serious." As they jounced along the dirt road in his Willys, Kerrie Ann knew just how a pioneer mail-order bride would have felt pulling into town in a covered wagon, not knowing what awaited her. Ollie took his hand off the wheel to give her a reassuring pat on the knee. "Just be yourself."

She groaned. "That's what I'm worried about. Being myself is usually what gets me into trouble."

"Don't." He spoke sternly.

"Don't what?"

"Don't put yourself down. Why do you always assume people won't like you?"

"Let's just say I've had some bad experiences." She thought of all the times, coming to a new foster home, that she'd had high hopes, only to find herself damned before she could prove she was more than just what was in her case file. After a while, she'd stopped trying to make a good impression and had become the hostile kid they all expected her to be.

"Well, that's all in the past. You can be pretty likable when you want to be, you know that?" He smiled at her as they pulled up in front of his parents' modest shingled house.

"So could Typhoid Mary," she muttered.

"Trust me, I wouldn't subject either of us to the third degree if I thought that's what this was going to be. Relax, it's just lunch. And as far as I know, you aren't on the menu."

The thought did nothing to ease her anxiety.

She found his father, a big, top-heavy man with wind-scoured cheeks and a shock of black hair going gray, to be a man of few words. Over lunch she struggled to make conversation with him. She was beginning to wonder if she'd made any impact at all when, as she was prying at a crab leg in the delicious if somewhat complicated fish stew Ollie's mother had prepared, she looked up to find him eyeing her in amusement. "Here, let me show you," he said, demonstrating how to crack the shell, then extract the meat. "It just takes practice. You'll get the hang of it."

In her nervousness, she blurted, "That's what my teachers were always telling me in school, but somehow I never did get the hang of it."

At his parents' raised brows, Ollie was quick to inform them, "Kerrie Ann just got her GED."

"Congratulations. What are your plans now?" Ollie's dad spoke in a mild, conversational tone, but she sensed she was being put to the test and took care with her answer.

"I'd like to go to college. I thought about a career in nursing but decided I'd rather work with people in recovery, so now I'm looking to get a degree in social work." She felt her cheeks warm. Had she revealed too much? Or would they think it was just a lot of big talk from someone who wasn't cut out for a career? Kerrie Ann had her own doubts—a college degree seemed almost like wishing for the moon.

But Ollie's dad only smiled and said, "That's good, honest work."

Kerrie Ann found Ollie's mother easier to talk to but more intimidating in a way. Freddie Oliveira, a tall, angular woman with a freckled face and once-copper hair the color of an old penny, was the opposite of her taciturn husband. She was affable like Ollie, but without his goofy sensibility. Yet her keen gaze missed nothing, and throughout the meal Kerrie Ann felt those sharp blue eyes on her more than once, sizing her up while she did her best to make small talk.

It wasn't until they were alone in the kitchen, Kerrie Ann helping her wash up, that Freddie remarked, "So Ollie tells me you two are thinking of moving in together." She paused in the midst of scrubbing a pan to direct her pleasant, eagle-eyed gaze at Kerrie Ann.

Kerrie dropped her eyes, busying herself with the drying. "We've talked about it," she replied guardedly. After Lindsay and Randall were married, Randall was going to move in with her and Miss Honi, which meant Kerrie Ann would need to find another place to live, something she'd been planning to do anyway. Nevertheless, she wasn't sure she was ready to take that leap with Ollie. She cared about him deeply, she might even love him, but shacking up with him was a whole other level of commitment. A lot, too, depended on whether or not her daughter would be living with her.

"He's worried about leaving you guys in the lurch," she told Freddie, which was true as well. "He wants to find a place nearby so he can still help out around here." At the sharp look Freddie shot her, she hastened to add, "But I'm sure you don't need me to tell you that."

"No, and I don't need Ollie planning his life around us, either," Freddie replied crisply. "We're far from ready for the old folks' home, whatever my son might have told you. We'll manage."

"I'm sure you will, but he kind of feels responsible. You know?" She added, "I don't have parents of my own, but I like to think if I did, I'd feel the same way Ollie does." Kerrie Ann blushed once more, wondering if she'd overstepped her bounds.

Freddie's direct blue eyes remained pinned on her. "I understand you have a little girl," she said.

Kerrie Ann felt her heart sink, certain her fears were being realized: that this meet-and-greet would turn into a tribunal, not unlike the one in *The Witch of Blackbird Pond.*

"Yes," she said, with some of her old defiance as she met Freddie's gaze. "And the main thing right now is making a life for me and my daughter. I'm sure you heard what happened, so I don't have to tell you why she's not living with me. But I'm working to change that. I'm hoping to have her back before too long." Whatever Ollie's mother had been told, Kerrie Ann wanted her to know how important this was to her.

Freddie nodded. "How's that going?"

Kerrie Ann wasn't normally superstitious, but she hesitated before replying, not wanting to jinx anything. "With any luck, she'll be home in time for the wedding." Randall and Lindsay were getting married the third Sunday in June, and the date for the final custody hearing was set for the first week in May. Still a long way off, but Kerrie Ann's lawyer had assured her it was for the best, that it would allow enough time for the dust to settle and for her to show that she'd turned over a new leaf.

Kerrie Ann braced herself for a blast of contempt—how could an honest, hardworking mother of six begin to understand what it had been like for *her*?—and was surprised when Ollie's mother replied, "I'll keep my fingers crossed, in that case." As if musing aloud, she added, "The only thing I'm wondering is whether Ollie's ready to be a stepdad."

Kerrie Ann was so stunned that she almost dropped the saucepan she was drying. "Um, I . . . I don't know if that's gonna happen. I mean, I really care about him, but . . ." she stammered.

"Do you love him?" Freddie asked bluntly.

Backed into a corner, Kerrie Ann was forced to reply, "I think so. But I've only been in one other serious relationship before this, and that didn't go so well, so I'm not the best judge."

Ollie's mother offered her a piece of unexpected advice: "Well, I wouldn't wait too long to make up my mind if I were you. I nearly lost out on marrying his father that way."

"You did?"

"I was pretty full of myself back then," recalled Freddie with a dry chuckle as she plunged her hands back into the soapy water in the sink. "Thought I might do better, same as when you've got your eye on a flashy new car instead of appreciating the reliable one you've got."

"Even if I wanted a new car, I couldn't afford one," Kerrie Ann said with a laugh.

The older woman finished scrubbing the last pot and handed it to Kerrie Ann to dry. She squeezed out the dishrag, folding it neatly over the edge of the sink, a deep cast-iron one enameled in porcelain and with old-fashioned fixtures, which Ollie had pointed out to Kerrie Ann earlier on when showing her around the house. The kitchen sink was where he and his brothers and sisters had been bathed as infants, he'd told her. And where he'd learned the first rule of baking: that if you wanted to use the kitchen, you had to clean up afterward. Now it was the place where valuable advice was being imparted to Ollie's girlfriend regarding their possible future together.

At last Freddie turned toward her, wiping her

hands on her apron. "What I'm saying is, it's easy to take a man for granted when he's always there for you. But you can only get away with it for so long. I learned that the hard way after I'd dragged my heels on giving Al an answer to his proposal and he took a job on a commercial fishing boat up in Alaska. I didn't hear from him for a whole summer, and by the time he got back, I was beside myself. I didn't even wait for him to pop the question again. I told him I'd marry him before the words were even out of his mouth." She smiled then, a smile that radiated outward, lighting up her whole face and deepening the fine lines at the corners of her eyes. "After forty-two years, I can safely say I made the right choice. The ones built to last might not be as fun or flashy as some thrill ride, but they get you where you want to go."

Kerrie Ann smiled and nodded. No more was said on the subject, but she felt more relaxed around Freddie after that.

Now, months later, Kerrie Ann was on her way to San Luis Obispo to find out if she would pass muster with the judge presiding over her case. It was a mild day in May, sunny but breezy, and she was riding with Ollie along the now familiar route while her sister and Randall, accompanied by Miss Honi, brought up the rear in Randall's Audi. The final custody hearing wasn't until the following day, but Randall had generously offered to put them all up at a Sheraton near the courthouse, so she'd arrive fresh and rested tomorrow.

That night, lying in bed with Ollie, Kerrie Ann thought, *At least I won't have to face it alone.* She recalled his mother's words and found herself thinking of how he'd always been there for her.

"Tell it to me again," she said.

"It's gonna be okay," he repeated the words he'd spoken so many times that they were like a mantra.

"What if the judge can't see that I've changed?"

"He will."

"How can you be so sure?"

"Because you're the only one who doesn't see it."

"Is it that obvious?"

"Uh-huh." He edged closer, nibbling on her ear-lobe. "But don't forget, I liked you to begin with."

She turned her head to look at him. The room was dark and his face in shadow. There was only the gleam of his eyes. "What did you see in me?" she asked.

"I saw someone who'd been down but who never quit trying. That's what made me fall in love with you—that stubborn streak. You never give up. And you're not gonna now. Whatever happens tomorrow. One way or another, I know you'll work it out."

"I hope you're right." With a sigh, she snuggled up against him.

They made love that was as tender as it was passionate. Ollie kissed her all over, tiny kisses like a feather brushing over her skin. She'd taught him to rein in his natural exuberance in the bedroom, and he was demonstrating now just how well he'd learned that lesson. She moaned softly, opening herself to him, drawing comfort as well as pleasure from the sweet but insistent pressure of his fingers and exquisitely soft mouth. She gave to him in return, stroking and kissing him all over, taking him into her when neither could hold back a moment longer. As they rocked together in rhythm, she felt closer to him than she ever had to another living being except Bella. When she came, it was with a quiet intensity that was different than anything she had felt with the countless lovers before him; she felt free to just *be* and not have to fulfill a man's expectations by making the proper noises and thrashing about as if in the throes of mind-blowing ecstasy. With Ollie, she felt at home, not just with herself but in a safe place where no one could hurt her.

"That was nice," she murmured afterward as they lay in each other's arms.

"Nice? You mean I didn't rock your world?"

"That, too."

"Good because, dude, a guy's got his pride."

"Especially a stud like you." She smiled in the darkness.

He lifted his head to look at her, his mouth curled in amusement. "You making fun of me now?"

"No. I'd never make fun of you, Ollie." She spoke seriously, threading her fingers through his thick shock of hair and pulling his head down to kiss him on the lips. "You're too good."

"I didn't know there was such a thing as being too good."

"Not for everyone. Just some people."

"Like who, for instance?"

"For me. Maybe. I don't know."

"Why don't you let me be the judge of that?" He pulled her close, holding her protectively.

But as she drifted off to sleep, her only thought was of the judge to whom she'd have to answer in the courtroom tomorrow. Would he take as benevolent a view? When she stood before him, her deeds—and misdeeds—being weighed, would the good outweigh the bad? She could only hope so. Otherwise, what would have been the point? What would it matter how hard she had worked or how many hours she'd sat in those hard folding chairs at meetings if she didn't get her daughter back?

In the morning, she woke to a knot in her stomach. When she joined the others for breakfast, all she ordered was coffee. She shook her head when Miss Honi pressed a piece of toast on her and urged, "You got to eat, sugar. How else you gonna keep your strength up?"

"I don't think I could keep anything down," she said.

"I know the feeling," Lindsay sympathized.

471

"When it was me, I was so nervous, I thought I was going to throw up."

"Woulda served them right, those sons a bitches of Old Man Heywood, if you'd upchucked all over their fancy pinstripes," huffed Miss Honi. She cast a contrite glance at Randall. "Sorry. I know he's your kin and all, but after what that man put us through . . ."

"No need to apologize." Randall helped himself to a muffin. "My father and I aren't even on speaking terms at this point. In fact, I think it's safe to say he won't be attending the wedding."

"At least your stepmother is coming," Lindsay said.

"My father's wife, you mean," he corrected. "Or ex-wife, I should say."

"Whatever; I can't wait to meet her," said Lindsay, nibbling on half a toasted bagel smeared with cream cheese. "After all, I have her to thank for the fact that I'm not being evicted from my own home."

"Don't I get some of the credit?" Randall pretended to be put out.

"Ninety-nine point nine percent of it. But if I let you have it all, I'm afraid it would go to your head," she teased.

"Dude, isn't it enough that you're rich, famous, and good-looking?" Ollie ribbed him.

"Not to mention I landed the prettiest bookstore owner in Blue Moon Bay." Randall reached for

Lindsay's hand, leaning in to give her a proprietary kiss on the cheek.

Lindsay laughed. "The *only* bookstore owner in Blue Moon Bay, you mean."

Listening to them banter, Kerrie Ann found herself marveling at the change in her sister over the past year. Frankly, she wouldn't have thought this soft, less serious side of Lindsay existed if she weren't seeing it with her own eyes. If she'd changed, so had Lindsay. And maybe, thought Kerrie Ann, she'd had a small part in that transformation. Just as she herself was a different person partly due to Lindsay. But she still had one last hurdle to clear . . .

"It's no use, guys," she said, cutting through the repartee. "I know you're only trying to take my mind off what's ahead, but I won't be able to think about anything else until it's over."

Lindsay shot her a concerned look. "We didn't want to make it any worse by hashing it out over breakfast."

"Believe me, you couldn't make it any worse." Kerrie Ann's stomach executed another slow cartwheel and she pushed aside her coffee cup. She was jumpy enough as it was, her system pumping enough adrenaline to power her through the rest of the day without the aid of caffeine. "I just hope the judge doesn't decide that I'm still a lousy risk."

"I don't see how he could," said Lindsay. "Not after all you've accomplished."

"Anything's possible," Kerrie Ann said.

"If that's true, then he could just as easily decide you're a good bet," said Miss Honi more optimistically. She bit into a doughnut—she'd long since given up on Weight Watchers—brushing idly at the powdered sugar scattered over her lapels. Today's look was more toned down than usual; she was wearing emerald-green slacks with a candy-heart-pink jacket, a plain gold choker, and matching earrings. Fresh from the beauty parlor, with her upsweep firmly in place, she could have been a contestant in the Miss America pageant, senior division.

They finished breakfast, and Randall paid the check while the others fetched their luggage. Then they all headed to their respective cars for the drive to the courthouse. Kerrie Ann was silent on the way over, and for once Ollie didn't attempt to engage her in conversation; he seemed to sense that not only would it be futile, it might backfire. Whatever she had to say, she was saving it for the judge.

Her lawyer was waiting for her when they arrived.

"Ready?" Abel looked jaunty in a chalk-stripe suit, French cuffs, and a tie patterned with tiny porpoises.

Kerrie Ann managed a small smile. "As ready as I'll ever be."

"Good." He eyed her sternly. "Now, remember,

whatever they say, don't let it get to you. It's just words."

Recalling her outburst the last time, she nodded and said, "I'll try to keep that in mind."

He grinned, a dazzling display of white teeth against ebony skin. "Okay, then, let's go in there and show them what you're made of." He added with a chuckle, "Just don't show *too* much."

As the hearing got under way, it became increasingly harder for Kerrie Ann to maintain her composure as she sat listening to the Bartholds' attorney, Janice Chen, a five-foot-tall firecracker in a red suit and black patent-leather heels as shiny as her blunt-cut hair, go on and on about all the Bartholds had to offer and how Bella was thriving in their care.

"Your Honor, I think the results speak for themselves. Would her mother," the tiny woman flicked a hand toward Kerrie Ann, "be able to offer the same level of care? A woman with a known history of drug use who's repeatedly demonstrated a clear lack of judgment when it comes to her child? I think the answer is obvious. We believe the court would be doing this little girl a grave disservice by not awarding custody to my clients."

George Barthold took the stand next, looking somber and dignified. His face lit up only when speaking of Bella. "She's just the most amazing child. Bright, sweet-natured, and curious about everything. The pastor at our church was joking the other day that he's going to have to take a refresher course in order to keep up with all her questions." He chuckled softly. "Watching her blossom over the past year has brought me and my wife the greatest joy." He cast a glance at Carol, sitting ramrod-straight in the first row. "It would destroy us to lose her, but this isn't about us and what we want. It's about what's best for Bella. If we were to raise her, she couldn't have more devoted parents, I can promise you that."

When it was Carol Barthold's turn, she was the only one with the guts to raise the topic no one else had dared to mention. "That child belongs with us. Will her white mother be able to give her what we can? I went to the Phillips Exeter Academy on scholarship. I was the only African American girl in my class—the proverbial fly in the milk bucket." Behind Carol's haughty facade Kerrie Ann caught a glimpse of the girl who'd been on the outside looking in. "What saved me was the strong sense of identity my parents instilled in me. I want Bella to have that, too, to be proud of her black heritage."

Kerrie Ann began to tremble, partly in fear and partly in suppressed fury. On top of all her other sins, did she have to be punished because she was *white*? She silently blessed Abel when it was his turn to address the bench and he responded to Carol's argument, "Your Honor, I'm not even going to address the question of race—that's not the issue here. Let's stick to what matters. Yes, my client, Ms. McAllister, has made some mistakes in the past, but she recognizes those mistakes and has been doing her utmost to rectify them. She still regularly attends twelve-step meetings and has tested clean for drugs for over a year, not to mention she works two jobs. Can the Bartholds offer more in the way of material things? Undoubtedly. But shouldn't the love of a mother for her child and that of a child for her mother count more than dancing lessons and a shot at the Ivy League?"

The spark of hope in Kerrie Ann's breast sputtered, then flared. She risked a peek at the judge. He didn't appear unmoved. A good sign? Maybe, but she still had some heavy convincing of her own to do. And look what had happened the last time she'd spoken up in her own defense.

She broke out in a cold sweat as she approached the witness stand. If there was ever a time for her higher power to come to her aid, it was now. Taking her seat, she caught Lindsay's eye. Her sister looked tense, as if recalling her own recent ordeal. It was Ollie, beaming at Kerrie Ann with such love that it suffused his whole face as if a spotlight were shining on him, who gave her the extra push she needed.

"Your Honor, I'm not so good with words. I didn't get straight As in school, like my daughter," she began haltingly. "But I know one thing: I love that little girl with all my heart. Even at my lowest,

I never lost sight of that. I know I messed up, and I also know that if I spend the rest of my life trying to make up for that, it still won't be enough. But I'm trying my best. They say a leopard doesn't change its spots, and I used to believe that, but now I know it's not always true. I *have* changed. Not just what you see on the outside but on the inside, too. I promise if I get another chance, it'll be different the next time."

"The last time you were given that chance," the judge reminded her, "you left your child in her father's care—a known addict—and he put her at serious risk. It was lucky she was unharmed, or you would be here under very different circumstances, Ms. McAllister."

She hung her head. "I know that, Your Honor."

"And what do you have to say in your defense?"

"I made a mistake," she said in a small voice unlike that of the old smart-mouthed Kerrie Ann who'd had an excuse for everything. "I trusted him when I shouldn't have. He told me he was clean, and I believed him. I was wrong. I see that now, and it won't ever happen again."

"How do we know that?" interjected Ms. Chen with cool disdain. "This is a perfect example, Your Honor, of the point I was making earlier. I don't doubt that Ms. McAllister means well, but how can you expect a person who shows such poor judgment not to keep on making the same mistakes?"

Kerrie Ann became aware of a flurry of movement and looked up to find Lindsay on her feet, leaning across the balustrade to whisper something in Abel's ear. He nodded, then turned back to the bench, requesting, "Your Honor, Ms. McAllister's sister would like to have a word, if she may."

The judge gestured in assent, and Lindsay took the stand, saying in a strong, clear voice, "My name is Lindsay Bishop. I'm Ms. McAllister's sister. I'd like to state for the record that every word she said was true. She *has* changed. And I'm not just saying that because she's my sister." She paused, looking a little uncomfortable at being the center of attention. "You see, we didn't grow up together—we were put into foster care when Kerrie Ann was just three—and it's only recently that we've gotten to know each other. I won't deny that I had my doubts at first. But over time I came to see what a loyal, good-hearted person she is. Hardworking, too. I don't know how I'd manage without her. She's the best friend and sister—and employee—anyone could have." She smiled at Kerrie Ann. "She's a good mother, too. I've seen how she is with Bella. And I've watched her, time and again, deny herself something she wanted so she could put money aside for when her daughter comes home. That child means everything to her."

Kerrie Ann's eyes filled with tears. In the decade-plus of bouncing from one foster home to the next, followed by her years on the road, no one had ever stood up for her. And now here was her sister—a sister she hadn't even known existed until a relatively short while ago—saying the things Kerrie Ann had longed all her life to hear. Sticking up for her.

"What happened with Bella's father," Lindsay went on, "could've happened to anyone. In fact, I'm partly to blame. My sister was so sick that night that she could barely lift her head off the pillow, so of course she wasn't thinking straight. But I was there; I should've kept him from taking Bella. The only reason I didn't was because, like my sister, I thought he was a good dad. So don't judge her too harshly. It was a mistake, but an honest one."

The judge frowned, but his expression seemed more pensive than disapproving. His voice was kindly when he spoke. "Thank you, Ms. Bishop. I'll take that into consideration."

Next Bella's court-appointed attorney, the skinny, pop-eyed Ms. Travers, weighed in briefly, mainly to reiterate what was in the psychologist's report: that Bella appeared happy and well adjusted and showed no signs of any permanent trauma from her ordeal at her father's hands.

It was Mrs. Silvestre who proved to be the wild card. When it was her turn, she said with her usual crisp, dry delivery, "I, too, had my doubts about Ms. McAllister in the beginning. But the woman I see sitting before me now isn't the same one I first met over a year ago. Your Honor, I've been involved in hundreds of cases like this one, and most times I think the child in question would be better off with someone other than his or her biological parent or parents. But, in this case, I'd have to say the opposite is true. I believe Bella would be best placed with her mother."

Kerrie Ann was so stunned, it was all she could do to keep her mouth from dropping open. She smiled at Mrs. Silvestre as she stepped down from the stand. Mrs. Silvestre didn't smile back.

By the time both lawyers had given their closing remarks, Kerrie Ann felt more numb than anything. Gone was her righteous indignation of the past. There were no bad guys here, just ordinary people caught in a bad situation. Besides, she wasn't the only one who was scared. She'd seen the fear in the Bartholds' eyes when Mrs. Silvestre was on the stand. Despite everything they had to offer, they had to know they were in a vulnerable position.

The judge, after a brief recess to review the file, finally arrived at a decision. "I'm granting custody to the mother. On a pro-tem basis." He cast a stern look at Kerrie Ann. "Ms. McAllister, I want to see you back here in six months before anything is finalized." A gasp went up from the other table, followed by a muffled cry—from Carol Barthold—and he turned to address the couple, saying gently, "I don't doubt you'd make excellent parents. But this child already has a mother. And while I can't condone some of Ms. McAllister's actions in the past, I do recognize that she's made significant strides since then." He brought his gaze back to Kerrie Ann. "Ms. McAllister, you realize I'm not giving you *carte blanche* here?"

"Yes, Your Honor." She broke into a grin. "I even know what that means—that I'm not getting a free ride," she said, happy that she'd looked up the term after coming across it in one of her books.

"Quite right," he said, struggling to suppress a small smile of his own.

Then they were all trooping out of the court-room. Suddenly Kerrie Ann could breathe again. Lindsay, Randall, Miss Honi, and Abel all took turns hugging and congratulating her before Ollie, not to be outdone, swooped in to give her a kiss that, if it had been in a movie, would have been worthy of a leading man. At the moment he looked even better to her than Brad Pitt.

Kerrie Ann, laughing and crying at the same time, turned to Abel. "Where's Bella? Can I take her home with me now?"

He nodded, saying gravely, "Yes, but I think I should have a word with the Bartholds first."

"No. Let me talk to them," she said, surprising herself. Moments ago she wouldn't have thought she'd ever want to see their faces again, much less speak with them.

Abel gave her a dubious look. "All right. But

482

keep in mind, they're probably feeling pretty raw right now."

"I know," she said. "I've been there, remember?"

She was on her way back into the courtroom when the Bartholds emerged. They looked utterly devastated. She'd been so angry at them for such a long time that it took her a moment to recognize the emotion that welled up in her: sympathy. She knew exactly what they were going through.

"I just want you to know there's no hard feelings," she said to them.

George Barthold gave a stiff nod. "Thank you," he said in the dull voice of someone shell-shocked.

Carol Barthold wasn't so restrained. She glared at Kerrie Ann. "You're doing her a disservice, you know that, don't you? She belongs with *us*."

George Barthold placed a hand on his wife's arm. "I'm sorry," he apologized to Kerrie Ann. "We're both a little upset right now, as you can imagine."

"I know." Strangely, she felt no urge to lash out at them. "I . . . I just wanted to thank you for taking such good care of her. I also want you to know that I'll be taking good care of her, too, so you shouldn't worry."

"Can we still see her? It doesn't have to be on a regular basis . . ." His voice caught. "Just so she doesn't forget us." Gone was his usual authoritative tone. He was all but begging.

Kerrie Ann paused to consider. She wanted no

part of the Bartholds, and she was sure they wanted no part of her. But like it or not, they were a part of her child's life and had been for some time. She didn't doubt that Bella cared for them deeply and that over time, if the scales of justice had tipped the other way, she would have come to think of them as her mom and dad. She also thought about what the old Kerrie Ann would have done: She would have used George's humbling himself to dig the knife in a little deeper.

"I'm sure something could be arranged," she said.

George Barthold took her hand, squeezing it hard and saying with real emotion, "Thank you."

Minutes later she was holding Bella on her lap, drinking in her little-girl scent as she sat with chin resting atop Bella's braided head. "It's all settled, baby. You're coming home with me, just like I promised." Bella wriggled closer, as if not quite ready to take her mother at her word. "We'll be staying at Aunt Lindsay's, but only for a little while—just until we get our own place."

Bella lifted her head to say, "I like it at Aunt Lindsay's. Why can't we live there?"

"You're welcome to stay as long as you like," Lindsay assured her, reaching down to stroke Bella's cheek. "And after that you and your mom will be visiting all the time."

At the plaintive look Bella gave her, Kerrie Ann pointed out, "When your aunt Lindsay gets married, it would be kind of tight with all of us living under one roof. We wouldn't want poor old Uncle Randall to have to sleep in the doghouse, would we?"

"No, thanks," laughed Randall, casting a wry glance at Lindsay. "I've already been there once and don't plan on going back."

Randall had been a good sport about the unusual living arrangements he was entering into. Having Miss Honi around was no problem—he adored her, and vice versa. But with Kerrie Ann and now her daughter on board, quarters would be cramped. *It's time*, she thought once again.

The only question was, would they move in with Ollie or strike out on their own?

As if echoing her thoughts, Bella asked, "But where will we go, Mommy?"

Kerrie Ann looked up just then and caught Ollie's eye. He was gazing at her steadily and a bit worriedly, as if fearful of what her answer would be. She hesitated for a moment, not sure, either.

None of this would have been possible without Ollie, she realized. He hadn't just rescued Bella—he'd rescued her. In the warmth of his love, she'd blossomed and come into her own. She knew she would never have to worry about Ollie dumping her or cheating on her. And he would be a father to Bella, who adored him. Ever since the night he'd swooped in, like Prince Caspian from the Chronicles of Narnia, and carried her to safety,

Bella had looked up to him the way she would a favorite uncle or older brother, tagging after him whenever she came for a visit or they went to visit her.

But while those were all good reasons, there was only one that mattered: Did she love him enough to make it work?

The answer, when it came, was so clear that she wondered why it had taken her so long to arrive at it. Hugging her daughter tightly, she smiled up at Ollie as she spoke. "How would you like to go to a place where there's always lots of cake to eat?"

Eileen Goudge is the *New York Times* best-selling author whose novels include *The Diary*, *Domestic Affairs*, *Woman in Red*, *One Last Dance*, *Garden of Lies*, and *Thorns of Truth*. There are more than five million copies of her books in print worldwide. She lives with her husband, entertainment reporter Sandy Kenyon, in New York City.

Center Point Publishing
600 Brooks Road • PO Box 1
Thorndike ME 04986-0001 USA

(207) 568-3717

US & Canada:
1 800 929-9108
www.centerpointlargeprint.com